Queens of Romance

A collection of bestselling novels by the world's leading romance writers

Three stories from international bestselling author

NORA ROBERTS

"You can't bottle wish fulfilment, but Nora Roberts certainly knows how to put it on the page."
—*New York Times*

"Roberts' bestselling novels are some of the best in the romance genre. They are thoughtfully plotted, well-written stories featuring fascinating characters."
—*USA TODAY*

"The publishing world might be hard-pressed to find an author with a more diverse style or fertile imagination than Roberts."
—*Publishers Weekly*

"Her stories have fuelled the dreams of twenty-five million readers."
—*Enterta...*

"Everything Nora Rob...
—*Rom...*

100 Reasons to Celebrate

We invite you to join us in celebrating
Mills & Boon's centenary. Gerald Mills and
Charles Boon founded Mills & Boon Limited
in 1908 and opened offices in London's Covent
Garden. Since then, Mills & Boon has become
a hallmark for romantic fiction, recognised
around the world.

We're proud of our 100 years of publishing
excellence, which wouldn't have been achieved
without the loyalty and enthusiasm of our
authors and readers.

Thank you!

Each month throughout the year there will
be something new and exciting to mark the
centenary, so watch for your favourite authors,
captivating new stories, special limited
edition collections…and more!

NORA ROBERTS

Summer Delights

Containing

**Impulse,
The Best Mistake
& Temptation**

Impulse

NORA ROBERTS

The
Queens of Romance
Collection

MILLS & BOON
100 YEARS
of pure reading pleasure

Number one *New York Times* bestselling author **Nora Roberts** is "a storyteller of immeasurable diversity and talent" according to *Publishers Weekly*. She has published over one hundred and sixty novels, her work has been optioned and made into films, and her books have been translated into over twenty-five different languages and published all over the world.

As part of her incredible success, Nora has established a large and loyal romance audience, who took her to their hearts in 1981 when her very first book, *Irish Thoroughbred*, was published.

The last decade has seen over one hundred of Nora's books become *New York Times* bestsellers – many of them reaching the number one position. Nora is truly a publishing phenomenon.

Chapter 1

She knew it was crazy. That was what she liked best about it. It was crazy, ridiculous, impractical and totally out of character. And she was having the time of her life. From the balcony of her hotel suite Rebecca could see the sweep of the beach, the glorious blue of the Ionian Sea, blushed now with streaks of rose from the setting sun.

Corfu. Even the name sounded mysterious, exciting, glamorous. And she was here, really here. Practical, steady-as-a-rock Rebecca Malone, who had never traveled more than five hundred miles from Philadelphia, was in Greece. Not just in Greece, she thought with a grin, but on the exotic island of Corfu, in one of the most exclusive resorts in Europe.

First-class, she thought as she leaned out to let the sweet breeze ruffle over her face. As long as it lasted, she was going first-class.

Her boss had thought she was suffering from temporary

insanity. Edwin McDowell of McDowell, Jableki and Kline was never going to understand why a promising young CPA would resign from her position with one of the top accounting firms in Philadelphia. She'd made a good salary, she'd enjoyed excellent benefits, and she'd even had a small window in her office.

Friends and associates had wondered if she'd suffered a breakdown. After all, it wasn't normal, and it certainly wasn't Rebecca's style to quit a solid, well-paying job without the promise of a better one.

But she'd given her two weeks' notice, cleared out her desk and had cheerfully walked out into the world of the unemployed.

When she'd sold her condo and then in one frantic week, auctioned off every possession she owned—every stick of furniture, every pot and pan and appliance—they'd been certain she'd gone over the edge.

Rebecca had never felt saner.

She owned nothing that didn't fit in a suitcase. She no longer had any tax-deferred investments or retirement plans. She'd cashed in her certificates of deposit, and the home entertainment center she'd thought she couldn't live without was now gracing someone else's home.

It had been more than six weeks since she'd even looked at an adding machine.

For the first—and perhaps the only—time in her life, she was totally free. There were no responsibilities, no pressures, no hurried gulps of cold coffee. She hadn't packed an alarm clock. She no longer owned one. Crazy? No. Rebecca shook her head and laughed into the breeze. For as long as it lasted, she was going to grab life with both hands and see what it had to offer.

Aunt Jeannie's death had been her turning point. It had

come so suddenly, so unexpectedly, leaving Rebecca without any family. Aunt Jeannie had worked hard for most of her sixty-five years, always punctual, always responsible. Her position as head librarian had been her whole life. She'd never missed a day, never failed to do her duty. Her bills had been paid on time. Her promises had always been kept.

More than once Rebecca had been told she took after her mother's older sister. She was twenty-four, but she was—had been—as solid and sturdy as her maiden aunt. Two months into retirement, two months after dear Aunt Jeannie began to make plans to travel, to enjoy the rewards she'd worked so hard to earn, she was gone.

After Rebecca's grief had come the anger, then the frustration, then slowly, the realization that she was traveling the same straight road. She worked, she slept, she fixed well-balanced meals that she ate alone. She had a small circle of friends who knew she could be counted on in a crisis. Rebecca would always find the best and most practical answer. Rebecca would never drop her own problems in your lap—because she didn't have any. Rebecca, bless her, was a port in any storm.

She hated it, and she'd begun to hate herself. She had to do something.

And she was doing it.

It wasn't running away as much as it was breaking free. All her life she'd done what was expected of her and tried to make as few waves as possible while doing it. All through school a crushing shyness had kept her more comfortable with her books than with other teenagers. In college a need to succeed and justify her aunt's faith had locked her tightly into her studies.

She had always been good with figures—logical, thorough,

patient. It had been easy, perhaps too easy, to pour herself into that one area, because there, and really only there, had she felt confident.

Now she was going to discover Rebecca Malone. In the weeks or months of freedom she had, she wanted to learn everything there was to know about the woman within. Perhaps there wasn't a butterfly inside the cocoon she'd wrapped herself in so comfortably, but whatever she found—whoever she found—Rebecca hoped she would enjoy her, like her, perhaps even respect her.

When the money ran out, she'd get another job and go back to being plain, practical Rebecca. Until that time she was rich, rootless and ready for surprises.

She was also hungry.

Stephen saw her the moment she entered the restaurant. It wasn't that she was particularly striking. Beautiful woman passed through the world every day and they usually warranted a glance. But there was something about the way this one walked, as if she were ready for anything, even looking forward to it. He stopped, and because business was slow at this hour he took a second, longer look.

She was tall for a woman, and more angular than slender. Her skin was pale, and that made him think she had only just arrived at the resort or was shy of the sun. The white sundress that left her shoulders and back bare accented the lack of color and gave dramatic contrast to her short cap of raven hair.

She paused, then seemed to take a deep breath. Stephen could almost hear her satisfied sigh. Then she smiled at the headwaiter, and followed him to her table, tossing her head back, so that her hair, which she wore arrow-straight, swung away from her chin.

A nice face, Stephen concluded. Bright, intelligent, eager. Especially the eyes. They were pale, an almost translucent gray. But there was nothing pale in their expression. She smiled at the waiter again, then laughed and looked around the restaurant. She looked as if she'd never been happier in her life.

She saw him. When Rebecca's gaze first skimmed over the man leaning against the bar, her automatic shyness kicked in and had her looking away. Attractive men had stared at her before—though it wasn't exactly a daily event. She'd never been able to handle it with the aplomb—or even cynicism—of most of her contemporaries. To cover her momentary embarrassment, she lifted her menu.

He hadn't meant to linger more than a few moments longer, but the impulse came suddenly. Stephen flicked a hand at the waiter and had him scurrying over, nodding quickly at Stephen's murmured request and hurrying off. When he returned it was to deliver a bottle of champagne to Rebecca's table.

"Compliments of Mr. Nickodemus."

"Oh." Rebecca followed the waiter's gaze over to the man by the bar. "Well, I—" She brought herself up short before she could stammer. A sophisticated woman wouldn't stutter over a gift of champagne, she reminded herself. She'd accept it graciously, with dignity. And maybe—if she wasn't a complete fool—she'd relax enough to flirt with the man who offered it.

Stephen watched the expressions pass across her face. Fascinating, he mused, and realized that the vague boredom he'd been feeling had vanished. When she lifted her head and smiled at him, he had no idea that her heart was pounding. He saw only a casual invitation, and he answered it.

He wasn't just attractive, Rebecca realized as he crossed

to her table. He was gorgeous. Eye-popping, mouth-dropping gorgeous. She had an image of Apollo and ancient Greek warriors. Thick blond hair streaked by the sun fell over the collar of his shirt. Smooth, bronzed skin was marred—and somehow enhanced—by a faint scar under his jawline. A strong jaw, she thought. A strong face, with the darkest, deepest blue eyes she'd ever seen.

"Good evening, I'm Stephen Nickodemus." His voice wasn't accented, it was rounded, rich. He might have come from anywhere. Perhaps it was that, more than anything else, that intrigued her.

Lecturing herself on poise and image, she lifted her hand. "Hello. I'm Rebecca, Rebecca Malone." She felt a quick flutter when he brushed his lips over her knuckles. Feeling foolish, she drew her hand away and balled it in her lap. "Thank you for the champagne."

"It seemed to suit your mood." He studied her, wondering why he was getting such a mix of signals. "You are by yourself?"

"Yes." Perhaps it was a mistake to admit it, but if she was going to live life to the fullest she had to take some risks. The restaurant wasn't crowded, but they were hardly alone. Take the plunge, she told herself, and tried another smile. "The least I can do is offer you a glass."

Stephen took the seat across from her, brushing the waiter aside to pour the wine himself. "You are American?"

"It shows."

"No. Actually, I thought you were French until you spoke."

"Did you?" That pleased her. "I've just come from Paris." She had to force herself not to touch her hair. She'd had it cut, with trepidation and delight, in a French salon.

Stephen touched his glass to hers. Her eyes bubbled with life as cheerfully as the wine. "Business?"

"No, just pleasure." What a marvelous word, she thought. *Pleasure.* "It's a wonderful city."

"Yes. Do you go often?"

Rebecca smiled into her glass. "Not often enough. Do you?"

"From time to time."

She nearly sighed at that. Imagine anyone speaking of going to Paris "from time to time." "I nearly stayed longer, but I'd promised myself Greece."

So she was alone, restless, and on the move. Perhaps that was why she had appealed to him, because he was, too. "Is Corfu your first stop?"

"Yes." She sipped at her drink. A part of her still believed it was all a dream. Greece, champagne, the man. "It's beautiful. Much more beautiful than I imagined it could be."

"It's your first trip, then?" He couldn't have said why that pleased him. "How long do you stay?"

"As long as I like." She grinned, savoring the feeling of freedom. "And you?"

He lifted his glass. "Longer, I think, than I had planned." When the waiter appeared at his side, Stephen handed over the menu, then spoke to him in soft, quick Greek. "If you don't object, I'd like to guide you through your first meal on the island."

The old Rebecca would have been too nervous to sit through a meal with a stranger. The new Rebecca took a second, deeper sip of champagne. "I'd love it. Thank you."

It was easy. Easy to sit, to laugh, to sample new and exotic tastes. She forgot that he was a stranger, forgot that the world she was living in now was only temporary. They didn't speak of anything important—only of Paris, and the weather, and the wine. Still, she was sure it was the most interesting conversation of her life. He looked at her when he spoke to her, looked at her as though he were delighted to spend an hour talking of nothing. The last man she'd had dinner with had wanted her to give him a discount when she did his taxes.

Stephen wasn't asking her for anything more than her company for dinner. When he looked at her it seemed unlikely that he'd care if she knew how to fill out Schedule C.

When he suggested a walk along the beach, she agreed without a qualm. What better way to end an evening than a walk in the moonlight?

"I was looking out at this from my window just before dinner." Rebecca stepped out of her shoes, then dangled them from her fingers as she walked. "I didn't think it could look more beautiful than it did at sunset."

"The sea changes, like a woman, in the light." He paused to touch a flame to the end of a slim cigar. "So men are drawn to her."

"Are you? Drawn to the sea?"

"I've spent my time on her. I fished in these waters as a boy."

She'd learned at dinner that he'd grown up traveling the islands with his father. "It must have been exciting, moving from place to place, seeing new things almost every day."

He shrugged. He'd never been sure whether the restlessness had been born in him or had been a product of his upbringing. "It had its moments."

"I love to travel." Laughing, she tossed her shoes aside, then stepped into the surf. The champagne was making her head swim and the moonlight felt as soft as rain. "I adore it." She laughed again when the spray washed up to dampen her skirts. The Ionian Sea. She was standing in it. "On a night like this I think I'll never go home."

She looked so vibrant, so alive, standing in the surf with her white skirts billowing. "Where's home?"

She glanced over her shoulder. The flirtatious look was totally unplanned and completely devastating. "I haven't decided. I want to swim." On impulse, she dived into the surf.

Stephen's heart stopped when she disappeared. He'd already kicked off his shoes and started forward when she rose up again. For a second time, his heart stopped.

She was laughing, her face lifted to the moonlight. Water cascaded from her hair, from her skin. The drops that clung to her were the only jewels she wore. Beautiful? No, she wasn't beautiful. She was electric.

"It's wonderful. Cool and soft and wonderful."

With a shake of his head, he stepped in far enough to take her hand and pull her toward shore. She was a little mad, perhaps, but engagingly so. "Are you always so impulsive?"

"I'm working on it. Aren't you?" She combed her hand through her dripping hair. "Or do you always send champagne to strange women?"

"Either way I answer that could be trouble. Here." He shrugged out of his jacket and draped it over her shoulders. Unframed, washed clean, her face glowed in the moonlight. There was a graceful kind of strength in it, to the sweep of cheekbone, the slightly pointed chin. Delicate—except for the eyes. One look there showed power, a power that was still. "You're irresistible, Rebecca."

She stared at him, confused all over again, as he gathered the neck of the jacket close around her throat. "I'm wet," she managed.

"And beautiful." With his hands still on the jacket, he brought her toward him. "And fascinating."

That made her laugh again. "I don't think so, but thanks. I'm glad you sent me the champagne and guided me through my first meal." Her nerves began to jangle. His eyes stayed on hers, journeying only once to her mouth, which was still damp from the sea. Their bodies were close, close enough to brush. Rebecca began to shiver, and she knew it had nothing to do with wet clothes and the breeze.

"I should go in…change my dress."

There was something about her. The impulsiveness, the easy flirtatiousness, hid an unmistakable innocence that baffled and attracted him. Whatever it was, he wanted more.

"I'll see you again."

"Yes." She prayed for her heartbeat to slow. "It's not a very big island."

He smiled at that, slowly. She felt, with a mixture of relief and regret, the relaxation of his hands. "Tomorrow. I have business early. I'll be done by eleven, if that suits you. I'll show you Corfu."

"All right." Better judgment and nerves be damned. She wanted to go with him. "I'll meet you in the lobby." Carefully, because she suddenly wasn't sure she could manage it, she stepped back. Moonlight silhouetted him against the sea. "Good night, Stephen."

She forgot to be sophisticated and dashed toward the hotel.

He watched her go. She puzzled him, puzzled him as no woman had since he'd been a boy and too young to understand that a woman was not meant to be understood. And he wanted her. That wasn't new, but the desire had come with surprising speed and surprising force.

Rebecca Malone might have started out as an impulse, but she was now a mystery. One he intended to solve. With a little laugh, he bent to scoop up the shoes she'd forgotten. He hadn't felt quite so alive in months.

Chapter 2

Stephen wasn't the kind of man who rearranged his schedule to spend the day with a woman. Especially a woman he barely knew. He was a wealthy man, but he was also a busy man, driven by both pride and ambition to maintain a high level of involvement in all his projects. He shouldered responsibility well and had learned to enjoy the benefits of hard work and dedication.

His time on Corfu wasn't free—or rather hadn't been planned as free. Mixing business and pleasure wasn't his style. He pursued both, separately, with utter concentration. Yet he found himself juggling appointments, meetings, conference calls, in order to have the afternoon open for Rebecca.

He supposed any man would want to get to know a woman who flirted easily over a champagne flute one moment and dived fully dressed into the sea the next.

"I've postponed your meeting with Theoharis until five-thirty this evening." Stephen's secretary scribbled on a notepad she had resting on her lap. "He will meet you for early cocktails in the suite. I've arranged for hors d'oeuvres and a bottle of ouzo."

"Always efficient, Elana."

She smiled and tucked a fall of dark hair behind her ear. "I try."

When Stephen rose to pace to the window, she folded her hands and waited. She had worked for him for five years, she admired his energy and his business acumen, and—fortunately for both of them—had long since gotten over an early crush. There was often speculation about their personal relationship, but though he could be friendly—even kind when it suited him—with Stephen, business was business.

"Contact Mithos in Athens. Have him telex that report by the end of the day. And I want to hear from Lereau by five, Paris time."

"Shall I call and give him a nudge?"

"If you think it's necessary." Restless, he dug his hands in his pockets. Where had this sudden discontent come from? he wondered. He was wealthy, successful, and free, as always, to move from place to place. As he stared out at the sea, he remembered the scent of Rebecca's skin. "Send flowers to Rebecca Malone's suite. Wildflowers, nothing formal. This afternoon."

Elana made a note, hoping she'd get a look at this Rebecca Malone before long. She had already heard through the grapevine that Stephen had had dinner with an American woman. "And the card?"

He wasn't a man for poetry. "Just my name."

"Anything else?"

"Yes." He turned and offered her a half smile. "Take some time off. Go to the beach."

Pad in hand, she rose. "I'll be sure to work it in. Enjoy your afternoon, Stephen."

He intended to. As she left him, Stephen glanced at his watch. It was fifteen minutes before eleven. There was work he could do to fill in the time, a quick call that could be made. Instead, he picked up Rebecca's shoes.

After three tries, Rebecca settled on an outfit. She didn't have an abundance of clothes, because she'd preferred to spend her funds on travel. But she had splurged here and there on her route through Europe. No tidy CPA suits, she thought as she tied a vivid fuchsia sash at the waist of her sapphire-colored cotton pants. No sensible shoes or pastel blouses. The last shock of color came from a primrose-hued blouse cut generously to layer over a skinny tank top in the same shade as the slacks.

The combination delighted her, if only because her firm had preferred quiet colors and clean lines.

She had no idea where she was going, and she didn't care.

It was a beautiful day, even though she'd awoken with a dull headache from the champagne, and the disorientation that went with it. A light, early breakfast on her terrace and a quick dip in the sea had cleared both away. She still had trouble believing that she could lounge through a morning as she pleased—and that she'd spent the evening with a man she'd just met.

Aunt Jeannie would have tut-tutted and reminded her of the dangers of being a woman alone. Some of her friends would have been shocked, others envious. But they would all have been astonished that steady Rebecca had strolled in the moonlight with a gorgeous man with a scar on his jawline and eyes like velvet.

If she hadn't had his jacket as proof, she might have thought she'd dreamed it. There had never been anything wrong with her imagination—just the application of it. Often she'd pictured herself in an exotic place with an exotic man, with moonlight and music. Imagined herself, she remembered. And then she'd turned on her calculator and gotten down to business.

But she hadn't dreamed this. She could still remember the giddy, half-terrified feeling that had swarmed through her when he'd gathered her close. When his mouth had been only an inch from hers and the sea and the champagne had roared in her head.

What if he had kissed her? What tastes would she have found? Rich, strong ones, she mused, almost able to savor them as she traced a fingertip over her lips. After just one evening she was absolutely certain there would be nothing lukewarm about Stephen Nickodemus. She wasn't nearly so certain about Rebecca.

She probably would have fumbled and blushed and stammered. With a shake of her head, she pulled a brush through her hair. Exciting men didn't tumble all over themselves to kiss neat, practical-minded women.

But he'd asked to see her again.

Rebecca wasn't certain whether she was disappointed or relieved that he hadn't pressed his advantage and kissed her. She'd been kissed before, held before, of course. But she had a feeling—a very definite feeling—that it wouldn't be the same with Stephen. He might make her want more, offer more, than she had with any other man.

Crossing bridges too soon, she decided as she checked the contents of her big straw bag. She wasn't going to have an affair with him, or with anyone. Even the new, improved

Rebecca Malone wasn't the type for a casual affair. But maybe— She caught her lower lip between her teeth. If the time was right she might have a romance she'd remember long after she left Greece.

For now, she was ready, but it was much too early to go down. It would hardly make her look like a well-traveled woman of the world if she popped down to the lobby and paced for ten minutes. This was her fantasy, after all. She didn't want him to think she was inexperienced and overeager.

Only the knock on the door prevented her from changing her mind about her outfit one more time.

"Hello." Stephen studied her for a moment, unsmiling. He'd nearly been certain he'd exaggerated, but she was just as vibrant, just as exciting, in the morning as she had been in the moonlight. He held out her shoes. "I thought you might need these."

She laughed, remembering her impulsive dunk in the sea. "I didn't realize I'd left them on the beach. Come in a minute." With a neatness ingrained in her from childhood, she turned to take them to the bedroom closet. "I'm ready to go if you are."

Stephen lifted a brow. He preferred promptness, but he never expected it in anyone but a business associate. "I've got a Jeep waiting. Some of the roads are rough."

"Sounds great." Rebecca came out again, carrying her bag and a flat-brimmed straw hat. She handed Stephen his jacket, neatly folded. "I forgot to give this back to you last night." Should she offer to have it cleaned? she wondered when he only continued to look at her. Fiddling with the strap of her bag, she decided against it. "Does taking pictures bother you?"

"No, why?"

"Good, because I take lots of them. I can't seem to stop myself."

She wasn't kidding. As Stephen drove up into the hills, she took shots of everything. Sheep, tomato plants, olive groves and straggly sage. He stopped so that she could walk out near the edge of a cliff and look down at a small village huddled near the sea.

She wouldn't be able to capture it on film; she wasn't clever enough. But she knew she'd never forget that light, so pure, so clear, or the contrast between the orange tiled roofs and the low white-washed walls and the deep, dangerous blue of the water that flung itself against the weathered rock that rose into harsh crags. A stork, legs tucked, glided over the water, where fishing boats bobbed.

There were nets drying on the beach and children playing. Flowers bloomed and tangled where the wind had planted them, more spectacular than any planned arrangement could ever be.

"It's beautiful." Her throat tightened with emotion, and with a longing she couldn't have defined. "So calm. You imagine women baking black bread and the men coming home smelling of fish and the sea. It looks as though it hasn't changed in a hundred years."

"Very little." He glanced down himself, surprised and more than a little pleased that she would be touched by something so simple. "We cling to antiquity."

"I haven't seen the Acropolis yet, but I don't think it could be any more spectacular than this." She lifted her face, delighted by the way the wind whipped at it. Here, high above the sea, she absorbed everything—the salty, rough-edged bite of the wind, the clarity of color and sound, and the man beside her. Letting her camera dangle from its strap, she turned to him. "I haven't thanked you for taking the time to show me all of this."

He took her hand, not to raise it to his lips, just to hold it. It was a link he hadn't known he wanted. "I'm enjoying seeing the familiar through someone else's eyes. Your eyes."

Suddenly the edge of the cliff seemed too close, the sun too hot. Could he do that just by touching her? With an effort, Rebecca smiled, keeping her voice light. "If you ever come to Philadelphia, I'll do the same for you."

It was odd. She'd looked almost frightened for a moment. Fragile and frightened. Stephen had always carefully avoided women who were easily bruised. "I'll consider that a promise."

They continued to drive, over roads that jarred and climbed and twisted. She saw her first of the *agrimi*, the wild goat of Greece, and the rocky pastures dotted with sturdy sheep. And everywhere, rich and defiant, was the intense color of flowers.

He didn't complain when she asked him to stop so that she could snap pictures of tiny blue star blossoms that pushed their way through cracks in the rock. He listened to her delight as she framed a thick, thorny stem topped with a ragged yellow flower. It made him realize, and regret, that it had been years since he'd taken the time to look closely at the small, vital things that grew around him.

He looked now at Rebecca standing in the sunlight, her hat fluttering around her face and her laugh dancing on the air.

Often the road clung to cliffs that plunged dizzily into the sea. Rebecca, who was too timid to fight rush-hour traffic, found it exhilarating.

She felt almost like another person. She *was* another person, she thought, laughing as she held on to her hat to keep the wind from snatching it away.

"I love it!" she shouted over the wind and the noise of the engine. "It's wild and old and incredible. Like no place I've ever been."

Still laughing, she lifted her camera and snapped his picture as he drove. He wore sunglasses with amber lenses and had a cigar clamped between his teeth. The wind blew through his hair and chased the smoke behind them. He stopped the Jeep, took the camera and snapped a picture of her in turn.

"Hungry?"

She dragged her tousled hair back from her face. "Starving."

He leaned over to open her door. A current passed through her, sharp and electric, strong enough to make him pause with his arm across her body and his face close to hers. It was there again, he thought as he waited and watched. The awareness, ripe and seductive. And the innocence, as alluring as it was contradictory. In a test—a test for both of them—he lifted a hand to stroke her cheek. It was as soft as her scent.

"Are you afraid of me, Rebecca?"

"No." That was true; she was nearly sure of it. "Should I be?"

He didn't smile. Through the amber lenses she saw that his eyes were very intense. "I'm not entirely sure." When he pulled away he heard her release an unsteady breath. He wasn't feeling completely steady himself. "We'll have to walk a little first."

Confused, her mind churning, she stepped out onto the dirt path. A woman on a simple date didn't tremble every time a man got close, Rebecca told herself as Stephen lifted the picnic basket out of the back. She was behaving like a teenager, not a grown woman.

Troubled by his own thoughts, Stephen stopped beside her. He hesitated, then held out a hand. It felt good, simply good, when she put hers in it.

They walked through an olive grove in a companionable silence while the sun streamed down on dusty leaves and rocky ground. There was no sound of the sea here, but when the wind was right she could hear the screech of a gull far away. The island was small, but here it seemed uninhabited.

"I haven't had a picnic in years." Rebecca spread the cloth. "And never in an olive grove." She glanced around, wanting to remember every leaf and pebble. "Are we trespassing?"

"No." Stephen took a bottle of white wine from the basket. Rebecca left him to it and started rummaging in search of food.

"Do you know the owner?"

"I'm the owner." He drew the cork with a gentle pop.

"Oh." She looked around again. It should have occurred to her that he would own something impressive, different, exciting. "It sounds romantic. Owning an olive grove."

He lifted a brow. He owned a number of them, but he had never thought of them as romantic. They were simply profitable. He offered her a glass, then tapped it with his own. "To romance, then."

She swept down her lashes, battling shyness. To Stephen, the gesture was only provocative. "I hope you're hungry," she began, knowing she was talking too fast. "It all looks wonderful." She took a quick sip of wine to ease her dry throat, then set it aside to finish unpacking the basket.

There were sweet black olives as big as a man's thumb, and there was a huge slab of sharp cheese. There were cold lamb and hunks of bread, and fruit so fresh it could have been just plucked from the stem.

Gradually she began to relax again.

"You've told me very little about yourself." Stephen topped off her wine and watched her bite into a ripe red plum. "I know little more than that you come from Philadelphia and enjoy traveling."

What could she tell him? A man like him was bound to be

bored with the life story of the painfully ordinary Rebecca Malone. Lies had never come easily to her, so she skirted between fact and fiction. "There's little more. I grew up in Philadelphia. I lost both of my parents when I was a teenager, and I lived with my aunt Jeannie. She was very dear, and she made the loss bearable."

"It's painful." He flicked his lighter at the end of a cigar, remembering not only the pain, but also the fury he had felt when his father had died and left him orphaned at sixteen. "It steals childhood."

"Yes." So he understood that. It made her feel close to him, close and comfortable. "Maybe that's why I like to travel. Every time you see a new place you can be a child again."

"So you don't look for roots?"

She glanced at him then. He was leaning back against the trunk of a tree, smoking lazily, watching carefully. "I don't know what I'm looking for."

"Is there a man?"

She moved her shoulders, determined not to be embarrassed. "No."

He took her hand, drawing her closer. "No one?"

"No, I..." She wasn't certain what she would have said, but could say nothing at all when he turned her palm upward and pressed his lips to its center. She felt the fire burst there, in her hand, then race everywhere.

"You're very responsive, Rebecca." He lowered her hand but kept it in his. He could feel the heat, but he wasn't sure whether it had sprung to her skin or to his own. "If there's no one, the men in your Philadelphia must be very slow."

"I've been too...busy."

His lips curved at that. There was a tremor in her voice, and there was passion in her eyes. "Busy?"

"Yes." Afraid she'd make a fool of herself, she drew her hand back. "This was wonderful." Trying to calm herself, she pushed a hand through her hair. "You know what I need?"

"No. Tell me."

"Another picture." She sprang to her feet and, steadier, grinned. "A memento of my first picnic in an olive grove. Let's see…you can stand right over there. The sun's good in front of that tree, and I should be able to frame in that section of the grove."

Amused, Stephen tapped out his cigar. "How much more film do you have?"

"This is the last roll—but I have scads back at the hotel." She flicked him a quick laughing glance. "I warned you."

"So you did." Competent hands, he thought as he watched her focus and adjust. He hadn't realized he could be as attracted to competence as he was to beauty. She mumbled to herself, tossing her head back so that her hair swung, then settled. His stomach tightened without warning.

Good God, he wanted her. She'd done nothing to make him burn and strain this way. He couldn't accuse her of taunting or teasing, and yet…he felt taunted. He felt teased. For the first time in his life he felt totally seduced by a woman who had done nothing more than give him a few smiles and a little companionship.

Even now she was chattering away as she secured her camera to the limb of a tree. Talking easily, as though they were just friends, as though she felt nothing more than a light, unimportant affection. But he'd seen it. Stephen felt his blood heat as he remembered the quick flash of arousal he'd seen on her face. He'd see it again. And more.

"I'm going to set the timer," Rebecca went on, blissfully unaware of Stephen's thoughts. "All you have to do is stand there. Once I get this damn thing set, I'm going to run over so it'll take one of both— There." She interrupted herself, crossed her fingers and ran to Stephen's side in a dash. "Unless I messed up, it'll snap all by itself in—"

The rest of the words slid down her throat as he crushed her against him and captured her mouth.

Chapter 3

Heat. Light. Speed. Rebecca felt them, felt each separate, distinct sensation. Urgency. Demand. Impatience. She tasted them, as clearly as wild honey, on his lips. Though she'd never experienced it, she had known exactly what it would be like to be with him, mouth to mouth and need to need.

In an instant the world had narrowed from what could be seen and understood to a pure, seamless blanket of emotion. It cloaked her, not softly, not in comfort, but tightly, hotly, irresistibly. Caught between fear and delight, she lifted a hand to his cheek.

God, she was sweet. Even as he dragged her closer, aroused by the simplicity of her acceptance, he was struck by—disarmed by—her sweetness. There had been a hesitation, almost too brief to be measured, before her lips had parted beneath his. Parted, invited, accepted.

There was a sigh, so soft it could barely be heard, as she

stroked her hands up his back to his shoulders. Curious, simple, generous. A man could drown in such sweetness, fall prisoner to such pliancy. And be saved by it. Beneath the patterned shade of the olive tree, she gave him more than passion. She gave him hope.

Charmed, he murmured some careless Greek phrase lovers might exchange. The words meant nothing to her, but the sound of them on the still air, the feel of them stroking across her lips…seduction. Glorious seduction.

Pleasure burst in her blood, in her head, in her heart, thousands of tiny bubbles of it, until she was straining against him.

The quiet explosion rocked him. It tightened his chest, fuddled his mind. She fitted into his arms as if she'd been born for him. As if, somehow, they had known each other before, loved before, hungered before. Something seemed to erupt between them, something molten, powerful, dangerous. But it wasn't new. It was ancient, a whispering echo of ageless passions.

She began to tremble. How could this be so right, so familiar? It wasn't possible to feel safe and threatened at the same time. But she did. She clung to him while a dim, floating image danced through her head. She had kissed him before. Just like this. As her mind spun, she heard her own mindless murmurs answer his. As freely, as inescapably as the sun poured light, response flowed from her. She couldn't stop it. Frightened by her sudden loss of control, she struggled against him, against herself.

He slipped his hands up to her shoulders, but not to free her, to look at her. To look at how their coming together had changed her. It had changed him. Passion had made her eyes heavy, seductive. Fear had clouded them. Her lips were full, softened and parted by his. Her breath shivered through them.

Under his hands he could feel the heat of her skin and the quick, involuntary trembling of her muscles.

No pretense here, he decided as he studied her. He was holding both innocence and delight in his hands.

"Stephen, I—"

"Again."

Then his face filled her vision and she was lost.

Differently. Should she have known that one man could hold one woman in so many different ways? That one man could kiss one woman with such stunning variety? There was gentleness now, as familiar and as novel as the urgency. His lips persuaded rather than demanded. They savored instead of devouring. Her surrender came as quietly, and as unmistakably, as her earlier passion. The trembling stopped; the fear vanished. With a complete trust that surprised them both, she leaned against him, giving.

More aroused by her serenity than by the storm that had come before, Stephen pulled back. He had to, or what had begun would finish without either of them saying a word. As he swore and pulled out a cigar, Rebecca placed a hand on the olive tree for support.

Moments, she thought. It had been only moments, and yet she felt as though years had passed, racing backward or forward, perhaps spinning in circles. In a place like this, with a man like this, what difference did it make what year it was? What century?

Half terrified, she lifted a hand to her lips. Despite her fear, they curved under her touch. She could still taste him. Still feel him. And nothing, nothing, would ever be quite the same again.

He stared out at the rough and dusty land he'd known as a boy, and beyond, to the stark, tumbling rocks where he and other wild things had climbed.

What was he doing with her? Furious with himself, he drew on the cigar. What was he feeling? It was new, and far from comfortable. And it was comfort he preferred, he reminded himself. Comfort and freedom. Bringing himself under control, he turned to her again, determined to treat what had happened as a man should—lightly.

She just stood there, with the sun and the shade falling over her. There was neither recrimination nor invitation in her eyes. She didn't flinch or step forward, but merely stood, watching him with the faintest of smiles, as if… As if, Stephen realized, she knew what questions he was asking himself— and the answers.

"It grows late."

She felt the ache and fought not to let it show on her face. "I guess you're right." She dragged a hand through her hair—it was the first sign of her agitation—then walked over to pick up her camera. "I should have a picture to remember all this by," she said, forcing brightness into her voice. Her breath caught when his fingers closed over her arm and whirled her around.

"Who are you?" he demanded. "What are you?"

"I don't know what you mean." The emotion burst out before she could stop it. "I don't know what you want."

With one jerk he had her tumbling against him. "You know what I want."

Her heart was in her throat, beating wildly. She found it strange that it was not fear but desire that she felt. She hadn't known she was capable of feeling a need that was so unreasonable, so reckless. It was almost purifying to experience it, and to see it mirrored in his eyes.

"It takes more than one afternoon." Didn't it? Her voice rose as she tried to convince herself. "It takes more than a picnic and a walk in the moonlight for me."

"One moment the temptress, the next the outraged innocent. Do you do it to intrigue me, Rebecca?" She shook her head, and his fingers tightened. "It works," he murmured. "You've hardly been out of my mind since I first saw you. I want to make love with you, here, in the sun."

Color flooded her face, not because she was embarrassed, but because she could imagine it, perfectly. And then what? Carefully she leveled her breathing. Whatever impulses she had followed, whatever bridges she had burned, she still needed answers.

"No." It cost her to go against her own needs and say it. "Not when I'm unsure and you're angry." She took a deep breath and kept her eyes on him. "You're hurting me, Stephen. I don't think you mean to."

Slowly he released her arm. He was angry, furious, but not at her refusal. The anger stemmed from the need she pulled from him, a need that had come too fast and too strong for him to channel. "We'll go back."

Rebecca merely nodded, then knelt to gather the remains of the picnic.

He was a busy man, much too busy to brood about a woman he barely knew and didn't understand at all. That was what Stephen told himself. He had reports to read, calls to make and paperwork—which he had both a talent and a distaste for—to deal with. A couple of simple kisses weren't enough to take a man's mind off his work.

But there hadn't been anything simple about them. Disgusted, Stephen pushed away from his desk and wandered to the terrace doors. He'd left them open because the breeze, and the fragrances it brought, helped him forget he was obligated to be inside.

For days he'd worked his way through his responsibilities, trying to ignore the nagging itch at the back of his mind—the itch that was Rebecca. There was no reason for him to stay on Corfu. He could have handled his business in Athens, or Crete, or in London, for that matter. Still, he'd made no plan to leave, though he'd also made no attempt to approach her.

She…concerned him, he decided. To be drawn to an attractive woman was as natural as breathing. To have the attraction cause discomfort, confusion, even annoyance was anything but natural. A taste of her hadn't been enough. Yet he hesitated.

She was…mysterious. Perhaps that was why he couldn't push her from his mind. On the surface she appeared to be an attractive, free-spirited woman who grabbed life with both hands. Yet there were undercurrents. The hints of innocence, of shyness. The sweetness. The complexity of her kept him wondering, thinking, imagining.

Perhaps that was her trick. Women had them…were entitled to them. It was a waste of time to begrudge them their illusions and their feminine magic. More than a waste of time, it was foolish, when a man could enjoy the benefits. But there was more, and somehow less, to Rebecca than innate feminine magic.

When he had kissed her, though it had been the first time, it had been like coming back to a lover, to a love, after a painful separation. When his lips had found hers, something had filled him. A heat, an impatience, a knowledge.

He knew her, knew more than her name and her background and the color of her eyes. He knew all of her. Yet he knew nothing.

Fantasies, he told himself. He didn't have time for them. Leaning a hip against the railing, he lit a cigar and watched the sea.

As always, it pulled at him, bringing back memories of a

childhood that had been careless and too short. There were times, rare times, when he allowed himself to regret. Times when the sun was a white flash of heat and the water was blue and endless. His father had taught him a great deal. How to fish, how to see both beauty and excitement in new places, how to drink like a man.

Fifteen years, Stephen thought, a smile ghosting around his mouth. He still missed him, missed the companionship, the robust laughter. They had been friends, as well as parent and child, with a bond as easy, and as strong, as any Stephen had ever known. But his father had died as he would have wanted to, at sea and in his prime.

He would have taken one look at Rebecca, rolled his eyes, kissed his fingers and urged his son to enjoy. But Stephen wasn't the boy he had once been. He was more cautious, more aware of consequences. If a man dived into the sea, he should know the depth and the currents.

Then he saw her, coming from the sea. Water ran down her body, glistening in the strong sun, sparkling against skin that had warmed in the last few days to a dusky gold. As he looked, as he wanted, he felt his muscles clench, one by one, shoulders, stomach, thighs. Without his being aware, his fingers tightened, snapping the cigar in two. He hadn't known that desire could arouse a reaction so akin to anger.

She stopped, and though he knew she was unaware of him, she might easily have been posing. To taunt, to tease, to invite. As drops of water slid down her, she stretched, lifting her face skyward. Her skimpy suit rested low over her boyish hips, shifted enticingly over the subtle curve of her breasts. At that moment, she was totally absorbed in her own pleasure and as unself-conscious as any young animal standing in the sun. Nothing had ever been so alluring.

Then, slowly, seductively, she combed her fingers through her hair, smiling, as if she enjoyed the wet, silky feel of it. Watching her, he felt the air back up and clog in his lungs. He could have murdered her for it, for making him want so unreasonably what he did not yet understand.

She plucked a long, mannish T-shirt from a straw bag and, after tugging it on, strolled barefoot into the hotel.

He stood there, waiting for the need to pass. But it built, layered with an ache that infuriated him and a longing that baffled him.

He should ignore her. Instinct warned him that if he didn't his life would never be the same. She was nothing more than a distraction, a momentary impulse he should resist. He should turn away, go back to work. He had commitments, obligations, and no time to waste on fantasies. With an oath, he tossed the broken cigar over the rail.

There were times, he thought, when a man had to trust in fate and dive in.

Chapter 4

Rebecca had hardly shut the door behind her before she turned back to answer the knock. The sun and the water had left her pleasantly tired, but all thoughts of a lazy catnap vanished when she saw Stephen.

He looked wonderful. Cool, a little windblown, intense. For days she'd wondered about him, wondered and wished. She felt her pulse skip and her lips curve just at the sight of him. With an effort, she kept her voice breezy.

"Hello. I wasn't sure you were still on the island."

It wasn't really a lie, she told herself. An offhand inquiry had assured her that Mr. Nickodemus hadn't checked out, but she hadn't actually seen him.

"I saw you come up from the beach."

"Oh." Unconsciously she tugged at the hem of her cover-up. To Stephen the small gesture was one more contradictory signal. "I can't seem to get enough of the sun and the sea. Would you like to come in?"

By way of an answer he stepped through and shut the door behind him. It made a very quiet, a very final sound. Rebecca's carefully built poise began to crumble. "I never thanked you for the flowers." She made a gesture indicating the vase near the window, then brought her hands back together and linked them in front of her. "They're still beautiful. I…I thought I might run into you, in the dining room, on the beach, or…" Her words trailed off when he lifted a hand to her hair.

"I've been busy." He watched her eyes, eyes that were as clear as rainwater, blur at the slight touch. "Business."

It was ridiculous, she knew, but she wasn't at all sure she could speak. "If you have to work, I doubt you could pick a more beautiful place."

He stepped closer. She smelled of the water and the sun. "You're enjoying the resort, and the island."

Her hand was in his now, caught lightly. It took only that to make her knees weak. "Yes, very much."

"Perhaps you'd like to see it from a different perspective." Deliberately, wanting to test them both, he lifted her hand to his lips. He grazed her knuckles—it was barely a whisper of contact—and felt the jolt. She felt it, and he could see that she did, so it couldn't just be his imagination. "Spend the day with me tomorrow on my boat."

"What?"

He smiled, delighted with her response. "Will you come with me?"

Anywhere. Astonished, she stepped back. "I haven't any plans."

"Good." He closed the distance between them again. Her

hands fluttered up in flustered defense, then settled again when he made no attempt to touch her. "Then I'll make them for you. I'll come for you in the morning. Nine?"

A boat. He'd said something about a boat. Rebecca drew in a deep breath and tried to pull herself together. This wasn't like her—going off into daydreams, feeling weak-kneed, being flooded with waves of desire. And it felt wonderful.

"I'd like that." She gave him what she hoped was an easy woman-of-the-world smile.

"Until tomorrow, then." He started for the door, then turned, a hand on the knob. "Rebecca, don't forget your camera."

She waited until he'd closed the door before she spun in three quick circles.

When Stephen had said "boat," Rebecca had pictured a trim little cabin cruiser. Instead, she stepped onto the glossy mahogany deck of a streamlined hundred-foot yacht.

"You could live on this," Rebecca said, then wished she'd bitten her tongue. But he only laughed.

"I often do."

"Welcome aboard, sir," a white-uniformed man with a British accent said.

"Grady. This is my guest, Miss Malone."

"Ma'am." Grady's cool British reserve didn't flicker for an instant, but Rebecca felt herself being summed up.

"Cast off when you're ready." Stephen took Rebecca's arm. "Would you like a tour?"

"Yes." A yacht. She was on a yacht. It took all her willpower to keep her camera in the bag. "I'd love to see it all."

He took her below, through four elegantly appointed cabins. Her comment about living on board had been said impulsively, but she could see now that it could be done easily, even luxuriously.

Above there was a large glassed-in cabin in which one could stretch out comfortably, out of the sun, and watch the sea, whatever the weather. She had known that there were people who lived like this. Part of her job had been to research and calculate so that those who did paid the government as little as possible. But to be there, to see it, to be surrounded by it, was entirely different from adding figures on paper.

There was a masculine feel to the cabin, to the entire boat—leather, wood, muted colors. There were shelves filled with books and a fully stocked bar, as well as a stereo system.

"All the comforts of home," Rebecca murmured, but she'd noted that there were doors and panels that could be secured in case of rough weather. What would it be like to ride out a storm at sea, to watch the rain lash the windows and feel the deck heave?

She gave a quick gasp when she felt the floor move. Stephen took her arm again to steady her.

"We're under way." Curious, he turned her to face him. "Are you afraid of boats?"

"No." She could hardly admit that the biggest one she'd been on before this had been a two-passenger canoe at summer camp. "It just startled me." Under way, she thought as she prayed that her system would settle. It was such an exciting, adventurous word. "Can we go out on deck? I'd like to watch."

It was exciting. She felt it the moment the wind hit her face and rushed through her hair. At the rail, she leaned out, delighted to see the island shrink and the sea spread. Because she couldn't resist and he didn't laugh at her, she took half a dozen pictures as the boat sped away from land.

"It's better than flying," she decided. "You feel a part of it. Look." With a laugh, she pointed. "The birds are chasing us."

Stephen didn't bother to glance at the gulls that wheeled and called above the boat's wake. He preferred to watch the delight and excitement bloom on her face. "Do you always enjoy so completely?"

"Yes." She tossed her hair away from her face, only to have the wind rush it back again. With another laugh, she stretched back from the railing, her face lifted to the sun. "Oh, yes."

Irresistible. With his hands at her waist, he spun her toward him. It was like holding a live wire. The shock rippled from her to him, then back again. "Everything?" His fingers spread over her back and, with the slightest pressure, moved her forward until their thighs met.

"I don't know." Instinctively she braced her hands on his shoulders. "I haven't tried everything." But she wanted to. Held close, with the sound of the water and the wind, she wanted to. Without giving a thought to self-preservation, she leaned toward him.

He swore, lightly, under his breath. Rebecca jolted back as if he had shouted at her. Stephen caught her hand as he nodded to the steward, who had just approached with drinks. "Thank you, Victor. Just leave everything." His voice was smooth enough, but Rebecca felt the tension in his hand as he led her to a chair.

He probably thought she was a fool, she decided. All but tumbling into his arms every time he touched her. He was obviously a man of the world—and a kind man, she added as she sipped her mimosa. Not all powerful men spoke kindly to those who worked for them. Her lips curved, a little wryly, as she sipped again. She knew that firsthand.

His body was in turmoil. Stephen couldn't remember, even

in his youth, having had a woman affect him so irrationally. He knew how to persuade, how to seduce—and always with finesse. But whenever he was around this woman for more than five minutes he felt like a stallion being spurred and curbed at the same time.

And he was fascinated. Fascinated by the ease with which she went into his arms, by the trust he saw when he looked down into her eyes. As he had in the olive grove, he found himself believing he'd looked into those eyes, those rainwater-clear eyes, a hundred times before.

Still churning, he took out a cigar. The thought was fanciful, but his desire was very real. If there couldn't be finesse, perhaps there could be candor.

"I want you, Rebecca."

She felt her heart stop, then start up again with slow, dull throbs. Carefully she took another sip, then cleared her throat. "I know." It amazed her, flattered her, terrified her.

She seemed so cool. He envied her. "Will you come with me, to my cabin?"

She looked at him then. Her heart and her head were giving very different answers. It sounded so easy, so…natural. If there was a man she could give herself to, wholly, he was with her now. Complications, what complications there were, were her own.

But no matter how far she had run from Philadelphia and her own strict upbringing, there were still lines she couldn't cross.

"I can't."

"Can't?" He lit his cigar, astonished that they were discussing making love as though it were as casual a choice as what dinner entrée to chose. "Or won't?"

She drew a breath. Her palms were damp on the glass, and she set it down. "Can't. I want to." Her eyes, huge and lake-pale, clung to his. "I very much want to, but…"

"But?"

"I know so little about you." She picked up her glass again because her empty hands tended to twist together. "Hardly more than your name, that you own an olive grove and like the sea. It's not enough."

"Then I'll tell you more."

She relaxed enough to smile. "I don't know what to ask."

He leaned back in his chair, the tension dissolving as quickly as it had built. She could do that to him with nothing more than a smile. He knew no one who could excite and solace with so little effort.

"Do you believe in fate, Rebecca? In something unexpected, even unlooked-for, often a small thing that completely and irrevocably changes one's life?"

She thought of her aunt's death and her own uncharacteristic decisions. "Yes. Yes, I do."

"Good." His gaze skimmed over her face, quickly, then more leisurely. "I'd nearly forgotten that I believe it, too. Then I saw you, sitting alone."

There were ways and ways to seduce, she was discovering. A look, a tone, could be every bit as devastating as a caress. She wanted him more in that moment than she had ever known she could want anything. To give herself time, and distance, she rose and walked to the rail.

Even her silence aroused him. She had said she knew too little about him. He knew even less of her. And he didn't care. It was dangerous, possibly even destructive, but he didn't care. As he watched her with the wind billowing her shirt and her hair he realized that he didn't give a damn about where she had come from, where she had been, what she had done.

When lightning strikes, it destroys, though it blazes with

power. Rising, he went to her and stood, as she did, facing the sea.

"When I was young, very young," he began, "there was another moment that changed things. My father was a man for the water. He lived for it. Died for it." When he went on it was almost as if he were speaking to himself now, remembering. Rebecca turned her head to look at him. "I was ten or eleven. Everything was going well, the nets were full. My father and I were walking along the beach. He stopped, dipped his hand into the water, made a fist and opened it. 'You can't hold it,' he said to me. 'No matter how you try or how you love or how you sweat.' Then he dug into the sand. It was wet and clung together in his hand. 'But this,' he said, 'a man can hold.' We never spoke of it again. When my time came, I turned my back on the sea and held the land."

"It was right for you."

"Yes." He lifted a hand to catch at the ends of her hair. "It was right. Such big, quiet eyes you have, Rebecca," he murmured. "Have they seen enough, I wonder, to know what's right for you?"

"I guess I've been a little slow in starting to look." Her blood was pounding thickly. She would have stepped back, but he shifted so that she was trapped between him and the rail.

"You tremble when I touch you." He slid his hands up her arms, then down until their hands locked. "Have you any idea how exciting that is?"

Her chest tightened, diminishing her air even as the muscles in her legs went limp. "Stephen, I meant it when I said…" He brushed his lips gently over her temple. "I can't. I need to…" He feathered a kiss along her jawline, softly. "To think."

He felt her fingers go lax in his. She was suddenly fragile, outrageously vulnerable, irresistibly tempting. "When I kissed you the first time I gave you no choice." His lips trailed over her face, light as a whisper, circling, teasing, avoiding her mouth. "You have one now."

He was hardly touching her. A breath, a whisper, a mere promise of a touch. The slow, subtle passage of his lips over her skin couldn't have been called a kiss, could never have been called a demand. She had only to push away to end the torment. And the glory.

A choice? Had he told her she had a choice? "No, I don't," she murmured as she turned to find his lips with hers.

No choice, no past, no future. Only now. She felt the present, with all its needs and hungers, well up inside her. The kiss was instantly hot, instantly desperate. His heart pounded fast and hard against hers, thunderous now, as he twisted a hand in her hair to pull her head back. To plunder. No one had ever taken her like this. No one had ever warned her that a touch of violence could be so exciting. Her gasp of surprise turned into a moan of pleasure as his tongue skimmed over hers.

He thought of lightning bolts again, thought of that flash of power and light. She was electric in his arms, sparking, sizzling. Her scent, as soft, as seductive, as a whisper, clouded his mind, even as the taste of her heightened his appetite.

She was all woman, she was every woman, and yet she was like no other. He could hear each quick catch of her breath above the roar of the motor. With her name on his lips, he pressed them to the vulnerable line of her throat, where the skin was heated from the sun and as delicate as water.

She might have slid bonelessly to the deck if his body hadn't pressed hers so firmly against the rail. In wonder, in panic, she felt his muscles turn to iron wherever they touched her. Never before had she felt so fragile, so at the mercy of her own desires. The sea was as calm as glass, but she felt herself tossed, tumbled, wrecked. With a sigh that was almost a sob, she wrapped her arms around him.

It was the defenselessness of the gesture that pulled him back from the edge. He must have been mad. For a moment he'd been close, much too close, to dragging her down to the deck without a thought to her wishes or to the consequences. With his eyes closed, he held her, feeling the erratic beat of her heart, hearing her shallow, shuddering breath.

Perhaps he was still mad, Stephen thought. Even as the ragged edges of desire eased, something deeper and far more dangerous bloomed.

He wanted her, in a way no man could safely want a woman. Forever.

Fate, he thought again as he stroked her hair. It seemed he was falling in love whether he wished it or not. A few hours with her and he felt more than he had ever imagined he could feel.

There had been a few times in his life when he had seen and desired on instinct alone. What he had seen and desired, he had taken. Just as he would take her. But when he took, he meant to keep.

Carefully he stepped back. "Maybe neither of us has a choice." He dipped his hands into his pockets. "And if I touch you again, here, now, I won't give you one."

Unable to pretend, knowing they were shaking, she pushed her hands through her hair. She didn't bother to disguise the tremor in her voice. She wouldn't have known how. "I won't want one." She saw his eyes darken quickly, dangerously, but she didn't know his hands were balled into fists, straining.

"You make it difficult for me."

A long, shuddering breath escaped her. No one had ever

wanted her this way. Probably no one ever would again. "I'm sorry. I don't mean to."

"No." Deliberately he relaxed his hands. "I don't think you do. That's one of the things about you I find most intriguing. I will have you, Rebecca." He saw something flicker in her eyes.... Excitement? Panic? A combination of the two, perhaps. "Because I'm sure of it, because I know you're sure of it, I'll do my best to give you a little more time."

Her natural humor worked through the sliver of unease she felt. "I'm not sure whether I should thank you politely or run like hell."

He grinned, surprising himself, then flicked a finger down her cheek. "I wouldn't advise running, *matia mou*. I'd only catch you."

She was sure of that, too. One look at his face, even with the smile that softened it, and she knew. Kind, yes, but with a steely underlying ruthlessness. "Then I'll go with the thank-you."

"You're welcome." Patience, he realized, would have to be developed. And quickly. "Would you like to swim? There's a bay. We're nearly there."

The water might, just might, cool her off. "I'd love it."

Chapter 5

The water was cool and mirror-clear. Rebecca lowered herself into it with a sigh of pure pleasure. Back in Philadelphia she would have been at her desk, calculator clicking, the jacket of her neat business suit carefully smoothed over the back of her chair. Her figures would always tally, her forms would always be properly filed.

The dependable, efficient Miss Malone.

Instead, she was swimming in a crystal-clear bay, letting the water cool and the sun heat. Ledgers and accounts were worlds away. Here, as close as a handspan, was a man who was teaching her everything she would ever want to know about needs, desires, and the fragility of the heart.

He couldn't know it, she thought. She doubted she'd ever have the courage to tell him that he was the only one who had ever made her tremble and burn. A man as physically aware as he would only be uncomfortable knowing he held an inexperienced woman in his arms.

The water lapped around her with a sound as quiet as her own sigh. But he didn't know, because when she was in his arms she didn't feel awkward and inexperienced. She felt beautiful, desirable and reckless.

With a laugh, Rebecca dipped under the surface to let the water, and the freedom, surround her. Who would have believed it?

"Does it always take so little to make you laugh?"

Rebecca ran a hand over her slicked-back hair. Stephen was treading water beside her, smoothly, hardly making a ripple. His skin was dark gold, glistening-wet. His hair was streaked by the sun and dampened by the water, which was almost exactly the color of his eyes. She had to suppress an urge to just reach out and touch.

"A secluded inlet, a beautiful sky, an interesting man." With another sigh, she kicked her legs up so that she could float. "It doesn't seem like so little to me." She studied the vague outline of the mountains, far out of reach. "I promised myself that no matter where I went, what I did, I'd never take anything for granted again."

There was something in the way she said it, some hint of sadness, that pulled at him. The urge to comfort wasn't completely foreign in him, but he hadn't had much practice at it. "Was there a man who hurt you?"

Her lips curved at that, but he couldn't know that she was laughing at herself. Naturally, she'd dated. They had been polite, cautious evenings, usually with little interest on either side. She'd been dull, or at least she had never worked up the nerve to spread her wings. Once or twice, when she'd felt a tug, she'd been too shy, too much the efficient Rebecca Malone, to do anything about it.

With him, everything was different. Because she loved him. She didn't know how, she didn't know why, but she loved him as much as any woman could love any man.

"No. There's no one." She closed her eyes, trusting the water to carry her. "When my parents died, it hurt. It hurt so badly that I suppose I pulled back from life. I thought it was important that I be a responsible adult, even though I wasn't nearly an adult yet."

Strange that she hadn't thought of it quite that way until she'd stopped being obsessively responsible. Stranger still was how easy it was to tell him what she'd never even acknowledged herself.

"My aunt Jeannie was kind and considerate and loving, but she'd forgotten what it was like to be a young girl. Suddenly I realized I'd missed being young, lazy, foolish, all the things everyone's entitled to be at least once. I decided to make up for it."

Her hair was spread out and drifting on the water. Her eyes were closed, and her face was sheened with water. Not beautiful, Stephen told himself. She was too angular for real beauty. But she was fascinating…in looks, in philosophy…more, in the open-armed way she embraced whatever crossed her path.

He found himself looking around the inlet as he hadn't bothered to look at anything in years. He could see the sun dancing on the surface, could see the ripples spreading and growing from the quiet motion of their bodies. Farther away was the narrow curving strip of white beach, deserted now, but for a few birds fluttering over the sand. It was quiet, almost unnaturally quiet, the only sound the soft, monotonous slap of water against sand. And he was relaxed, totally, mind and body. Perhaps he, too, had forgotten what it was like to be young and foolish.

On impulse he put a hand on her shoulder and pushed her under.

She came up sputtering, dragging wet hair out of her eyes. He grinned at her and calmly continued to tread water. "It was too easy."

She tilted her head, considering him and the distance between them. Challenge leaped into her eyes, sparked with amusement. "It won't be the next time."

His grin only widened. When he moved, he moved fast, streaking under and across the water like an eel. Rebecca had time for a quick squeal. Dragging in a deep breath, she kicked out. He caught her ankle, but she was ready. Unresisting, she let him pull her under. Then, instead of fighting her way back to the surface, she wrapped her arms around him and sent them both rolling in an underwater wrestling match. They were still tangled, her arms around him, her hands hooked over his shoulders, when they surfaced.

"We're even." She gasped for air and shook the water out of her eyes.

"How do you figure?"

"If we'd had a mat I'd have pinned you. Want to go for two out of three?"

"I might." He felt her legs tangle with his as she kicked out lazily. "But for now I prefer this."

He was going to kiss her again. She saw it in his eyes, felt it in the slight tensing of the arm that locked them torso to torso. She wasn't sure she was ready. More, she was afraid she was much too ready.

"Stephen?"

"Hmm?" His lips were a breath away from hers. Then he found himself underwater again, his arms empty. He should have been furious. He nearly was when he pushed to surface. She was shoulder-deep in the water, a few feet away. Her laughter rolled over him, young, delighted, unapologetic.

"It was too easy." She managed a startled "whoops" when he struck out after her. She might have made it—she had enough of a lead—but he swam as though he'd been born in the water. Still, she was agile, and she almost managed to dodge him, but her laughter betrayed her. She gulped in water, choked, then found herself hauled up into his arms in thigh-deep water.

"I like to win." Deciding it was useless to struggle, she pressed a hand to her heart and gasped for air. "It's a personality flaw. Sometimes I cheat at canasta."

"Canasta?" The last thing he could picture the slim, sexy bundle in his arms doing was spending a quiet evening playing cards.

"I can't help myself." Still breathless, she laid her head on his shoulder. "No willpower."

"I find myself having the same problem." With a careless toss, he sent her flying through the air. She hit the water bottom first.

"I guess I deserved that." She struggled to her feet, water raining off her. "I have to sit." Wading through the water, she headed for the gentle slope of beach. She lay, half in and half out of the water, not caring that the sand would cling to her hair and skin. When he dropped down beside her, she reached out a hand for his. "I don't know when I've had a nicer day."

He looked down to where her fingers linked with his. The gesture had been so easy, so natural. He wondered how it could both comfort and arouse. "It's hardly over."

"It seems like it could last forever." She wanted it to go on and on. Blue skies and easy laughter. Cool water and endless hours. There had been a time, not so long before, when the days had dragged into nights and the nights into days. "Did you ever want to run away?"

With her hand still in his, he lay back to watch a few scattered rags of clouds drift. How long had it been, he wondered, since he'd really watched the sky? "To where?"

"Anywhere. Away from the way things are, away from what you're afraid they'll always be." She closed her eyes and could see herself brewing that first cup of coffee at exactly 7:15, opening the first file at precisely 9:01. "To drop out of sight," she murmured, "and pop up somewhere else, anywhere else, as someone completely different."

"You can't change who you are."

"Oh, but you can." Her tone suddenly urgent, she rose on her elbow. "Sometimes you have to."

He reached up to touch the ends of her hair. "What are you running from?"

"Everything. I'm a coward."

He looked into her eyes. They were so clear, so full of enthusiasm. "I don't think so."

"But you don't know me." A flicker of regret, then uncertainty, ran across her face. "I'm not sure I want you to."

"Don't I?" His fingers tightened on her hair, keeping her still. "There are people and circumstances that don't take months or years before they're understood. I look at you and something fits into place, Rebecca. I don't know why, but it is. I know you." He tugged her down for the lightest, the briefest, of kisses. "And I like what I see."

"Do you?" She smiled. "Really?"

"Do you imagine I spend the day with a woman only

because I want to sleep with her?" She shrugged, and though her blush was very faint, he noticed it and was amused by it. How many women, he wondered, could kiss a man into oblivion, then blush? "Being with you, Rebecca, is a difficult pleasure."

She chuckled and began to draw circles in the wet sand. What would he say, what would he think, if he knew what she was? Or, more accurately, what she wasn't? It didn't matter, she told herself. She couldn't let it spoil what there was between them.

"I think that's the most wonderful compliment I've ever had."

"Where have you been?" he murmured.

When she moved restlessly, he held her still. "Don't. I'm not going to touch you. Not yet."

"That's not the problem." With her eyes closed, she tilted her chin up and let the sun beat down on her face. "The problem is, I want you to touch me, so much it frightens me." Taking her time, she sat up, gathering her courage. She wanted to be honest, and she hoped she wouldn't sound like a fool. "Stephen, I don't sleep around. I need you to understand, because this is all happening so quickly. But it's not casual."

He lifted a hand to her chin and turned her to face him. His eyes were as blue as the water, and, to her, as unfathomable. "No, it's not." He made the decision quickly, though he had been turning the idea over in his mind all day. "I have to go to Athens tomorrow. Come with me, Rebecca."

"Athens?" she managed, staring at him.

"Business. A day, two at the most. I'd like you with me." And he was afraid, more than he cared to admit, that when he returned she might be gone.

"I…" What should she say? What was right?

"You told me you'd planned to go." He'd push if necessary.

Now that the idea had taken root, Stephen had no intention of going anywhere without her.

"Yes, but I wouldn't want to be in the way while you're working."

"You'll be in my way whether you're here or there."

Her head came up at that, and the look she gave him was both shy and stunning. He stifled the need to take her again, to roll until she was beneath him on the sand. He'd said he'd give her time. Perhaps what he'd really meant was that he needed time himself.

"You'll have your own suite. No strings, Rebecca. Just your company."

"A day or two," she murmured.

"It's a simple matter to have your room held for you here for your return."

Her return. Not his. If he left Corfu tomorrow she would probably never see him again. He was offering her another day, perhaps two. Never take anything for granted, she remembered. Never again.

Athens, she thought. It was true that she had planned to see it before she left Greece. But she would have gone alone. A few days before, that had been what she thought she wanted. The adventure of seeing new places, new people, on her own. Now the thought of going with him, of having him beside her when she first caught sight of the Acropolis, of having him want her with him, changed everything.

"I'd love to go with you." She rose quickly and dived into the water. She was in over her head.

Chapter 6

Athens was neither East nor West. It was spitted meat and spices roasting. It was tall buildings and modern shops. It was narrow, unpaved streets and clamorous bazaars. It had been the scene of revolution and brutality. It was ancient and civilized and passionate.

Rebecca quite simply fell in love at first sight.

She'd been seduced by Paris and charmed by London, but in Athens she lost her heart. She wanted to see everything at once, from sunrise to moonlight, and the heat-drenched afternoon between.

All that first morning, while Stephen was immersed in business meetings, she wandered. The hotel he'd chosen was lovely, but she was drawn to the streets and the people. Somehow she didn't feel like a visitor here. She felt like someone who had returned home after a long, long journey. Athens was waiting for her, ready to welcome her back.

Incredible. All her life she had accepted the parameters set for her. Now she was touring Old Athens, with its clicking worry beads and its open-fronted shops, where she could buy cheap plaster copies of monuments or elegant antiques.

She passed tavernas, but she was too excited to be tempted by the rich smells of coffee and baking. She heard the clear notes of a flute as she looked up and saw the Acropolis.

There was only one approach. Though it was still early, other tourists were making their way toward the ruins in twos and in groups. Rebecca let her camera hang by its strap. Despite the chattering around her, she felt alone, but beautifully so.

She would never be able to explain what it felt like to stand in the morning sun and look at something that had been built for the gods—something that had endured war and weather and time. It had been a place of worship. Even now, after centuries had passed, Rebecca felt the spiritual pull. Perhaps the goddess Athena, with her gleaming helmet and spear, still visited there.

Rebecca had been disappointed that Stephen couldn't join her on her first morning in Athens. Now she was glad to be alone—to sit and absorb and imagine without having to explain her thoughts.

How could she, after having seen so much, go back to so little? Sighing, she wandered through the temples. It wasn't just the awe she felt here, or the excitement she had felt in London and Paris, that had changed her. It was Stephen and everything she'd felt, everything she'd wanted, since she'd met him.

Perhaps she would go back to Philadelphia, but she would never be the same person. Once you fell in love, completely, totally in love, nothing was ever the same.

She wished it could be simple, the way she imagined it was simple for so many other women. An attractive man, a physical tug. But with Stephen, as with Athens, she'd lost her heart. However implausible it seemed, she had recognized the man, as well as the city, as being part of her, as being for her. Desire, when tangled up with love, could never be simple.

But how could you be sure you were in love when it had never happened to you before? If she were home, at least she would have a friend to talk to. With a little laugh, Rebecca walked out into the sunlight. How many times had she been on the receiving end of a long, scattered conversation from a friend who had fallen in love—or thought she had. The excitement, the unhappiness, the thrills. Sometimes she'd been envious, and sometimes she'd been grateful not to have the complication in her own life. But always, always, she'd offered calm, practical, even soothing advice.

Oddly enough, she didn't seem to be able to do the same for herself.

All she could think of was the way her heart pounded when he touched her, how excitement, panic and anticipation fluttered through her every time he looked at her. When she was with him, her feelings and fantasies seemed reasonable. When she was with him, she could believe in fate, in the matching of soul to soul.

It wasn't enough. At least that was what she would have told another woman. Attraction and passion weren't enough. Yet there was no explaining, even to herself, the sense of rightness she experienced whenever she was with him. If she were a fanciful person she would say it was as though she'd been waiting for him, waiting for the time and the place for him to come to her.

It sounded simple—if fate could be considered simple. Yet

beneath all the pleasure and that sense of reunion was guilt. She couldn't shake it, and she knew she wouldn't be able to ignore it much longer. She wasn't the woman she had let him believe her to be. She wasn't the well-traveled at-loose-ends free spirit she pretended to be. No matter how many ties she'd cut, she was still Rebecca Malone. How would he feel about her once he knew how limited and dull her life had been?

How and when was she going to tell him?

A few more days, she promised herself as she began the walk back. It was selfish, perhaps it was even dangerous, but she wanted just a few more days.

It was midafternoon before she returned to the hotel. Ignoring the fact that she might be considered overeager, she went straight to Stephen's suite. She couldn't wait to see him, to tell him everything she'd seen, to show him everything she'd bought. Her easy smile faded a bit when his secretary Elana opened the door.

"Miss Malone." Gracious and self-confident, Elana waved her in. "Please sit down. I'll let Stephen know you're here."

"I don't want to interrupt." Rebecca shifted her bags, feeling gauche and foolish.

"Not at all. Have you just come in?"

"Yes, I…" For the first time, Rebecca noticed that her skin was damp and her hair tousled. In contrast, Elana was cool and perfectly groomed. "I really should go."

"Please." Elana urged Rebecca to a chair. "Let me get you a drink." With a half smile, Elana began to pour a tall glass of iced juice. She had expected Stephen's mystery lady to be smooth, controlled and stunning. It pleased her a great deal to find Rebecca wide-eyed, a little unsure, and clearly a great deal in love.

"Did you enjoy your morning?"

"Yes, very much." She accepted the glass and tried to relax. Jealousy, she realized, feeling herself flush at the re-alization. She couldn't remember ever having experienced the sensation before. Who wouldn't be jealous? she asked herself as she watched Elana walk to the phone. The Greek woman was gorgeous, self-contained, coolly efficient. Above all, she had a relationship with Stephen that Rebecca knew nothing about. How long has she known him? Rebecca wondered. And how well?

"Stephen's just finishing up some business," Elana said as she hung up the phone. With easy, economical moves, she poured herself a drink, then walked to the chair facing Rebecca. "What do you think of Athens?"

"I love it." Rebecca wished she'd taken the time to brush her hair and freshen her makeup. Lecturing herself, she sipped at her juice. "I'm not sure what I expected, but it's everything and more."

"Europeans see it as the East, Orientals see it as the West." Elana crossed her legs and settled back. It surprised her to realize that she was prepared to like Rebecca Malone. "What Athens is is Greek—and, more particularly, Athenian." She paused, studying Rebecca over the rim of her glass. "People often view Stephen in much the same way, and what he is is Stephen."

"How long have you worked for him?"

"Five years."

"You must know him well."

"Better than some. He's a demanding and generous employer and an interesting man. Fortunately, I like to travel and I enjoy my work."

Rebecca rubbed at a spot of dust on her slacks. "It never

occurred to me that farming required so much traveling. I never realized how much was involved in growing olives."

Elana's brows rose in obvious surprise, but she continued smoothly when Rebecca glanced back at her. "Whatever Stephen does, he does thoroughly." She smiled to herself, satisfied. She hadn't been certain until now whether the American woman was attracted to Stephen or to his position. "Has Stephen explained to you about the dinner party this evening?"

"He said something about a small party here at the hotel. A business dinner."

"Men take these things more lightly than women." Feeling friendlier, Elena offered her first genuine smile. "It will be small, but quite extravagant." She watched as Rebecca automatically lifted a hand to her hair. "If you need anything—a dress, a salon—the hotel can accommodate you."

Rebecca thought of the casual sportswear she'd tossed into her bag before the impulsive trip to Athens. "I need everything."

With a quick, understanding laugh, Elana rose. "I'll make some calls for you."

"Thank you, but I don't want to interfere with your work."

"Seeing that you're comfortable is part of my work." They both glanced over when the door opened. "Stephen. You see, she hasn't run away." Taking her glass and her pad, she left them alone.

"You were gone a long time." He hated the fact that he'd begun to watch the clock and worry. He'd imagined her hurt or abducted. He'd begun to wonder if she would disappear from his life as quickly as she'd appeared in it. Now she was here, her eyes alive with pleasure, her clothes rumpled and her hair windblown.

"I guess I got caught up exploring." She started to rise, but before she could gain her feet he was pulling her out of the chair, seeking, finding her mouth with his.

His desperation whipped through her. His hunger incited her own. Without thought, without hesitation, she clung to him, answering, accepting. Already seduced, she murmured something, an incoherent sound that caught in her throat.

Good God, he thought, it wasn't possible, it wasn't sane, to want like this. Throughout the morning while all the facts and figures and demands of business had been hammering at him, he'd thought of her, of holding her, of tasting her, of being with her. When she had stayed away for so long he'd begun to imagine, then to fear, what his life would be like without her.

It wasn't going to happen. He scraped his teeth over her bottom lip, and she gasped and opened for him. He wouldn't let it happen. Where she came from, where she intended to go, no longer mattered. She belonged to him now. And, though he'd only begun to deal with it, he belonged to her.

But he needed some sanity, some logic. Fighting himself, Stephen drew her away from him. Her eyes remained closed, and her lips remained parted. A soft, sultry sound escaped them as her lashes fluttered upward.

"I…" She took a deep breath and let it out slowly. "I should go sightseeing more often."

Gradually he realized how hard his fingers were pressing into her arms. As if he were afraid she would slip away. Cursing himself, he relaxed. "I would have preferred to go with you."

"I understand you're busy. I'd have bored you silly, poking into every shop and staring at every column."

"No." If there was one thing he was certain of, it was that she would never bore him. "I'd like to have seen your first impression of Athens."

"It was like coming home," she told him, then hurried on because it sounded foolish. "I couldn't get enough." Laughing at herself, she gestured toward her bags. "Obviously. It's so different from anywhere I've ever been. At the Acropolis I couldn't even take any pictures, because I knew they couldn't capture the feeling. Then I walked along the streets and saw old men with *kom—konbou—*" She fumbled over the Greek and finally made a helpless gesture.

"Kombouloi," he murmured. "Worry beads."

"Yes, and I imagined how they might sit in those shadowy doorways watching the tourists go by, day after day, year after year." She sat, pleased to share her impressions with him. "I saw a shop with all these costumes, lots of tinsel, and some really dreadful plaster copies of the monuments."

He grinned and sat beside her. "How many did you buy?"

"Three or four." She bent down to rattle through her bags. "I bought you a present."

"A plaster statue of Athena?"

She glanced up, eyes laughing. "Almost. Then I found this tiny antique shop in the old section. It was all dim and dusty and irresistible. The owner had a handful of English phrases, and I had my phrase book. After we'd confused each other completely, I bought this."

She drew out an S-shaped porcelain pipe decorated with paintings of the wild mountain goats of Greece. Attached to it was a long wooden stem, as smooth as glass, tipped by a tarnished brass mouthpiece.

"I remembered the goats we'd seen on Corfu," she explained as Stephen examined it. "I thought you might like it, though I've never seen you smoke a pipe."

With a quiet laugh, he looked back at her, balancing the gift in both hands. "No, I don't—at least not of this nature."

"Well, it's more ornamental than functional, I suppose. The man couldn't tell me much about it—at least not that I could understand." She reached out to run a finger along the edge of the bowl. "I've never seen anything like it."

"I'm relieved to hear it." When she sent him a puzzled look, he leaned over to brush her lips with his. "*Matia mou,* this is a hashish pipe."

"A hashish pipe?" She stared, first in shock, then in fascination. "Really? I mean, did people actually use it?"

"Undoubtedly. Quite a number, I'd say, since it's at least a hundred and fifty years old."

"Imagine that." She pouted, imagining dark, smoky dens. "I guess it's not a very appropriate souvenir."

"On the contrary, whenever I see it I'll think of you."

She glanced up quickly, unsure, but the amusement in his eyes had her smiling again. "I should have bought you the plaster statue of Athena."

Taking her hands, he drew her to her feet. "I'm flattered that you bought me anything." She felt the subtle change as his fingers tightened on hers. "I want time with you, Rebecca. Hours of it. Days. There's too much I need to know." When she lowered her gaze, he caught her chin. "What are those secrets of yours?"

"Nothing that would interest you."

"You're wrong. Tomorrow I intend to find out all there is to know." He saw the quick flicker of unease in her eyes. Other men, he thought with an uncomfortable surge of jealousy. The hell with them. "No more evasions. I want you, all of you. Do you understand?"

"Yes, but—"

"Tomorrow." He cut her off, suddenly, completely, frustratingly Greek. "I have business that can't be avoided now. I'll come for you at seven."

"All right."

Tomorrow was years away, she told herself. She had time to decide what she would say, how she would say it. Before tomorrow came tonight. She would be everything she'd ever wanted to be, everything he wanted her to be.

"I'd better go." Before he could touch her again, she bent to gather her bags. "Stephen…" She paused at the door and turned to look at him as he stood in the middle of the room, comfortable with the wealth that surrounded him, confident with who and what he was. "You might be disappointed when you find out."

She left quickly, leaving him frowning after her.

Chapter 7

She was as nervous as a cat. Every time she looked in the mirror Rebecca wondered who the woman was who was staring back at her. It wasn't a stranger, but it was a very, very different Rebecca Malone.

Was it just the different hairstyle, poufed and frizzed and swept around her face? Could it be the dress, the glittery spill of aquamarine that left her arms and shoulders bare? No, it was more than that. More than makeup and clever stylists and glamorous clothes. It was in her eyes. How could she help but see it? How could anyone? The woman who looked back from the mirror was a woman in love.

What was she going to do about it? What could she do? she asked herself. She was still practical enough to accept that some things could never be changed. But was she bold enough, or strong enough, to take what she wanted and live with the consequences?

When she heard the knock on the door, Rebecca took a deep breath and picked up the useless compact-size evening bag she'd bought just that afternoon. It was all happening so fast. When she'd come back from Stephen's suite there had been a detailed message from Elana listing appointments—for a massage, a facial, hairstyling—along with the name of the manager of the hotel's most exclusive boutique. She hadn't had time to think, even for a minute, about her evening with Stephen. Or about any tomorrows.

Perhaps that was best, she decided as she pulled open the door. It was best not to think, not to analyze. It was best to accept and to act.

She looked like a siren, some disciple of Circe, with her windswept hair and a dress the color of seductive seas. Had he told himself she wasn't beautiful? Had he believed it? At that moment he was certain he'd never seen, never would see, a more exciting woman.

"You're amazing, Rebecca." He took her hand and drew her to him so that they stood in the doorway together. On the threshold.

"Why? Because I'm on time?"

"Because you're never what I expect." He brought her hand to his lips. "And always what I want."

Because she was speechless, she was glad when he closed the door at her back and led her to the elevators. He looked different from the man she had first met, the one who dressed with such casual elegance. Tonight there was a formality about him, and the sophistication she had sensed earlier was abundantly apparent in the ease with which he wore the black dinner jacket.

"The way you look," he told her, "it seems a shame to waste the evening on a business dinner."

"I'm looking forward to meeting some of your friends."

"Associates," he said with an odd smile. "When you've been poor—and don't intend to be poor again—you rarely make friends in business."

She frowned. This was a side of him, the business side, that she didn't know. Would he be ruthless? She looked at him, saw it, and accepted it. Yes, a man like Stephen would always be ruthless with what belonged to him. "But enemies?"

"The same rule, in business, applies to friends and enemies. My father taught me more than fishing, Rebecca. He also taught me that to succeed, to attain, you must learn not only how to trust, but how far."

"I've never been poor, but I imagine it's frightening."

"Strengthening." He took her hand again when the elevator doors opened. "We have different backgrounds, Rebecca, but, fortunately, we've come to the same place."

He had no idea *how* different. Trust. He had spoken of trust. She discovered she wanted to tell him, tell him everything. Tell him that she knew nothing of elegant parties and glamorous life-styles. She was a fraud, and when he found out he might laugh at her and brush her aside. But she wanted him to know.

"Stephen, I want to—"

"Stephen. Once more you outdo us all in your choice of women."

"Dimitri."

Rebecca stopped, caught on the brink of confession. The man who faced her was classically handsome. His silver mane contrasted with bronzed skin lined by a half century of sun. He wore a mustache that swept majestically over gleaming teeth.

"It was kind of you to invite us here this evening, but it would be kinder still to introduce me to your lovely companion."

"Rebecca Malone, Dimitri Petropolis."

A diamond glittered on the hand he lifted to clasp Rebecca's. The hand itself was hard as rock. "A pleasure. Athens is already abuzz with talk of the woman who arrived with Stephen."

Certain he was joking, she smiled. "Then Athens must be in desperate need of news."

His eyes widened for a moment, then creased at the corners when he laughed. "I have no doubt you will provide an abundance of it."

Stephen slipped a hand under Rebecca's elbow. The look he sent Dimitri was very quick and very clear. They had competed over land, but there would be no competition over Rebecca.

"If you'll excuse us a moment, Dimitri, I'd like to get Rebecca some champagne."

"Of course." Amused—and challenged—Dimitri brushed at his mustache as he watched them walk away.

Rebecca had no way of knowing that to Stephen a small dinner party meant a hundred people. She sipped her first glass of wine, hoping she wouldn't embarrass them both by being foolishly shy and tongue-tied. In the past, whenever she had found herself in a crowd, she had always looked for the nearest corner to fade into. Not tonight, she promised herself, straightening her shoulders.

There were dozens of names to remember, but she filed them away as easily as she had always filed numbers. In the hour before dinner, while the guests mixed and mingled, she found herself at ease. The stomach flutters and hot blushes she'd often experienced at parties and functions simply didn't happen.

Perhaps she was the new Rebecca Malone after all.

She heard business discussed here and there. Most of it

seemed to be hotel and resort business—talk of remodeling and expansions, mergers and takeovers. She found it odd that so many of the guests were in that trade, rather than prosperous farmers or olive growers.

Stephen came up behind her and murmured in her ear, "You look pleased with yourself."

"I am." He couldn't know that she was pleased to find herself at ease and comfortable in a party of strangers. "So many interesting people."

"Interesting." He brushed a finger over her wispy bangs. "I thought you might find it dull."

"Not at all." She took a last sip of champagne, then set the glass aside. Instantly a waiter was at her side, offering another. Stephen watched her smile her thanks.

"So you enjoy parties?"

"Sometimes. I'm enjoying this one, and having a chance to meet your associates."

Stephen glanced over her shoulder, summing up the looks and quiet murmurs. "They'll be talking about you for weeks to come."

She only laughed, turning in a slow circle. Around her was the flash of jewels and the gleam of gold. The sleek and the prosperous, the rich and the successful. It pleased her that she'd found more to talk about than tax shelters.

"I can't imagine they have so little on their minds. This is such a gorgeous room."

She looked around the huge ballroom, with its cream-and-rose walls, its glittering chandeliers and its gleaming floors. There were alcoves for cozy love seats and tall, thriving ornamental trees in huge copper pots. The tables, arranged to give a sense of intimacy, were already set with ivory cloths and slender tapers.

"It's really a beautiful hotel," she continued. "Everything about it runs so smoothly." She smiled up at him. "I'm torn between the resort in Corfu and this."

"Thank you." When she gave him a blank look, he tipped up her chin with his finger. "They're mine."

"Your what?"

"My hotels," he said simply, then led her to a table.

She spoke all through dinner, though for the first fifteen minutes she had no idea what she said. There were eight at Stephen's table, including Dimitri, who had shifted name cards so that he could sit beside her. She toyed with her seafood appetizer, chatted and wondered if she could have made a bigger fool out of herself.

He wasn't simply prosperous. He wasn't simply well-off. There was enough accountant left in Rebecca to understand that when a man owned what Stephen owned he was far, far more than comfortable.

What would he think of her when he found out what she was? Trust? How could she ever expect him to trust her now? She swallowed without tasting and managed to smile. Would he think she was a gold digger, that she had set herself up to run into him?

No, that was ridiculous.

She forced herself to look over and saw that Stephen was watching her steadily. She picked up her fork with one hand and balled up the napkin in her lap with the other.

Why couldn't he be ordinary? she wondered. Someone vacationing, someone working at the resort? Why had she fallen in love with someone so far out of her reach?

"Have you left us?"

Rebecca jerked herself back to see Dimitri smiling at her. Flushing, she noticed that the next course had been served while she'd been daydreaming. "I'm sorry." With an effort she began to toy with the *salata Athenas*.

"A beautiful woman need never apologize for being lost in her own thoughts." He patted her hand, then let his fingers linger. He caught Stephen's dark look and smiled. If he didn't like the boy so much, he thought, he wouldn't get nearly so much pleasure from irritating him. "Tell me, how did you meet Stephen?"

"We met in Corfu." She thought of that first meal they had shared…quiet, relaxed, alone.

"Ah, soft nights and sunny days. You are vacationing?"

"Yes." Rebecca put more effort into her smile. If she stared into her salad she would only embarrass herself, and Stephen. "He was kind enough to show me some of the island."

"He knows it well, and many of the other islands of our country. There's something of the gypsy in him."

She had sensed that. Hadn't that been part of the attraction? Hadn't Rebecca just discovered the gypsy in herself? "Have you know him long?"

"We have a long-standing business relationship. Friendly rivals, you might say. When Stephen was hardly more than a boy he accumulated an impressive amount of land." He gestured expansively. "As you can see, he used it wisely. I believe he has two hotels in your country."

"Two? More?" Rebecca picked up her glass and took a long swallow of wine.

"So you see, I had wondered if you had met in America and were old friends."

"No." Rebecca nodded weakly as the waiter removed the salad and replaced it with moussaka. "We only just met a few days ago."

"As always, Stephen moves quickly and stylishly." Dimitri

took her hand again, more than a little amused by the frown he saw deepening in Stephen's eyes. "Where is it in America you are from?"

"Philadelphia." Relax, she ordered herself. Relax and enjoy. "That's in the Northeast."

It infuriated Stephen to watch her flirting so easily, so effectively, with another man. She sat through course after course, barely eating, all the while gifting Dimitri with her shy smiles. Not once did she draw away when the older man touched her hand or leaned close. From where he sat, Stephen could catch a trace of her scent, soft, subtle, maddening. He could hear her quiet laugh when Dimitri murmured something in her ear.

Then she was standing with him, her hand caught in his, as he led her to the dance floor.

Stephen sat there, battling back a jealousy he despised, and watched them move together to music made for lovers. Under the lights her dress clung, then swayed, then shifted. Her face was close, too damn close, to Dimitri's. He knew what it was like to hold her like that, to breathe in the scent of her skin and her hair. He knew what it was to feel her body brush against his, to feel the life, the passion, bubbling. He knew what it was to see her eyes blurr, her lips part, to hear that quiet sigh.

He had often put his stamp on land, but never on a woman. He didn't believe in it. But only a fool sat idly by and allow another man to enjoy what was his. With a muttered oath, Stephen rose, strode out onto the dance floor and laid a hand on Dimitri's shoulder.

"Ah, well." The older man gave a regretful sigh and stepped aside. "Until later."

Before she could respond, Rebecca was caught against

Stephen. With a sigh of her own, she relaxed and matched her steps to his. Maybe it was like a dream, she told herself as she closed her eyes and let the music fill her head. But she was going to enjoy every moment until it was time to wake up.

She seemed to melt against him. Her fingers moved lightly through his hair as she rested her cheek against his. Was this the way she'd danced with Dimitri? Stephen wondered, then cursed himself. He was being a fool, but he couldn't seem to stop himself. Then again, he'd had to fight for everything else in his life. Why should his woman be any different?

He wanted to drag her off then and there, away from everyone, and find some dark, quiet place to love her.

"You're enjoying yourself?"

"Yes." She wouldn't think about what he was, not now. Soon enough the night would be over and tomorrow would have to be faced. While the music played and he held her, she would only think of what he meant to her. "Very much."

The dreamy tone of her voice almost undid him. "Apparently Dimitri entertained you well."

"Mmm. He's a very nice man."

"You moved easily from his arms to mine."

Something in his tone pried through the pleasure she felt. Carefully she drew back so that she could see his face. "I don't think I know what you mean."

"I believe you do."

She was tempted to laugh, but there was no humor in Stephen's eyes. Rebecca felt her stomach knot as it always did when she was faced with a confrontation. "If I do, then I'd have to think you ridiculous. Maybe we'd better go back to the table."

"So you can be with him?" Even as the words came out he realized the unfairness, even the foolishness, of them.

She stiffened, retreating as far as she could from anger. "I don't think this is the place for this kind of discussion."

"You're quite right." As furious with himself as he was with her, he pulled her from the dance floor.

Chapter 8

"Stop it." By the time he'd dragged her to the elevators, Rebecca had gotten over her first shock. "What's gotten into you?"

"I'm simply taking you to a more suitable place for our discussion." He pulled her into the elevator, then punched the button for their floor.

"You have guests," she began, but he sent her a look than made her feel like a fool. Falling back on dignity, she straightened her shoulders. "I prefer to be asked if I want to leave, not dragged around as though I were a pack mule."

Though her heart was pounding, she sailed past him when the doors opened, intending to breeze into her own rooms and slam the door in his face. In two steps he had her arm again. Rebecca found herself guided, none too gently, into Stephen's suite.

"I don't want to talk to you," she said, because she was certain her teeth would begin to chatter at any moment. She didn't argue well in the best of circumstances. Faced with Stephen's anger, she was certain she would lose.

He said nothing as he loosened his tie and the first two buttons of his shirt. He went to the bar and poured two brandies. He was being irrational and he knew it, but he seemed unable to control it. That was new, he decided. But there had been many new emotions in him since Rebecca.

Walking back to Rebecca, he set one snifter by her elbow. When he looked at her…he wanted to shout, to beg, to demand, to plead. As a result, his voice was clipped and hard.

"You came to Athens with me, not with Dimitri or any other man."

She didn't touch the snifter. She was certain her hands would shake so hard that it would slip out of her grip. "Is that a Greek custom?" It amazed her—and bolstered her confidence—to hear how calm her voice was. "Forbidding a woman to speak to another man?"

"Speak?" He could still see the way Dimitri had bent his head close to hers. Dimitri, who was smooth and practiced. Dimitri, whose background would very likely mirror Rebecca's. Old money, privileged childhoods, quiet society. "Do you allow every man who speaks to you to hold you, to touch you?"

She didn't blush. Instead, the color faded from her cheeks. She shook, not with fear but with fury. "What I do, and with whom I do it, is my business. Mine."

Very deliberately he lifted his snifter and drank. "No."

"If you think that because I came here with you you have the right to dictate to me you're wrong. I'm my own person, Stephen." It struck her even as she said it that it was true. She was her own person. Each decision she made was her own. Filled with a new sense of power, she stepped forward. "No one owns me, not you, not anyone. I won't be ordered, I won't be forced, I won't be pressured." With a flick of her skirts, she turned. He had her again quickly, his hands on both of her arms, his face close.

"You won't go back to him."

"You couldn't stop me if that was what I wanted." She tossed her head back challengingly. "But I have no intention of going back downstairs to Dimitri, or anyone else." She jerked her arms free. "You idiot. Why should I want to be with him when I'm in love with you?"

She stopped, her eyes wide with shock, her lips parted in surprise. Overwhelmed by a combination of humiliation and fury, she spun around. Then she was struggling against him. "Leave me alone! Oh, God, just leave me alone!"

"Do you think I could let you go now?" He caught her hair in his hand, dragging it back until her eyes met his. In them she saw triumph and desire. "I feel as though I've waited all my life to hear you say those words." He rained kisses over her face until her struggles ceased. "You drive me mad," he murmured. "Being with you, being without you."

"Please." Colors, shapes, lights were whirling in her head. "I need to think."

"No. Ask me for anything else, but not more time." Gathering her close, he buried his face in her hair. "Do you think I make a fool of myself over every woman?"

"I don't know." She moaned when his lips trailed down her throat. Something wild and terrifying was happening inside her body. "I don't know you. You don't know me."

"Yes, I do." He pulled away just far enough to look down at her. "From the first moment I saw you, I knew you. Needed you. Wanted you."

It was true. She knew it, felt it, but she shook her head in denial. "It's not possible."

"I've loved you before, Rebecca, almost as much as I do now." He felt her go still. The color fled from her face again, but her eyes stayed steady on his.

"I don't want you to say what isn't real, what you're not sure of."

"Didn't you feel it, the first time I kissed you?" When he saw the acknowledgment in her eyes, his grip tightened. He could feel her heart thundering, racing to match the rhythm of his own. "Somehow you've come back to me, and I to you. No more questions," he said, before she could speak. "I need you tonight."

It was real. She felt the truth and the knowledge when his mouth found hers. If it was wrong to go blindly into need, then she would pay whatever price was asked. She could no longer deny him...or herself.

There was no gentleness in the embrace. It was as it had been the first time, lovers reunited, a hunger finally quenched. All heat and light. She gave more than she'd known she had. Her mouth was as avid as his, as seeking. Her murmurs were as desperate. Her hands didn't shake as they moved over him. They pressed, gripped, demanded. Greedy, she tugged the jacket from his shoulders.

Yes, he'd come back to her. If it was madness to believe it, then for tonight she'd be mad.

The taste of her, just the taste of her, was making his head swim and his blood boil. He nipped at her lip, then sucked until he heard her helpless whimper. He wanted her helpless. Something fierce and uncivilized inside him wanted her weak and pliant and defenseless. When she went limp in his arms he dived into her mouth and plundered. Her response tore at him, so sweet, so vulnerable, then suddenly so ardent.

Her hands, which had fluttered helplessly to her side, rose

up again to pull at his shirt, to race under it to warmed flesh. She could only think of how right it felt to touch him, to press against him and wait for him to light new fires inside her.

With an oath, he swept her up into his arms and carried her to the bedroom.

The moon was waning and offered only the most delicate light. It fell in slants and shadows on the bed, dreamlike. But the vibrating of Rebecca's pulse told her this was no dream. There was the scent of jasmine from the sprigs in the vase beside the bed. It was a scent she would always remember, just as she would remember how dark and deep were the color of his eyes.

Needful, desperate, they tumbled onto the bed.

He wanted to take care with her. She seemed so small, so fragile. He wanted to show her how completely she filled his heart. But his body was on fire, and she was already moving like a whirlwind beneath him.

His mouth was everywhere, making her shudder and arch and ache. Desires she'd never known sprang to life inside her and took control. Delirious, she obeyed them, reveled in them, then searched for more.

They rolled across the bed in a passionate war that would have two victors, touching, taking, discovering. Impatient, he peeled the dress from her, moaning as he found her breasts with his hands, his lips, his teeth. Unreasoning desire catapulted through him when he felt her soar.

Her body felt like a furnace, impossibly hot, impossibly strong. Sensations rammed into her, stealing her breath. Mindless and moaning, she writhed under him, open for any demand he might make, pulsing for any new knowledge he might offer.

Finally, finally, she knew what it was to love, to be loved.

o be wanted beyond reason. Naked, she clung to him, awash
n the power and the weakness, the glory and the terror.

He raced over her as if he already knew what would make
er tremble, what would make her yearn. Never before had
he been so aware, so in tune with another.

She made him feel like a god. He touched, and her skin
ibrated under his hand. He tasted, and her flavor was like no
ther. She was moist, heated, and utterly willing. She seemed
o explode beneath him, lost in pleasure, drugged by passion.
No other woman had ever driven him so close to madness. Her
ead was thrown back, and one hand was flung out as her
ingers dug into the sheets. Wanton, waiting, wild.

With her name on his lips, he drove into her. His breath
aught. His mind spun. Her cry of pain and release echoed in
is head, bringing him both triumph and guilt. His body went
igid as he fought to claw his way back. Then she seemed to
lose around him, body, heart, soul. As helpless as she, he
rossed the line into madness and took her with him.

Chapter 9

Aftershocks of passion wracked her. Stunned and confused, she lay in the shadowed light. Nothing had prepared her for this. No one had ever warned her that pleasure could be so huge or that need could be so jagged. If she had known… Rebecca closed her eyes and nearly laughed out loud. If she had known, she would have left everything behind years ago and searched the world for him.

Only him. She let out a quiet, calming sigh. Only him.

He was cursing himself, slowly, steadily, viciously. Innocent. Dear God. She'd been innocent, as fresh and untouched as spring, and he'd used her, hurt her, taken her.

Disgusted with himself, he sat up and reached for a cigar. He needed more than tobacco. He needed a drink, but he didn't trust his legs to carry him.

The flick of his lighter sounded like a gunshot. For an instant his face, hardened by anger and self-loathing, was illuminated.

"Why didn't you tell me?"

Still floating on an ocean of pleasure, she blinked her eyes open. "What?"

"Damn it, Rebecca, why didn't you tell me you hadn't been with a man before? That this—that I was your first?"

There was an edge of accusation in his voice. For the first time, she realized she was naked. Her cheeks grew hot as she fumbled for the sheet. One moment there was glory; the next, shame. "I didn't think of it."

"Didn't think of it?" His head whipped around. "Don't you think I had a right to know? Do you think this would have happened if I had known?"

She shook her head. It was true that she hadn't thought of it. It hadn't mattered. He was the first, the last, the only. But now it occurred to her that a man like him might not want to make love with an inexperienced woman. "I'm sorry." Her heart seemed to shrivel in her breast. "You said that you loved me, that you wanted me. The rest didn't seem to matter."

She'd cried out. He'd heard the shock and pain in her voice. And he hadn't been able to stop himself. Yes, he needed a drink. "It mattered," he tossed back as he rose and strode into the other room.

Alone, she let out a shuddering breath. Of course it mattered. Only a fool would have thought otherwise. He'd thought he was dealing with an experienced, emotionally mature woman who knew how to play the game. Words like *love* and *need* and *want* were interchangeable. Yes, he'd said he loved her, but to many love was physical and physical only.

She'd made a fool of herself and she'd infuriated him, and all because she'd begun a relationship built on illusions.

She'd knowingly taken the risk, Rebecca reminded herself as she climbed out of bed. Now she'd pay the price.

He was calmer when he started back to the bedroom. Calmer, though anger still bubbled inside him. First he would show her how it should have been, how it could be. Then they had to talk, rationally, coherently.

"Rebecca…" But when he looked at the bed it was empty.

She was wrapped in a robe and was hurling clothing into her suitcase when she heard him knock. With a shake of her head, she rubbed the tears from her cheeks and continued her frenzied packing. She wouldn't answer…. She wouldn't answer and be humiliated again.

"Rebecca." The moment of calm he'd achieved had vanished. Swearing through gritted teeth, he pounded on the door. "Rebecca, this is ridiculous. Open this door."

Ignoring him, she swept bottles and tubes of toiletries off the bureau and into her bag. He'd go away, she told herself, hardly aware that she'd begun to sob. He'd go away and then she'd leave, take a cab to the airport and catch the first plane to anywhere.

The sound of splintering wood had her rushing into the parlor in time to see the door give way.

She'd thought she'd seen fury before, but she'd been wrong. She saw it now as she stared into Stephen's face. Speechless, she looked from him to the broken door and back again.

Elana, tying the belt of her robe, rushed down the hall. "Stephen, what's happened? Is there a—"

He turned on her, hurling one short sentence in clipped Greek at her. Her eyes widened and she backed away, sending Rebecca a look that combined sympathy and envy.

"Do you think you have only to walk away from me?" He pushed the door back until it scraped against the battered jamb.

"I want—" Rebecca lifted a hand to her throat as if to push the words out. "I want to be alone."

"The hell with what you want." He started toward her, only to stop dead when she cringed and turned away. He'd forgotten what it was like to hurt, truly hurt, until that moment. "I asked you once if you were afraid of me. Now I see that you are." Searching for control, he dipped his hands into the pockets of the slacks he'd thrown on. She looked defenseless, terrified, and tears still streaked her cheeks. "I won't hurt you again. Will you sit?" When she shook her head, he bit off an oath. "I will."

"I know you're angry with me," she began when he'd settled into a chair. "I'll apologize if it'll do any good, but I do want to be alone."

His eyes had narrowed and focused. "You'll apologize? For what?"

"For…" What did he expect her to say? Humiliated, she crossed her arms and hugged her elbows. "For what happened…for not…explaining," she finished lamely. "For whatever you like," she continued as the tears started again. "Just leave me alone."

"Sweet God." He rubbed a weary hand over his face. "I can think of nothing in my life I've handled as badly as this." He rose, but stopped again when she automatically retreated. "You don't want me to touch you." His voice had roughened. He had to swallow to clear his throat. "I won't, but I hope you'll listen."

"There's nothing more to say. I understand how you feel and why you feel it. I'd rather we just left it at that."

"I treated you inexcusably."

"I don't want an apology."

"Rebecca—"

"I don't." Her voice rose, stopping his words, stopping her tears. "It's my fault. It's been my fault all along. No, no, no!"

she shouted when he took another step. "I don't want you to touch me. I couldn't bear it."

He sucked in his breath, then let it out slowly. "You twist the knife well."

But she was shaking her head and pacing the room now. "It didn't matter at first—at least I didn't think it would matter. I didn't know who you were or that I would fall in love with you. Now I've waited too long and ruined everything."

"What are you talking about?"

Perhaps it was best, best for both of them, to lay out the truth. "You said you knew me, but you don't, because I've done nothing but lie to you, right from the first moment."

Slowly, carefully, he lowered himself to the arm of a chair. "What have you lied to me about?"

"Everything." Her eyes were drenched with regret when she looked at him. "Then, tonight… First I found out that you own hotels. *Own* them."

"It was hardly a secret. Why should it matter?"

"It wouldn't." She dropped her hands to her sides. "If I was what I'd pretended to be. After we'd made love and you—I realized that by pretending I'd let you have feelings for someone who didn't even exist."

"You're standing in front of me, Rebecca. You exist."

"No. Not the way you think, not the way I've let you think."

He prepared himself for the worst. "What have you done? Were you running away from America?"

"No. Yes." She had to laugh at that. "Yes, I was running." She gathered what composure she had left and folded her hands. "I did come from Philadelphia, as I told you. I've lived there all my life. Lived there, went to school there, worked there." She found a tissue in the pocket of her robe. "I'm an accountant."

He stared at her, one brow lifting, as she blew her nose. "I beg your pardon?"

"I said, I'm an accountant." She hurled the words at him, then whirled away to face the window. Stephen started to rise, then thought better of it.

"I find it difficult to imagine you tallying ledgers, Rebecca. If you'd sit down, maybe we could talk this through."

"Damn it, I said I'm an accountant. A CPA, specializing in corporate taxes. Up until a few weeks ago I worked for McDowell, Jableki and Kline in Philadelphia."

He spread his hands, taking it all in. "All right. What did you do? Embezzle?"

She tossed back her head and nearly exploded with laughter. If she said yes he'd probably be intrigued. But the time for intrigue was over. The time for the truth was now. "No. I've never done anything illegal in my life. I've never even had a parking ticket. I've never done anything at all out of the ordinary until a few weeks ago."

She began to pace again, too agitated to keep still. "I'd never traveled, never had a man send a bottle of champagne to my table, never walked along the beach in the moonlight, never had a lover."

He said nothing, not because he was angry or bored but because he was fascinated.

"I had a good job, my car was paid for, I had good, conservative investments that would have ensured me a comfortable retirement. In my circle of friends I'm known as dependable. If someone needs a sitter they know they can call Rebecca. If they need advice or someone to feed their fish while they're on vacation they don't have to worry. I was never late for work, never took five minutes extra for lunch."

"Commendable," he said, and earned a glare.

"Just the type of employee I imagine you'd like to hire."

He swallowed a chuckle. He'd been prepared for her to confess she had a husband, five husbands, a prison record. Instead she was telling him she was an accountant with an excellent work record. "I have no desire to hire you, Rebecca."

"Just as well." She turned away and started to prowl the room again. "You'd undoubtedly change your mind after I tell you the rest."

Stephen crossed his ankles and settled back. God, what a woman she was. "I'm anxious to hear it."

"My aunt died about three months ago, suddenly."

"I'm sorry." He would have gone to her then, but he could see she was far from ready. "I know how difficult it is to lose family."

"She was all I had left." Because she needed something to do, she pushed open the balcony doors. Warm, fragrant night air rushed in. "I couldn't believe she was gone. Just like that. No warning. Of course, I handled the funeral arrangements. No fuss, no frills. Just the way Aunt Jeannie would have wanted. She was a very economical woman, not only in finances but in dress, in speech, in manner. As long as I can remember, people compared me to her."

Stephen's brow lifted again as he studied the woman being buffeted by the breeze—the short red silk robe, the tousled hair.

"Soon after her death—I don't know if it was days or a week—something just snapped. I looked at myself, at my life, and I hated it." She dragged her hair back, only to have the wind catch it again. "I was a good employee, just like my aunt, a good credit risk, a dependable friend. Law-abiding, conservative and boring. Suddenly I could see myself ten, twenty, thirty years down the road, with nothing more than I had at that moment. I couldn't stand it."

She turned around. The breeze caught at the hem of her robe and sent it dancing around her legs. "I quit my job, and I sold everything."

"Sold?"

"Everything I owned—car, apartment, furniture, books, absolutely everything. I turned all the cash into traveler's checks, even the small inheritance from my aunt. Thousands of dollars. I know it might not sound like a lot to you, but it was more than I'd ever imagined having at once."

"Wait." He held up a hand, wanting to be certain he understood everything. "You're telling me that you sold your possessions, *all* your possessions?"

She couldn't remember ever having felt more foolish, and she straightened her shoulders defensively. "Right down to my coffeepot."

"Amazing," he murmured.

"I bought new clothes, new luggage, and flew to London. First-class. I'd never been on a plane before in my life."

"You'd never flown, but took your first trip across the Atlantic."

She didn't hear the admiration in his voice, only the amusement. "I wanted to see something different. To *be* something different. I stayed at the Ritz and took pictures of the changing of the guard. I flew to Paris and had my hair cut." Self-consciously she lifted a hand to it.

Because he could see that she was overwrought, he was careful not to smile. "You flew to Paris for a haircut."

"I'd heard some women discussing this stylist, and I— Never mind." It was no use trying to explain that she'd gone to the same hairdresser, to the same shops, for years. The same everything. "Right after Paris, I came here," she went on. "I met you. Things happened. I let them happen." Tears threatened. She could only pray he didn't see them. "You were exciting, and attracted to me. Or attracted to who you thought I was. I'd never had a romance. No one had ever looked at me the way you did."

Once more he chose his words carefully. "Are you saying that being with me was different? An adventure, like flying to a Paris salon?"

She would never be able to explain what being with him had meant to her. "Apologies and explanations really don't make any difference now. But I am sorry, Stephen. I'm sorry for everything."

He didn't see the tears, but he heard the regret in her voice. His eyes narrowed. His muscles tensed. "Are you apologizing for making love with me, Rebecca?"

"I'm apologizing for whatever you like. I'd make it up to you if I could, but I don't know how, unless I jump out the window."

He paused, as if he were considering it. "I don't think this requires anything quite that drastic. Perhaps if you'd sit down calmly?"

She shook her head and stayed where she was. "I can't handle any more of this tonight, Stephen. I'm sorry. You've every right to be angry."

He rose, the familiar impatience building. But she was so pale, looked so fragile, sounded so weary. He hadn't treated her gently before. At least he could do so now.

"All right. Tomorrow, then, after you've rested." He started to go to her, then checked himself. It would take time to show her that there were other ways to love. Time to convince her that love was more, much more than an adventure. "I want you to know that I regret what happened tonight. But that, too, will wait until tomorrow." Though he wanted to touch a hand to her cheek, he kept it fisted in his pocket. "Get some rest."

She had thought her heart was already broken. Now it shattered. Not trusting her voice, she nodded.

He left her alone. The door scraped against the splintered jamb as he secured it. She supposed there might have been a woman somewhere who'd made a bigger fool of herself. At the moment, it didn't seem to matter.

At least there was something she could do for both of them. Disappear.

Chapter 10

It was her own fault, she supposed. There were at least half a dozen promising accounting positions in the want ads. Not one of them interested her. Rebecca circled them moodily. How could she be interested in dental plans and profit sharing? All she could think about, all she'd been able to think about for two weeks, was Stephen.

What had he thought when he'd found her gone? Relief? Perhaps a vague annoyance at business left unfinished? Pen in hand, Rebecca stared out of the window of the garden apartment she'd rented. In her fantasies she imagined him searching furiously for her, determined to find her, whatever the cost. Reality, she thought with a sigh, wasn't quite so romantic. He would have been relieved. Perhaps she wasn't sophisticated, but at least she'd stepped out of his life with no fuss.

Now it was time to get her own life in order.

First things first. She had an apartment, and the little square of lawn outside the glass doors was going to make her happy. That in itself was a challenge. Her old condo had been centrally located on the fifth floor of a fully maintained modern building.

This charming and older development was a good thirty miles from downtown, but she could hear the birds in the morning. She would be able to look out at old oaks and sweeping maples and flowers she would plant herself. Perhaps it wasn't as big a change as a flight to Paris, but for Rebecca it was a statement.

She'd bought some furniture. *Some* was the operative word. Thus far she'd picked out a bed, one antique table and a single chair.

Not logical, Rebecca thought with a faint smile. No proper and economical living room suite, no tidy curtains. Even the single set of towels she'd bought was frivolous. And exactly what she'd wanted. She would do what she'd secretly wanted to do for years—buy a piece here, a piece there. Not because it was a good buy or durable, but because she wanted it.

She wondered how many people would really understand the satisfaction of making decisions not because they were sensible but because they were desirable. She'd done it with her home, her wardrobe. Even with her hair, she thought, running a hand through it. Outward changes had led to inner changes. Or vice versa. Either way, she would never again be the woman she'd been before.

Or perhaps she would be the woman she'd always been but had refused to acknowledge.

Then why was she circling ads in the classifieds? Rebecca asked herself. Why was she sitting here on a beautiful morning planning a future she had no interest in? Perhaps it was true that she would never have the one thing, the one person, she really wanted. There would be no more picnics or walks in the moonlight or frantic nights in bed. Still, she had the memories, she had the moments, she had the dreams. There would be no regrets where Stephen was concerned. Not now, and not ever. And if she was now more the woman she had been with him, it had taken more than a change in hairstyle.

She was stronger. She was surer. She was freer. And she'd done it herself.

She could think of nothing she wanted less than to go back into someone else's firm, tallying figures, calculating profit and loss. So she wouldn't. Rebecca sank into the chair as the thought struck home.

She wouldn't. She wouldn't go job hunting, carrying her résumé, rinsing sweaty palms in the rest room, putting her career and life in someone else's hands again. She'd open her own firm. A small one, certainly. Personalized. Exclusive, she decided, savoring the word. Why not? She had the skill, the experience, and—finally—she had the courage.

It wouldn't be easy. In fact, it would be risky. The money she had left would have to go toward renting office space, equipment, a phone system, advertising. With a bubbling laugh, she sprang up and searched for a legal pad and a pencil. She had to make lists—not only of things to do but of people to call. She had enough contacts from her McDowell, Jableki and Kline days. Maybe, just maybe, she could persuade some of her former clients to give her a try.

"Just a minute," she called out when she heard the knock on the door. She scribbled a reminder to look for file cabinets as she went to answer. She'd much rather have some good solid oak file cabinets than a living room sofa.

She knew better than to open the door without checking the security peephole, but she was much too involved with her plans to think about such things. When she opened the door, she found herself face-to-face with Stephen.

Even if she could have spoken, he wasn't in the mood to let her. "What in the hell do you think you're doing?" he demanded as he slammed the door behind him. "Do you deliberately try to drive me mad, or does it come naturally to you?"

"I—I don't—" But he was already yanking her against him. Whatever words she might have spoken dissolved into a moan against his lips. Her pad fell to the floor with a slap. Even as her arms came up around him he was thrusting her away.

"What kind of game are you playing, Rebecca?" When she just shook her head, he dug his hands into his pockets and paced the wide, nearly empty room. He was unshaven, disheveled and absolutely gorgeous. "It's taken me two weeks and a great deal of trouble to find you. I believe we'd agreed to talk again. I was surprised to discover you'd not only left Athens, but Europe." He swung back and pinned her with a look. "Why?"

Still reeling from his entrance, she struggled not to babble. "I thought it best that I leave."

"You thought?" He took a step toward her, his fury so palatable that she braced herself. "You thought it best," he repeated. "For whom?"

"For you. For both of us." She caught herself fiddling with the lapels of her robe and dropped her hands. "I knew you were angry with me for lying to you and that you regretted what had happened between us. I felt it would be better for both of us if I—"

"Ran away?"

Her chin came up fractionally. "Went away."

"You said you loved me."

She swallowed. "I know."

"Was that another lie?"

"Please don't." She turned away, but there was nowhere to go. "Stephen, I never expected to see you again. I'm trying to make some sense out of my life, to do things in a way that's not only right but makes me happy. In Greece, I guess, I did what made me happy, but I didn't think about what was right. The time with you was…"

"Was what?"

Dragging both hands through her hair, she turned to him again. It was as if the two weeks had never been. She was facing him again, trying to explain what she feared she could never explain. "It was the best thing that ever happened to me, the most important, the most unforgettable, the most precious. I'll always be grateful for those few days."

"Grateful." He wasn't sure whether to laugh or murder her. Stepping forward, he surprised them both by slipping his hands lightly around her throat. "For what? For my giving you your first fling? A fast, anonymous romance with no consequences?"

"No." She lifted a hand to his wrist but made no attempt to struggle. "Did you come all this way to make me feel more guilty?"

"I came all this way because I finish what I begin. We'd far from finished, Rebecca."

"All right." Be calm, she told herself. When a man was this close to the edge, a woman's best defense was serenity. "If you'll let me go, we'll talk. Would you like some coffee?"

His fingers tightened reflexively, then slowly relaxed. "You've bought a new pot."

"Yes." Was that humor in his eyes? she wondered. "There's only one chair. Why don't you use it while I go into the kitchen?"

He took her arm. "I don't want coffee, or a chair, or a pleasant conversation."

It seemed serenity wouldn't work. "All right, Stephen. What do you want?"

"You. I'd thought I'd made that fairly obvious." When she frowned, he glanced around the apartment. "Now tell me, Rebecca, is this what you want? A handful of rooms to be alone in?"

"I want to make the best of the rest of my life. I've already apologized for deceiving you. I realize that—"

"Deceiving me." He held up a finger to stop her. "I've wanted to clear that point up myself. How did you deceive me?"

"By letting you think that I was something I'm not."

"You're not a beautiful, interesting woman? A passionate woman?" He lifted a brow as he studied her. "Rebecca, I have too much pride to ever believe you could deceive me that completely."

He was confusing her—deliberately, she was sure. "I told you what I'd done."

"What you'd done," he agreed. "And how you'd done it." He brought his hand to her throat again, this time in a caress. His anger hadn't made her knees weak. She felt them tremble now at his tenderness. "Selling your possessions and flying to Paris for a new hairstyle. Quitting your job and grabbing life with both hands. You fascinate me." Her eyes stayed open wide when he brushed his lips over hers. "I think the time is nearly over when you'll be so easily flattered. It's almost a pity." He drew her closer, slowly, while his mouth touched hers. Relief coursed through him as he felt her melt and give. "Do you think it was your background that attracted me?"

"You were angry," she managed.

"Yes, angry at the idea that I had been part of your experiment. Furious," he added before he deepened the kiss. "Furious that I had been of only passing interest." She was heating in his arms, just as he remembered, just as he needed, softening, strengthening. "Shall I tell you how angry? Shall I tell you that for two weeks I couldn't work, couldn't think, couldn't function, because you were everywhere I looked and nowhere to be found?"

"I had to go." She was already tugging at his shirt to find the flesh beneath. To touch him again, just for a moment. To be touched by him. "When you said you regretted making love…" Her own words brought her back. Quickly she dropped her hands and stepped away.

He stared at her for a moment, then abruptly swore and began to pace. "I've never thought myself this big a fool. I hurt you that night in a much different way than I'd believed. Then I handled it with less finesse than I might the most unimportant business transaction." He paused, sighing. For the first time she saw clearly how incredibly weary he was.

"You're tired. Please, sit down. Let me fix you something."

He took a moment to press his fingers to his eyes. Again he wanted to laugh—while he strangled her. She was exactly what he needed, what he understood. Yet at the same time she baffled him.

"You weaken me, Rebecca, and bring out the fool I'd forgotten I could be. I'm surprised you allowed me to set foot into your home. You should have—" As quickly as the anger had come, it faded. As quickly as the tension had formed, it eased. Everything he'd needed to see was in her eyes. Carefully now, he drew a deep breath. A man wasn't always handed so many chances at happiness.

"Rebecca, I never regretted making love with you." He stopped her from turning with the lightest of touches on her shoulder. "I regretted only the way it happened. Too much need and too little care. I regret, I'll always regret, that for your first time there was fire but no warmth." He took her hands in his and brought them to his lips.

"It was beautiful."

"In its way." His fingers tightened on hers. Still so innocent, he thought. Still so generous. "It was not kind or patient or tender, as love should be the first time."

She felt hope rise in her heart again. "None of that mattered."

"It mattered, more than I can ever tell you. After, when you told me everything, it only mattered more. If I had done what my instincts told me to do that night you would never have left me. But I thought you needed time before you could bear to have me touch you again." Slowly, gently, he drew the tip of her finger into his mouth and watched her eyes cloud over. "Let me show you what I should have shown you then." With her hands locked in his, he looked into her eyes. "Do you want me?"

It was time for the truth. "Yes."

He lifted her into his arms and heard her breath catch. "Do you trust me?"

"Yes."

When he smiled, her heart turned over. "Rebecca, I must ask you one more thing."

"What is it?"

"Do you have a bed?"

She felt her cheeks heat even as she laughed. "In there."

She was trembling. It reminded him how careful he had to be, how precious this moment was to both of them. The sun washed over the bed, over them, as he lay beside her. And kissed her—only kissed her, softly, deeply, thoroughly, until her arms slipped from around him to fall bonelessly to her sides. She trembled still as he murmured to her, as his lips brushed over her cheeks, her throat.

He had shown her the desperation love could cause, the sharp-edged pleasure, the speed and the fury. Now he showed her that love could mean serenity and sweetness.

And she showed him.

He had thought to teach her, not to learn, to reassure her but not to be comforted. But he learned, and he was comforted. The need was there, as strong as it had been the first time. But strength was tempered with patience. As he slipped his hands down her robe to part it, to slide it away from her skin, he felt no need to hurry. He could delight in the way the sun slanted across her body, in the way her flesh warmed to his touch.

Her breath was as unsteady as her hands as she undressed him. But not from nerves. She understood that now. She felt strong and capable and certain. Anticipation made her tremble. Pleasure made her shudder. She gave a sigh that purred out of her lips as she arched against his seeking hands. Then he nipped lightly at her breast and she bounded from serenity to passion in one breathless leap.

Still he moved slowly, guiding her into a kind of heated torment she'd never experienced. Desire boiled in her, and his name sprang to her lips and her body coiled like a spring. Chaining down his own need, he set hers free and watched as she flew over the first peak.

"Only for me," he murmured as she went limp in his arms. "Only for me, Rebecca." With his own passions strapped, he slipped into her, determined to watch her build again. "Tell me you love me. Look at me and tell me."

She opened her eyes. She could barely breathe. Somehow the strength was pouring back into her, but so fast, so powerfully. Sensation rolled over sensation, impossibly. She moved with him, pressed center to center, heart to heart, but all she could see were his eyes, so dark, so blue, so intense. Perhaps she was drowning in them.

"I love you, Stephen."

Then she was falling, fathoms deep, into his eyes, into the sea. With her arms locked around him, she dragged him under with her.

He pulled her against him so that he could stroke her hair and wait for his pulse to level. She'd been innocent. But the surprise, the one he'd been dealing with for weeks, was that until Rebecca he'd been just as innocent. He'd known passion, but he'd never known intimacy, not the kind that reached the heart as fully as the body. And yet...

"We've been here before," he murmured. "Do you feel it, too?"

She linked her fingers with his. "I never believed in things like that until you. When I'm with you it's like remembering." She lifted her head to look at him. "I can't explain it."

"I love you, Rebecca, only more knowing who you are, why you are."

She touched a hand to his cheek. "I don't want you to say anything you don't really feel."

"How can a woman be so intelligent and still so stupid?" With a shake of his head, Stephen rolled on top of her. "A man doesn't travel thousands of miles for this, however delightful it may be. I love you, and though it annoyed me for quite some time I'm accustomed to it now."

"Annoyed you."

"Infuriated." He kissed her to cut off whatever retort she might make. "I'd seen myself remaining free for years to come. Then I met a woman who sold her coffeepot so she could take pictures of goats."

"I certainly have no intention of interfering with your plans."

"You already have." He smiled, holding her still when she tried to struggle away. "Marriage blocks off certain freedoms and opens others."

"Marriage?" She stopped struggling but turned her head to avoid another kiss.

"Soon." He nuzzled her neck. "Immediately."

"I never said I'd marry you."

"No, but you will." With his fingertips only, he began to arouse her. "I'm a very persuasive man."

"I need to think." But she was trembling again. "Stephen, marriage is very serious."

"Deadly. And I should warn you that I've already decided to murder any man you look at for more than twenty seconds."

"Really?" She turned her head back, prepared to be angry. But he was smiling. No one else had ever smiled at her in quite that way. "Really?"

"I can't let you go, Rebecca. Can't and won't. Come back with me. Marry me. Have children with me."

"Stephen—"

He laid a finger to her lips. "I know what I'm asking you. You've already started a new life, made new plans. We've had only days together, but I can make you happy. I can promise to love you for a lifetime, or however many lifetimes we have. You once dived into the sea on impulse. Dive with me now, Rebecca. I swear you won't regret it."

Gently she pressed her lips to his fingertip, then drew his hand away. "All my life I've wondered what I might find if I had the courage to look. I found you, Stephen." With a laugh she threw her arms around him. "When do you want to leave?"

* * * * *

The Best Mistake

NORA ROBERTS

Chapter 1

No one answered the door. Coop glanced at the scrawled note in his hand to make sure he had the right address. It checked out, and since the tidy two-story Tudor in the neat, tree-lined neighborhood was precisely what he was after, he knocked again. Loudly.

There was a car in the drive, an aging station wagon that could use a good wash and a little bodywork. Somebody was in there, he thought, scowling up at the second-floor window, where music pumped out—high-volume rock with a thumping backbeat. He stuffed the note and his hands in his pockets and took a moment to survey the surroundings.

The house was trim, set nicely off the road behind clipped bayberry hedges. The flower garden, in which spring blossoms were beginning to thrive, was both colorful and just wild enough not to look static.

Not that he was a big flower lover, but there *was* something to be said for ambience.

There was a shiny red tricycle beside the driveway, and that made him a little uneasy. He wasn't particularly fond of kids. Not that he disliked them. It was just that they always seemed a kind of foreign entity to him, like aliens from an outlying planet: they spoke a different language, had a different culture. And, well, they were short, and usually sticky.

Still, the ad had talked of quiet, privacy, and a convenient distance from Baltimore. That was exactly what he was looking for.

He knocked again, only to have a thundering wave of music wash out the window over him. The rock didn't bother him. At least he understood it. But he wasn't a man to kick his heels outside a closed door for long, so he tried the knob.

When it turned, he pushed the door open and walked in. In an old habit, he pushed back the dark hair that fell over his forehead and scanned the none-too-neat living room he'd entered.

There was a lot of clutter, and he, a bachelor who'd spent a great deal of his thirty-two years living alone, wondered over it. He wasn't fussy or obsessive, he often told himself. It was simply that everything had a place, and it was easier to find if it had been put there. Obviously his prospective landlord didn't agree.

There were toys that went along with the tricycle outside, piles of magazines and newspapers, a pint-size fielder's cap that declared for the O's.

At least the kid had taste, Coop decided, and moved on.

There was a small powder room done in an amazing combination of purple and green, and a den that had been converted into a makeshift office. File drawers were open, papers spilling out. In the kitchen dishes waited in the sink to be washed, and lurid drawings, created by a child with a wild imagination, decorated the front of the refrigerator.

Maybe, he thought, it was just as well no one had answered the door.

He considered backtracking and wandering upstairs. As long as he was here, it made sense to check the rest of the place out. Instead, he stepped outside to get the lay of the land. He spotted open wooden steps leading to a short deck. The private entrance the ad had mentioned, he mused, and climbed.

The glass door was open, and the music rolling through it was overwhelming. He caught the smell of fresh paint, one he'd always enjoyed, and stepped inside.

The open area combined kitchen and living space cleverly enough. The appliances weren't new, but they were gleaming. The tile floor had been scrubbed recently enough for him to identify pine cleaner beneath the scent of paint.

Feeling more hopeful, he followed the music, snooping a bit as he went. The bathroom was as scrupulously clean as the kitchen, and, fortunately, a plain glossy white. Beside the sink was a book on home repair, open to the plumbing section. Wary, Coop turned on the tap. When the water flowed out fast and clear, he nodded, satisfied.

A small room with definite office potential and a nice view of the yard was across the hall. The ad had claimed two bedrooms.

The music led him to it, a fair-sized room that fronted the house, with space enough for his California king. The floor, which seemed to be a random-width oak in good condition, was covered with splattered drop cloths. There were paint cans, trays, brushes, extra rollers. A laborer in baggy overalls and bare feet completed the picture. Despite the hair-concealing cap and oversize denim, Coop recognized a woman when he saw one.

She was tall, and the bare feet on the stepladder were long and narrow and decorated with paint splotches and hot-pink toenails. She sang, badly, along with the music.

Coop rapped on the door jamb. "Excuse me."

She went on painting, her hips moving rhythmically as she started on the ceiling border. Stepping across the drop cloths, Coop tapped her on the back.

She screamed, jumped and turned all at once. Though he was quick on his feet, he wasn't fast enough to avoid the slap of the paintbrush across his cheek.

He swore and jerked backward, then forward again to catch her before she tumbled off the ladder. He had a quick, and not unpleasant, impression of a slim body, a pale, triangular face dominated by huge, long-lashed brown eyes, and the scent of honeysuckle.

Then he was grunting and stumbling backward, clutching the stomach her elbow had jammed into. She yelled something while he fought to get his breath back.

"Are you crazy?" he managed, then shot up a hand as she hefted a can, slopping paint over the sides as she prepared to use it as a weapon. "Lady, if you throw that at me, I'm going to have to hurt you."

"What?" she shouted.

"I said, don't throw that. I'm here about the ad."

"What?" she shouted again. Her eyes were still wide and full of panic, and she looked capable of anything.

"The ad, damn it." Still rubbing his stomach, Coop marched to the portable stereo and shut it off. "I'm here about the ad," he repeated, his voice loud in the sudden silence.

The big brown eyes narrowed with suspicion. "What ad?"

"The apartment." He swiped a hand over his cheek, studied the smear of white on it, and swore again. "The apartment."

"Really?" She kept her eyes glued to his. He looked tough, she thought. Like a brawler with those broad shoulders, lean athletic build and long legs. His eyes, a light, almost translucent green, looked anything but friendly, and the faded Baltimore Orioles T-shirt and battered jeans didn't contribute any sense of respectability. She figured she could outrun him, and she could certainly outscream him. "The ad doesn't start to run until tomorrow."

"Tomorrow?" Nonplussed, he reached into his pocket for his scribbled note. "This is the right address. The ad was for this place."

She stood her ground. "It doesn't run until tomorrow, so I don't see how you could know about it."

"I work at the paper." Moving cautiously, he held out the note. "Since I've been looking for a place, I asked one of the girls in Classifieds to keep an eye out." He glanced down at his note again. "Two-bedroom apartment on second floor, private entrance, quiet neighborhood convenient for commuters."

She only continued to frown at him. "That's right."

Realizing his inside track wasn't strictly ethical, he winced. "Look, I guess she got a little overenthusiastic. I gave her a couple of tickets to a game, and she must've figured she'd do me a favor and pass the information along a little early."

When he saw that her grip on the can had relaxed, he tried a smile. "I knocked, then I came around back." Probably best not to mention he'd wandered through the house first.

"The ad didn't run the address."

"I work at the paper," he repeated. He was taking a good look at her now. There was something vaguely familiar about her face. And what a face it was. All slashing cheekbones and liquid eyes, that creamy porcelain skin women's face cream ads always raved about. Her mouth was wide, with an alluringly full lower lip. At the moment, the face continued to frown.

"They had the address for billing," he continued. "Since I had a couple of hours, I thought I'd come by and check it out. Look, I can come back tomorrow, if you'd feel more comfortable. But I'm here now." He shrugged. "I can show you my press pass."

He pulled it out for her, and was pleased when she narrowed her eyes to study it. "I do a column. J. Cooper McKinnon on sports. 'All in the Game'?"

"Oh." It meant nothing to her. The sports page wasn't her choice of reading material. But the smile had appeased her. He didn't look so much like a thug when he smiled. And the smear of paint decorating the lean, tanned face added just enough comedy to soothe her. "I guess it's all right, then. I wasn't expecting to show the apartment for a couple of days yet. It's not ready." She held up the can, set it down again. "I'm still painting."

"I noticed."

She laughed at that. It was a full-throated, smoky sound that went with the natural huskiness of her voice. "Guess you did. I'm Zoe Fleming." She crouched down to dampen a rag with paint remover.

"Thanks." He rubbed the rag over his cheek. "The ad said immediate occupancy."

"Well, I figured I'd be finished in here by tomorrow, when the ad was scheduled to run. Are you from the area?"

"I've got a place downtown. I'm looking for something with a little more space, a little more atmosphere."

"This is a pretty good-sized apartment. It was converted

about eight years ago. The guy who owned it had it done for his son, and when he died, the son sold it and moved to California. He wanted to write sitcoms."

Coop walked over to check out the view. He moved fluidly, Zoe thought, like a man who knew how to stay light and ready on his feet. She'd had the impression of wiry strength when her body tumbled into his. And good strong hands. Quick ones, too. She pursed her lips. It might be handy to have a man around.

"Is it just you, Mr. McKinnon?" She thought wistfully how nice it would be if he had a family—another child for Keenan to play with.

"Just me." The place felt right, he decided. It would be good to get out of a box that was just one more box in a building of boxes, to smell grass now and then. Barbecue smoke. "I can move in over the weekend."

She hadn't thought it would be so easy, and she nibbled her lip as she thought it through. She'd never been a landlady before, but she'd been a tenant, and she figured she knew the ropes. "I'll need first and last months' rent."

"Yeah."

"And, ah, references."

"I'll give you the number of the management company that handles my building. You can call Personnel at the paper. Have you got a lease for me to sign?"

She didn't. She'd checked out a book from the library, and she'd meant to type up a scaled-down copy of a lease from it the next morning. "I'll have it tomorrow. Don't you want to look at the rest of the apartment, ask any questions?" She'd been practicing her landlady routine for days.

"I've seen it. It's fine."

"Well." That deflated her a bit. "I guess I can cancel the ad."

There was a sound like a herd of rampaging elephants. Zoe glanced toward the open door and crouched to intercept the missile that hurtled through.

It was a boy, Coop saw when she scooped the child up. He had glossy golden hair, red sneakers, and jeans that were streaked with some unidentifiable substance that looked like it would easily transfer to other surfaces. He carried a plastic lunch box with a picture of some apocalyptic space battle on it, and a sheet of drawing paper that was grimy at the edges.

"I drew the ocean," he announced. "And a million people got ate by sharks."

"Gruesome." Zoe shuddered obligingly before accepting his sloppy kiss. She set him down to admire the drawing. "These are really big sharks," she said, cagily distinguishing the shark blobs from the people blobs.

"They're monster sharks. Mutant monster sharks. They have teeth."

"So I see. Keenan, this is Mr. McKinnon. Our new tenant."

Keenan wrapped one arm around Zoe's leg for security as he eyed the stranger. His eyes were working their way up to Coop's face when they lit on the T-shirt. "That's baseball. I'm gonna learn. Mama's getting a book so's she can teach me."

A book. Coop barely checked a snort. As if you could learn the greatest game invented by a man from a book. What kind of nerd did the kid have for a father?

"Great." It was all Coop intended to say. He'd always thought it wise to avoid entangling himself in a conversation with anyone under sixteen.

Keenan had other ideas. "If you're going to live here, you have to pay rent. Then we can pay the mortgage and stuff and go to Disney World."

What *was* the kid? An accountant?

"Okay, old man." Zoe laughed and ruffled his hair. "I can handle it from here. Go on down and put your stuff away."

"Is Beth coming to play with me tonight?"

"Yes, Beth's coming. Now scoot. I'll be down in a minute."

"'Kay." He made a dash for the door, stopping when his mother called him. It only took one look, the raised brow for him to remember. He looked back at Coop, flashed a quick, sunny grin. "Bye, mister."

The herd of elephants rampaged again, then there was the crash of a door slamming. "He makes an entrance," Zoe said as she turned back to Coop. "The dramatic flair comes from my mother. She's an actress, off-off-Broadway." Tilting her head, Zoe rested one bare foot on the bottom rung of the stepladder. "You look like you're ready to change your mind. You have a problem with children?"

"No." The kid might have thrown him off, but Coop doubted it would be a problem. The boy would hardly be beating a path to his door. And if he did, Coop thought, he could send him off again quickly enough. "No, he's, ah, cute."

"Yes, he is. I won't claim he's an angel, but he won't make a nuisance of himself. If he gives you any trouble, just let me know."

"Sure. Look, I'll come by tomorrow to sign the lease and give you a check. I'll pick up the keys then."

"That'll be fine."

"Any special time good for you?"

She looked blank for a moment. "What's tomorrow?"

"Friday."

"Friday." She closed her eyes and flipped through her messy internal calendar. "I'm working between ten and two. I think." She opened her eyes again, smiled. "Yeah, I'm pretty sure. Anytime after two-thirty?"

"Fine. Nice meeting you, Mrs. Fleming."

She took his offered hand. "It's Miss," she said easily. "I'm not married. And since we'll be living together, so to speak, you can make it Zoe."

Chapter 2

No one answered the door. Again. Coop checked his watch and saw that it was quarter to three. He didn't like to think he was a man obsessed with time, but as his living centered around deadlines, he did respect it. There was no rusting station wagon in the driveway this time, but he walked around the back of the house, hoping. Before he could start up the stairs to the apartment, he was hailed from across the chain-link fence.

"Young man! Yoo-hoo, young man!" Across the yard next door came a flowered muumuu, topped with a curling thatch of brightly hennaed hair that crowned a wide face. The woman hurried to the fence in a whirl of color. It wasn't just the dress and the improbable hair, Coop noted. The face itself was a rainbow of rich red lipstick, pink cheeks and lavender eye shadow.

When she reached the fence, she pressed a many-ringed

hand over the wide shelf of her breasts. "Not as young as I used to be," she said. "I'm Mrs. Finkleman."

"Hi."

"You're the young man who's going to live upstairs." Mrs. Finkleman, a born flirt, patted her curls. "Zoe didn't tell me you were so handsome. Single, are you?"

"Yeah," Coop said cautiously. "Miss Fleming was supposed to meet me. She doesn't seem to be home."

"Well, that's Zoe, flying here, flying there." Mrs. Finkleman beamed and leaned comfortably on the fence, as if she were settling in for a nice cozy gossip. "Got a dozen things on her plate at once, that girl does. Having to raise that sweet little boy all alone. Why, I don't know what I'd have done without my Harry when our young ones were coming up."

Coop was a reporter, after all. That, added to the fact that he was curious about his landlady, put him in interview mode. "The kid's father doesn't help out any?"

Mrs. Finkleman snorted. "Don't see hide nor hair of him. From what I'm told, he lit out the minute he found out Zoe was expecting. Left her high and dry, and her hardly more than a child herself. Far as I know, he's never so much as seen the boy. The little sweetheart."

Coop assumed she was referring to Keenan. "Nice kid. What's he, five, six?"

"Just four. Bright as a button. They grow them smarter these days. Teach them faster, too. The little love's in pre-school now. He'll be home any minute."

"His mother went to pick him up, then?"

"Oh, no, not her week for car pool. Alice Miller—that's the white house with blue trim, down the block?—it's her week. She has a boy and a girl. Little darlings. The youngest, Steffie, is Keenan's age. Now her oldest, Brad, there's a pistol for you."

As she began to fill Coop in on the neighborhood rascal, he decided it was time to draw the interview to a close. "Maybe you could tell Miss Fleming I was by? I can leave a number where she can reach me when—"

"Oh, goodness." Mrs. Finkleman waved a hand. "I do run on. Nearly forgot why I came out here in the first place. Zoe called and asked me to look out for you. Got held up at the flower shop. She works there three days a week. That's Floral Bouquet, down in Ellicott City? Nice place, but expensive. Why, it's a crime to charge so much for a daisy."

"She got held up," Coop prompted.

"Her relief had car trouble, so Zoe's going to be a little late. Said you could go right on into the kitchen there, where she left the lease and the keys."

"That's fine. Thanks."

"No problem at all. This is a friendly neighborhood. Always somebody to lend a helping hand. I don't think Zoe mentioned what you did for a living."

"I'm a sportswriter for the *Dispatch*."

"You don't say? Why, my Harry's just wild for sports. Can't budge him from in front of the TV when a game's on."

"That's what makes this country great."

Mrs. Finkleman laughed and gave Coop's arm an affectionate bat that might have felled a lesser man. "You men are all the same. You can come over and talk sports with Harry anytime. Me, if it's not baseball, it isn't worth talking about."

Coop, who'd been about to retreat, brightened. "You like baseball?"

"Son, I'm a Baltimore native." As if that said it all. "Our boys are going to go all the way this year. Mark my word."

"They could do it, if they heat those bats up. The pitching

rotation's gold this year, and the infield's tight as a drum. What they need—"

Coop was interrupted by a cheerful toot. He glanced over to see Keenan burst out of a red sedan and rocket across the side yard.

"Hi, mister. Hi, Mrs. Finkleman. Carly Myers fell down, and there was blood." The big brown eyes gleamed wickedly. "Lots and lots of it, and she screamed and cried." He demonstrated, letting go with a piercing yell that had Coop's ears ringing. "Then she got a Band-Aid with stars on it." Keenan thought it would have been worth losing some blood for such a neat badge of honor. "Where's Mama?"

"Little lamb." Mrs. Finkleman leaned over the fence to pinch Keenan's cheek. "She's working a little late. She said you could come stay with me until she gets home."

"Okay." Keenan liked his visits next door, since they always included cookies and a rock on Mrs. Finkleman's wonderfully soft lap. "I gotta put my lunch box away."

"Such a good boy," Mrs. Finkleman cooed. "You come on over when you're done. Why don't you show the nice man inside so he can wait for your mother?"

"Okay."

Before Coop could take evasive action, his hand was clutched by Keenan's. He'd been right, he thought with a wince. It was sticky.

"We've got cookies," Keenan told him, cannily deducing that he could have double his afternoon's treat if he played his cards right.

"Great."

"We baked them ourselves, on our night off." Keenan sent Coop a hopeful look. "They're really good."

"I bet." Coop caught the back door before it could slam shut.

"There." Keenan pointed to a ceramic cookie jar in the shape of a big yellow bird on the counter. "In Big Bird."

"Okay, okay." Since it seemed like the best way to appease the kid, Coop reached in and pulled out a handful of cookies. When he dumped them on the table, Keenan's eyes went as wide as saucers. He could hardly believe his luck.

"You can have one, too." He stuffed an entire chocolate chip deluxe in his mouth and grinned.

"That good, huh?" With a shrug, Coop sampled one himself. The kid, Coop decided after the first bite, knew his cookies. "You'd better get next door."

Keenan devoured another cookie, stalling. "I gotta wash out my thermos, 'cause if you don't, it smells."

"Right." Cooper sat at the table to read through the lease while the boy dragged a stool in front of the sink.

Keenan squirted dishwashing liquid in the thermos, and then, when he noticed Coop wasn't paying any attention, he squirted some more. And more. He turned the water up high and giggled when soap began to bubble and spew. With his tongue caught between his teeth, he jiggled the stopper into the sink and began to play dishwasher.

Coop forgot about him, reading quickly. The lease seemed standard enough, he decided. Zoe had already signed both copies. He dashed his signature across from hers, folded his copy, then set the check he'd already written on the table. He'd picked up the keys and rose to tuck his copy in his pocket when he spotted Keenan.

"Oh, God."

The boy was drenched, head to foot. Soap bubbles dotted his face and hair. A good-sized puddle was forming on the tile at the base of the stool.

"What are you doing?"

Keenan looked over his shoulder, smiled innocently. "Nothing."

"Look, you've got water everywhere." Coop looked around for a towel.

"Everywhere," Keenan agreed, and, testing the opposition, he slapped his hands in the sink. Water and suds geysered.

"Cut it out! Jeez! Aren't you supposed to be somewhere else?" He grabbed a dish towel and advanced, only to be slapped in the face by the next geyser. His eyes narrowed. "Look, kid—"

He heard the front door slam. Like mother, like son, he thought.

"Keenan?" Zoe called out. "I hope you haven't been into those cookies."

Coop looked at the crumbs on the table, on the floor, floating in the soapy water.

"Oh, hell," he muttered.

"Oh, hell," Keenan echoed, beaming at him. He giggled and danced on his stool. "Hi, Mom."

Zoe, her arms full of day-old irises, took in the scene with one glance. Her son was as wet as a drowned dog, her kitchen looked as though a small hurricane had blown through. Hurricane Keenan, she thought. And her new tenant looked damp, frazzled, and charmingly sheepish.

Like a boy caught with his hand in the cookie jar, she noted, glancing at the telltale crumbs.

"Been playing dishwasher again?" With a calm that baffled Coop, she set the flowers down. "I'm just not sure it's the right career choice, Keen-man."

Keenan fluttered his long, wet lashes. "He wanted cookies."

Coop started to defend himself, then simply scowled at the boy.

"I'm sure he did. Go on into the laundry room and get out
of those wet clothes."

"Okay." He jumped from the stool, splashing more water
before he zoomed away. He stopped only long enough to give
his mother a wet kiss before he disappeared into an adjoining room.

"Sorry I'm late," Zoe said easily, yanking the stopper out
of the sink then walking to a cupboard to get a vase.

Coop opened his mouth. He started to explain what had
gone on in the past ten minutes, but realized he wasn't at all
sure. "I signed the lease."

"I see that. Would you mind putting some water in this?"
She held out the vase. "I need to get a mop."

"Sure."

She was probably going to wallop the kid with it, Coop
thought, and felt a quick tug of regret and guilt. But the sounds
from the laundry room where she'd disappeared weren't those
he associated with corporal punishment. They were a young
boy's giggles, a woman's lusty laugh. Coop stood, a vase of
water in his hands, and wondered at it.

"You're standing in a puddle," Zoe commented when she
came back with a mop and pail.

"Oh, right." Coop glanced down at his wet hightops,
shifted. "Here's your vase."

"Thanks." She tended to her flowers first. "You met Mrs.
Finkleman, I hear."

"News travels fast."

"Around here it does." When she handed him a dishcloth
to dry his face with, he caught her scent—much more
potent, much more colorful, than the flowers. She was
wearing jeans and a baggy T-shirt with Floral Bouquet
across the chest. Her hair, he noted, was some elusive shade

between brown and blond. She wore it tied back in a jaunty ponytail.

When she lifted her brows, he realized he'd been staring. "Sorry. I mean—I'm sorry about the mess."

"Were you playing dishwasher, too?"

"Not exactly." It was impossible not to smile back, to ignore the quick pull of attraction.

It wouldn't be so bad, he mused, having a pretty landlady sharing the house with her, maybe an occasional meal. Or an occasional—

"Mama!" Keenan stood in the doorway, wearing nothing but skin. "I can't find my pants."

"In the basket by the washing machine," she told him without taking her eyes from Coop's.

He'd forgotten about the kid, let himself fantasize a little before remembering she didn't come as a single. He took a long mental step backward and jingled the keys to his new apartment.

"I've got some boxes out in the car," he told her. "I'm going to move some things in this afternoon."

"That's fine." It was silly to feel disappointed, Zoe thought. Foolish to have felt that fast feminine flutter when she recognized interest in his eyes. More foolish to feel let down because the interest had blanked out when her child called her. "Do you need any help?"

"No, I can handle it. I've got a game to cover tonight, so I'm going to move the rest in tomorrow." He backed toward the door. "Thanks."

"Welcome aboard, Mr. McKinnon."

"Coop," he said as he stepped outside. "It's Coop."

Coop, she thought, leaning on the mop handle. It had seemed like such a good idea to make use of the apartment upstairs. The extra income would take some of the pressure off, and maybe add a few bonuses. Like that trip to Disney World that Keenan wanted so badly.

It had been a risk to buy the house, but she'd wanted her son to grow up in a nice neighborhood, with a yard, maybe a dog when he was a little older. The rental income would take away some of the risk.

But she hadn't realized it could add another, more personal risk. She hadn't realized how awkward it might be to have a tenant who was male, single, and absolutely gorgeous.

She laughed at herself. Dream on, Zoe, she thought. J. Cooper McKinnon was just like the rest, who ran like a hound when they heard the patter of little feet.

Something crashed in the laundry room. She just shook her head.

"Come on, sailor," she called to Keenan. "It's time to swab the deck."

Chapter 3

"Pretty good digs, Coop. Really, pretty good." Ben Robbins, a staff reporter for the *Dispatch,* sipped a cold one while surveying Coop's apartment. "I didn't think much of it when we hauled all your junk up here, but it ain't half-bad."

It was a lot better than not half-bad, and Coop knew it. He had everything exactly where he wanted it. The living room was dominated by his long, low-slung sofa of burgundy leather and his big-screen television, so perfect for viewing games. A couple of brass lamps, a nicely worn coffee table scuffed from the heels of the dozens of shoes that had rested on it and a single generous chair completed the formal section of the room.

There was an indoor basketball hoop, small-scaled, for practice—and because shooting a little round ball helped him think. A used pinball machine called Home Run, a stand that held two baseball bats, his tennis racket and a hockey stick, a pair of old boxing gloves hanging on the wall and a scarred Fooz Ball table made up the recreation area.

Coop wouldn't have called them toys. They were tools.

He'd chosen blinds, rather than curtains, for the windows. Blinds, he thought, that would close out the light if a man decided to treat himself to an afternoon nap.

The bedroom held little other than his bed, a nightstand and another TV. The room was for sleeping—or, if he got lucky, another type of sport.

But it was his office that pleased him most. He could already imagine himself spending hours there at his computer, a game playing on his desktop TV. He'd outfitted it with a big swivel chair, a desk that had just the right number of scars and burns, a fax, a dual-line phone and a VCR—to play back those controversial calls or heart-stopping plays.

With all the plaques and photos and sports memorabilia scattered about, it was home.

His home.

"Looks like the neighborhood bar," Ben said, and stretched out his short, hairy legs. "Where the jocks hang out."

Coop considered that the highest of compliments. "It suits me."

"To the ground," Ben agreed, and toasted Coop with his bottle of beer. "A place where a man can relax, be himself. You know, since I started living with Sheila, I've got little china things all over, and underwear hanging in the bathroom. The other day she comes home with a new bedspread. It's got *flowers* all over. Pink flowers." He winced as he drank. "It's like sleeping in a meadow."

"Hey." With all the smug righteousness of the unencumbered, Coop propped his feet on the coffee table. "Your choice, pal."

"Yeah, yeah. Too bad I'm nuts about her. And her a⃫
Oakland fan, too."

"Takes all kinds. Talk is the A's are trading Remirez."

Ben snorted. "Yeah, yeah, pull the other one, champ."

"That's the buzz." Coop shrugged, took a pull on his ow⃫
beer. "Sending him to K.C. for Dunbar, and that rookie fielde⃫
Jackson."

"They got to be crazy. Remirez hit .280 last season."

".285," Coop told him. "With twenty-four baggers. Led th⃫
team in errors, too."

"Yeah, but with a bat like that… And Dunbar, what's he⃫
Maybe he hit .220?"

"It was .218, but he's like a vacuum cleaner at second⃫
Nothing gets by him. And the kid's got potential. Big, strap⃫
ping farm boy with an arm like a bullet. They need new blood⃫
Most of the starting lineup's over thirty."

They argued baseball and finished their beers in complet⃫
male harmony.

"I've got a game to cover."

"Tonight? I thought the O's were in Chicago until tomorrow.⃫

"They are." Coop pocketed his tape recorder, his pad, ⃫
pencil. "I'm covering the college game. There's a hot thir⃫
baseman who's got the scouts drooling. Thought I'd take ⃫
look, cop an interview."

"What a job." Ben hauled himself to his feet. "Going t⃫
games, hanging around locker rooms."

"Yeah, it's a rough life." He slung an arm over Ben's shoul⃫
ders as they headed out. "So, how's the story on neutering pet⃫
going?"

"Stuff it, Coop."

"Hey, some of us hang around the pound, some of us han⃫
around the ballpark."

And a hell of a day it was for it, too, Coop thought. Balmy and clear-skied. He could almost smell roasting peanuts and hot dogs.

"While you're hanging around a bunch of sweaty college boys in jockstraps, I'll be snuggled up with a woman."

"Under a flowered bedspread."

"Yeah, but she says flowers make her feel sexy. And I'm here to tell you— My, oh, my…"

When Ben's small, square face went lax, Coop turned. He felt his own jaw drop. And, if he wasn't mistaken, his tongue landed on his shoes.

She was wearing what had to be the shortest skirt ever devised by man. Beneath it were a pair of endless legs that were molded into black fishnet hose. She swayed when she walked. How could she help it, when she stood in black sky-scraper heels?

A tiny white bustier exposed a delicious amount of cleavage. Around her neck was a shiny black bow tie that, for reasons utterly inexplicable to Coop, made every male cell in his body sizzle.

Her hair was down, falling straight as a pin to her shoulders in a melding of tones that made him think of wild deer leaping through a sunlit forest.

She stopped, smiled, said something, but his mind had checked out the moment his eyes landed on her legs.

"…if you've settled in okay."

"Ah…" He blinked like a man coming out of a coma. "What?"

"I said I haven't had a chance to check and see if you've settled in okay."

"Fine." He folded his tongue back in his mouth and got a grip on himself. "Just fine."

"Good. Keenan came down with a cold, so things hav been hectic. I caught a glimpse of you hauling things up th steps a couple of days ago."

"Hauling," he repeated. "Yeah. Ben," he said when hi friend jabbed him. "This is Ben. He's been giving me a han moving."

"Hi, Ben. I'm Zoe."

"Hi, Zoe," Ben said stupidly. "I'm Ben."

She just smiled. It was the outfit, she knew. As much as sh hated it, she couldn't help but be amused by how it affecte certain members of the species. "Do you work at the paper, too?"

"Yeah, I'm, ah, doing a story on neutering pets."

"Really?" She almost felt sorry for him, the way hi Adam's apple was bobbing. "I'll be sure to look for it. I'r glad you're settling in okay. I've got to get to work."

"You're going out?" Coop said. "In that?"

Her lips twitched. "Well, this is my usual outfit when I'r carpooling, but I thought I'd wear it to work tonight. A Shadows? I'm a waitress. Nice meeting you, Ben."

She walked to her car. No, Coop thought, swayed to it, i those long, lazy strides. They were both still staring when sh pulled out of the drive and cruised down the street.

"Your landlady," Ben said in a reverential whisper. "Tha was your landlady."

"I think it was." She hadn't looked like that when he signe the lease. Beautiful, yes—she'd been beautiful, but in a whole some, unthreatening sort of way. She hadn't looked so…so… Words failed him. She was a mother, for God's sake, h reminded himself. She wasn't supposed to look like tha "She's got a kid."

"Yeah? What kind?"

"Human, I think."

"Come on."

"A boy," Coop said absently. "This high." He held a hand, palm down, about three feet from the ground.

"She may have a kid, but she's also got legs. This high." Ben waved a hand in front of his own throat. "You got a charmed life, Coop. My landlord's got arms like cinder blocks, and a tattoo of a lizard. You got one who looks like a centerfold."

"She's a mother," Coop said under his breath.

"Well, I wouldn't mind coming home to her for milk and cookies. See you at the sweatshop."

"Sure." Coop stood where he was, frowning at the quiet street. Mothers weren't supposed to look like that, he thought again. They were supposed to look…motherly. Safe. Comfortable. He blew out a breath, willed away the knot in his stomach.

She wasn't *his* mother, he reminded himself.

By midnight, Zoe's feet were screaming. Her back ached, and her arms felt as though she'd been hauling boulders rather than drink trays. She'd deflected six propositions, two of them good-hearted enough to amuse, one of them insulting enough to earn the gentleman in question a bruised instep, courtesy of one of her stiletto heels. The others had been the usual, and easily ignored.

It went with the territory, and it didn't bother her overmuch.

The lounge earned its name from the shadowy effect of neon and all the dim corners. The decor was fifties tacky, and the waitresses were dolled up like old-fashioned mindless floozies to match.

But the tips were excellent, and the clientele, for the most part, harmless.

"Two house wines, white, a Black Russian and a coffee, light." After calling out her order to the bartender, Zoe took a moment to roll her shoulders.

She hoped Beth had gotten Keenan to bed without any fuss. He'd been cranky all day—which meant he was nearly over his sniffles. He'd put up quite a fuss that morning, Zoe remembered, when she'd nixed the idea of him going to school.

Didn't get that from me, she thought. She'd never fussed about not going to school. Now, at twenty-five, she deeply regretted letting her education slide. If she'd applied herself, tried for college, she could have developed a skill, had a career.

Instead, she had a high school diploma she'd barely earned, and was qualified for little more than serving drinks to men whose eyes tried to crawl down her cleavage.

But she wasn't one for regrets. She'd done what she'd done, and she had the greatest prize of all. Keenan. In a couple of years, she figured, she'd have saved enough that she could turn in her bustier and take a night course. Once she had a few business courses under her belt, she could open her own flower shop. And she wouldn't have to leave Keenan with sitters at night.

She served her drinks, took an order from another table and thanked God her break was coming up in five minutes.

When she saw Coop walk in, her first thought was Keenan. But the sick alarm passed almost as quickly as it had come. Coop was relaxed, obviously scoping the place out. When his eyes met hers, he nodded easily and made his way through the scattered tables.

"I thought I'd stop in for a drink."

"This is the place for it. Do you want to sit at the bar, or do you want a table?"

"A table. Got a minute?"

"At quarter after I've got fifteen of them. Why?"

"I'd like to talk to you."

"Okay. What can I get you?"

"Coffee, black."

"Coffee, black. Have a seat."

He watched her head toward the bar and tried not to dwell on how attractive she looked walking away. He hadn't come in because he wanted a drink, but because she seemed like a nice woman in a tight skirt—spot, he corrected. A tight spot.

Get hold of yourself, Coop, he warned himself. He knew better than to let a pair of long legs cloud his judgment. He'd only come in to ask a few questions, get the full story. That was what he did, and he was good at it. Just as he was good at dissecting a game, any game, and finding those small triumphs and small mistakes that influenced the outcome.

"We've been busy tonight." Zoe set two coffees on the table before sliding onto a chair across from Coop. She let out a long, heartfelt sigh, then smiled. "This is the first time I've been off my feet in four hours."

"I thought you worked in a flower shop."

"I do, three days a week." She slid her cramped feet out of her shoes. "Around Mother's Day, Christmas, Easter—you know, the big flower days, I can squeeze in more." She sipped the coffee she'd loaded with sugar and let it pump into her system. "It's just a small shop, and Fred—that's the owner—only keeps on a couple of part-timers. That way he doesn't have to pay any of the bennies, like hospitalization, sick leave."

"That's lousy."

"Hey, it's a job. I like it. It's just Fred and Martha—she's his wife. They've taught me a lot about flowers and plants."

Someone pumped quarters into the juke. The room heated up with music. Coop leaned over the table so that she could hear him. For a moment he lost the thread somewhere in her big brown eyes.

"Have I met you somewhere before?" he asked her.

"In the apartment."

"No, I mean..." He shook his head, let it go. "Uh, why here?"

"Why here what?"

"Why do you work here?"

She blinked, those long lashes fluttering down, then up. "For a paycheck."

"It doesn't seem like you should be working in a bar."

"Excuse me?" Zoe wasn't sure if she should be amused or insulted. She chose the former simply because it was her nature. "Do you have a problem with cocktail waitresses?"

"No, no. It's just that, you're a mother."

"Yes, I am. I have a son to prove it." She laughed and leaned her chin on her fist. "Are you thinking it would be more appropriate for me to be home baking cookies or knitting a scarf?"

"No." Though it embarrassed him that he did. "It's that outfit," he blurted out. "And the way all these men look at you."

"If a woman's going to wear something like this, men are going to look. Looking's all they do," she added. "If it makes you feel better, I don't dress like this for PTA meetings."

He was feeling more ridiculous every second. "Look, it's none of my business. I just have a habit of asking questions. Seems to me you could do better than this. I mean, you've got the flower job, and the rent—"

"And I have a mortgage, a son who seems to outgrow his clothes and shoes every other week, a car payment, grocery bills, doctor bills."

"Doctor? Is the kid sick?"

Zoe rolled her eyes. Just when she was starting to get irritated, he deflated her. "No. Kids Keenan's age are always bringing some germ or other home from school. He needs regular checkups with his pediatrician, with the dentist. Those things aren't free."

"No, but there are programs. Assistance." He stopped, because those big brown eyes had turned fierce.

"I'm perfectly capable of earning a living, and of taking care of my child."

"I didn't mean—"

"Maybe I don't have a college degree or any fancy skills, but I can pay my own way, and my son doesn't lack for anything." She jammed her feet into the backbreaking heels and stood. "We've been doing just fine on our own, and I don't need some nosy jock reporter coming in here and telling me how to be a mother. Coffee's on the house, you jerk."

He winced as she stormed away from the table, then let out a long breath. Handled that one *real* well, Coop.

He wondered if there would be an eviction notice on his door in the morning.

Chapter 4

She didn't kick him out. She had thought of it, but had decided the satisfaction she'd gain didn't quite equal the rental income. Besides, she'd heard it all before.

One of the reasons she'd moved from New York was that she'd grown impossibly weary of friends and family telling her how to run her life. How to raise her son.

Baltimore had been a clean slate.

She'd had enough money put aside to afford a nice two-bedroom apartment and invest the rest. And because she was willing to work at any job, and work hard, she'd rarely been unemployed. It had been difficult for her to put Keenan in day-care. But he'd thrived. He had his mother's knack for making friends.

Now, two years after the move, she had a house, and a yard, in the kind of neighborhood she wanted for her son. And she'd paid for every bit of it on her own.

Too many people had told her she was crazy, that she was too young, that she was throwing her life and her chances away. With a grunt, Zoe shoved the lawn mower around and began to cut another strip of grass. *Her* grass, she thought with clenched teeth.

She'd proved them wrong. She'd had her baby, kept her baby, and she was making a decent life for him. She and Keenan weren't statistics. They were a family.

They didn't need anyone to feel sorry for them, or to offer handouts. She was taking care of everything, one step at a time. And she had plans. Good, solid plans.

The tap on her shoulder made her jump. When she whipped her head around and looked at Coop, her hands tightened on the mower. "What?"

"I want to apologize," he shouted. When she only continued to glare at him, he reached down and shut off the engine. "I want to apologize," he repeated. "I was out of line last night."

"Really?"

"I'm sort of addicted to poking into other people's business."

"Maybe you should go cold turkey." She reached down to grab the pull cord. His hand closed over hers. She stared at it a moment. He had big hands, rough-palmed. She remembered the impression she'd gotten of strength and energy. Now the hand was gentle and hard to resist.

She hadn't felt a man's hands—hadn't wanted to feel a man's hands—in a very long time.

"Sometimes I push the wrong buttons," Coop continued. He was staring at their hands, as well, thinking how small hers felt under his. How soft. "It's earned me a fist in the face a time or two." He tried a smile when her gaze slid up to his.

"That doesn't surprise me."

She didn't smile back, but he sensed a softening. The roar of the mower had awakened him. When he'd looked out and seen her marching along behind it in baggy shorts, a T-shirt and a ridiculous straw hat, he'd wanted to go back to bed. But he'd been compelled to seek her out.

It was only a flag of truce, he told himself. After all, he had to live with her. More or less.

"I didn't mean to be critical. I was curious about you. And the kid," he added quickly. "And maybe seeing you in that outfit last night pushed a few of my buttons."

She lifted a brow. That was honest enough, she thought. "All right. No permanent damage."

It had been easier than he'd expected. Coop decided to press his luck. "Listen, I've got to cover the game this afternoon. Maybe you'd like to come along. It's a nice day for baseball."

She supposed it was. It was warm and sunny, with a nice, freshening breeze. There were worse ways to spend the day than in a ballpark with an attractive man who was doing his best to pry his foot out of his mouth.

"It sounds like fun—if I didn't have to work. But Keenan would love it." She watched his jaw drop, and smothered a smile.

"Keenan? You want me to take him?"

"I can't think of anything he'd rather do. Some of the kids play in their yards, and they let him chase the ball. But he's never seen the real thing, except on TV." She smiled now, guilelessly, and held back a hoot of laughter. She could all but see Coop's mind working.

"I don't know too much about kids," he said, backpedaling cautiously.

"But you know about sports. It'll be great for Keenan to

experience his first real game with an expert. When are you leaving?"

"Ah…a couple of hours."

"I'll make sure he's ready. This is awfully nice of you." While he stood staring, she leaned over and kissed his cheek. After one hard tug, she had the mower roaring again.

Coop stood planted like a tree when she strolled away. What the hell was he supposed to do with a kid all afternoon?

He bought popcorn, hot dogs and enormous cups of soft drinks. Coop figured food would keep the kid quiet. Keenan had bounced on the seat of the car throughout the drive to Camden Yards, and since they had arrived he'd goggled at everything.

Coop had heard "What's that?" and "How come?" too many times to count. Nervous as a cat, he settled into the press box with his laptop.

"You can watch through the window here," he instructed Keenan. "And you can't bother anybody, because they're working."

"Okay." Almost bursting with excitement, Keenan clutched his hot dog.

There were lots of people in the press box, some with neat computers, like Coop, others with headphones. A few of them had smiled at him, and all of them had said hello to Coop. Keenan knew Coop was important. As his mother had instructed, he kept close and didn't ask for any presents. Even though there had been really neat stuff at the stands. His mother had given him five whole dollars and told him he could buy a souvenir. But there'd been so many he didn't know which to pick. And Coop had walked so fast he'd hardly been able to look.

But it didn't matter, because he was at a real ball game.

Wide-eyed, he stared down at the field. It was bigger than anything he'd imagined. He knew where the pitcher would stand, and he recognized home plate, but he wasn't sure of anything else.

The big scoreboard exploded with pictures, and words he couldn't read. Circling it all were the stands, filled with more people than he'd ever seen.

When they announced the lineup, he looked down at the players with naked admiration. The national anthem began, and, recognizing it, Keenan stood up, as he'd been taught.

Coop glanced over, saw the boy standing, with a hot dog in one hand and a big, dazzling grin on his face. Suddenly he remembered his first time at a ballpark. His eager hand gripping his father's, his eyes trying to see everything at once, and his heart so full of the excitement, of the game, of just being a boy.

As the players took the field, Coop reached over and tugged on Keenan's bright hair. "Pretty cool, huh?"

"It's the best ever. Those are our guys, right?"

"Those are our guys. They're gonna kick butt."

Keenan giggled and leaned closer to the glass to watch the first pitch. "Kick butt," he said with relish.

He didn't, as Coop had expected, fidget, whine or make a general nuisance of himself. Because he was accustomed to working under noisy and confusing conditions, Keenan's constant questions didn't annoy him overmuch. At least, he thought, the kid had the good sense to ask.

Between innings, Keenan peered over Coop's shoulder and sounded out the words that were popping up on the computer screen, and he did transfer some mustard from his hands onto Coop's sleeve. But it wasn't the disaster Coop had envisioned.

Coop even felt a quick tug of pride when the play-by-play announcer called Keenan over and let the boy sit in his lap for an inning.

Most kids would've been running around the booth begging for more candy. But this one, Coop thought, had come for the game.

"How come he didn't run all the way? How come he didn't?" Keenan shifted from foot to foot. His bladder was past full, but he couldn't bear to miss a minute.

"The throw went to second, so he was forced out," Coop explained. "See, the second baseman caught the ball and stepped on the bag to retire the side."

"Retire the side," Keenan repeated reverently. "But we're still winning?"

"The O's are up by one going into the top of the ninth. Looking at the batting order, I'd say they'll put in a south-paw."

"Southpaw," Keenan repeated, as if it were gospel.

"A left-handed reliever. Probably Scully." He glanced over and noted that Keenan was holding his crotch. "Uh, got a problem?"

"Nuh-uh."

"Let's hit the john—the bathroom." He took Keenan's hand and hoped it wasn't too late. As they passed through the door, Scully was announced as the relief.

"Just like you said." Keenan looked up at Coop with dazzling admiration. "You're smarter than anybody."

Coop felt a grin break out over his face. "Let's just say I know the game."

When they arrived home, Keenan was wearing a new Orioles jersey and carrying an autographed baseball in a pint-size baseball glove. He waved a pennant in his other hand as he scrambled up the steps.

"Look! Look what Coop got me!" He barreled into his mother who'd barely walked in the door herself. "We went into the locker room with the real Orioles, and they signed the baseball for me. To keep."

"Let's see." She took the ball and examined it. "This is really special, Keenan."

"I'm gonna keep it forever. And I got this shirt, too, like they wear. And a glove. It even fits."

Emotion backed up in her throat. "It certainly does. Looks like you're all ready to play ball."

"I'm gonna play third base, 'cause it's the…the…"

"Hot corner," Coop supplied.

"Yeah. Can I go show Mr. Finkleman? Can I show him my baseball?"

"Sure."

"He's gonna be surprised." He turned and threw his arms around Coop's legs. "Thanks, thanks for taking me. I liked it best of anything. Can we go again, and take Mama?"

"Uh, yeah, I guess. Sure." Feeling awkward again, he patted Keenan's head.

"Okay!" Giving Coop one last squeeze, Keenan raced out the door to show off his treasures.

"You didn't have to buy him all that stuff," Zoe began. "Taking him was enough."

"No big deal. He didn't ask for it, or anything." Coop stuck his hands in his pockets. "He got such a charge out of meeting the players, and one thing kind of led to another."

"I know. I hear our team won."

"Yeah. Clipped them by one. I had to stop by the paper and file the story, or we'd have been here sooner."

"I just got in myself." On impulse, she walked over, wrapped her arms around him and hugged. Coop's hands stayed paralyzed in his pockets. "I owe you. You gave him a great day. He won't forget it." She drew back. "Neither will I."

"It's no big deal. He just hung out in the press box."

"It's a very big deal, especially since I trapped you into it." She laughed and tossed back her hair. "You were so transparent this morning, Coop. The idea of having a four-year-old tagging along terrified you. But you did good, real good. Anyway— Sorry," she said when the phone rang. "Hello? Oh, hi, Stan. Tonight? I'm not scheduled." Letting out a breath, she sat on the arm of a chair. "I'll have to let you know. No, Stan, I can't tell you now. I have to see if I can find a sitter. An hour, then. Yes, I understand you're in a jam. I'll call you back."

"Problem?"

"Hmmm… Two of the waitresses called in sick for tonight. They're short-staffed." She was already dialing the phone. "Hi, Mrs. Finkleman. Yeah, I know. He had a great time. Mm-hmm…" Zoe's gaze flicked up to Coop as Mrs. Finkleman told her how important it was for a boy to have a man in his life. "I'm sure you're right. I was wondering if you're busy tonight. Oh. That's right, I forgot. No, it's nothing. Have a good time."

Zoe hung up and pursed her lips. "It's their bingo night," she told Coop. "Beth's got a date. Maybe Alice." She reached for the phone again, shook her head. "No, she's having her in-laws over for dinner." Her eyes lit on Coop and narrowed in speculation. "You didn't have any problem with Keenan today."

"No," Coop said slowly, wary of another trap. "He was cool."

"Stan doesn't need me in until nine. Keenan goes to bed at eight, so you wouldn't have to do anything but hang around, watch television or whatever."

"Hang around here, while you work?" He took a step back. "Just me and the kid—like a baby-sitter? Listen…"

"I'll pay you. Beth gets two an hour, but I can up the ante."

"I don't want your money, Zoe."

"That's so sweet." She smiled, took his hand and squeezed. "Really, so sweet of you. If you could come down about eight-thirty."

"I never said—"

"You can help yourself to anything in the kitchen. I'll make some brownies, if I have time. I'd better call Stan back before he pulls out what's left of his hair." She picked up the phone, beamed at Coop. "Now I owe you two."

"Yeah, right." He hurried out before she could find some way to owe him three.

Chapter 5

For the next couple of hours, Coop immersed himself in "All in the Game," his weekly syndicated column. The kid had given him the hook, he thought. The first visit to a ball game, the passing on of tradition, and the bond that was forged over the cheers, the crack of the bat, the peanut shells.

It was a good piece, Coop decided, and wrote easily. He supposed since he owed the idea to Keenan the least he could do was hang around downstairs and eat brownies while the kid slept.

He wandered back down just as Zoe came through the kitchen door.

She hadn't been sure he'd come. She knew she'd hustled him, and after she'd finished being amused by it, she felt guilty. But here he was, right on time, standing at the foot of the steps.

"I pushed you into a corner…." she began.

"Yeah, you did." She looked so somber, he had to smile. "You've got a real talent for it."

She shrugged her shoulders and smiled back at him. "Sometimes being pushy's the only way to get things done, but I always feel bad about it after. I did bake brownies."

"I could smell them all the way upstairs." When she didn't move, he tilted his head. Funny, though she was wearing that sexy waitress rig again, she didn't seem so outrageous. Except for that bow tie, he thought. Something about that black tie around that slim white throat shot straight to his libido.

"You going to let me in, or do you want me to stand out here?"

"I have this guilt thing," she explained, "whenever I have to ask anyone for a favor. And it was so sweet of you to take Keenan to the game, especially when…"

"When I'd been asking you out?"

She shrugged her shoulders again, let them fall. He was looking at her that way again, and something in her body was reacting helplessly. Better, she thought, to set the rules quickly. "I don't go out with men. I should have told you straight out."

He had to force himself not to lift a hand to that neat little bow and tug. "At all?"

"It's just easier not to. They're not interested in Keenan, or they pretend they are so they can talk me into bed." When he rocked back on his heels and cleared his throat, she laughed. "What they don't know is that they're clear as cellophane. You see, Keenan and I are a team. As a sportswriter, you should know what that means."

"Sure. I get it."

"Anyway, you gave him a really wonderful day, and I feel like I'm twisting your arm about tonight."

He decided, after a moment, that she wasn't doing it on

purpose. There was just too much sincerity in that glorious face for a con. And if there was a twinge of guilt because he had given considerable thought to talking her into bed, that was his problem.

"Look, he's asleep, right?"

"Yes. All the excitement wore him out."

"So, I'll eat your brownies and watch your TV. No big deal." Her smile came easily now, beautifully, and made his mouth water. "I left the number of the club by the phone, just in case. The Finklemans should be home by eleven. She'd come over and relieve you if you want."

"We'll play it by ear."

"Thanks, really." She stepped back into the kitchen to let him in. "My shift ends at two, at closing."

"Long day for you."

"I've got tomorrow off." After grabbing her purse, she took a quick look around. "Make yourself at home, okay?"

"I will. See you."

She hurried out, those incredibly sexy heels clicking across the tile. Coop let out a long breath and told himself to settle down. The lady had just set the ground rules. Fun and games were out.

She had the face of a siren, the body of a goddess, and legs designed to make a strong man whimper—but deep in her heart she was Betty Crocker.

Coop took a deep sniff and decided to content himself with a plate of double fudge brownies.

The storm rolled in just before midnight. Coop had taken Zoe at her word and made himself at home. He was stretched out on her couch, sunk deep in the cushions, with his feet propped comfortably on her coffee table. He was dozing in front of an old war movie, his only regret being that he hadn't thought to bring a couple of beers down with him.

Zoe's selection ran to milk, juice and some unidentified green liquid.

He'd poked around a little—it was simply in his nature. The clutter ran throughout the house, but he began to see a pattern to it. Obviously she wasn't a detail person, but the general lack of order made the house comfortable, even cozy. Coop wasn't sure if the result was by design or simply because she was a woman who worked two jobs and had a kid to raise.

And from the library books he'd found stacked here and there, it seemed she spent most of her free time reading up on flowers, car repair, tax laws and time management.

He couldn't help but think it was a waste of a perfectly stunning woman, this voluntary burial of self in books and nowhere part-time jobs.

But it wasn't his problem.

The crash of thunder from outside harmonized nicely with the artillery barrage on the TV screen. Coop had just decided that this baby-sitting racket was a snap.

Then he heard the wailing.

Marines didn't wail, he thought fuzzily, especially when they were battling Nazi scum. He yawned, circled his neck until it cracked, then spotted Keenan.

The boy stood at the base of the stairs in Batman pajamas, a battered stuffed dog clutched in one arm and tears pouring down his face.

"Mama!" His voice sharpened like an ice pick, then hitched. "Where's my mama?"

"She's at work." Coop straightened on the sofa and stared helplessly. "Something wrong?"

A flash of lightning lit the room. By the time the thunder

rolled in answer, Keenan screamed like a banshee and launched himself into Coop's lap.

"I'm scared. There's monsters outside. They're coming to get me."

"Hey…" Coop gave the head buried in his chest an inadequate pat. "Hey, it's just a thunderstorm."

"Monsters," Keenan sobbed. "I want Mama."

"Well, she's—" He started to swear, caught himself. The poor kid was shaking. With an instinct he didn't recognize, Coop cuddled Keenan in his lap. "You don't like storms, huh?" All Keenan could do was shake his head and burrow deeper. "They're just like fireworks. You know, on the Fourth of July, or after your team wins the pennant? They probably just had a big game up there. They're celebrating."

"Monsters," Keenan repeated, but he'd calmed enough to lift his head and look at Coop. "Big black monsters with sharp teeth." He jolted at the next clap of thunder. Fresh tears started to roll. "They want to eat me."

"Nah." Experimentally, Coop tested Keenan's biceps. "You're too tough."

"I am?"

"You bet. Any monsters who looked in here would see you and run for their lives. They'd never take on Coop and the Keen-man."

Keenan sniffled, rubbed a fist over his eyes. "Really?"

"Absolutely." Coop saw Keenan's lower lip tremble when thunder grumbled. "Home run," he said, and Keenan's trembling mouth curved in a hesitant smile.

"Can I stay out here with you?"

"Sure. I guess."

Keenan, an expert in such matters, settled himself comfortably in Coop's lap, laid his head against Coop's heart and sighed.

                              * * *

Zoe was swaying with fatigue by the time she let herself in. It was nearly 3:00 a.m., and she'd been up and going for twenty hours straight. All she wanted was to fall facedown on her bed and sleep.

She saw them in the gray light of the snowy television screen. They were curled together on the couch, the boy snuggled deep against the man. Something shifted inside her at the sight of them, both sleeping deeply, Keenan's tousled golden hair beneath Coop's broad, tanned hand.

She set her purse and her keys aside without taking her eyes off them.

How small her son looked, and how safe.

She slipped out of her shoes and walked to them on stockinged feet. In a natural gesture, she brushed a hand over Coop's hair before gently lifting her son. Keenan stirred, then settled against her.

"Mama."

"Yes, baby," she murmured. She nuzzled him as she carried him away, caught the scent of man mixed with boy.

"The monsters came, but we scared them away."

"Of course you did."

"Coop said the thunder's just fireworks. I like fireworks."

"I know." She laid him in his bed, smoothing the sheets, his hair, kissing his soft cheeks. "Go back to sleep now."

But he already had. She watched him a moment longer in the faint glow of his night-light, then turned and went back downstairs to Coop.

He was sitting up now, his head in his hands, the heels rubbing against his eyes. She switched off the buzzing television set, then sat on the arm of the couch. Any man who could sleep so comfortably with a child, to her mind, had unlimited potential.

She wondered, just for an instant, what it would feel like to curl up beside him.

"The storm woke him?"

"Yeah." His voice was rusty. He cleared it. "He was pretty spooked."

"He said you chased the monsters away."

"Seemed like the right thing to do." He turned his head to look at her. Those big brown eyes were sleepy and smiling. The quick hitch in his heartbeat warned him to be on his way. But he lingered. "He's okay now?"

"He's fine. You'd make a good daddy."

"Oh, well…" That had him moving. He stood, working out the kinks. "That's not my line. But it was no big deal."

"It was to me." She'd embarrassed him, she noted, and she hadn't meant to. "Why don't I fix you breakfast tomorrow?"

"Huh?"

"Pay you back with pancakes. Mrs. Finkleman tells me you bring in a lot of pizza and Chinese, so I don't imagine you cook. Do you like pancakes?"

"Who doesn't?"

"Then let me know when you're up and around. I'll flip some for you." She lifted a hand, brushed the hair from his brow. "Thanks for helping me out."

"No problem." He took a step away, swore under his breath and turned back. "Listen, I've just got to do this, okay?"

Before she could respond, he took her face in his hands and closed his mouth over hers.

The kiss was quick, and it was light, and it sent sparks snapping down her nerve ends.

When she didn't move a muscle, he lifted his head, looked at her. She was staring at him, her eyes heavy and dark. He thought he saw the same stunned reaction in them that was curling somewhere in his gut. She opened her mouth as if to speak, but he shook his head and kissed her again. Longer, deeper, until he felt her bones begin to melt. Until he heard the small whimper of pleasure purr in her throat.

Her hands slid up his arms, gripped, then moved up to tangle in his hair. They stood there, locked against each other.

One of them quivered, perhaps both. It didn't seem to matter as the warm taste of her seeped into his mouth, into his blood. It was like a dream that he hadn't yet shaken off, one that tempted him to sink back in, to forget reality.

She'd forgotten it. All she knew for one glorious moment was that she was being held in strong arms, that her mouth was being savored wonderfully, and that needs, so long dormant, were swimming to the surface and breaking into life.

Touch me. She wondered if she said it, or if the words simply whirled hazily in her head. But his hand, hard and sure, ran once down her body, kindling fires.

She remembered what it was to burn, and what it was like when the flames died out and left you alone.

"Coop." Oh, she wanted, so badly, just to let it happen. But she wasn't a young, reckless girl this time. And she had more to think of than herself. "Coop. No."

His mouth clung to hers for another moment, his teeth nipping. But he drew back. He was, he realized, as breathless as a man who'd slid headfirst into home plate.

"Now I'm supposed to say I'm sorry."

She shook her head. "No, you're not. I'm not."

"Good." The hands that were resting on her shoulders kneaded once, then slipped away into his pockets. "Me neither. I've been thinking about doing that since I first saw your feet."

Her brows rose. Surely she'd heard him wrong. "My what?"

"Your feet. You were standing on the ladder, painting. You weren't wearing any shoes. You've got tremendously sexy feet."

"Really?" It amazed her that he could tie her into helpless knots one minute, then make her laugh the next. "Thanks. I think."

"I guess I'd better go."

"Yeah, you'd better."

He nodded, started out. This time, when he stopped, she braced, and she yearned. But he simply turned and looked at her. "I'm not going to try to talk you into bed. But I want you there. I figured I should let you know."

"I appreciate it," she said in a shaky voice.

When the door closed behind him, she let her weak legs fold and sat down on the couch. What, she asked herself, was she supposed to do now?

Chapter 6

When Coop dragged himself out of bed, it was nearly noon. He stumbled into the shower and nearly drowned himself before both of his eyes opened. Wet and out of sorts, he rubbed himself down, gave a moment's thought to shaving, then dismissed the idea.

He tugged on gym shorts and a T-shirt before heading directly to the coffeemaker. While it brewed, he opened his front door and let the full power of the sun shock him the rest of the way awake.

They were in the yard, Zoe and Keenan, laughing as mother tried to help son hit fungoes with a plastic bat. The kid wasn't having much luck, Coop noted. But he was sure having fun. He started to step back inside before either of them spotted him. But the jock in him had him kibitzing.

"He'll never hit anything standing that way," Coop called out, and had two pair of big brown eyes looking up in his direction.

"Hi, Coop. Hi. I'm playing baseball." Thrilled to have an audience, Keenan waved his bat and nearly caught his mother on the chin.

"Watch it, champ," she said, and shifted out of range. "Good morning," she called out. "Want your breakfast?"

"Yeah, maybe."

Keenan took another pathetic swing and had Coop muttering under his breath. Swung like a girl. Somebody had to show the kid how to hold a bat, didn't they? he asked himself as he started down.

"You're choking it too much."

Zoe's brows drew together. "The book I got said—"

"Book." He cursed automatically. Keenan echoed him. "Sorry," he muttered when Zoe gave him a narrow-eyed look. "Now listen, you learn how to add and subtract from books. You don't learn baseball. Just like a girl." He crouched down and adjusted Keenan's hands.

Zoe had been ready to concede to the expert, but the last statement stopped her. "Excuse me? Are you implying that females can't play sports?"

"Not what I said. Swing from the shoulders," he told Keenan. Coop might have been grouchy, but he wasn't stupid. "There are plenty of terrific female athletes. Keep your eye on the ball, kid." He kept one hand around Keenan's and lightly tossed the ball up in the air with the other. The bat connected with a hollow thud.

"I hit it! I hit it really, really hard!"

"Major league stuff." Coop slid his eyes back up to Zoe's. "I thought you were making pancakes."

"I was— I am." She blew out a breath. "I guess you're taking over."

"Well, I don't know diddly about pancakes, and you

don't know squat about baseball. Why don't we both do what we know?"

"Like it's a big deal to hit a stupid ball with a stupid bat," she muttered as she strode to the back door.

"You can't do it."

She stopped dead in her tracks, eyes narrowed, turned. "I certainly can."

"Yeah, right. Okay, Keenan, let's try it again."

"I believe it's my turn." Challenge in her every movement, Zoe slipped the bat from her son's hands.

"Are you going to hit it, Mama? Are you?"

"You bet I am." She held out a hand for the ball Coop was holding. She tossed it up, swung, and batted the ball to the chain-link fence bordering the side yard. Keenan let out a cheer and raced to retrieve it.

Coop sniffed, smiled. "Not bad, for a girl. But anybody can hit a fungo."

"Keenan's too young for anything but a plastic ball."

"No, a fungo's when you toss it up yourself and hit it."

"Oh."

"I'm gonna throw it, Coop. You catch."

"Sure, zip it in here."

It took Keenan three tries, running in closer each time, to send the ball anywhere near Coop.

"I suppose you don't think I could hit it if you threw it at me…." Zoe began.

"Pitch it to you," Coop said patiently. "I would pitch it to you."

"All right, pitch it to me, then." She raised the bat.

"Fine, but you might want to turn a little more to the side. That's it," he said, backing away. "Zoe, you're holding the bat like you're going to use it to hammer a nail. Okay, here it comes."

He tossed the ball soft and underhand, but she still had to grit her teeth to keep herself from jerking away. Because her pride and her son's respect for women were at stake, she swung hard. No one was more stunned than Zoe when she connected. Coop snatched the ball an instant before it could smash his nose.

"Well." Zoe handed the bat back to a wide-eyed Keenan, dusted her hands. "I'll go see about those pancakes."

"She hit it really hard," Keenan said admiringly.

"Yeah." Coop watched the back door swing shut behind her. "Your mother's really...something, kid."

"Will you pitch to me, Coop? Will you?"

"Sure. But let's work on that stance, huh? You gotta look like a ballplayer."

When Zoe finished flipping the last pancake on the stack, she looked out the window and saw her son swing the bat. The ball didn't go far, but Coop made a pretense of a diving catch, missing, while Keenan danced gleefully in place.

"Too hot to handle," Coop claimed, and Keenan jumped on top of him. "Hey, there's no tackling in baseball. Football's out of season." He scooped the wriggling boy up and held him upside down. Somewhere along the line, his sour mood had vanished.

It became a habit to spend time with the boy. Nothing planned, just playing a little catch in the yard or showing Keenan how to dunk baskets in the apartment. It wasn't as though he were attached to the kid, Coop assured himself. But when he had some free time and the boy wanted to hang around, what was the harm? Maybe it was sort of nice to see those big eyes all full of hero worship. And maybe it wasn't so much of a hardship to listen to that rollicking belly laugh Keenan burst into when something struck his fancy.

If the boy sometimes came along with the bonus of his mother, it wasn't exactly a hardship.

The fact was, he had seen a great deal more of Keenan than Zoe since the night of the thunderstorm. She was friendly enough, but she'd been careful—or so it seemed to Coop—not to be alone with him.

That was something he was going to fix, he decided as he shut down his computer.

He grabbed a couple of miniature race cars, some of the flotsam and jetsam of boyhood that Keenan had left in his apartment. If Coop knew Zoe as he thought he was beginning to, the toys would be an easier entry than a bouquet of long-stemmed roses.

Jiggling the cars in his hand, he strode down the steps to knock on her kitchen door.

In the laundry room, Zoe slammed down the lid on the washer. "Who is it?"

"It's Coop."

She hesitated, started the machine. "Come on in. I'll be right out." She hefted a basket of clean laundry, as much out of defense as out of necessity, and went into the kitchen.

God, he looked good. She had really, really tried not to dwell on how good the man looked. So damn male, she thought, the rangy, athletic body, the muscles, the dark, untidy hair, and those wonderful pale green eyes. She wished her heart wouldn't always stutter when he aimed one of his cocky grins in her direction.

"Hi." She plopped the basket on the kitchen table and immediately began busying her hands folding socks.

"Hi." The kitchen was cluttered, as always. She really

needed someone to help her organize, he thought. God, she smelled fantastic. "Keenan left these upstairs." Coop set the cars on the table. "I thought he might be looking for them."

"Thanks."

"So where is he?"

"In school."

"Oh, right." Coop knew Keenan's schedule as well as he knew yesterday's box scores. "You just get in from the flower shop?"

"Mmm-hmm… Business is picking up. We've got a couple of weddings. Actually, I could work full-time for the next three weeks, but it just doesn't fit Keenan's schedule."

"What do you mean?" Idly he plucked a shirt from the basket.

"Well, the spring weddings. The arrangements take a lot of extra hands, so Fred asked if I could put in full days for a while."

"So, that's good, right?"

"The school Keenan goes to is really more of a preschool than day-care. It doesn't stay open after three. And I have the car pool next week, anyway. Plus, I promised to take him and some of the other kids swimming at the community center on Friday. He's really looking forward to it."

"Yeah, he mentioned it." About twenty times, Coop recalled.

"I don't want to let him down."

"So, I'll do it."

She looked back up, socks dangling from her hands. "What?"

He couldn't believe he'd said that. He stared at her for another moment, then shrugged. "I said I'd do it. It's no big deal. He can hang with me when he gets home from school."

She tilted her head. "Don't you have a job?"

"That's what I call it, since they pay me." He smiled,

finding the idea went down easily. "I do most of my writing here, and he could tag along when I go in to the paper or on an interview. He'd probably get a kick out of it."

"I'm sure he would." She narrowed her eyes. Why couldn't she get a handle on J. Cooper McKinnon? "But why would you?"

He wasn't sure he had the answer to that, so he punted. "Why not? He's not that much of a pest."

With a laugh, she went back to her laundry. "Maybe he's not, but you forgot the car pool."

"I can drive. What's the big deal about hauling a bunch of kids to school and back?"

"I can't begin to tell you," she murmured. It was, perhaps, something every adult should experience for himself. "And the swimming."

"I was captain of the swim team in college. All-state."

She glanced up at that. "I thought you played baseball. Uh, Keenan mentioned it."

"Yeah, I did. Two hundred and twelve RBIs my last season. I played basketball, too, averaged forty-two points a game." He was bragging, Coop realized. Like some gawky teenager trying to impress the head cheerleader. He frowned down at the little cars, began to slide one over the table.

"Keenan says you make great engine noises."

"Yeah, it's a talent."

He'd embarrassed himself, Zoe realized, and she wanted to hug him. "Tell you what. Why don't we take it a day at a time? If you decide you can't handle it—"

His eyes flashed up at that. "I think I can handle one scrawny kid and a few of his pals."

"Okay. If you decide you don't *want* to handle it, no hard feelings."

"Fine. When do you want to start?"

"Tomorrow would be great."

"Okay." That was settled. Now, he thought, it was on to other business. "How about dinner?"

Her eyes widened in surprise. "Um…sure. We're just going to have chicken. I'll probably fry it."

"No." He stepped closer. She stepped back. "I mean, why don't we have dinner? Out. You and me."

"Oh, well…" Good answer, she thought foolishly. Very succinct. She took another step in retreat. "I have to work tonight."

"Tomorrow."

"I don't really go out."

"I've noticed. What are you backing away from, Zoe?"

"You." Annoyed with herself, she held up a hand. And found it pressed against his chest. "I don't want to date anyone. Start anything. I have very good reasons."

"You'll have to tell me about them sometime." He reached up, combed a hand through her hair and loosened the band that held it back.

"You're not going to kiss me again."

"Sure I am." He touched his lips to hers to prove it. His eyes remained open as he drew her lower lip into his mouth, as he used his tongue, his teeth, to tease and seduce. "You've got an incredible mouth."

She couldn't get her breath. Even as she gasped for it, her vision dimmed. It was all she wanted. It seemed her life depended on keeping her lips against his. This wasn't fair, she thought dimly as she began to sink into the glory of sensation. Too long, she told herself. Surely she was reacting this way only because it had been so terribly long since she'd allowed herself to feel only as a woman.

She was melting against him like wax. He hadn't known how painfully erotic it would be to feel that long, lean body go fluid. He'd only meant to kiss her, to test them both, but his hands were already reaching, stroking, exploring.

His touch, those hard, callused hands against her bare skin, all but brought her to her knees.

"I have to think."

"Think later." He pressed his mouth to her throat.

Oh, it was glorious, glorious to ache again. But she knew too well what came from soothing that ache. "Coop, we can't do this."

"Yes, we can. I'll show you."

With a laugh that came out half moan, she turned her head away. "My head's spinning. You have to stop. God, do you have any idea what you're doing to me?"

"I haven't even started. Come upstairs, come upstairs with me, Zoe. I want to feel you under me. I want to feel myself inside you."

"I want to." She trembled, the needs exploding inside her like firebombs. "Coop, I need to think first. I have to think. I haven't been with anyone in five years."

His mouth stopped its desperate journey over her throat. Slowly he drew back to look at her. Her eyes were clouded, and her mouth was swollen and ripe. "No one?"

"No." She swallowed and prayed for her system to level before she gave in to the urge to rip off his clothes and cut loose. "Since before Keenan was born. I feel like all those needs dried up—like old leaves. You've set a match to them, and I don't know how to handle it."

"The kid's father," Coop said carefully. "You're still in love with him."

"No." She might have laughed at that, if she weren't so

shaken. "He has nothing to do with it. Well, of course he does, but... I have to sit down." She walked unsteadily to a chair. "I knew this was going to happen. I think I knew it the first time I saw you. There's been no one, because I didn't want anyone. Because Keenan was all that mattered to me. I have plans." That came out as an accusation, and her eyes darkened. "Damn it, I have plans. I want to go back to school. I want to have my own flower shop one day." Her voice began to catch, alarming him.

"Zoe—"

But she barreled right over him. "And everything was going along fine. I got the house. I wanted him to have a house, and a yard, and neighbors. Everyone said I was crazy, that I'd never be able to do it, that I'd be sorry I'd given everything up to raise a child on my own. But I'm not sorry. He's the best thing that ever happened to me. And I've done a good job. Keenan's happy, and he's bright and funny and wonderful. We have a good life, and I know I can make it even better. I haven't needed anyone. And... Oh, God, I'm in love with you."

The hand he'd lifted awkwardly to pat her head froze. "What?"

"Oh, what a mess. What a mess." She plucked a tiny sock out of the laundry basket and wiped her eyes. "Maybe it's just hormones. It could be, you know. But I walked in and you were sleeping with him on the couch. It was so sweet. Then you were kissing me and everything went crazy. Then you're out in the yard looking so smug and male, showing Keenan how to hit that silly ball. And you're eating pancakes and looking at me. I can hardly breathe when you're looking at me."

Somewhere along the line, his mind had gone blank. "I think I missed a step."

"No, you didn't." She sniffled and struggled to get herself under control. "I've just taken too many. It's my fault. You've been nice to Keenan, and you've been honest with me." She sighed, dropped the damp sock in her lap. "Believe me, I know my emotions are my responsibility." Because he was still staring at her, like a man who'd just had the friendly family dog lunge for his throat, she smiled. "I'm sorry, Coop. I shouldn't have dumped all that on you. I didn't even know it was all bottled up."

This time he took a step back. "Zoe, I like the kid. Who wouldn't? And I'm attracted to you. But—"

"There's no need to explain." Steady now, she rose. "Really, there isn't. I don't expect anything from you, and I'm sorry if I made you uncomfortable. But I feel a lot better." And, oddly enough, she did. "When I go to bed with you, we'll understand each other."

"When you—"

"I think we both know that's going to happen," she said calmly. "We both want it to, and it's smarter to face that than to live with all this tension. Keenan's been wanting to spend the night with a friend of his. I'll arrange it." She laughed a little at Coop's expression. "It's a little hard to be spontaneous with a four-year-old around. I hope you don't mind planning out a night together."

"No, I mean, I don't— God, Zoe."

"If you'd rather not, or if you want some time to decide, that's all right."

He studied her face, felt that same greedy tug, and a flare of something entirely different. Entirely new. "No, I want you. Whenever."

"How about Monday night?"

"I've got a twilight doubleheader on Monday." He couldn't

believe he was standing here planning out a wild night of love like a dentist's appointment.

"Ah...Wednesday?"

He nodded. "Wednesday's good for me. Do you want to go out somewhere?"

It was sweet, she thought, really sweet of him to ask. "It's not necessary." She laid a hand on his cheek. "I don't need flowers and candlelight. I'll come upstairs after Keenan's settled."

"Good. Fine. I...better get back to work."

"Do you still want to have Keenan tomorrow?"

"Yeah, no problem. Tell him to come on up." Coop backed toward the door as Zoe began folding laundry again. "I guess I'll see you."

She listened to him walk up the steps. He was certainly a mistake, she told herself. But she'd made others. Life got too mundane when you avoided all the wrong turns.

Chapter 7

"He shoots, he scores!" Coop made appropriate crowd noises as Keenan dunked the basket.

"I can do it again! I can, okay?" From his perch on Coop's shoulders, Keenan swung his sneakered feet.

"Okay, you've drawn the foul." Coop scooped the palm-sized ball up and passed it into Keenan's eager hands. "It's game point, kid, ten seconds to play. This free throw is all-or-nothing. Got it?"

"Got it!"

"A hush falls over the crowd as Fleming steps up to the line. He's played the game of his life tonight, but it all comes down to this one shot. He eyes the basket. You eyeing the basket?"

"Eyeing it," Keenan said, with his tongue caught between his teeth.

"He sets…and shoots." Coop winced as the little rubber

ball circled the rim, then watched through squinted eyes as it tipped in and dropped through the net.

"And the crowd goes wild!" Coop danced around the sofa while Keenan hooted and clapped on his shoulders. When he dumped the boy on the cushions of the sofa, Keenan let go with one of the rolling belly laughs that always made Coop grin. "You're a natural."

"You shoot it, Coop! You!"

Obliging, Coop executed a quick turnaround jump shot. This wasn't such a bad way to spend a rainy afternoon, he decided. And it helped keep his mind off how he was going to spend the rainy night ahead.

It was Wednesday.

"Okay, time out. I've got to finish up my piece on the track meet."

"Are we going to go to the paper again? It's neat there."

"Not today. I'm going to fax it in when it's done. You watch some tube." Coop hit the remote, then handed it over.

"Can I get a drink?"

"Yeah, there's some of that juice your mom sent up for you. Stay out of trouble, right?"

"Right."

When Coop headed into his office, Keenan scrambled up from the couch. He liked it best when he got to stay with Coop after school. They always got to do something neat, and Coop never asked if he'd washed his hands or said too many cookies would spoil his appetite.

Best of all, he liked when Coop picked him up. It was different than when his mother did. He liked when she held him, nuzzled him after his bath or rocked him when he had a bad dream. But Coop smelled different, and felt different.

He knew why, Keenan thought as he wandered into the

kitchen. It was because Coop was a daddy instead of a mom.

He liked to pretend Coop was his daddy, and figured that maybe if he didn't do anything bad, Coop wouldn't go away.

After a couple of tugs, Keenan had the refrigerator open. He was proud that Coop had hung the pictures he had drawn for him on the door. He peered inside, saw the jug of juice his mother had bought for him. And the green bottles Coop liked.

"B-E-E-R," Keenan said to himself. He remembered that he'd asked Coop if he could have a taste from the bottle, and that Coop had told him he couldn't until he was big. After Coop had let him sniff the beer, Keenan had been glad he wasn't big yet.

There was a new bottle in the fridge today, and Keenan knit his brow and tried to recognize the letters. *C-H-A-R-D-O-N—* There were too many letters to read, so he lost interest.

He took out the jug, gripping it manfully and setting it on the floor. Humming to himself, he dragged a chair over to get cups from the cabinet. One day he'd be as tall as Coop and wouldn't need to stand on a chair. He leaned forward on his toes.

The crash and the howl had Coop leaping up, rapping his knee hard against the desk. Papers scattered as he raced out of the office and into the kitchen.

Keenan was still howling. A chair was overturned, juice was glugging cheerfully onto the floor, and the refrigerator was wide open. Coop splashed through the puddle and scooped Keenan up.

"Are you hurt? What'd you do?" When his only answer was another sob, he stood Keenan on the kitchen table and searched for blood. He imagined gaping wounds, broken bones.

"I fell down." Keenan wriggled back into Coop's arms.

"Okay, it's okay. Did you hit your head?"

"Nuh-uh." With a sniffle, Keenan waited for the kisses he expected after a hurt. "I fell on my bottom." Keenan's lip poked out. "Kiss it."

"You want me to kiss your— Come on, kid, you're joking."

The lip trembled, another tear fell. "You gotta kiss where it hurts. You gotta, or it won't get better."

"Oh, man." Flummoxed, Coop dragged a hand through his hair. He was desperately relieved that no blood had been spilled, but if anyone, anyone, found out what he was about to do, he'd never live it down. He turned Keenan around and gave the little rump a quick kiss. "Does that do it?"

"Uh-huh." Keenan knuckled his eyes, then held out his arms. "Will you pick me up?"

"Yeah." He didn't feel as ridiculous as he'd expected when the boy's arms went around his neck. "Okay now?"

With his head resting on Coop's shoulder, he nodded. "I didn't mean to do it. I spilled all the juice."

"No big deal." Hardly realizing he did so, Coop turned his head to brush his lips over Keenan's hair. Something was shifting inside him, creaking open.

"You aren't mad at me? You won't go away?"

"No." What the hell was going on? Coop wondered as unexplored and unexpected emotions swirled inside him. "No, I'm not going anywhere."

"I love you," Keenan said, with the simple ease of a child.

Coop closed his eyes and wondered how a grown man was supposed to handle falling for a four-year-old boy.

Well, here she was, Zoe thought as she stood at the bottom of the steps leading to Coop's apartment. All she had to do was go upstairs, open the door and start an affair. Her stomach clenched.

Silly to be nervous, she told herself, and climbed the first step. She was a normal woman with normal needs. If her emotions were too close to the surface, she would deal with it. It was much more difficult to be hurt when you had no expectations.

She'd had expectations once, but she knew better now.

This was simply a physical attraction between two single, healthy people. She'd nearly backed down a step before she forced herself to move forward. All the practical details had been seen to. Her son was safely tucked away for the night at his sleep-over. She'd arranged for birth control—that wasn't an oversight she would make again.

No regrets, she promised herself as she lifted a hand to knock. She knew how useless they were.

He answered so quickly, she nearly jumped. Then they stood and stared at each other.

She'd worn a dress, one of those thin, breezy sundresses designed to make a man give thanks for the end of winter. Her hair was loose, falling over thin raspberry-colored straps and bare, peach-toned shoulders. There were nerves in her eyes.

"Hi." He glanced down to the cordless phone she held. "Expecting a call?"

"What? Oh." She laughed, miserably self-conscious. "No, I just don't like to be out of touch when Keenan's not home."

"He's all settled at his pal's?"

"Yeah." She stepped inside, set the phone on the counter. "He was so excited, he—" She broke off when her sandal stuck to the floor.

Coop grimaced. "I guess I missed some of it. We had a spill."

"Oh?"

"The kid took a tumble, sheared off ten years of my life. No blood lost, though. Just a half gallon of orange juice."

When she only smiled, he stepped to the refrigerator. Why in hell was he babbling? "Want some wine?"

"That would be nice." Why, he's as nervous as I am, she realized, and she loved him for it. "Keenan's having a wonderful time staying with you. I have to study the sports pages now just to keep up with what he's talking about."

"He catches on fast."

"So do I. Go ahead," she said as he handed her a glass of wine, "Ask me about stats. I know all about RBIs and ERAs." She took a sip, then gestured with her glass. "I think the Orioles would have taken the second game of that doubleheader the other night if they'd put in a relief pitcher in the second inning."

His lips twitched. "Do you?"

"Well, the starter had lost his stuff, obviously. The guy who was announcing—"

"The play-by-play man."

"Yes, he said so himself."

"So, you watched the game."

"I watch 'Sesame Street,' too. I like to keep up with Keenan's interests." She trailed off when Coop reached out to twine a lock of her hair around his finger.

"He's got a thing for dinosaurs, too."

"I know, I've checked a half dozen books out of the library. We've—" The fingers trailed over her shoulder. "We've been down to the natural history museum twice."

She set the glass aside and fell into his arms.

He kissed her as though he'd been starved for her taste. The impact was fast, deep, desperate. The little purring sounds that vibrated in her throat had his muscles turning into bundles of taut wire.

"I wasn't sure you'd come."

"Neither was I. I—"

"Can't think of anything but you," he said as he swept her off her feet. "I thought we'd take this slow."

"Let's not," she murmured, pressing her lips to his throat as he carried her into the bedroom.

She had a quick impression of Spartan neatness and simple masculine colors and lines before they tumbled onto the bed.

Neither of them was looking for patience. They rolled together, a tangle of limbs grasping, groping, glorying. The sheer physicality of it, flesh to flesh, mouth to mouth, had Zoe's head reeling. Oh, she wanted to be touched like this, to feel so desperately like a woman, with a man's hand streaking over her, with his lips savoring every thud of her pulse.

So she lost herself. No more nerves, no more fears. And if she loved, it only made the joy of mating more lovely.

She was every man's fantasy. Stunningly responsive, breathlessly aggressive. And so beautiful, he thought. Undraped, the exquisite body was so slim, so perfect, he couldn't believe it had ever carried a child. In the gilded light of dusk, her face was elegant, heart-stopping. Whenever he touched, wherever he touched, he could see the bold echo of her pleasure reflected in her eyes.

He watched those eyes glaze over, felt her body tense, heard her strangled cry of release. Swamped with the power of it, he drove her upward again until they were both panting for air, until she reared up from the bed and wrapped herself around him.

Damp skin slid over damp skin, hungry mouth sought hungry mouth. They rolled over the bed again, moaning, quivering. Then his hands gripped hers, and his mouth crushed her mouth. And he thrust inside her, hard and deep.

She felt the sensation as if it were a lance through her

system, painful, glorious. For an instant, neither of them moved, they just stayed tensed and shuddering on the edge.

Then it was all movement, all speed, a wild race that ended with them both plunging deliriously over the finish line.

It wasn't exactly the way he'd imagined, Coop thought. They were sprawled across his bed, Zoe curled against him. The light was nearly gone, and the room was full of shadows.

He'd imagined they would progress to the bedroom by stages. They were both adults and had known that was the ultimate goal, but he'd thought they would move slowly.

Then she'd been standing there smiling, the nerves shining in her eyes… He'd never wanted anything or anyone more in his life.

Still, he thought she deserved more than a quick tussle, however rewarding. But the night was young.

He flexed his arm to bring her head a little closer, brushed his lips over her temple. "Okay?"

"Mmm… At the very least." Her body felt golden. She was surprised her skin didn't glow in the dark.

"I rushed you a little."

"No, perfect timing."

He began to trail a finger up and down her arm. He wanted her again. Good God, his system was already churning to life. A little control, Coop, he ordered himself. "You're going to stay?"

She opened her eyes, looking into his. "Yes."

"I'm going to go get the wine."

"That's good." She sighed as he left the bed. She'd forgotten how to deal with the after, she realized. Or with the before and during, for that matter, she thought with a wry smile. Though she thought she'd done pretty well so far.

She hadn't known how much had been bottled up inside her. Or just how much she'd needed to feel like a woman again. But then, she hadn't known she could love again.

She shifted, slipping under the tangled sheets, automatically lifting them to her breasts when Coop came back with the wine and glasses.

The sight of her in his bed shot to his loins, with a quick detour through the heart. He said nothing, pouring wine, offering her a fresh glass and settling beside her.

"Why haven't you been with anyone?" The moment the question was out, he wished for a rusty knife to hack off his tongue. "Sorry, none of my business."

"It's all right." Because I haven't fallen in love with anyone before you, she thought. But that wasn't what he wanted to hear, she knew. Nor was it really what he'd asked.

"You want to know about Keenan's father."

"None of my business," he repeated. "Sorry, it's the reporter in me."

"It was a long time ago—a lifetime ago. I don't mind telling you. I grew up in New York. I think I mentioned that my mother's an actress. I was the result of a second marriage. She's had five. So far."

"Five?"

Zoe chuckled into her wine, sipped. "Clarice falls in love and changes husbands the way some women change hairstyles. My father lasted about four years before they parted amicably. Clarice always has friendly divorces. I didn't see much of him, because he moved to Hollywood. He does commercials and voice-overs mostly. Anyway, I think she was on husband number four when I was in high school. He had some pull with the Towers Modeling Agency. They're pretty big."

"I've heard of them."

"Well, he got me in. I started doing some shoots. And I caught on."

"That's it," Coop said, interrupting her. "I knew I'd seen your face before."

She moved her shoulders. "Five, six years ago, it was hard to avoid it. I did twenty covers in one month, the year after I graduated school."

"Cover of *In Sports,* swimsuit edition."

She smiled. "You've got a good memory. That was six years ago."

He remembered the long, sand-dusted legs, the lush wet red excuse for a bathing suit, the laughing, seductive face. He gulped down wine. "It was a hell of a shot."

"And a long, grueling shoot. Anyway, I was making a lot of money, getting a lot of press, going to lots of parties. I met Roberto at one of them."

"Roberto." Coop grimaced at the sound of the name.

"Lorenzi. Tennis player. You might have heard of him."

"Lorenzi? Sure—took the French Open three years ago in straight sets, then blew Wimbledon in the semis. He's got a bad attitude and likes to race cars and chase women on the side. Hasn't been seeded above twenty-fifth in the last two years. Got some bad press this spring when he tipped back too many vinos and punched out a photographer." Coop started to drink, stopped. "Lorenzi? He's Keenan's father? But he's—"

"A womanizer?" Zoe supplied. "A creep, a rich, spoiled egotist? I know—now. What I saw then was a gorgeous, charming man who sent me roses and jetted me off to Monte Carlo for intimate dinners. I was dazzled. He told me he loved me, that he adored me, worshiped me, he couldn't live without me. I believed him, and we became lovers. I thought, since he was my first, he'd be my only. Anyway, I didn't realize he was already getting tired of me when I found out I was pregnant. When I told him, he was angry, then he was very calm, very reasonable. He assumed I'd want an abortion and agreed to pay all the expenses, even to make the arrangements."

"A real prince."

"It was a logical assumption," Zoe said calmly. "I had a career on fast forward, in a field that wouldn't wait while I put on weight and suffered from morning sickness. He, of course, had no intention of marrying me, and thought, rightly enough, that I knew the rules of the game. I did know them," she said quietly. "But something had changed when the doctor confirmed the pregnancy. After the disbelief, the panic, even the anger, I felt good. I felt right. I wanted the baby, so I quit my job, moved away from New York and read everything I could get my hands on about parenting."

"Just like that?"

"Well, there were some scenes, some dire predictions, and a lot of anger, but that's how it worked. Roberto and I parted less than amicably, but with the agreement that he would stay out of my life and I would stay out of his."

"What have you told Keenan?"

"It's tough." And it never failed to make her feel guilty. "So far I've just told him his father had to go away, that he wasn't going to come back. He's happy, so he doesn't ask a lot of questions."

"Are you? Happy?"

"Yes." She smiled and touched his cheek. "I am. All my life I wanted a home, a family, something solid and settled. I didn't even know it until Keenan. He changed my life."

"No urge to go back and smile for the camera?"

"Oh, no. Not even a twinge."

He cupped a hand behind her neck, studying her. "It's such a face," he murmured. Right now he liked the idea of having it all to himself.

Chapter 8

The concept of car pools obviously had been devised by someone with a foul and vicious sense of humor. Having lived most of his life in cities where public transportation or a quick jog would get a man from his home to his office, Coop had never experienced the adult version.

But he'd heard rumors.

Arguments, petty feuds, crowded conditions, spilled coffee.

After a week as designated driver, Coop had no doubt the kiddie version was worse. Infinitely worse.

"He's pinching me again, Mr. McKinnon. Brad's pinching me."

"Cut it out, Brad."

"Carly's looking at me. I told her to stop looking at me."

"Carly, don't look at Brad."

"I'm going to be sick. Mr. McKinnon, I'm going to be sick right now."

"No, you're not."

Though Matthew Finney made gagging noises that had the other kids screeching, Coop gritted his teeth and kept driving. Matt threatened to be sick twice a day unless he rode in the front seat. After five miserable days Coop had his number. But that did very little to soothe his nerves.

Keenan, who had waited all week for his turn in the front, swiveled in his seat to make monster faces at Matt. This incited a small riot of elbow jabs, howls, screaming giggles and shoves.

"Keenan, turn around!" Coop snapped. "You guys straighten up back there. Cut it out! If I have to stop this car..." He trailed off, shuddered. He'd sounded like his own mother. Now Coop was afraid *he* would be sick. "Okay, first stop. Matt, scram."

Fifteen minutes later, his back seat thankfully empty, Coop pulled into the drive and rested his throbbing head on the steering wheel. "I need a drink."

"We got lemonade," Keenan told him.

"Great." He reached over to unbuckle Keenan's seat belt. All he needed was a pint of vodka to go with it.

"Can we go swimming again soon?"

The idea of taking a herd of screaming kids back to the community pool anytime within the next century had a stone lodging in Coop's heart. "Ask your mother."

Coop started to look in the back seat and realized he couldn't face it. Earlier in the week he'd made that mistake, and discovered wads of chewing gum on the rug, cookie crumbs everywhere, and a mysterious green substance smeared on the seat.

In his weakened state, even a candy wrapper was likely to tip the balance.

"Yoo-hoo!" Mrs. Finkleman stripped off her flowered garden gloves and headed across the lawn in a flowing tent dress and electric-blue sandals. "How was your swim, little man?"

"We had races, and Brad dunked Carly and made her cry even though Coop told him not to, and I can hold my breath underwater for twelve seconds."

"My goodness." She laughed and ruffled Keenan's hair. "You'll be in the Olympics next." Her shrewd eyes took in Coop's haggard face. "You look a little frazzled, Coop. Keenan, why don't you run in and tell Mr. Finkleman you want a piece of that cherry cobbler he baked today?"

"Okay!" He tugged on Coop's hand. "Do you want some? Do you wanna come?"

"I'll pass. You go ahead."

Mrs. Finkleman chuckled as Keenan darted away and scrambled up the steps. "Little angel. We'll keep him entertained for a couple of hours—or he'll keep us entertained. You look like you could use a few minutes in a quiet room."

"Padded room," Coop muttered. "How does anyone survive kids?"

"It's easier if you go through the stages with them. Once you've walked the floor all night with a colicky baby, nothing much fazes you." She sighed. "Except science projects. Science projects always took me to the edge. And that first driving lesson." She shook her head at the memory. "That can bring you to your knees." She beamed and patted his arm. "But there's years yet to worry about that. And you've been doing a fine job. Why, Harry and I were just saying how nice it is that Zoe and Keenan have a man in their lives. Not that Zoe hasn't been handling everything. Raising that sweet-natured boy all alone, and working two jobs and tending the house. But it does my heart good to see you and that little angel playing ball in the yard, or the way Zoe lights up when you're around. You make a lovely little family. Now, you go and take a nice nap. We'll keep an eye on your boy."

"I'm not— He's not—" But even as Coop stammered, she was drifting away.

Family? he thought as a ball of ice formed in his stomach. They weren't a family. Oh, no, he promised himself as he walked around the house to his steps. He hadn't taken that on.

He liked the kid, sure. What wasn't to like? And he was damn near nuts about the mother. But that didn't make them a family. That didn't make things permanent. Maybe he'd volunteered to spend time with the kid, taught him a few things about ball, pitched him a few, but that didn't make him Daddy.

He headed straight for the refrigerator, popped the top off a beer and took a long pull.

Sure, maybe he enjoyed having the kid around, and Lord knows he enjoyed being with Zoe. He'd even been sort of pleased when a woman at the pool mistook Keenan for his and commented on what a handsome son he had. But that didn't mean he was going to start thinking about family health insurance or college funds.

He was single. He liked being single. It meant coming and going as he pleased, planning all-night poker games, spending all day with the sports channel blaring.

He liked working in his own space—that was why he did the bulk of his writing at home, rather than at the paper. He didn't like people messing with his things or structuring his time or planning outings.

Family life—as he remembered from his childhood—was lousy with outings.

No way was he changing his nice comfortable existence to accommodate a family.

So he'd made a mistake, Coop decided, and stretched out on the couch with his beer. He'd given Zoe and the kid a little too much of his time, a little too much of his attention. It hadn't been anything he didn't want to give, but he could see now that the gesture could be misconstrued. Particularly since Zoe had once brought up the *L* word. Only once, he reminded himself, and he'd like to think that had just been a woman thing.

Still, if he didn't back off, they might start to depend on him. He shifted uncomfortably as the idea flitted through his mind that he might also come to depend on them.

It was time to reestablish himself as the tenant upstairs.

Keenan raced out of the house next door the minute his mother pulled her car in the drive.

"Hi, Mama, hi! I held my breath for twelve seconds underwater!"

Zoe caught him on the fly and swung him twice. "You must be hiding gills in there," she said, tickling his ribs. "Hi, Mrs. Finkleman."

"Hi yourself. We've had ourselves a fine hour. I sent Coop up for a nap when they got home. He looked like he'd had a rough day."

"Thanks." She kissed Keenan's waiting lips, then smacked her own. "Mmm… Cherries."

"Mr. Finkleman baked them, and they were good."

"I bet. Did you say thank you?"

"Uh-huh. Matt almost threw up in Coop's car."

"Threw up," Zoe said as she carried Keenan inside.

"Uh-huh. 'Cause it was my turn to ride in the front. I had the best time, and Coop helped me to swim without my bubbles. He said I was a champ."

"That's just what you are." She collapsed with him on a

chair. The idea of fixing dinner, changing into her uniform and serving drinks for six hours loomed heavily. "Give me a hug," she demanded, then soothed herself with some nuzzling. "Definitely a champion hugger. Why don't you come in the kitchen and tell me what else you did today while I fix dinner?"

A half hour later, as Zoe was draining pasta and Keenan was entertaining himself with crayons and paper on the kitchen floor, she heard the sound of Coop's feet on the stairs. Her heart sped up. The normal, healthy reaction made her smile. Imagine, she thought, believing herself immune to men.

She left the pasta draining in the sink and went to the back door just as he came to the foot of the steps.

"Hi."

"How's it going?" Coop jingled the keys in his pocket. Did she look all lit up? he wondered. She was smiling, and despite the shadows of fatigue under them, her eyes did have the prettiest lights in them.

"I was just going to call upstairs. I thought you'd like some dinner after a hard day at the pool." She opened the screen door and leaned out to kiss him. The smile dimmed a bit when he eased back. "It's just chicken and pasta."

It smelled nearly as good as she did. He glanced inside— the homey scene, cluttered counters, fresh flowers, steam rising from a pan on the stove, the child sprawled on the floor, the pretty woman offering him food and kisses.

A definite trap.

"Thanks, but I'm on my way out."

"Oh. I thought you had a couple hours before game time." She laughed at his arched brow. "I guess I've been paying more attention to the sports scene. Baltimore versus Toronto, game one of three."

"Yeah." When she starts to take an interest in *your* interests, she's really shutting the cage door. "I've got some stuff to do."

"Can I go with you?" Keenan dashed to the door to tug on Coop's slacks. "Can I go to the game? I like watching them with you best."

Coop could almost hear the locks clicking into place. "I've got too much to do," he said, with an edge to his voice that had Keenan's lips quivering. "Look, it's not just a game, it's my job."

"You said I was good luck."

"Keenan." Zoe put her hand on her son's shoulder to draw him back, but her eyes stayed on Coop's. "Did you forget Beth was coming over to stay with you tonight? She'll be here soon, and you're going to watch a tape of your favorite movie."

"But I wanna—"

"Now go wash your hands for dinner."

"But—"

"Go on now."

The way Keenan's face crumpled would have softened an ogre's heart. Dragging his feet, he headed out of the kitchen.

"I can't take him with me everywhere…." Coop began defensively.

"Of course not. He's just overtired. I couldn't have let him go, in any case." She hesitated, wishing she could ignore her instincts. "Is everything all right?"

"Everything's fine." He didn't know why he shouted it. He didn't know why he felt like something slimy stuck to the bottom of a shoe. "I have a life, you know. I don't need kids climbing up my back or you fixing me dinner. And I don't have to explain myself."

Her eyes turned very cool, her face very composed. "You

certainly don't. I appreciate you helping me out the past couple of weeks. Let me know if I can return the favor."

"Look, Zoe—"

"I've got to get dinner on the table, or I'll be late for work." She let the screen door slam between them. "Enjoy the game."

She knew exactly how long he continued to stand there while she worked at the stove. Knew exactly when he turned and walked away.

It wasn't unexpected, she reminded herself. This backing away was typical, even understandable. Perhaps it had taken Coop a few weeks to completely comprehend that she didn't come as a single. She was part of a pair, a ready-made family, with its share of responsibilities and problems and routines.

And he was opting out.

He might not even know it yet, she thought, but he was in the first stages of a full retreat.

Her eyes blurred, her chest heaved. Resolutely she choked the tears back. She would indulge herself with a nice long cry later, she promised. But for now she had a little boy to soothe.

When he came back in, she crouched down until they were eye-to-eye.

"You had a good time with Coop today, didn't you?"

Keenan sniffled, nodded.

"And he's taken you a lot of places. You've had fun, and done a lot of new things."

"I know."

"You should be grateful for that, baby, instead of pouting because you can't have more."

She straightened again and hoped she could take her own advice.

Chapter 9

"You're spending a lot of time around here." Ben edged a hip onto the corner of Coop's desk. All around Coop's cubicle phones rang, keyboards clattered.

"So?" Without taking his eyes from the computer screen, Coop hammered out the draft of his weekly column.

"I just figured you had it made in that apartment of yours. I mean, great location." He thought of Zoe. "Great view. You didn't spend as much time in here when you lived downtown."

"I needed a change of scene."

"Yeah." Ben snorted and picked up a baseball from Coop's desk. "Trouble in paradise?"

"I don't know what you're talking about. And I've got a column to write."

"Pretty obvious the last few weeks that you've been stuck on the landlady." He tossed the ball from one hand to the other.

"I mean, when a man hauls a kid around, buys little baseball jerseys, it follows that he's hooking a line into Mom."

Coop's eyes flashed up. "I like the kid, okay? I don't have to use a four-year-old to get a woman. The kid's cool."

"Hey, I got nothing against rug rats. Might even have a few of my own one day. The thing is, when a woman's got one, a man has to play Daddy if he wants the inside track."

"Who says I have to play at anything to get a woman?"

"Not me. But it was you who couldn't shoot hoop last week because you were taking the family to the aquarium." Ben winked, set the ball down. "Still, I bet you scored better than I did." Ben jerked back as Coop lunged for his throat.

"It's not like that," Coop said between his teeth.

"Hey, hey. Just yanking your chain. I wouldn't have made any cracks if I'd known you were serious about her."

Coop's grip loosened. "I didn't say I was serious. I said it wasn't like that."

"Whatever you say."

Disgusted with himself, Coop dropped back in his chair. He and Ben had been riding each other about women for better than five years. No reason to overreact, he thought. Or to make a fool of himself. "Sorry. I've got a lot on my mind."

"Forget it. What you need's a distraction. You coming to the poker game tonight?"

"Yeah."

"Good. Losing money should put you back on track."

Something had to, Coop thought as he sat back alone in his cubicle to stare at his screen. For the past three days he'd slept little, eaten less, and gone around in a constant state of flux.

Because he was avoiding the issue, he decided. Opting to

bunt, when he should be swinging away. The only solution to getting his life back in order was to face the problem head-on.

He flicked off his terminal.

The beautiful thing about an afternoon off, Zoe thought, was the solitude. No customers to talk to, no orders to fill. It meant she didn't have to be salesclerk, or waitress, or Mom, or anything but Zoe.

Sitting on the back stoop, she struggled to understand the assembly instructions for the new barbecue grill she'd bought. She was going to surprise Keenan with hamburgers.

She liked the quiet—her kind of quiet, which meant there was music throbbing from the kitchen radio. She liked the loneliness—her kind of loneliness, which meant Keenan would dash toward her shortly with open arms and chattering voice.

She knew the upstairs apartment was empty, and she tried not to think about that. Tried not to think about the fact that Coop had been away more than he'd been home in the last few days.

Foolish of her to have thought he was different. He'd wanted her, he'd had her, and now he'd lost interest. Well, she had wanted him, so they were even there. If her heart was suffering it would pass. It had passed before. She and Keenan could get along fine on their own. Just like always.

Her screwdriver slipped, scraped her knuckles, had her swearing.

"What the hell are you doing?"

Eyes hot, she looked up at Coop. "Baking a cake. What does it look like I'm doing?"

"You can't put something together if you're going to spread parts all over the damn place." Automatically he bent down to organize. She rapped his hand away with the rubber grip of the screwdriver.

"I don't need you to put things together for me. I'm not some poor helpless female who needs a man to pick up the slack. I managed just fine before you came along."

Stung, he rammed his hands in his pockets. "Fine. Do it yourself."

"I am doing it myself. I like doing it myself."

"Terrific. And when the thing topples over, you won't have anyone else to blame."

"That's right." She blew her hair out of her eyes. "I accept when something's my fault." She picked up a wrench and locked a bolt in place. "Do you plan to hover over me all afternoon?"

"I want to talk to you."

"So talk."

He had it well planned. He was a writer, after all. "I realize the way I've been hanging around with you and the kid—"

"His name is Keenan," Zoe said between her teeth.

"I know what his name is. The way I've been hanging around the last few weeks might give the wrong impression."

"Oh, really?" She looked up again, tapping the wrench against her palm.

"He's a great kid, he kind of grows on you. I've gotten a kick out of spending time with him."

Though she hated herself for it, Zoe softened. She understood that he was genuinely fond of Keenan. That only made it all the more difficult. "He likes spending time with you. It's been good for him."

"Well, yeah, on the one hand. On the other, I started thinking that he—that you—that both of you might get the wrong idea. I mean, tossing a ball around or taking him to a game, that's cool. I just don't want him thinking it's like—permanent."

"I see." She was calm now, frigidly so. It would help keep the hurt in check. "You're afraid he might begin to see you as a father figure."

"Well, yeah. Kind of."

"That's natural enough. But then, he spends a lot of time with Mr. Finkleman, too, and with Billy Bowers down the street."

"Finkleman's old enough to be his grandfather, and the Bowers kid is eighteen." Coop backed off, realizing there was a touch of jealousy in the defense. "And they don't have the same sort of thing going with you."

She arched both brows. "Thing?"

"Relationship," he said tightly. "Whatever the hell you want to call it. Damn it, we only slept together once."

"I'm aware of that." Carefully she set the wrench aside. It would give her only momentary pleasure to heave it at his head.

"That came out wrong," he said, furious with himself. "It sounded like it didn't mean anything. It did, Zoe." A great deal, he was afraid. A very great deal. "It's just that…"

"Now you're terrified that Keenan and I will trap you into a family. That you'll wake up one morning and be Daddy, with a wife and a mortgage and a small boy who needs attention."

"Yes. No. Something like that." He was burying himself, he realized, and he suddenly didn't know why. "I just want to make myself clear."

"Oh, I think you have. Perfectly." She rubbed her hands on her knees as she studied him. "You needn't worry, Coop. I advertised for a tenant, not a father for my child, or a husband for myself. I slept with you because I wanted to, not because I thought I could lure you to the altar."

"I didn't mean it like that." Frustrated, he dragged a hand through his hair. However well he'd planned this little scene, it was going all wrong. "I wanted you. I still do. But I know how badly you were let down before. I don't want to hurt you, Zoe. Or the kid. I just don't want you thinking I'd slide into the gap."

The anger came back, one swift wave of it that reddened her vision. She was on her feet before either of them realized she'd moved. "Keenan and I don't have a gap. We're a family, as real and as complete and as full a family as any could be." She jabbed the wrench at his chest. "Just because Daddy doesn't make three doesn't mean we're less of a unit."

"I didn't mean—"

"I'll tell you what you mean. You see a woman and a small boy and you think they're just pining away for some big strong man to come along and fulfill them. Well, that's bull. If I needed a man, I'd have one. And if I thought Keenan needed a father to make him happy, I'd find him one. And," she continued, advancing and giving him another jab, "if you think you're at the head of some fictional list, you're wrong. Maybe I'm in love with you, but that's not enough. It's not just me, and it's not just you. Keenan comes first. When and if I want a father for Keenan, he'll be someone with compassion and patience, someone willing to adjust his life to make room for my son. So relax, Cooper. You're in the clear."

"I didn't come here to fight with you."

"Good, because I'm finished."

He grabbed her arm before she could turn away. "I haven't. I'm trying to be straight with you, Zoe. I care about you, okay? About both of you. I just don't want it to get out of hand."

"Out of whose hands?" she retorted. "Yours? Then that's no problem, is it? Because you know how to hold on to everything inside, really tight. Just keep holding on to it, Coop.

Don't worry about me or about Keenan. We'll be fine." She jerked her arm free and sat again. Picking up the instruction sheet, she gave it her full attention.

Now why, he wondered, did he feel as though he'd just been rejected? Shaking his head, Coop took a step in retreat. "As long as we're clear."

"We are."

"I've, ah, got a little time, if you want me to help you put that grill together."

"No thanks. I can do it." She slanted him a look. "I'm going to grill burgers later. You're welcome to join us. Unless you're afraid it will lead to a commitment."

She shoots, he thought wryly, she scores. "Thanks anyway. I've got plans. Maybe I could take a rain check."

"Fine. You know where to find us."

He got drunk. Not sloppily, but thoroughly. When Coop poured himself out of the cab and staggered toward the house, he already knew he'd hate himself in the morning. But it was tonight he had to deal with.

He leaned heavily against Zoe's front door and waited for the porch to settle down under his feet. She might think they'd finished, he told himself blearily, but she was wrong. Dead wrong.

He'd thought of a dozen things he had to say to her.

There was no time like the present.

Lifting a fist, he pounded on the door. "Come on, Zoe." He pounded again. "I know you're in there." He saw a light flick on inside and kept on pounding. "Come on, come on. Open up."

"Coop?" From the other side of the door, Zoe belted her hastily donned robe. She'd been home from the lounge for barely twenty minutes, and in bed for less than five. "It's after two o'clock in the morning. What do you want?"

"I want to talk to you. Let me in."

"We'll talk in the morning."

"You just said it was morning."

When he pounded again, she flicked off the locks. "Stop that—you'll wake Keenan." Furious, she yanked open the door and had the surprise of a hundred-and-seventy-pound male tumbling against her. "Are you hurt? What happened?" The alarm signals that had screamed on shifted when she caught the scent of beer. "You're drunk."

"Mostly." He started to straighten, then lost himself in the smell of her. "God, you feel good. What d'you wash this in?" He nuzzled her hair. "Smells like moonbeams."

"Really drunk," she said with a sigh. "Sit down. I'll get you some coffee."

"Don't want coffee. Doesn't sober you up, only wakes you up. And I'm awake, and I have something to say to you." He drew away then, and discovered he wasn't as steady as he'd hoped. "But I'll sit down." He did, heavily. "Hate getting drunk. Haven't done it like this since I played minor league. Did I tell you I played minor league ball? Triple A."

"No." Baffled, she stood her ground and watched him.

"Right out of high school. Two years. Thought I'd make it to the show. The majors. But I didn't, so I went to college, and now I write about people who did."

"I'm sorry."

"No." He waved that away. "I like writing. Always did. Like watching the games and seeing all the little dramas. If I'd've played, I'd be nearly washed up now. I'm almost thirty-three. Old man for the game." He focused on her, smiled. "You're the most beautiful woman I've ever seen in my life. You know, the kid looks just like you. Look at him, see you. It's spooky. I see you all the time. Minding my own business, and pop! There's your face in my head. What d'ya make of that?"

"I don't know." She wanted to be angry with him, really she did. But he was so foolishly drunk. "Why don't I take you upstairs, Coop? Put you to bed."

"I want you in my bed, Zoe. I want to make love with you. I want to touch you again."

She wanted that, too. Very much. But new lines had been drawn. "You said you wanted to talk to me."

"Do you know what your skin feels like? I can't describe it, it's all soft and smooth and warm. I started thinking about your skin when I was playing poker and getting drunk tonight. I won, too. Took a big pot with a pair of sixes. Pulled in over two hundred and fifty dollars."

"Congratulations."

"But I kept thinking about you. You have this little dimple right here." He nearly poked himself in the eye, then dragged a finger down his cheek to the corner of his mouth. "I kept thinking about that little dimple, and your skin, and those big eyes and killer legs. And I kept thinking how I like to watch you with the kid, like I do sometimes from upstairs, when you don't know. Didn't know that, did you?"

"No," she said quietly. "I didn't."

"Well, see…" He gestured wildly. "You've got this way of running your hand over his hair. It gets to me." He shook his head. "It really gets to me. Keenan loves me, you know. He told me he did. So did you."

"I know."

"And I meant everything I said this afternoon."

"I know." Sighing, she walked over to undo his shoelaces.

"Every word, Zoe. I've got my life set, just like I want it."

"Okay." She pried off his shoes, hefted his legs onto the couch.

"So you can stop popping into my head, 'cause it's not changing anything."

"I'll keep that in mind."

He was asleep before she bent over and kissed his cheek.

Chapter 10

As hangovers went, Coop knew, this would be a champ. He didn't have to open his eyes, he didn't have to move, not when his head was already beating like the army drum corps.

He wasn't sure how he'd managed to get home and into bed, but the blur of the evening wasn't comforting. Still, he thought it best to wait to tax his brain.

Cautious, close to fearful, he opened his eyes. The little face directly above him had him jerking back, then moaning at the pain.

"Good morning," Keenan said cheerfully. "Did you sleep over?"

"I don't know." Coop lifted a hand to his head. "Where's your mother?"

"She's making my lunch. She said I could come in and look at you if I didn't wake you up. I didn't wake you up, did I? I was really quiet."

"No." Coop closed his eyes again and prayed for oblivion.

"Are you sick? Do you have a tempature?" Keenan laid a small, light hand on Coop's aching forehead. "Mama can make it better. She always makes it better." Very gently, Keenan replaced his hand with a kiss. "Does that help?"

Oh, hell, Coop thought. Even a hangover didn't have a chance against this kid. "Yeah, thanks. What time is it?"

"The big hand's on the ten and the little hand's on the eight. You can sleep in my bed until you're better, and play with my toys."

"Thanks." Coop made the supreme effort and sat up. When his head rolled, he did his best to catch it in his hands. "Keenan, be a pal and ask your mom for some aspirin."

"Okay." He raced off, and the sound of his sneakers pounding the floor had Coop shuddering.

"Headache?" Zoe asked a moment later.

Coop lifted his head. She was still in her robe. The robe he remembered from the night before. He was beginning to remember quite a bit from the night before. "If you're going to yell at me, could you do it later?"

In answer, she held out aspirin and a glass filled with reddish liquid.

"What is it?"

"A remedy from Joe the bartender. He guarantees it'll take the edge off."

"Thanks."

There was a blast of a horn from outside that cut through Coop's skull like a dulled knife. While he was dealing with the shock of that, Keenan came racing back.

"Bye, Mama, bye!" He gave her a smacking kiss, then turned to hug Coop. "Bye."

As the door slammed behind him, Coop gulped down Joe's remedy.

"Do you want coffee?" Zoe ran her tongue around her teeth and tried not to smile. "Some breakfast?"

"You're not going to yell at me?"

"For barging in here, drunk, in the middle of the night? And for passing out on my sofa?" She paused just long enough to make her point. "No, I'm not going to yell at you. I figure you're suffering enough."

"I am, I promise you." He got up to follow her into the kitchen. "Not just physically. I feel like a total jerk."

"You *were* a total jerk." She poured a mug of coffee, set it on the table for him. "My mother's third husband had a fondness for bourbon. He swore eggs the morning after were the cure. How do you want them?"

"Scrambled would be good." He sat gingerly at the table. "I'm sorry, Zoe."

She kept her back to him. "For?"

"For being a jackass yesterday afternoon, and a bigger jackass last night."

"Oh, that." With the bacon frying, she chose a small bowl to scramble eggs in. "I don't imagine it's the first or the last time you'll be one."

"You didn't…" He shifted miserably. "Ah, you didn't tell Keenan I was…"

"Drunk and disorderly?" A half smile on her face, she glanced over her shoulder. "I told him you weren't feeling well and went to sleep on the couch. Which was close enough."

"Thanks. I wouldn't want him to think…you know. I don't make a habit out of it."

"So you said last night." She turned the bacon, whipped the eggs.

He watched her, gradually getting past the astonishment that she wasn't going to rub his nose in the mess he'd made of things. Remembering the afternoon before, when she'd stood up to him with all that pride and fury shining in her eyes. And the other night, when he'd fallen asleep on her couch— the way she'd looked when she slipped the boy from his arms into hers and carried him into bed.

A dozen other pictures, captured in so short a time, flitted through his head, until they were whittled down to one. This one. Zoe standing at the stove, with the morning sun streaming over her tousled hair, her robe flowing down, breakfast smells warming the room.

How could he have thought he didn't want this? Just this. And what did he do now that he knew the truth?

"Food should help." She set the plate in front of him. "I've got to get ready for work."

"Can you— Have you got a minute?"

"I suppose." She poured herself another cup of coffee. "I don't have to be in until ten."

He began to eat while thoughts scrambled in his brain. "This is good. Thanks."

"You're welcome." She leaned back against the counter. "Did you want something else?"

"Yeah." He ate more, hoping eggs equaled courage. Then he put his fork down. It was the ninth inning, he thought, and there were already two outs. "You. I want you."

She smiled a little. "Coop, I doubt you're in any shape for that, and I really have to go to work, so—"

"No, I don't mean that. I mean I do, but not—" He broke off, took a long, deep breath. "I want you to marry me."

"I beg your pardon?"

"I think you should marry me. It's a good idea." Somewhere in the back of his mind, he realized, he'd been working on this all along. He had it figured. "You can quit your night job and go back to school if you want. Or open that flower shop. Whatever. I think that's what we should do."

"Really." Because her hand was unsteady, she set her coffee down. "Well that's very generous of you, Coop, but I don't have to get married to do any of those things. So thanks just the same."

He stared. "No? You're saying no? But you love me. You said it. Twice you said it."

"We can make it three," she said evenly. "Yes, I love you. No, I won't marry you. Now I really have to get ready for work."

"Just a damn minute." Hangover forgotten, he pushed back from the table and rose. "What kind of game is this? You love me, your kid's crazy about me, we're terrific in bed, I even know how to drive a damn car pool, but you won't marry me."

"You're such an idiot. You're such a fool. Do you think because I didn't put up a struggle before I fell into your bed that you can have everything your own way? When you want it, how you want it? Well, you're wrong. And you *are* a jackass."

He winced as she stormed from the room. Strike one, he thought. And he hadn't even seen the pitch.

But the game wasn't over, he thought grimly, until the fat lady sang.

Zoe was still steaming when she came home from work. Of all the arrogant, interfering, self-absorbed idiots she'd ever known, J. Cooper McKinnon took the gold medal. Imagine him telling her that marrying him was a good idea, then ticking off all the advantages she'd gain.

Oh, he thought he was a prize.

One day he's telling her to get any ideas of sneaking him into a relationship out of her head. As if she'd been baiting traps for him. The next he's taking pity on her and offering her a big male helping hand.

She should have bitten it off.

Not once, not once had he said what she would bring to him, what he felt for her, what he wanted. Not once had he brought up the fact that he could or would accept another man's child as his own.

She jerked open the front door, slammed it. He could take his half-baked proposal and sit on it.

"Mama! Hey, Mama!" Keenan zipped into the living room and grabbed her hand. "Come on, come on. We've got a surprise."

"What surprise? What are you doing home, Keenan? You're supposed to be at the Finklemans'."

"Coop's here." He tugged manfully on her hand. "We have a surprise. And we have a secret. And you have to come *now!*"

"All right, I'm coming." She braced herself and let Keenan drag her into the kitchen.

There were flowers, banks of them, vases and baskets overflowing on the counters, on the floor, on the windowsills. There was music, some soft, dreamy classical sonata, on the radio. The table was set, crystal she'd never seen before glinting in the sunlight, a bottle of champagne chilling in a silver bucket. And Coop was standing there, in a neatly pressed shirt and slacks.

"It's a surprise," Keenan announced gleefully. "We made everything look nice so you'd like it. And Mrs. Finkleman said we could use the glasses and the plates. And Mr. Finkleman made his special chicken 'cause it's resistible."

"Irresistible," Coop said, his eyes on Zoe. "You, ah, said

you didn't need flowers and candlelight, but I've never taken you out on a date. I thought this was the next-best thing."

"Do you like it, Mama? Do you?"

"Yes, it's very nice." She bent down to kiss Keenan. "Thank you."

"I get to go to the Finklemans' so you can have romance."

"Ah, come on, kid." Coop scooped Keenan up. "Let's get you started. You were supposed to keep quiet about it," he muttered when he carried the boy outside.

"What's romance?"

"I'll tell you later."

Satisfied with that, Keenan draped his arm around Coop's neck. "Are you gonna tell Mama the secret about us all getting married?"

"That's the plan."

"And you'll live with us and you can be my Daddy and that'll be okay?"

"That'll be great. It'll be perfect." He stopped by the fence to press a kiss to Keenan's mouth. "I love you, Keenan."

"Okay." He squeezed his arms hard around Coop's neck. "Bye."

"Bye."

"Yoo-hoo!" Mrs. Finkleman stood at the back door. She sent Coop a wink and an exaggerated thumbs-up sign before whisking Keenan inside.

She was standing pretty much where Coop had left her when he came back. He wasn't sure whether or not that was a good sign.

"So, ready for some champagne?"

"Coop, this is very nice of you, but—"

"Like the flowers?" Nervous as a cat, he popped the cork.

"Yes, they're wonderful, but—"

"I couldn't get them where you work, or I'd have spoiled the surprise. Keenan really gave me a hand setting things up." He handed her the glass, and when she was distracted, he leaned in for a slow, warm kiss. "Hi."

"Coop." She had to wait for her heart to finish its lazy somersault. "I know you must have gone to a lot of trouble—"

"I should have gone to it before. I didn't know I wanted to."

"Oh, Lord." She turned away and struggled to get her emotions under control. "I've given you the wrong impression this time. I don't need the trappings. I don't have to have romantic evenings and—" she waved toward the tapers on the table, waiting to be lit "—candlelight."

"Sure you do. So do I, when they're with you."

"You're trying to charm me," she said unsteadily. "That's new."

"You know what I am. The way this house is set up, we've practically been living together for the past month or so. People get to know each other quicker that way than just by socializing. So you know what I am, and you fell for me anyway."

She took a drink. "You're awfully smug about it. I told you my feelings are my responsibility, and that holds true. A romantic dinner doesn't change it."

It looked like strike two, but Coop knew that if he was going to go down, he'd go down swinging. "So I want to give you a nice evening. Is something wrong with that? I want to do better than propose over scrambled eggs when I've got a hangover." His voice had risen, and he bit down on it. "Damn it, this is my first time, have a little tolerance. No, don't say anything, let me finish this. You don't need me." He took another long breath. "Not for taking care of things, for you or the kid, I mean, for mowing the grass or putting stupid barbecue grills together. What about what I need, Zoe?"

She blinked at him. "Well, that's just it. Don't you see? You made it clear that you don't need or want ties. I come with ties, Coop."

"I made it clear," he muttered. "I didn't make anything clear, because I didn't know. Didn't want to know. I was scared. There. You feel better knowing that?" He glared at her. "I was scared, because I need you. Because I need to see your face and hear your voice and smell your hair. I just need you to be there. And I need to help you mow the grass and put the grill together. I need you to need me back."

"Oh." She shut her eyes. "I like hearing that."

"Then tell me you will." He took her arms until she opened her eyes again. "It's my last swing, Zoe. Marry me."

"I—" Yes. She wanted to say yes. "It's not just me, Coop."

"You think I don't want the kid? God, open your eyes. I'm crazy about him. I fell for him before I fell for you. I want to marry both of you, then maybe have another kid or two so can start out on the ground floor. We already worked that out."

"You— Who did what?"

He swore, stepped back, shrugged. "I kind of ran it by the kid. I figured I should smooth the way a little, and find out where he stood." When she just stared, he jammed his hands in his pockets. "It didn't seem fair not to bring him into it since he'd be mine."

"Yours," she murmured, staring blindly into her wine.

"Since you two are a team, it would be sort of like an expansion. Anyway, he's for it. So it's two against one."

"I see."

"Maybe I don't know a lot about the daddy stuff, but I love him. That's a good start."

She looked at him again, looked into his eyes. Her heart opened, flooded. "It's a good one, all right."

"I love you." His hands relaxed in his pockets. "That's the first time I've said that to a woman—except my mother. I love you, Zoe. So why don't you marry me and give me and the kid a break?"

"It looks like I'm outvoted." She lifted a hand to his cheek.

"Is that a yes?"

"That's definitely a yes." She laughed as he swung her into his arms. "Daddy."

"I like the sound of that." He crushed his lips down on hers. "I like it a lot."

* * * * *

Temptation

NORA ROBERTS

This book is dedicated with
gratitude and affection
to Nancy Jackson

Chapter 1

"If there's one thing I hate," Eden mumbled, "it's six o'clock in the morning."

Sunlight poured through the thinly screened windows of the cabin and fell on the wooden floor, the metal bars of her bunk, and her face. The sound of the morning bell echoed dully in her head. Though she'd known that long, clanging ring for only three days, Eden already hated it.

For one fanciful moment, she buried her face under the pillow, imagining herself cuddled in her big four-poster. The Irish-linen sheets would smell ever-so-slightly of lemon. In her airy pastel bedroom, the curtains would be drawn against the morning, the scent of fresh flowers sweetening the air.

The pillowcase smelled of feathers and detergent.

With a grunt, Eden tossed the pillow to the floor, then struggled to sit up. Now that the morning bell had stopped, she could hear the cries of a couple of excited crows. From the cabin directly across the compound came a happy blast of rock music. With glazed eyes, she watched Candice Bartholomew bound out of the adjoining bunk. Her sharp-featured pixie's face was split by a grin.

"Morning." Candy's long, clever fingers ran through her thatch of red hair like scoops, causing it to bounce into further disarray. Candy was, Eden had always thought, all bounce. "It's a beautiful day," she announced, in a voice as cheerful as the rest of her. Watching her friend stretch in frilly baby-doll pajamas, Eden gave another noncommittal grunt. She swung her bare legs off the mattress and contemplated the accomplishment of putting her feet on the floor.

"I could grow to hate you." Eden's voice, still husky with sleep, carried the rounded tones of her finishing-school education. Eyes shut, she pushed her own tousled blond hair away from her face.

Grinning, Candy tossed open the cabin door so that she could breathe in the fresh morning air while she studied her friend. The strong summer sunlight shot through Eden's pale hair, making it look fragile where it lay against her forehead and cheeks. Her eyes remained shut. Her slender shoulders slumped, she let out an enormous yawn. Candy wisely said nothing, knowing Eden didn't share her enthusiasm for sunrise.

"It can't be morning," Eden grumbled. "I swear I only lay down five minutes ago." Resting her elbows on her knees, she dropped her face into her hands. Her complexion was creamy, with just a suggestion of rose on the crest of her cheekbones. Her nose was small, with a hint of an upward tilt at the tip. What might have been a coolly aristocratic face was gentled by a full, generous mouth.

Candy took in one last breath of air, then shut the door. "All you need is a shower and some coffee. The first week of camp's the toughest, remember?"

Eden opened wide, lake-blue eyes. "Easy for you to say. You're not the one who fell in the poison ivy."

"Still itching?"

"A little." Because her own foul mood was making her feel guilty, Eden managed a smile. Everything softened, eyes, mouth, voice. "In any case, this is the first time we're the campees instead of the campers." Letting out another fierce yawn, she rose and tugged on a robe. The air coming through the screens was fresh as a daisy, and chilly enough to make Eden's toes curl. She wished she could remember what she'd done with her slippers.

"Try under the bunk," Candy suggested.

Eden bent down and found them. They were embroidered pink silk, hardly practical, but it hadn't seemed worthwhile to invest in another pair. Putting them on gave her an excuse to sit down again. "Do you really think five consecutive summers at Camp Forden for Girls prepared us for this?"

Haunted by her own doubts, Candy clasped her hands together. "Eden, are you having second thoughts?"

Because she recognized distress in the bubbly voice, Eden buried her own doubts. She had both a financial and emotional interest in the newly formed Camp Liberty. Complaining wasn't going to put her on the road to success. With a shake of her head, she walked over to squeeze Candy's shoulder. "What I have is a terminal case of morning crankiness. Let me get that shower, then I'll be ready to face our twenty-seven tenants."

"Eden." Candy stopped her before she closed the bathroom door. "It's going to work, for both of us. I know it."

"I know it, too." Eden closed the bathroom door and leaned

against it. She could admit it now, while she was alone. She was scared to death. Her last dime, and her last ray of hope, were tied up in the six cabins, the stables and the cafeteria that were Camp Liberty. What did Eden Carlbough, former Philadelphia socialite, know about managing a girls' summer camp? Just enough to terrify her.

If she failed now, with this, could she pick up the pieces and go on? Would there be any pieces left? Confidence was what was needed, she told herself as she turned the taps on. Once inside the narrow shower stall, she gave the tap optimistically marked HOT another twist. Water, lukewarm, dripped out halfheartedly. Confidence, Eden thought again as she shivered under the miserly spray. Plus some cold hard cash and a whole barrel of luck.

She found the soap and began to lather with the soft-scented French milled she still allowed herself to indulge in. A year ago she would never have considered something as lowly as soap an indulgence.

A year ago.

Eden turned so that the rapidly cooling water hit her back. A year ago she would have risen at eight, had a leisurely, steaming shower, then breakfasted on toast and coffee, perhaps some shirred eggs. Sometime before ten, she would have driven to the library for her volunteer morning. There would have been lunch with Eric, perhaps at the Deux Cheminées before she gave her afternoon to the museum or one of Aunt Dottie's charities.

The biggest decision she might have made was whether to wear her rose silk suit or her ivory linen. Her evening might have been spent quietly at home, or at one of Philadelphia's elegant dinner parties.

No pressure. No problems. But then, Papa had been alive.

Eden sighed as she rinsed away the last of the lather. The light French scent clung to her even as she dried her skin with the serviceable camp-issue towel. When her father had been alive, she had thought that money was simply something to spend and that time was forever. She had been raised to plan a menu, but not to cook; to run a home, but not to clean it.

Throughout her childhood, she had been carelessly happy with her widowed father in the ageless elegance of their Philadelphia home. There had always been party dresses and cotillions, afternoon teas and riding lessons. The Carlbough name was an old and respected one. The Carlbough money had been a simple fact of life.

How quickly and finally things could change.

Now she was giving riding instructions and juggling columns in a ledger with the vain hope that one and one didn't always make two.

Because the tiny mirror over the tiny sink was dripping with condensation, Eden rubbed it with the towel. She took a miserly dab of the half pot of imported face cream she had left. She was going to make it last through the summer. If *she* lasted through the summer herself, another pot would be her reward.

Eden found the cabin empty when she opened the bathroom door. If she knew Candy, and after twenty years she certainly did, the redhead would be down with the girls already. How easily she became acclimatized, Eden thought; then she reminded herself it was time she did the same. She took her jeans and her red T-shirt with CAMP LIBERTY emblazoned on the chest, and began to dress. Even as a teenager, Eden had rarely dressed so casually.

She had enjoyed her social life—the parties, the well-chaperoned ski trips to Vermont, the trips to New York for shopping or the theater, the vacations in Europe. The prospect of earning a living had never been considered, by her, or her father. Carlbough women didn't work, they chaired committees.

College years had been spent with the idea of rounding out her education rather than focusing on a career. At twenty-three, Eden was forced to admit she was qualified to do absolutely nothing.

She could have blamed her father. But how could she blame a man who had been so indulgent and loving? She had adored him. She could blame herself for being naive and shortsighted, but she could never blame her father. Even now, a year after his sudden death, she still felt pangs of grief.

She could deal with that. The one thing she had been taught to do, the one thing she felt herself fully qualified to accomplish, was to cover emotion with poise, with control, or with disdain. She could go day after day, week after week through the summer, surrounded by the girls at camp and the counselors Candy had hired, and none of them would know she still mourned her father. Or that her pride had been shattered by Eric Keeton.

Eric, the promising young banker with her father's firm. Eric, always so charming, so attentive, so suitable. It had been during her last year of college that she had accepted his ring and made her promises to him. And he had made promises to her.

When she discovered the hurt was still there, Eden coated it, layer by layer, with anger. Facing the mirror, she tugged her hair back in a short ponytail, a style her hairdresser would have shuddered at.

It was more practical, Eden told her reflection. She was a practical woman now, and hair waving softly to the shoulders would just have got in the way during the riding lessons she was to give that morning.

For a moment, she pressed her fingers against her eyes. Why were the mornings always the worst? She would wake, expecting to come out of some bad dream and find herself at home again. But it wasn't her home any longer. There were strangers living in it now. Brian Carlbough's death had not been a bad dream, but a horrible, horrible reality.

A sudden heart attack had taken him overnight, leaving Eden stunned with shock and grief. Even before the grief could fade, Eden had been struck with another shock.

There had been lawyers, black-vested lawyers with long, technical monologues. They had had offices that had smelled of old leather and fresh polish. With solemn faces and politely folded hands, they had shattered her world.

Poor investments, she had been told, bad market trends, mortgages, second mortgages, short-term loans. The simple fact had been, once the details had been sifted through, there had been no money.

Brian Carlbough had been a gambler. At the time of his death, his luck had turned, and he hadn't had time to recoup his losses. His daughter had been forced to liquidate his assets in order to pay off the debts. The house she had grown up in and loved was gone. She had still been numbed by grief when she had found herself without a home or an income. Crashing down on top of that had been Eric's betrayal.

Eden yanked open the cabin door and was met by the balmy morning air of the mountains. The breathtaking view of greening hills and blue sky didn't affect her. She was back in Philadelphia, hearing Eric's calm, reasonable voice.

The scandal, she remembered and began marching toward the big cabin where mess would be served. *His* reputation. *His* career. Everything she had loved had been taken away, but he had only been concerned with how he might be affected.

He had never loved her. Eden jammed her hands into her pockets and kept walking. She'd been a fool not to see it from the beginning. But she'd learned, Eden reminded herself. How she'd learned. It had simply been a merger to Eric, the Carlbough name, the Carlbough money and reputation. When they had been destroyed, he had cut his losses.

Eden slowed her quick pace, realizing she was out of breath, not from exertion but from temper. It would never do to walk into breakfast with her face flushed and her eyes gleaming. Giving herself a moment, she took a few deep breaths and looked around her.

The air was still cool, but by midmorning the sun would be warm and strong. Summer had barely begun.

And it was beautiful. Lining the compound were a half-dozen small cabins with their window flaps open to the morning. The sound of girlish laughter floated through the windows. Along the pathway between cabins four and five was a scattering of anemones. A dogwood, with a few stubborn blooms clinging to it, stood nearby. Above cabin two, a mockingbird chattered.

Beyond the main camp to the west were rolling hills, deeply green. Grazing horses and trees dotted them. There was an openness here, a sense of space which Eden found incredible. Her life had always been focused on the city. Streets, buildings, traffic, people, those had been the familiar. There were times when she felt a quick pang of need for what had been. It was still possible for her to have all that. Aunt Dottie had offered her home and her love. No one would ever know how long and hard Eden had wrestled with the temptation to accept the invitation and let her life drift.

Perhaps gambling was in Eden's blood, too. Why else would she have sunk what ready cash she had had left into a fledgling camp for girls in the hills?

Because she had had to try, Eden reminded herself. She had had to take the risk on her own. She could never go back into the shell of the fragile porcelain doll she had been. Here, centered in such open space, she would take the time to learn about herself. What was inside Eden Carlbough? Maybe, just maybe, by expanding her horizons, she would find her place.

Candy was right. Eden took a long last breath. It was going to work. They were going to make it work.

"Hungry?" Her hair damp from whatever shower she'd popped into, Candy cut across Eden's path.

"Starved." Content, Eden swung a friendly arm around Candy's shoulder. "Where did you run off to?"

"You know me, I can't let any part of this place run by itself." Like Eden, Candy swept her gaze over the camp. Her expression reflected everything inside her—the love, the fear, the fierce pride. "I was worried about you."

"Candy, I told you, I was just cranky this morning." Eden watched a group of girls rush out of a cabin and head for breakfast.

"Eden, we've been friends since we were six months old. No one knows better than I what you're going through."

No, no one did, and since Candy was the person she loved best, Eden determined to do a better job of concealing the wounds that were still open. "I've put it behind me, Candy."

"Maybe. But I know that the camp was initially my venture, and that I roped you in."

"You didn't rope me in. I wanted to invest. We both know it was a pitifully small amount."

"Not to me. The extra money made it possible for me to include the equestrian program. Then, when you agreed to come in and give riding lessons…"

"Just keeping a close eye on my investment," Eden said

lightly. "Next year I won't be a part-time riding instructor and bookkeeper. I'll be a full-fledged counselor. No regrets, Candy." This time she meant it. "It's ours."

"And the bank's."

Eden shrugged that away. "We need this place. You, because it's what you've always wanted to do, always worked and studied toward. Me…" She hesitated, then sighed. "Let's face it, I haven't got anything else. The camp's putting a roof over my head, giving me three meals a day and a goal. I need to prove I can make it."

"People think we're crazy."

The pride came back, with a feeling of recklessness Eden was just learning to savor. "Let them."

With a laugh, Candy tugged at Eden's hair. "Let's eat."

Two hours later, Eden was winding up the day's first riding lesson. This was her specialty, her contribution to the partnership she and Candy had made. It had also been decided to trust Eden with the books, mainly because no one could have been more inept with figures than Candice Bartholomew.

Candy had interviewed and hired a staff of counselors, a nutritionist and a nurse. They hoped to have a pool and a swimming instructor one day, but for now there was supervised swimming and rowing on the lake, arts and crafts, hiking and archery. Candy had spent months refining a program for the summer, while Eden had juggled the profit-and-loss statements. She prayed the money would hold out while Candy ordered supplies.

Unlike Candy, Eden wasn't certain the first week of camp would be the toughest. Her partner had all the training, all the qualifications for running the camp, but Candy also had an optimist's flair for overlooking details like red ink on the books.

Pushing those thoughts aside, Eden signaled from the center

of the corral. "That's all for today." She scanned the six young faces under their black riding hats. "You're doing very well."

"When can we gallop, Miss Carlbough?"

"After you learn to trot." She patted one of the horses' flanks. Wouldn't it be lovely, she thought, to gallop off into the hills, riding so fast even memories couldn't follow? Foolish, Eden told herself; she gave her attention back to the girls. "Dismount, then cool down your horses. Remember, they depend on you." The breeze tossed her bangs, and she brushed at them absently. "Remember to put all the tack in its proper place for the next class."

This caused the groans she expected. Riding and playing with the horses was one thing, tidying up afterward was another. Eden considered exerting discipline without causing resentment another accomplishment. Over the past week, she'd learned to link the girls' faces and names. The eleven- and twelve-year-olds in her group had an enthusiasm that kept her on her toes. She'd already separated in her mind the two or three she instructed who had the kind of horse fever she recognized from her own adolescence. It was rewarding, after an hour on her feet in the sun, to answer the rapid-fire questions. Ultimately, one by one, she nudged them toward the stables.

"Eden!" Turning, she spotted Candy hustling toward her. Even from a distance, Eden recognized concern.

"What's happened?"

"We're missing three kids."

"What?" Panic came first, and quickly. Years of training had her pulling it back. "What do you mean, missing?"

"I mean they're nowhere in camp. Roberta Snow, Linda Hopkins and Marcie Jamison." Candy dragged a hand through her hair, a habitual gesture of tension. "Barbara was lining up her group for rowing, and they didn't show. We've looked everywhere."

"We can't panic," Eden said, as much to warn herself as Candy. "Roberta Snow? Isn't she the little brunette who stuck a lizard down one of the other girls' shirts? And the one who set off the morning bell at 3:00 a.m.?"

"Yes, that's her." Candy set her teeth. "The little darling. Judge Harper Snow's granddaughter. If she's skinned her knee, we'll probably face a lawsuit." With a shake of her head, Candy switched to an undertone. "The last anyone saw of her this morning, she was walking east." She pointed a finger, paint-spattered from her early art class. "No one noticed the other girls, but my bet is that they're with her. Darling Roberta is an inveterate leader."

"If she's walking that way, wouldn't she run into that apple orchard?"

"Yeah." Candy shut her eyes. "Oh, yeah. I'm going to have six girls up to their wrists in modeling clay in ten minutes, or I'd go off myself. Eden, I'm almost sure they headed for the orchard. One of the other girls admitted she heard Roberta planning to sneak over there for a few samples. We don't want any trouble with the owner. He's letting us use his lake only because I begged, shamelessly. He wasn't thrilled about having a girls' summer camp for a neighbor."

"Well, he has one," Eden pointed out. "So we'll all have to deal with it. I'm the one most easily spared around here, so I'll go after them."

"I was hoping you'd say that. Seriously, Eden, if they've snuck into that orchard, which I'd bet my last dime they have, we could be in for it. The man made no bones about how he feels about his land and his privacy."

"Three little girls are hardly going to do any damage to a

bunch of apple trees." Eden began to walk, with Candy scurrying to keep pace.

"He's Chase Elliot. You know, Elliot Apples? Juice, cider, sauce, jelly, chocolate-covered apple seeds, whatever can be made from an apple, they do it. He made it abundantly clear that he didn't want to find any little girls climbing his trees."

"He won't find them, I will." Leaving Candy behind, Eden swung over a fence.

"Put Roberta on a leash when you catch up to her." Candy watched her disappear through the trees.

Eden followed the path from the camp, pleased when she found a crumpled candy wrapper. Roberta. With a grim smile, Eden picked it up and stuffed it in her pocket. Judge Snow's granddaughter had already earned a reputation for her stash of sweets.

It was warm now, but the path veered through a cool grove of aspens. Sunlight dappled the ground, making the walk, if not her errand, pleasant. Squirrels dashed here and there, confident enough in their own speed not to be alarmed at Eden's intrusion. Once a rabbit darted across her path, and disappeared into the brush with a frantic rustle. Overhead a woodpecker drummed, sending out an echo.

It occurred to Eden that she was more completely alone than she had ever been before. No civilization here. She bent down for another candy wrapper. Well, very little of it.

There were new scents here, earth, animal, vegetation, to be discovered. Wildflowers sprang up, tougher and more resilient than hothouse roses. It pleased her that she was even beginning to be able to recognize a few. They came back, year after year, without pampering, taking what came and thriving on it. They gave her hope. She could find a place here. Had found a place, she corrected herself. Her friends in

Philadelphia might think her mad, but she was beginning to enjoy it.

The grove of aspens thinned abruptly, and the sunlight was strong again. She blinked against it, then shielded her eyes as she scanned the Elliot orchards.

Apple trees stretched ahead of her as far as she could see, to the north, south and east. Row after row after row of trees lined the slopes. Some of them were old and gnarled, some young and straight. Instantly she thought of early spring and the overwhelming scent of apple blossoms.

It would be magnificent, she thought as she stepped up to the fence that separated the properties. The fragrance, the pretty white-and-pink blossoms, the freshly green leaves, would be a marvelous sight. Now the leaves were dark and thick, and instead of blossoms, she could see fruit in the trees closest to her. Small, shiny, and green they hung, waiting for the sun to ripen them.

How many times had she eaten applesauce that had begun right here? The idea made her smile as she began to climb the fence. Her vision of an orchard had been a lazy little grove guarded by an old man in overalls. A quaint picture, but nothing as huge and impressive as the reality.

The sound of giggling took her by surprise. Shifting toward the direction of the sound, Eden watched an apple fall from a tree and roll toward her feet. Bending, she picked it up, tossing it away as she walked closer. When she looked up, she spotted three pairs of sneakers beneath the cover of leaves and branches.

"Ladies." Eden spoke coolly and was rewarded by three startled gasps. "Apparently you took a wrong turn on your way to the lake."

Roberta's triangular, freckled face appeared through the leaves. "Hi, Miss Carlbough. Would you like an apple?"

The devil. But even as she thought it, Eden had to tighten her lips against a smile. "Down," she said simply, then stepped closer to the trunk to assist.

They didn't need her. Three agile little bodies scrambled down and dropped lightly onto the ground. In a gesture she knew could be intimidating, Eden lifted her left eyebrow.

"I'm sure you're aware that leaving camp property unsupervised and without permission is against the rules."

"Yes, Miss Carlbough." The response would have been humble if it hadn't been for the gleam in Roberta's eye.

"Since none of you seem interested in rowing today, Mrs. Petrie has a great deal of washing up to be done in the kitchen." Pleased by her own inspiration, Eden decided Candy would approve. "You're to report to Miss Bartholomew, then to Mrs. Petrie for kitchen detail."

Only two of the girls dropped their heads and looked down at the ground.

"Miss Carlbough, do you think it's fair to give us extra kitchen detail?" Roberta, one half-eaten apple still in hand, tilted her pointed chin. "After all, our parents are paying for the camp."

Eden felt her palms grow damp. Judge Snow was a wealthy and powerful man with a reputation for indulging his granddaughter. If the little monster complained... No. Eden took a deep breath and not by a flicker showed her anxiety. She wouldn't be intimidated or blackmailed by a pint-size con artist with apple juice on her chin.

"Yes, your parents are paying for you to be entertained, instructed and disciplined. When they signed you up for Camp Liberty, it was with the understanding that you would obey the rules. But if you prefer, I'd be glad to call your parents and discuss this incident with them."

"No, ma'am." Knowing when to retreat, Roberta smiled charmingly. "We'll be glad to help Mrs. Petrie, and we're sorry for breaking the rules."

And I'm sure you have a bridge I could buy, Eden thought, but she kept her face impassive. "Fine. It's time to start back."

"My hat!" Roberta would have darted back up the tree if Eden hadn't made a lucky grab for her. "I left my hat up there. Please, Miss Carlbough, it's my Phillies cap, and it's autographed and everything."

"You start back. I'll get it. I don't want Miss Bartholomew to worry any longer than necessary."

"We'll apologize."

"See that you do." Eden watched them scramble over the fence. "And no detours," she called out. "Or I keep the cap." One look at Roberta assured her that that bit of blackmail was all that was needed. "Monsters," she murmured as they jogged back into the grove, but the smile finally escaped. Turning back, she studied the tree.

All she had to do was climb up. It had looked simple enough when Roberta and her partners-in-crime had done it. Somehow, it didn't look as simple now. Squaring her shoulders, Eden stepped forward to grab a low-hanging branch. She'd done a little mountain-climbing in Switzerland; how much harder could this be? Pulling herself up, she hooked her foot in the first vee she found. The bark was rough against her palm. Concentrating on her goal, she ignored the scrapes. With both feet secured, she reached for the next branch and began to work her way up. Leaves brushed her cheeks.

She spotted the cap hanging on a short branch, two arms' lengths out of reach. When she made the mistake of looking down, her stomach clenched. So don't look, Eden ordered herself. What you can't see can't hurt you. She hoped.

Eden cautiously inched her way out to the cap. When her fingers made contact with it, she let out a low breath of relief. After setting it on her own head, she found herself looking out, beyond the tree, over the orchard.

Now it was the symmetry that caught her admiration. From her bird's height, she could see the order as well as the beauty. She could just barely glimpse a slice of the lake beyond the aspens. It winked blue in the distance. There were barnlike buildings, and what appeared to be a greenhouse, far off to the right. About a quarter of a mile away, there was a truck, apparently abandoned, on a wide dirt path. In the quiet, birds began to sing again. Turning her head, she saw the bright yellow flash of a butterfly.

The scent of leaves and fruit and earth was tangy, basic. Unable to resist, Eden reached out and plucked a sun-warmed apple.

He'd never miss it, she decided as she bit into the skin. The tart flavor, not quite ripe, shot into her mouth. She shivered at the shock of it, the sensual appeal, then bit again. Delicious, she thought. Exciting. Forbidden fruit usually was, she remembered, but she grinned as she took a third bite.

"What in the devil are you doing?"

She started, almost unseating herself, as the voice boomed up from below. She swallowed the bite of apple quickly before peering down through the leaves.

He stood with his hands on his hips, narrow, lean, spare. A faded denim workshirt was rolled up past the elbows to show tan and muscle. Warily, Eden brought her eyes to his face. It was tanned like his arms, with the skin drawn tight over bone. His nose was long and not quite straight, his mouth full and firm and frowning. Jet-black and unruly, his hair fell over his brow and curled just beyond the collar of his shirt. Pale, almost translucent green eyes scowled up at her.

An apple, Eden, and now the serpent. The idea ran through her head before she drew herself back.

Wonderful, she thought. She'd been caught pinching apples by the foreman. Since disappearing wasn't an option, she opened her mouth to start a plausible explanation.

"Young lady, do you belong at the camp next door?"

The tone brought on a frown. She might be penniless, she might be scrambling to make a living, but she was still a Carlbough. And a Carlbough could certainly handle an apple foreman. "Yes, that's right. I'd like to—"

"Are you aware that this is private property, and that you're trespassing?"

The color of her eyes deepened, the only outward sign of her embarrassed fury. "Yes, but I—"

"These trees weren't planted for little girls to climb."

"I hardly think—"

"Come down." There was absolute command in his tone. "I'll have to take you back to the camp director."

The temper she had always gently controlled bubbled up until she gave serious consideration to throwing what was left of the apple down on his head. No one, absolutely no one, gave her orders. "That won't be necessary."

"I'll decide what's necessary. Come down here."

She'd come down all right, Eden thought. Then, with a few well-chosen words, he'd be put precisely in his place. Annoyance carried her from branch to branch, leaving no room for thoughts of height or inexperience. The two scrapes she picked up on the trip were hardly felt. Her back was to him as she lowered herself into a vee of the trunk. The pleasure of demolishing him with icy manners would be well worth the embarrassment of having been caught in the wrong place at the wrong time. She imagined him cringing and babbling an incoherent apology.

Then her foot slipped, and her frantic grab for a limb was an inch short of the mark. With a shriek that was equal parts surprise and dismay, she fell backward into space.

The breath whooshed back out of her as she connected with something solid. The tanned, muscled arms she'd seen from above wrapped around her. Momentum carried them both to the ground and, like the apple, they rolled. When the world stopped spinning, Eden found herself beneath a very firm, very long body.

Roberta's cap had flown off and Eden's face, no longer shadowed by the brim, was left unguarded in the sunlight. Chase stared down at her and felt soft breasts yield under him.

"You're not twelve years old," he murmured.

"Certainly not."

Amused now, he shifted his weight, but didn't remove it. "I didn't get a good look at you when you were in the tree." He had time to make up for that now, he decided, and he looked his fill. "You're quite a windfall." Carelessly, he brushed stray strands of hair away from her face. His fingertips were as rough against her skin as the bark had been to her palms. "What are you doing in a girls' summer camp?"

"Running it," she said coldly. It wasn't a complete lie. Because it would have bruised her dignity even more to squirm, she settled on sending him an icy look. "Would you mind?"

"Running it?" Since she had dropped out of one of his trees, he had no qualms about ignoring her request. "I met someone. Bartholomew—red hair, appealing face." He scanned Eden's classic features. "You're not her."

"Obviously not." Because his body was too warm, too male, and too close, she sacrificed some dignity by putting her hands to his shoulders. He didn't budge. "I'm her partner. Eden Carlbough."

"Ah, of the Philadelphia Carlboughs."

The humor in his voice was another blow to her pride. Eden combated it with a withering stare. "That's correct."

Intriguing little package, he thought. All manners and breeding. "A pleasure, Miss Carlbough. I'm Chase Elliot of the South Mountain Elliots."

Chapter 2

Perfect, just perfect, Eden thought as she stared up at him. Not the foreman, but the bloody owner. Caught stealing apples by, falling out of trees on and pinned to the ground under, the owner. She took a deep breath.

"How do you do, Mr. Elliot."

She might have been in the front parlor pouring tea, Chase thought; he had to admire her. Then he burst out laughing. "I do just fine, Miss Carlbough. And you?"

He was laughing at her. Even after the scandal and shame she had faced, no one had dared laugh at her. Not to her face. Her lips trembled once before she managed to control them. She wouldn't give the oaf the pleasure of knowing how much he infuriated her.

"I'm quite well, thank you, or will be when you let me up."

City manners, he thought. Socially correct and absolutely

meaningless. His own were a bit cruder, but more honest. "In a minute. I'm finding this conversation fascinating."

"Then perhaps we could continue it standing up."

"I'm very comfortable." That wasn't precisely true. The soft, slender lines of her body were causing him some problems. Rather than alleviate them, Chase decided to enjoy them. And her. "So, how are you finding life in the rough?"

He was still laughing at her, without troubling to pretend otherwise. Eden tasted the fury bubbling up in her throat. She swallowed it. "Mr. Elliot—"

"Chase," he interrupted. "I think, under the circumstances, we should dispense with formalities."

Control teetered long enough for her to shove against his shoulders again. It was like pushing rock. "This is ridiculous. You *have* to let me up."

"I rarely have to do anything." His voice was a drawl now, and insolent, but no less imposing than the bellow that had first greeted her. "I've heard a lot about you, Eden Carlbough." And he'd seen the newspaper pictures that he now realized had been just shy of the mark. It was difficult to capture that cool sexuality in two dimensions. "I never expected a Carlbough of Philadelphia to fall out of one of my trees."

Her breathing became unsteady. All the training, the years she'd spent being taught how to coat every emotion with politeness, began to crack. "It was hardly my intention to fall out of one of your trees."

"Wouldn't have fallen out if you hadn't climbed up." He smiled, realizing how glad he was that he'd decided to check this section of the orchard himself.

This couldn't be happening. Eden closed her eyes a moment and waited for things to fall back into their proper places. She couldn't be lying flat on her back under a stranger. "Mr.

Elliot." Her voice was calm and reasonable when she tried it again. "I'd be more than happy to give you a complete explanation if you'd let me up."

"Explanation first."

Her mouth quite simply fell open. "You are the most unbelievably rude and boorish man I have ever met."

"My property," he said simply. "My rules. Let's hear your explanation."

She almost shuddered with the effort to hold back the torrent of abuse that leaped to her tongue. Because of her position, she had to squint up at him. Already a headache was collecting behind her eyes. "Three of my girls wandered away from camp. Unfortunately, they climbed over the fence and onto your property. I found them, ordered them down and sent them back to the camp, where they are being properly disciplined."

"Tar and feathers?"

"I'm sure you'd prefer that, but we settled on extra kitchen detail."

"Seems fair. But that doesn't explain you falling out of my tree and into my arms. Though I've about decided not to complain about that. You smell like Paris." To Eden's amazement, he leaned down and buried his face in her hair. "Wicked nights in Paris."

"Stop it." Now her voice wasn't calm, wasn't disciplined.

Chase felt her heart begin to thud against his own. It ran through his mind that he wanted to do more than sample her scent. But when he lifted his head, her eyes were wide. Along with the awareness in them was a trace of fear.

"Explanation," he said lightly. "That's all I intend to take at the moment."

She could hear her own pulse hammering in her throat. Of its own accord, her gaze fell upon his mouth. Was she mad, or could she almost taste the surge of masculine flavor that would certainly be on his lips? She felt her muscles softening, then instantly stiffened. She might very well be mad. If an explanation was what it took, she'd give it to him and get away. Far away.

"One of the girls…" Her mind veered vengefully to Roberta. "One of them left her cap in the tree."

"So you went up after it." He nodded, accepting her explanation. "That doesn't explain why you were helping yourself to one of my apples."

"It was mealy."

Grinning again, he ran a hand along her jawline. "I doubt that. I'd imagine it was hard and tart and delicious. I had my share of stomachaches from green apples years ago. The pleasure's usually worth the pain."

Something uncomfortably like need was spreading through her. The fear of it chilled both her eyes and voice. "You have your explanation, and your apology."

"I never heard an apology."

She'd be damned, she'd be twice damned if she'd give him one now. Glaring at him, she nearly managed to look regal. "I want you to let me up this instant. You're perfectly free to prosecute if you feel the need for compensation for a couple of worm-filled apples, but for now, I'm tired of your ridiculous backwoods arrogance."

His apples were the best in the state, the best in the country. But at the moment, he relished the idea of her sinking her pretty white teeth into a worm. "You haven't had a taste of backwoods arrogance yet. Maybe you should."

"You wouldn't dare," she began, only to have the last word muffled by his mouth.

The kiss caught her completely off guard. It was rough and

demanding and as tart as the apple had been. Forbidden fruit. To a woman accustomed to coaxing, to requesting, the hard demand left her limp, unable to respond or protest. Then his hands were on her face, his thumbs tracing her jawline. Like the kiss, his palms were hard and thrilling.

He didn't regret it. Though he wasn't a man used to taking from a woman what wasn't offered, he didn't regret it. Not when the fruit was this sweet. Even though she lay very still, he could taste the panicked excitement on her lips. Yes, very sweet, he thought. Very innocent. Very dangerous. He lifted his head the moment she began to struggle.

"Easy," he murmured, still stroking her chin with his thumb. Her eyes were more frantic than furious. "It seems you're not the woman of the world you're reputed to be."

"Let me up." Her voice was shaking now, but she was beyond caring.

Getting to his feet, Chase brought her with him. "Want some help brushing off?"

"You are the most offensive man I've ever met."

"I can believe it. A pity you've been spoiled and pampered for so long." She started to turn away, but he caught her shoulders for one last look. "It should be interesting to see how long you last here without the basics—like hairdressers and butlers."

He's just like everyone else, she thought; she coated her hurt and doubt with disdain. "I'm very late for my next class, Mr. Elliot. If you'll excuse me?"

He lifted his hands from her shoulders, holding the palms out a moment before dropping them. "Try to keep the kids out of the trees," he warned. "A fall can be dangerous."

His smile had insults trembling on her lips. Clamping her tongue between her teeth, Eden scrambled over the fence.

He watched her, enjoying the view until she was swallowed up by the aspens. Glimpsing the cap at his feet, he bent down for it. As good as a calling card, he decided, tucking it into his back pocket.

Eden went through the rest of the day struggling not to think. About anything. She had deliberately avoided telling Candy about her meeting with Chase. In telling of it, she would have to think about it.

The humiliation of being caught up a tree was hard enough to swallow. Still, under other circumstances, she and Candy might have shared a laugh over it. Under any other circumstances.

But more than the humiliation, even more than the anger, were the sensations. She wasn't sure what they were, but each separate sensation she had experienced in the orchard remained fresh and vibrant throughout the day. She couldn't shake them off or cover them over, and she certainly couldn't ignore them. If she understood anything, she understood how important it was for her to close off her feelings before they could grow.

Ridiculous. Eden interrupted her own thoughts. She didn't know Chase Elliot. Moreover, she didn't want to know him. It was true that she couldn't block out what had happened, but she could certainly see that it never happened again.

Over the past year, she had taken control of the reins for the first time in her life. She knew what it was to fumble, what it was to fail, but she also knew she would never fully release those reins again. Disillusionment had toughened her. Perhaps that was the one snatch of silver lining in the cloud.

Because of it, she recognized Chase Elliot as a man who held his own reins, and tightly. She had found him rude and overbearing, but she had also seen his power and authority.

She'd had her fill of dominating men. Rough-edged or polished, they were all the same underneath. Since her experience with Eric, Eden's opinion of men in general had reached a low ebb. Her encounter with Chase had done nothing to raise it.

It was annoying that she had to remind herself continually to forget about him.

Learning the camp's routine was enough to occupy her mind. Since she didn't have Candy's years of training and experience in counseling, her responsibilities were relatively few and often mundane, but at least she had the satisfaction of knowing she was more than a spectator. Ambition had become a new vice. If her role as apprentice meant she mucked out stalls and groomed horses, then Eden was determined to have the cleanest stables and the glossiest horses in Pennsylvania. She considered her first blister a badge of accomplishment.

The rush after the dinner bell still intimidated Eden. Twenty-seven girls aged ten to fourteen swarmed the cafeteria. It was one of Eden's new duties to help keep order. Voices were raised on topics that usually ranged from boys to rock stars, then back to boys. With a little luck, there was no jostling or shoving in line. But luck usually required an eagle eye.

Camp Liberty's glossy brochures had promised wholesome food. Tonight's menu included crispy chicken, whipped potatoes and steamed broccoli. Flatware rattled on trays as the girls shuffled, cafeteria-style, down the serving line.

"It's been a good day." Candy stood beside Eden, her eyes shifting back and forth as she managed to watch the entire room at once.

"And nearly over." Even as she said it, Eden realized her back didn't ache quite as much as it had the first couple of days. "I've got two girls in the morning riding session who show real promise. I was hoping I could give them a little extra time a couple of days a week."

"Great, we'll check the schedule." Candy watched one of the counselors convince a camper to put a stem of broccoli on her plate. "I wanted to tell you that you handled Roberta and company beautifully. Kitchen detail was an inspiration."

"Thanks." Eden realized how low her pride had fallen when such a small thing made her glow. "I did have a twinge of guilt about dumping them on Mrs. Petrie."

"The report is they behaved like troopers."

"Roberta?"

"I know." Candy's smile was wry. Both women turned to see the girl in question, already seated and eating daintily. "It's like waiting for the other shoe to drop. Eden, do you remember Marcia Delacroix from Camp Forden?"

"How could I forget?" With the bulk of the campers seated, Eden and Candy joined the line. "She was the one who put the garter snake in Miss Forden's lingerie drawer."

"Yeah." She turned to give Roberta another look. "Do you believe in reincarnation?"

With a laugh, Eden accepted a scoop of potatoes. "Let's just say I'll be checking my underwear." Hefting the tray, she started forward. "You know, Candy, I—" She saw it as if in slow motion. Roberta, the devil's own gleam in her eyes, held her fork vertically, a thick blob of potatoes clinging to the tines. Aim was taken as Roberta pulled back the business end of the fork with an expert flick. Even as Eden opened her mouth, Roberta sent the blob sailing into the hair of the girl across from her. Pandemonium.

Globs of potatoes flew. Girls screamed. More retaliated. In a matter of seconds, floors, tables, chairs and adolescents were coated in a messy layer of white. Like a general leading the way into battle, Candy stepped into the chaos and lifted her whistle. Before she had the chance to blow it, she was hit, right between the eyes.

A shocked silence fell.

With her tray still in her hands, Eden stood, afraid to breathe. One breath, one little breath, she thought, and she would dissolve into helpless laughter. She felt the pressure of a giggle in her lungs as Candy slowly wiped the dollop of potato from the bridge of her nose.

"Young ladies." The two words, delivered in Candy's most ferocious voice, had Eden's breath catching in her throat. "You will finish your meal in silence. Absolute silence. As you finish, you will line up against this wall. When the dinner hour is over, you will be issued rags, mops and buckets. The mess area will shine tonight."

"Yes, Miss Bartholomew." The acknowledgment came in murmured unison. Only Roberta, her hands folded neatly, her face a picture of innocence, responded in clear tones.

After a long ten seconds of silent staring, Candy walked back to Eden and picked up her tray. "If you laugh," she said in an undertone, "I'll tie your tongue into a square knot."

"Who's laughing?" Eden desperately cleared her throat. "I'm not laughing."

"Yes, you are." Candy sailed, like a steamship, to the head table. "You're just clever enough to do it discreetly."

Eden sat, then carefully smoothed her napkin on her lap. "You've got mashed potatoes in your eyebrows." Candy glared at her, and she lifted her coffee cup to hide a grin behind it. "Actually, it's very becoming. You may have found an alternative to hair gel."

Candy glanced down at the cooling potatoes on her own plate. "Would you like to try some?"

"Now, darling, you're the one who's always telling me we have to set an example." Eden took a satisfying bite of her chicken. "Mrs. Petrie's a gem, isn't she?"

It took the better part of two hours to clean the mess area and to mop up the puddles of water spilled by the inexperienced janitorial crew. By lights-out most of the girls were too tired to loiter. A pleasant late-evening hush covered the camp.

If the mornings were the worst for Eden, the evenings were invariably the best. A long day of physical activity left her comfortably tired and relaxed. The sounds of night birds and insects were becoming familiar. More and more, she looked forward to an hour of solitude with a sky full of stars. There was no theater to dress for, no party to attend. The longer she was away from her former life-style, the less she missed it.

She was growing up, she reflected, and she liked the idea. She supposed maturity meant recognizing what was really important. The camp was important, her friendship with Candy vital. The girls under their care for the summer, even the dastardly Roberta Snow, were what really mattered. She came to realize that even if everything she had once had was handed back to her, she would no longer be able to treat it in the same way.

She had changed. And even though she was certain there were still more changes to come, she liked the new Eden Carlbough. This Eden was independent, not financially, but internally. She'd never realized how dependent she had been on her father, her fiancé, the servants. The new Eden could cope with problems, large ones, small ones. Her hands were no longer elegantly manicured. The nails were neat, but short and rounded, unpainted. Practical, Eden thought as she held one up for inspection. Useful. She liked what she saw.

She continued her nightly ritual by walking to the stables.

Inside it was cool and dark, smelling of leather, hay and horses. Just stepping inside helped to cement her confidence. This was her contribution. In most other areas, she still relied on pride and nerve, but here she had skill and knowledge.

She would check each of the six horses, then the tack, before she would consider her duties over for the day. Candy might be able to build a cathedral out of papier-mâché, but she knew nothing about strained tendons or split hooves.

Eden stopped at the first stall to stroke the roan gelding she called Courage. In her hand was a paper bag with six apple halves. It was a nightly ritual the horses had caught on to quickly. Courage leaned his head over the stall door and nuzzled her palm.

"Such a good boy," she murmured as she reached into the bag. "Some of the girls still don't know a bit from a stirrup, but we're going to change that." She held the apple in her palm and let him take it. While he chewed contentedly, Eden stepped into the stall to check him over. He'd been a bargain because of his age and his slight swayback. She hadn't been looking for thoroughbreds, but for dependability and gentleness. Satisfied that his grooming had been thorough, she latched the stall door behind her and went to the next.

Next summer they'd have at least three more mounts. Eden smiled as she worked her way from stall to stall. She wasn't going to question whether there would be a Camp Liberty next summer. There would be, and she'd be part of it. A real part.

She realized that she'd brought little with her other than money and a flair for horses. It was Candy who had the training, Candy who had had the three younger sisters and a family that had possessed more tradition than money. Unlike Eden, Candy had always known she would have to earn her own way and had prepared for it. But Eden was a quick learner. By Camp Liberty's second season, she would be a partner in more than name.

Her ambition was already spiraling upward. In a few years, Camp Liberty would be renowned for its equestrian program. The name Carlbough would be respected again. There might even come a time when her Philadelphia contemporaries would send their children to her. The irony of it pleased her.

After the fifth apple had been devoured, Eden moved to the last stall. Here was Patience, a sweet-tempered, aging mare who would tolerate any kind of ineptitude in a rider as long as she received affection. Sympathetic to old bones and muscles, Eden often spent an extra hour rubbing the mare down with liniment.

"Here you are, sweetheart." As the horse gnawed the apple, Eden lifted each hoof for inspection. "A pretty sketchy job," she mumbled before drawing a hoof pick out of her back pocket. "Let's see, wasn't it little Marcie who rode you last? I suppose this means we have to have a discussion on responsibility." With a sigh, Eden switched to another hoof. "I hate discussions on responsibility. Especially when I'm giving them." Patience snorted sympathetically. "Well, I can't leave all the dirty work to Candy, can I? In any case, I don't think Marcie meant to be inconsiderate. She's still a bit nervous around horses. We'll have to show her what a nice lady you are. There. Want a rubdown?" After sticking the pick back in her pocket, Eden rested her cheek against the mare's neck. "Oh, me too, Patience. A nice long massage with some scented oil. You can just lie there with your eyes closed while all the kinks are worked out, then your skin feels so soft, your muscles so supple." With a quick laugh, Eden drew away. "Well, since you can't oblige me, I'll oblige you. Just let me get the liniment."

Giving the mare a final pat, she turned. Her breath caught on a gasp.

Chase Elliot leaned against the open stall door. Shadows fell across his face, deepening its hollows. In the dim light, his eyes were like sea foam. She would have taken a step backward in retreat, but the mare blocked her way. He smiled at her predicament.

That triggered her pride. She could be grateful for that. It had thrown her that, in the shadowed light, he was even more attractive, more…compelling than he had been in the sun. Not handsome, she amended quickly. Certainly not in the smooth, conventional sense, the sense she had always gauged men's looks by before. Everything about him was fundamental. Not simple, she thought. No, not simple, but basic. Basic, like his kiss that morning. Warmth prickled along her skin.

"I'd be happy to help you with the massage." He smiled again. "Yours, or the mare's."

"No, thank you." She became aware that she was even more disheveled than she had been at their first meeting, and that she smelled, all too obviously, of horse. "Is there something I can do for you, Mr. Elliot?"

He liked her style, Chase decided. She might be standing in a stall that could use a bit of cleaning, but she was still the lady of the drawing room. "You've got a good stock here. A bit on the mature side, but solid."

Eden had to ward off a surge of pleasure. His opinion hardly mattered. "Thank you. I'm sure you didn't come to look over the horses."

"No." But he stepped inside the stall. The mare shifted to accommodate him. "Apparently you know your way around them." He lifted a hand to run it down the mare's neck. There was a simple gold ring on his right hand. Eden recognized its age and value, as well as the strength of the man who wore it.

"Apparently." There was no way past him, so she linked

her fingers together and waited. "Mr. Elliot, you haven't told me what you're doing here."

Chase's lips twitched as he continued to stroke the mare. Miss Philadelphia was nervous, he thought. She covered it well enough with frigid manners, but her nerves were jumping. It pleased him to know that she hadn't been able to brush off that quick, impulsive kiss any more than he had. "No, I haven't." Before she could avoid it, he reached down for her hand. An opal gleamed dully in the shadowed light, nestled in a circle of diamond chips that promised to catch heat and fire.

"Wrong hand for an engagement ring." He discovered that the fact pleased him, perhaps more than it should have. "I'd heard you and Eric Keeton were to be married last spring. Apparently it didn't come off."

She would like to have sworn, shouted, yelled. That's what *he* wanted, Eden told herself, letting her hand lie passive in his. "No, it didn't. Mr. Elliot, for a, let's say, country squire, you have boundless curiosity about Philadelphia gossip. Don't your apples keep you busy enough?"

He had to admire anyone who could shoot straight and smile. "I manage to eke out a bit of free time. Actually, I was interested because Keeton's a family connection."

"He is not."

There, he'd ruffled her. For the first time since her initial surprise, she was really looking at him. Take a good look, Chase thought. You won't see any resemblance. "Distant, certainly." Capturing her other hand, he turned the palms up. "My grandmother was a Winthrop, and a cousin of his grandmother. Your Philadelphia hands have a couple of blisters. You should take care."

"A Winthrop?" Eden was surprised enough at the name to forget her hands.

"We've thinned the blood a bit in the last few generations." She should be wearing gloves, he thought, as he touched a blister with his thumb. "Still, I'd expected an invitation and was curious why you dumped him."

"I didn't dump him." The words came out like poisoned honey. "But to satisfy your curiosity, and to use your own crude phrase, he dumped me. Now if you'd give me back my hands, I could finish for the day."

Chase obliged, but continued to block her way out of the stall. "I'd never considered Eric bright, but I'd never thought him stupid."

"What a delightful compliment. Please excuse me, Mr. Elliot."

"Not a compliment." Chase brushed at the bangs over her forehead. "Just an observation."

"Stop touching me."

"Touching's a habit of mine. I like your hair, Eden. It's soft, but it goes its own way."

"A veritable bouquet of compliments." She managed one small step backward. He had her pulse thudding again. She didn't want to be touched, not physically, not emotionally, not by anyone. Instinct warned her how easily he could do both. "Mr. Elliot—"

"Chase."

"Chase." She acknowledged this with a regal nod. "The morning bell goes off at six. I still have several things to do tonight, so if there's a purpose in your being here, could we get to it?"

"I came to bring you back your hat." Reaching in his back pocket, he pulled out the Phillies cap.

"I see." One more black mark against Roberta. "It's not mine, but I'd be happy to return it to its owner. Thank you for troubling."

"You were wearing it when you fell out of my tree." Chase ignored her outstretched hand and dropped the cap on her head. "Fits, too."

"As I've already explained—"

Eden's frigid retort was interrupted by the sound of running feet. "Miss Carlbough! Miss Carlbough!" Roberta, in an angelic pink nightgown and bare feet, skidded to a halt at the open stall. Beaming, she stared up at Chase. Her adolescent heart melted. "Hi."

"Hi."

"Roberta." Voice stern, teeth nearly clenched, Eden stepped forward. "It's almost an hour past lights-out."

"I know, Miss Carlbough. I'm sorry." When she smiled, Eden thought you could almost believe it. "I just couldn't get to sleep because I kept thinking about my cap. You promised I could have it back, but you never gave it to me. I helped Mrs. Petrie. Honest, you can ask. There were millions of pans, too. I even peeled potatoes, and—"

"Roberta!" The sharp tone was enough for the moment. "Mr. Elliot was kind enough to return your hat." Whipping it off her own head, Eden thrust it into the girl's hands. "I believe you should thank him, as well as apologize for trespassing."

"Gee, thanks." She treated him to a dazzling smile. "Are those your trees, really?"

"Yeah." With a fingertip, Chase adjusted the brim of her hat. He had a weakness for black sheep and recognized a kindred soul in Roberta.

"I think they're great. Your apples tasted a whole lot better than the ones we get at home."

"Roberta."

The quiet warning had the girl rolling her eyes, which only Chase could see. "I'm sorry I didn't show the proper respect for your property." Roberta turned her head to see whether Eden approved of the apology.

"Very nice, Roberta. Now straight back to bed."

"Yes, ma'am." She shot a last look at Chase. Her little heart fluttered. Crushing the cap down on her head, she raced to the door.

"Roberta." She whipped back around at the sound of Chase's voice. He grinned at her. "See you around."

"Yeah, see you." In love, Roberta floated off to her cabin. When the stable door slammed at her back, all Eden could manage was a sigh.

"It's no use," Chase commented.

"What isn't?"

"Pretending you don't get a kick out of her. A kid like that makes you feel good."

"You wouldn't be so sure of that if you'd seen what she can do with mashed potatoes." But Eden gave in enough to smile. "She's a monster, but an appealing one. Still, I have to admit, if we had twenty-seven Robertas in camp this summer, I'd end up in a padded room."

"Certain people just breed excitement."

Eden remembered the dinner hour. "Some call it chaos."

"Life flattens out quickly without a little chaos."

She looked at him, realizing she'd dropped her guard enough to have an actual conversation. And realizing as well that they'd stopped talking about Roberta. The stables suddenly seemed very quiet. "Well, now that we've gotten that settled, I think—"

He took a step forward. She took a step back. A smile played around his lips again as he reached for her hand. Eden bumped solidly into the mare before she managed to raise her free hand to his chest.

"What do you want?" Why was she whispering, and why was the whisper so tremulous?

He wasn't sure what he wanted. Once, quickly, he scanned her face before bringing his gaze back to hers with a jolt. Or perhaps he was. "To walk with you in the moonlight, I think. To listen to the owls hoot and wait for the nightingale."

The shadows had merged. The mare stood quietly, breathing softly. His hand was in Eden's hair now, as if it belonged there. "I have to go in." But she didn't move.

"Eden and the apple," he murmured. "I can't tell you how tempting I've found that combination. Come with me. We'll walk."

"No." Something was building inside her, too quickly. She knew he was touching more than her hand, more than her hair. He was reaching for something he should not have known existed.

"Sooner or later." He'd always been a patient man. He could wait for her the way he waited for a new tree to bear fruit. His fingers slid down to her throat, stroking once. He felt her quick shudder, heard the unsteady indrawn breath. "I'll be back, Eden."

"It won't make any difference."

Smiling, he brought her hand to his lips, turning it palm up. "I'll still be back."

She listened to his footsteps, to the creak of the door as he opened it, then shut it again.

Chapter 3

The camp was developing its own routine. Eden adjusted hers to it. Early hours, long, physical days and basic food were both a solace and a challenge. The confidence she'd once had to work at became real.

There were nights during the first month of summer that she fell into her bunk certain she would never be able to get up in the morning. Her muscles ached from rowing, riding and endless hiking. Her head spun from weekly encounters with ledgers and account books. But in the morning the sun would rise, and so would she.

Every day it became easier. She was young and healthy. The daily regimented exercise hardened muscles only touched on by occasional games of tennis. The weight she had lost over the months since her father's death gradually came back, so that her look of fragility faded.

To her surprise, she developed a genuine affection for the

girls. They became individuals, not simply a group to be coped with or income on the books. It surprised her more to find that same affection returned.

Right from the start, Eden had been certain the girls would love Candy. Everyone did. She was warm, funny, talented. The most Eden had hoped for, for herself, was to be tolerated and respected. The day Marcie had brought her a clutch of wildflowers, Eden had been too stunned to do more than stammer a thank-you. Then there had been the afternoon she had given Linda Hopkins an extra half hour in the corral. After her first gallop, Linda had thrown herself into Eden's arms for a fierce and delightful hug.

So the camp had changed her life, in so many more ways than she'd expected.

The summer grew hot with July. Girls darted around the compound in shorts. Dips in the lake became a glorious luxury. Doors and windows stayed open at night to catch even the slightest breeze. Roberta found a garter snake and terrorized her cabin mates. Bees buzzed around the wildflowers and stings became common.

Days merged together, content, but never dull, so that it seemed possible that summer could last forever. As the time passed, Eden began to believe that Chase had forgotten his promise, or threat, to come back. She'd been careful to stay well within the borders of the camp herself. Though once or twice she'd been tempted to wander toward the orchards, she stayed away.

It didn't make sense for her to still be tense and uneasy. She could tell herself he'd only been a brief annoyance. Yet every time she went into the stables in the evening, she caught herself listening. And waiting.

Late in the evening, with the heat still shimmering, Eden

stretched out on her bunk, fully dressed. Bribed by the promise of a bonfire the following night, the campers had quieted down early. Relaxed and pleasantly weary, Eden pictured it. Hot dogs flaming on sharpened sticks, marshmallows toasting, the blaze flickering heat over her face and sending smoke billowing skyward. Eden found herself looking forward to the evening every bit as much as the youngest camper. With her head pillowed on her folded arms, she stared up at the ceiling while Candy paced.

"I'm sure we could do it, Eden."

"Hmm?"

"The dance." Gesturing with the clipboard she was carrying, Candy stopped at the foot of the bunk. "The dance I've been talking about having for the girls. Remember?"

"Of course." Eden forced her mind back to business. "What about it?"

"I think we should go ahead with it. In fact, if it works out, I think it should be an annual event." Even after she plopped herself down on Eden's bed, her enthusiasm continued to bounce around the room. "The boys' camp is only twenty miles from here. I'm sure they'd go for it."

"Probably." A dance. That would mean refreshments for somewhere close to a hundred, not to mention music, decorations. She thought first of the red ink in the ledger, then about how much the girls would enjoy it. There had to be a way around the red ink. "I guess there'd be room in the mess area if we moved the tables."

"Exactly. And most of the girls have records with them. We could have the boys bring some, too." She began to scrawl on her clipboard. "We can make the decorations ourselves."

"We'd have to keep the refreshments simple," Eden put in

before Candy's enthusiasm could run away with her. "Cookies, punch, that sort of thing."

"We can plan it for the last week of camp. Kind of a cele-brational send-off."

The last week of camp. How strange, when the first week had been so wearing, that the thought of it ending brought on both panic and regret. No, summer wouldn't last forever. In September there would be the challenge of finding a new job, a new goal. She wouldn't be going back to a teaching job as Candy was, but to want ads and résumés.

"Eden? Eden, what do you think?"

"About what?"

"About planning the dance for the last week of camp?"

"I think we'd better clear it with the boys' camp first."

"Honey, are you okay?" Leaning forward, Candy took Eden's hand. "Are you worried about going back home in a few weeks?"

"No. Concerned." She gave Candy's hand a squeeze. "Just concerned."

"I meant it when I told you not to worry about a job right away. My salary takes care of the rent on the apartment, and I still have a little piece of the nest egg my grandmother left me."

"I love you, Candy. You're the best friend I've ever had."

"The reverse holds true, Eden."

"For that reason, there's no way I'm going to sit around while you work to pay the rent and put dinner on the table. It's enough that you've let me move in with you."

"Eden, you know I'm a lot happier sharing my apartment with you than I was living alone. If you look at it as a favor, you're going to feel pressured, and that's ridiculous. Besides, for the past few months, you were taking care of fixing all the meals."

"Only a small portion of which were edible."

"True." Candy grinned. "But I didn't have to cook. Listen, give yourself a little space. You'll need some time to find out what it is you want to do."

"What I want to do is work." With a laugh, Eden lay back on the bed again. "Surprise. I really want to work, to keep busy, to earn a living. The past few weeks have shown me how much I enjoy taking care of myself. I'm banking on getting a job at a riding stable. Maybe even the one I used to board my horse at. And if that doesn't pan out—" She shrugged her shoulders. "I'll find something else."

"You will." Candy set the clipboard aside. "And next year, we'll have more girls, a bigger staff and maybe even a profit."

"Next year, I'm going to know how to make a hurricane lamp out of a tuna can."

"And a pillow out of two washcloths."

"And pot holders."

Candy remembered Eden's one mangled attempt. "Well, maybe you should take it slow."

"There's going to be no stopping me. In the meantime, I'll contact the camp director over at—what's the name, Hawk's Nest?"

"Eagle Rock," Candy corrected her, laughing. "It'll be fun for us, too, Eden. They have counselors. *Male* counselors." Sighing, she stretched her arms to the ceiling. "Do you know how long it's been since I've spoken with a man?"

"You talked to the electrician just last week."

"He was a hundred and two. I'm talking about a man who still has all his hair and teeth." She touched her tongue to her upper lip. "Not all of us have passed the time holding hands with a man in the stables."

Eden plumped up her excuse for a pillow. "I wasn't hold
ing hands. I explained to you."

"Roberta Snow, master spy, gave an entirely different story.
With her, it appears to be love at first sight."

Eden examined the pad of callus on the ridge of her palm.
"I'm sure she'll survive."

"Well, what about you?"

"I'll survive, too."

"No, I mean, aren't you interested?" After folding her legs
under her, Candy leaned forward. "Remember, darling, I got
a good look at the man when I was negotiating for the use of
his lake. I don't think there's a woman alive who wouldn'
sweat a bit after a look at those spooky green eyes."

"I never sweat."

Chuckling, Candy leaned back. "Eden, you're talking to
the one who loves you best. The man was interested enough
to track you down in the stables. Think of the possibilities."

"It's possible that he was returning Roberta's cap."

"And it's possible that pigs fly. Haven't you been tempted
to wander over by the orchard, just once?"

"No." Only a hundred times. "Seen one apple tree, you've
seen them all."

"The same doesn't hold true for an apple grower who's
about six-two, with a hundred and ninety well-placed pounds
and one of the most fascinating faces this side of the
Mississippi." Concern edged into her voice. She had watched
her friend suffer and had been helpless to do more than offer
emotional support. "Have fun, Eden. You deserve it."

"I don't think Chase Elliot falls into the category of fun."
Danger, she thought. Excitement, sexuality and, oh yes, temp
tation. Tossing her legs over the bunk, Eden walked to the win
dow. Moths were flapping at the screen.

"You're gun-shy."

"Maybe."

"Honey, you can't use Eric as a yardstick."

"I'm not." With a sigh, she turned back. "I'm not pining or brooding over him, either."

The quick shrug was Candy's way of dismissing someone she considered a weasel. "That's because you were never really in love with him."

"I was going to marry him."

"Because it seemed the proper thing to do. I know you, Eden, like no one else. Everything was very simple and easy with Eric. It all fit—click, click, click."

Amused, Eden shook her head. "Is something wrong with that?"

"Everything's wrong with that. Love makes you giddy and foolish and achy. You never felt any of that with Eric." She spoke from the experience of a woman who'd fallen in love, and out again, a dozen times before she'd hit twenty. "You would have married him, and maybe you would even have been content. His tastes were compatible with yours. His family mixed well with yours."

Amusement fled. "You make it sound so cold."

"It was. But you're not." Candy raised her hands, hoping she hadn't gone too far. "Eden, you were raised a certain way, to be a certain way; then the roof collapsed. I can only guess at how traumatic that was. You've picked yourself up, but still you've closed pieces of yourself off. Isn't it time you put the past behind you, really behind you?"

"I've been trying."

"I know, and you've made a good start, with the camp, with your outlook. Maybe it's time you started looking for a little more, just for yourself."

"A man?"

"Some companionship, some sharing, some affection. You're too smart to think that you need a man to make things work, but to cut them off because one acted like a weasel isn't the answer, either." She rubbed at a streak of red paint on her fingernail. "I guess I still believe that everyone needs someone."

"Maybe you're right. Right now I'm too busy pasting myself back together and enjoying the results. I'm not ready for complications. Especially when they're six foot two."

"You were always the romantic one, Eden. Remember the poetry you used to write?"

"We were children." Restless, Eden moved her shoulders. "I had to grow up."

"Growing up doesn't mean you have to stop dreaming." Candy rose. "We've started one dream here, together. I want to see you have other dreams."

"When the time's right." Touched, Eden kissed Candy's cheek. "We'll have your dance and charm your counselors."

"We could invite some neighbors, just to round things out."

"Don't press your luck." Laughing, Eden turned toward the door. "I'm going for a walk before I check on the horses. Leave the light on low, will you?"

The air was still, but not quiet. The first nights Eden had spent in the hills, the country quiet had disturbed her. Now, she could hear and appreciate the night music. The chorus of crickets in soprano, the tenor crying of an owl, the occasional bass lowing of the cows on a farm half a mile away all merged into a symphony accompanied by the rustling of small animals in the brush. The three-quarter moon and a galaxy of stars added soft light and dramatic shadows. The erratic yellow beams of an army of fireflies was a nightly light show.

As she strolled toward the lake, she heard the rushing song

of peepers over the softer sound of lapping water. The air smelled as steamy as it felt, so she rounded the edge of the lake toward the cooler cover of trees.

With her mind on her conversation with Candy, Eden bent to pluck a black-eyed Susan. Twisting the stem between her fingers, she watched the petals revolve around the dark center.

Had she been a romantic? There had been poetry, dreamy, optimistic poetry, often revolving around love. Troubadour love, she thought now. The sort that meant long, wistful glances, sterling sacrifices and purity. Romantic, but unrealistic, Eden admitted. She hadn't written any poetry in a long time.

Not since she had met Eric, Eden realized. She had gone from dreamy young girl to proper young woman, exchanging verses for silver patterns. Now both the dreamy girl and the proper woman were gone.

That was for the best, Eden decided, and she tossed her flower onto the surface of the lake. She watched it float lazily.

Candy had been right. It had not been a matter of love with Eric, but of fulfilling expectations. When he had turned his back on her, he had broken not her heart, but her pride. She was still repairing it.

Eric had given her a suitable diamond, sent her roses at the proper times and had never been at a loss for a clever compliment. That wasn't romance, Eden mused, and it certainly wasn't love. Perhaps she'd never really understood either.

Was romance white knights and pure maidens? Was it Chopin and soft lights? Was it the top of the Ferris wheel? Maybe she'd prefer the last after all. With a quiet laugh, Eden wrapped her arms around herself and held her face up to the stars.

"You should do that more often."

She whirled, one hand pressing against her throat. Chase stood a few feet away at the edge of the trees, the edge of the shadows. It flashed through her mind that this was the third time she had seen him and the third time he had taken her by surprise. It was a habit she wanted to break.

"Do you practice startling people, or is it a natural gift?"

"I can't remember it happening much before you." The fact was, he hadn't come up on her, but she on him. He'd been walking since dusk, and had stopped on the banks of the lake to watch the water and to think of her. "You've been getting some sun." Her hair seemed lighter, more fragile against the honeyed tone of her skin. He wanted to touch it, to see if it was still as soft and fragrant.

"Most of the work is outdoors." It amazed her that she had to fight the urge to turn and run. There was something mystical, even fanciful, about meeting him here in the moonlight, by the water. Almost as if it had been fated.

"You should wear a hat." He said it absently, distracted by the pounding of his own heart. She might have been an illusion, long slender arms and legs gleaming in the moonlight, her hair loose and drenched with it. She wore white. Even the simple shorts and shirt seemed to glimmer. "I'd wondered if you walked here."

He stepped out of the shadows. The monotonous song of the crickets seemed to reach a crescendo. "I thought it might be cooler."

"Some." He moved closer. "I've always been fond of hot nights."

"The cabins tend to get stuffy." Uneasy, she glanced back and discovered she had walked farther than she'd intended. The camp, with its comforting lights and company, was very far away. "I didn't realize I'd crossed over onto your property."

"I'm only a tyrant about my trees." She was less of an illusion up close, more of a woman. "You were laughing before. What were you thinking of?"

Her mouth was dry. Even as she backed away, he seemed to be closer. "Ferris wheels."

"Ferris wheels? Do you like the drop?" Satisfying his own need, he reached for her hair. "Or the climb?"

At his touch, her stomach shot down to her knees. "I have to get back."

"Let's walk."

To walk with you in the moonlight. Eden thought of his words, and of fate. "No, I can't. It's late."

"Must be all of nine-thirty." Amused, he took her hand, then immediately turned it over. There was a hardening ridge of calluses on the pad beneath her fingers. "You've been working."

"Some people make a living that way."

"Don't get testy." He turned her hand back to run a thumb over her knuckles. Was it a talent of his, Eden wondered, to touch a woman in the most casual of ways and send her blood pounding? "You could wear gloves," Chase went on, "and keep your Philadelphia hands."

"I'm not in Philadelphia." She drew her hand away. Chase simply took her other one. "And since I'm pitching hay rather than serving tea, it hardly seems to matter."

"You'll be serving tea again." He could see her, seated in some fussy parlor, wearing pink silk and holding a china pot. But, for the moment, her hand was warm in his. "The moon's on the water. Look."

Compelled, she turned her head. There were such things as moonbeams. They gilded the dark water of the lake and silvered the trees. She remembered some old legend about three women, the moonspinners, who spun the moon on spindles. More romance. But even the new, practical Eden couldn't resist.

"It's lovely. The moon seems so close."

"Some things aren't as close as they seem; others aren't so far away."

He began to walk. Because he still had her hand, and because he intrigued her, Eden walked with him. "I suppose you've always lived here." Just small talk, she told herself. She didn't really care.

"For the most part. This has always been headquarters for the business." He turned to look down at her. "The house is over a hundred years old. You might find it interesting."

She thought of her home and of the generations of Carlboughs who had lived there. And of the strangers who lived there now. "I like old houses."

"Are things going well at camp?"

She wouldn't think of the books. "The girls keep us busy." Her laugh came again, low and easy. "That's an understatement. We'll just say their energy level is amazing."

"How's Roberta?"

"Incorrigible."

"I'm glad to hear it."

"Last night she painted one of the girls while the girl was asleep."

"Painted?"

Eden's laugh came again, low and easy. "The little darling must have copped a couple of pots of paint from the art area. When Marcie woke up, she looked like an Indian preparing to attack a wagon train."

"Our Roberta's inventive."

"To say the least. She told me she thought it might be interesting to be the first woman chief justice."

He smiled at that. Imagination and ambition were the qualities he most admired. "She'll probably do it."

"I know. It's terrifying."

"Let's sit. You can see the stars better."

Stars? She'd nearly forgotten who she was with and why she had wanted to avoid being with him. "I don't think I—" Before she'd gotten the sentence out, he'd tugged her down on a soft, grassy rise. "One wonders why you bother to ask."

"Manners," he said easily as he slipped an arm around her shoulders. Even as she stiffened, he relaxed. "Look at the sky. How often do you notice it in the city?"

Unable to resist, she tilted her face up. The sky was an inky black backdrop for countless pinpoints of lights. They spread, winking, shivering, overhead with a glory that made Eden's throat ache just in the looking. "It isn't the same sky that's over the city."

"Same sky, Eden. It's people who change." He stretched out on his back, crossing his legs. "There's Cassiopeia."

"Where?" Curious, Eden searched, but saw only stars without pattern.

"You can see her better from here." He pulled her down beside him, and before she could protest, he was pointing. "There she is. Looks like a W this time of year."

"Yes!" Delighted, she reached for his wrist and outlined the constellation herself. "I've never been able to find anything in the sky."

"You have to look first. There's Pegasus." Chase shifted his arm. "He has a hundred and sixty-six stars you can view with the naked eye. See? He's flying straight up."

Eyes narrowed, she concentrated on finding the pattern. Moonlight splashed on her face. "Oh yes, I see." She shifted a bit closer to guide his hand again. "I named my first pony Pegasus. Sometimes I'd imagine he sprouted wings and flew. Show me another."

He was looking at her, at the way the stars reflected in her eyes, at the way her mouth softened so generously with a smile. "Orion," he murmured.

"Where?"

"He stands with his sword behind him and his shield lifted in front. And a red star, thousands of times brighter than the sun, is the shoulder of his sword arm."

"Where is he? I—" Eden turned her head and looked directly into Chase's eyes. She forgot the stars and the moonlight and the soft, sweet grass beneath her. The hand on his wrist tightened until the rhythm of his pulse was the rhythm of hers.

Her muscles contracted and held as she braced for the kiss. But his lips merely brushed against her temple. Warmth spread through her as softly as the scent of honeysuckle spread through the air. She heard an owl call out to the night, to the stars, or to a lover.

"What are we doing here?" she managed.

"Enjoying each other." Without rushing, his lips moved over her face.

Enjoying? That was much too mild a word for what was burning through her. No one had ever made her feel like this, so weak and hot, so strong and desperate. His lips were soft, the hand that rested on the side of her face was hard. Beneath his, her heart began to gallop uncontrolled. Eden's fingers slipped off the reins.

She turned her head with a moan and found his mouth with hers. Her arms went around him, holding him close as her lips parted in demand. In all her life she had never known true hunger, not until now. This was breathless, painful, glorious.

He'd never expected such unchecked passion. He'd been prepared to go slowly, gently, as the innocence he'd felt in her required. Now she was moving under him, her fingers pressing and kneading the muscles of his back, her mouth hot and willing on his. The patience that was so much a part of him drowned in need.

Such new, such exciting sensations. Her body gave as his pressed hard against it. Gods and goddesses of the sky guarded them. He smelled of the grass and the earth, and he tasted of fire. Night sounds roared in her head, and her own sigh was only a dim echo when his lips slid down to her throat.

Murmuring his name, Eden combed her fingers through his hair. He wanted to touch her, all of her. He wanted to take her now. When her hand came to rest on his face, he covered it with his own and felt the smooth stone of her ring.

There was so much more he needed to know. So little he was sure of. Desire, for the moment, couldn't be enough. Who was she? He lifted his head to look down at her. Who the hell was she, and why was she driving him mad?

Pulling himself back, he tried to find solid ground. "You're full of surprises, Eden Carlbough of the Philadelphia Carlboughs."

For a moment, she could only stare. She'd had her ride on the Ferris wheel, a wild, dizzying ride. Somewhere along the line, she'd been tossed off to spiral madly in the air. Now she'd hit the ground, hard. "Let me up."

"I can't figure you, Eden."

"You aren't required to." She wanted to weep, to curl up into a ball and weep, but she couldn't focus on the reason. Anger was clearer. "I asked you to let me up."

He rose, holding out a hand to help her. Ignoring it, Eden got to her feet. "I've always felt it was more constructive to shout when you're angry."

She shot him one glittering look. Humiliation. It was something she'd sworn she would never feel again. "I'm sure you do. If you'll excuse me."

"Damn it." He caught her arm and swung her back to face him. "Something was happening here tonight. I'm not fool enough to deny that, but I want to know what I'm getting into."

"We were enjoying each other. Wasn't that your term?" Nothing more, Eden repeated over and over in her head. Nothing more than a moment's enjoyment. "We've finished now, so good night."

"We're far from finished. That's what worries me."

"I'd say that's your problem, Chase." But a ripple of fear—of anticipation—raced through her, because she knew he was right.

"Yeah, it's my problem." My God, how had he passed so quickly from curiosity to attraction to blazing need? "And because it is, I've got a question. I want to know why Eden Carlbough is playing at camp for the summer rather than cruising the Greek Isles. I want to know why she's cleaning out stables instead of matching silver patterns and planning dinner parties as Mrs. Eric Keeton."

"My business." Her voice rose. The new Eden wasn't as good as the old one at controlling emotion. "But if you're so curious, why don't you call one of your family connections? I'm sure any of them would be delighted to give you all the details."

"I'm asking you."

"I don't owe you any explanations." She jerked her arm away and stood trembling with rage. "I don't owe you a damn thing."

"Maybe not." His temper had cooled his passion and cleared his head. "But I want to know who I'm making love with."

"That won't be an issue, I promise you."

"We're going to finish what we started here, Eden." Without stepping closer, he had her arm again. The touch was far from gentle, far from patient. "That I promise you."

"Consider it finished."

To her surprise and fury, he only smiled. His hand eased on her arm to one lingering caress. Helpless against her response, she shivered. "We both know better than that." He touched a finger to her lips, as if reminding her what tastes he'd left there. "Think of me."

He slipped back into the shadows.

Chapter 4

It was a perfect night for a bonfire. Only a few wispy clouds dragged across the moon, shadowing it, then freeing it. The heat of the day eased with sunset, and the air was balmy, freshened by a calm, steady breeze.

The pile of twigs and sticks that had been gathered throughout the day had been stacked, tepeelike, in a field to the east of the main compound. In the clearing, it rose from a wide base to the height of a man. Every one of the girls had contributed to the making of it, just as every one of them circled around the bonfire now, waiting for the fire to catch and blaze. An army of hot dogs and marshmallows was laid out on a picnic table. Stacked like swords were dozens of cleaned and sharpened sticks. Nearby was the garden hose with a tub full of water, for safety's sake.

Candy held up a long kitchen match, drawing out the drama as the girls began to cheer. "The first annual bonfire at

Camp Liberty is about to begin. Secure your hot dogs to your sticks, ladies, and prepare to roast."

Amid the giggles and gasps, Candy struck the match, then held it to the dry kindling at the base. Wood crackled. Flames licked, searched for more fuel, and spread around and around, following the circle of starter fluid. As they watched, fire began its journey up and up. Eden applauded with the rest.

"Fabulous!" Even as she watched, smoke began to billow. Its scent was the scent of autumn, and that was still a summer away. "I was terrified we wouldn't get it started."

"You're looking at an expert." Catching her tongue between her teeth, Candy speared a hot dog with a sharpened stick. Behind her, the bonfire glowed red at the center. "The only thing I was worried about was rain. But just look at those stars. It's perfect."

Eden tilted her head back. Without effort, without thought, she found Pegasus. He was riding the night sky just as he'd been riding it twenty-four hours before. One day, one night. How could so much have happened? Standing with her face lifted to the breeze and her hands growing warm from the fire, she wondered if she had really experienced that wild, turbulent moment with Chase.

She had. The memories were too ripe, too real for dreams. The moment had happened, and all the feelings and sensations that had grown from it. Deliberately she turned her gaze to a riot of patternless stars.

It didn't change what she remembered, or what she still felt. The moment had happened, she thought again, and it had passed. Yet, somehow, she wasn't certain it was over.

"Why does everything seem different here, Candy?"

"Everything *is* different here." Candy took a deep breath, drawing in the scents of smoke, drying grass and roasting meat. "Isn't it marvelous? No stuffy parlors, no boring dinner parties, no endless piano recitals. Want a hot dog?"

Because her mouth was watering, Eden accepted the partially blackened wiener. "You simplify things, Candy." Eden ran a thin line of ketchup along the meat and stuck it in a bun. "I wish I could."

"You will once you stop thinking you're letting down the Carlbough name by enjoying a hot dog by a bonfire." When Eden's mouth dropped open, Candy gave her a friendly pat. "You ought to try the marshmallows," she advised before she wandered off to find another stick.

Is that what she was doing? Eden wondered, chewing automatically. Maybe, in a way that wasn't quite as basic as Candy had said, it was. After all, she had been the one who had sold the house that had been in the family for four generations. In the end, it had been she who had inventoried the silver and china, the paintings and the jewelry for auction. So, in the end, it had been she who had liquidated the Carlbough tradition to pay off debts and to start a new life.

Necessary. No matter how the practical Eden accepted the necessity, the grieving Eden still felt the loss, and the guilt.

With a sigh, Eden stepped back. The scene that played out in front of her was like a memory from her own childhood. She could see the column of gray smoke rising toward the sky, twirling and curling. At the core of the tower of wood, the fire was fiercely gold and greedy. The smell of outdoor cooking was strong and summery, as it had been during her own weeks at Camp Forden for Girls. For a moment, there was regret that she couldn't step back into those memories of a time when life was simple and problems were things for parents to fix.

"Miss Carlbough."

Brought out of a half-formed dream, Eden glanced down at Roberta. "Hello, Roberta. Are you having fun?"

"It's super!" Roberta's enthusiasm was evident from the smear of ketchup on her chin. "Don't you like bonfires?"

"Yes, I do." Smiling, she looked back at the crackling wood, one hand dropping automatically to Roberta's shoulder. "I like them a lot."

"I thought you looked sort of sad, so I made you a marshmallow."

The offering dripped, black and shriveled, from the end of a stick. Eden felt her throat close up the same way it had when another girl had offered her a clutch of wildflowers. "Thanks, Roberta. I wasn't sad really, I was just remembering." Gingerly, Eden pulled the melted, mangled marshmallow from the stick. Half of it plopped to the ground on the way to her mouth.

"They're tricky," Roberta observed. "I'll make you another one."

Left with the charred outer hull, Eden swallowed valiantly. "You don't have to bother, Roberta."

"Oh, I don't mind." She looked up at Eden with a glowing, generous grin. Somehow, all her past crimes didn't seem so important. "I like to do it. I thought camp was going to be boring, but it's not. Especially the horses. Miss Carlbough…" Roberta looked down at the ground and seemed to draw her courage out of her toes. "I guess I'm not as good as Linda with the horses, but I wondered if maybe you could—well, if I could spend some more time at the stables."

"Of course you can, Roberta." Eden rubbed her thumb and forefinger together, trying fruitlessly to rid herself of the goo. "And you don't even have to bribe me with marshmallows."

"Really?"

"Yes, really." Attracted despite herself, Eden ruffled Roberta's hair. "Miss Bartholomew and I will work it into your schedule."

"Gee, thanks, Miss Carlbough."

"But you'll have to work on your posting."

Roberta's nose wrinkled only a little. "Okay. But I wish we could do stuff like barrel racing. I've seen it on TV."

"Well, I don't know about that, but you might progress to small jumps before the end of camp."

Eden had the pleasure of seeing Roberta's eyes saucer with pleasure. "No fooling?"

"No fooling. As long as you work on your posting."

"I will. And I'll be better than Linda, too. Wow, jumps." She spun in an awkward pirouette. "Thanks a lot, Miss Carlbough. Thanks a lot."

She was off in a streak, undoubtedly to spread the word. If Eden knew Roberta, and she was beginning to, she was certain the girl would soon have talked herself into a gold medal for equestrian prowess at the next Olympic Games.

But, as she watched Roberta spin from group to group, Eden realized she wasn't thinking of the past any longer; nor was she regretting. She was smiling. As one of the counselors began to strum a guitar, Eden licked marshmallow goop from her fingers.

"Need some help with that?"

With her fingers still in her mouth, Eden turned. She should have known he'd come. Perhaps, in her secret thoughts, she had hoped he would. Now she found herself thrusting her still-sticky fingers behind her back.

He wondered if she knew how lovely she looked, with the fire at her back and her hair loose on her shoulders. There was a frown on her face now, but he hadn't missed that one quick flash of pleasure. If he kissed her now, would he taste that sweet, sugary flavor she had been licking from her fingers? Through it would he find that simmering, waiting heat he'd tasted once before? The muscles in his stomach tightened, even as he dipped his thumbs into his pockets and looked away from her toward the fire.

"Nice night for a bonfire."

"Candy claims she arranged it that way." Confident there was enough distance between them, and that there were enough people around them, Eden allowed herself to relax. "We weren't expecting any company."

"I spotted your smoke."

That made her glance up and realize how far the smoke might travel. "I hope it didn't worry you. We notified the fire department." Three girls streaked by behind them. Chase glanced their way and had them lapsing into giggles. Eden caught her tongue in her cheek. "How long did it take you to perfect it?"

With a half smile, Chase turned back to her. "What?"

"The deadly charm that has females crumpling at your feet?"

"Oh, that." He grinned at her. "I was born with it."

The laugh came out before she could stop it. To cover her lapse, Eden crossed her arms and took a step backward. "It's getting warm."

"We used to have a bonfire on the farm every Halloween. My father would carve the biggest pumpkin in the patch and stuff some overalls and a flannel shirt with straw. One year he dressed himself up as the Headless Horseman and gave every kid in the neighborhood a thrill." Watching the fire, he remembered and wondered why until tonight he hadn't thought of continuing the tradition. "My mother would give each of the kids a caramel apple, then we'd sit around the fire and tell ghost stories until we'd scared ourselves silly. Looking back, I think my father got a bigger kick out of it than any of us kids."

She could see it, just as he described, and had to smile again. For her, Halloween had been tidy costume parties where she'd dressed as a princess or ballerina. Though the memories were still lovely, she couldn't help wishing she'd seen one of the bonfires and the Headless Horseman.

"When we were planning tonight, I was as excited as any of the girls. I guess that sounds foolish."

"No, it sounds promising." He put a hand to her cheek, turning her slightly toward him. Though she stiffened, her skin was warm and soft. "Did you think of me?"

There it was again—that feeling of drowning, of floating, of going under for the third time. "I've been busy." She told herself to move away, but her legs didn't respond. The sound of singing and strumming seemed to be coming from off in the distance, with melody and lyrics she couldn't quite remember. The only thing that was close and real was his hand on her cheek.

"I-it was nice of you to drop by," she began, struggling to find solid ground again.

"Am I being dismissed?" He moved his hand casually from her cheek to her hair.

"I'm sure you have better things to do." His fingertip skimmed the back of her neck and set every nerve end trembling. "Stop."

The smoke billowed up over her head. Light and shadow created by the fire danced over her face and in her eyes. He'd thought of her, Chase reminded himself. Too much. Now he could only think what it would be like to make love with her near the heat of the fire, with the scent of smoke, and night closing in.

"You haven't walked by the lake."

"I told you, I've been busy." Why couldn't she make her voice firm and cool? "I have a responsibility to the girls, and the camp, and—"

"Yourself?" How badly he wanted to walk with her again, to study the stars and talk. How badly he wanted to taste that passion and that innocence again. "I'm a very patient man, Eden. You can only avoid me for so long."

"Longer than you think," she murmured, letting out a sigh of relief as she spotted Roberta making a beeline for them.

"Hi!" Delighted with the quick fluttering of her heart, Roberta beamed up at Chase.

"Hi, Roberta," he said. She was thrilled that he'd remembered her name. He gave her a smile, and his attention, without releasing Eden's hair. "You're taking better care of your cap, I see."

She laughed and pushed up the brim. "Miss Carlbough said if I wandered into your orchard again, she'd hold my cap for ransom. But if you invited us to come on a tour, that would be educational, wouldn't it?"

"Roberta." Why was it the child was always one step ahead of everyone else? Eden lifted her brow in a quelling look.

"Well, Miss Bartholomew said we should think of interesting things." Roberta put her most innocent look to good use. "And I think the apple trees are interesting."

"Thanks." Chase thought he heard Eden's teeth clench. "We'll give it some thought."

"Okay." Satisfied, Roberta stuck out a wrinkled black tube. "I made you a hot dog. You have to have a hot dog at a bonfire."

"Looks terrific." Accepting it, he pleased Roberta by taking a generous bite. "Thanks." Only Chase and his stomach knew that the meat was still cold on the inside.

"I got some marshmallows and sticks, too." She handed them over. "It's more fun to do it yourself, I guess." Because she was on the border between childhood and womanhood, Roberta picked up easily on the vibrations around her. "If you two want to be alone, you know, to kiss and stuff, no one's in the stables."

"Roberta!" Eden pulled out her best camp director's voice. "That will do."

"Well, my parents like to be alone sometimes." Undaunted, she grinned at Chase. "Maybe I'll see you around."

"You can count on it, kid." As Roberta danced off toward a group of girls, Chase turned back. The moment he took a step toward her, Eden extended her skewered marshmallow toward the fire. "Want to go kiss and stuff?"

It was the heat of the fire that stung her cheeks with color, Eden assured herself. "I suppose you think it would be terribly amusing for Roberta to go home and report that one of the camp directors spent her time in the stables with a man. That would do a lot for Camp Liberty's reputation."

"You're right. You should come to my place."

"Go away, Chase."

"I haven't finished my hot dog. Have dinner with me."

"I've had a hot dog already, thank you."

"I'll make sure hot dogs aren't on the menu. We can talk about it tomorrow."

"We will not talk about it tomorrow." It was anger that made her breathless, just as it was anger that made her unwise enough to turn toward him. "We will not talk about anything tomorrow."

"Okay. We won't talk." To show how reasonable he was, he bent down and closed the conversation, his mouth covering hers. He wasn't holding her, but it took her brain several long, lazy seconds before it accepted the order to back away.

"Don't you have any sense of propriety?" she managed in a strangled voice.

"Not much." He made up his mind, looking down at her eyes, dazed and as blue as his lake, that he wasn't going to take no for an answer—to any question. "We'll make it about nine tomorrow morning at the entrance to the orchard."

"Make what?"

"The tour." He grinned and handed her his stick. "It'll be educational."

Though she was in an open field, Eden felt her back press into a corner. "We have no intention of disrupting your routine."

"No problem. I'll pass it on to your co-director before I go back. That way, you'll be sure to be coordinated."

Eden took a long breath. "You think you're very clever, don't you?"

"Thorough, just thorough, Eden. By the way, your marshmallow's on fire."

With his hands in his pockets, he strolled off while she blew furiously on the flaming ball.

She'd hoped for rain but was disappointed. The morning dawned warm and sunny. She'd hoped for support but was faced with Candy's enthusiasm for a field trip through one of the most prestigious apple orchards in the country. The girls were naturally delighted with any shift in schedule, so as they walked as a group the short distance to the Elliot farm, Eden found herself separated from the excitement.

"You could try not to look as though you're walking to the guillotine." Candy plucked a scrawny blue flower from the side of the road and stuck it in her hair. "This is a wonderful opportunity—for the girls," she added quickly.

"You managed to convince me of that, or else I wouldn't be here."

"Grumpy."

"I'm not grumpy," Eden countered. "I'm annoyed at being manipulated."

"Just a small piece of advice." Picking another flower, Candy twirled it. "If I'd been manipulated by a man, I'd make certain he believed it was my idea in the first place. Don't you think it would throw him off if you walked up to the gates with a cheery smile and boundless enthusiasm?"

"Maybe." Eden mulled the idea over until her lips began to curve. "Yes, maybe."

"There now. With a little practice, you'll find out that deviousness is much better in some cases than dignity."

"I wouldn't have needed either if you'd let me stay behind."

"Darling, unless I miss my guess, a certain apple baron would have plucked you up from whatever corner you'd chosen to hide in, tossed you over his wonderfully broad shoulder and dragged you along on our little tour, like it or not." Pausing, Candy let a sigh escape. "Now that I think about it, that would have been more exciting."

Because she was well able to picture it herself, Eden's mood hardened again. "At least I thought I could count on support from my best friend."

"And you can. Absolutely." With easy affection, Candy draped an arm over Eden's shoulder. "Though why you think you need my support when you have a gorgeous man giving you smoldering kisses, I can't imagine."

"That's just it!" Because several young heads turned when she raised her voice, Eden fought for calm again. "He had no business pulling something like that in front of everyone."

"I suppose it is more fun in private."

"Keep this up, and you may find that garter snake in your underwear yet."

"Just ask him if he's got a brother, or a cousin. Even an uncle. Ah, here we are," she continued before Eden could reply. "Now smile and be charming, just like you were taught."

"You're going to pay for this," Eden promised her in an under-tone. "I don't know how, I don't know when, but you'll pay."

They brought the group to a halt when the road forked. On the left were stone pillars topped with an arching wrought-iron sign that read ELLIOT. Sloping away from the pillars was a wall a foot thick and high as a man. It was old and sturdy, proving to Eden that the penchant for privacy hadn't begun with Chase.

The entrance road, smooth and well-maintained, ribboned back over the crest of a hill before it disappeared. Along the road were trees, not apple but oak, older and sturdier than the wall.

It was the continuity that drew her, the same symmetry she had seen and admired in the groves. The stone, the trees, even the road, had been there for generations. Looking, Eden understood his pride in them. She, too, had once had a legacy.

Then he strode from behind the wall and she fought back even that small sense of a common ground.

In a T-shirt and jeans, he looked lean and capable. There was a faint sheen of sweat on his arms that made her realize he'd already been working that morning. Drawn against her will, she dropped her gaze to his hands, hands that were hard and competent and unbearably gentle on a woman's skin.

"Morning, ladies." He swung the gates open for them.

"Oh Lord, he's something," Eden heard one of the counselors mumble. Remembering Candy's advice, she straightened her shoulders and fixed on her most cheerful smile.

"This is Mr. Elliot, girls. He owns the orchards we'll tour today. Thank you for inviting us, Mr. Elliot."

"My pleasure—Miss Carlbough."

The girlish murmurs of agreement became babbles of excitement as a dog sauntered to Chase's side. His fur was the color of apricots and glistened as though it had been polished in the sunlight. The big, sad eyes studied the group of girls before the dog pressed against Chase's leg. Eden had time to think that a smaller man might have been toppled. The dog was no less than three feet high at the shoulder. More of a young lion than a house pet, she thought. When he settled to sit at Chase's feet, Chase didn't have to bend to lay a hand on the dog's head.

"This is Squat. Believe it or not, he was the runt of his litter. He's a little shy."

Candy gave a sigh of relief when she saw the enormous tail thump the ground. "But friendly, right?"

"Squat's a pushover for females." His gaze circled the group. "Especially so many pretty ones. He was hoping he could join the tour."

"He's neat." Roberta made up her mind instantly. Walking forward, she gave the dog's head a casual pat. "I'll walk with you, Squat."

Agreeable, the dog rose to lead the way.

There was more to the business of apples than Eden had imagined. It wasn't all trees and plump fruit to be plucked and piled into baskets for market. Harvesting wasn't limited to autumn with the variety of types that were planted. The season, Chase explained, had been extended into months, from early summer to late fall.

They weren't just used for eating and baking. Even cores and peelings were put to use for cider, or dried and shipped to

Europe for certain champagnes. As they walked, the scent of ripening fruit filled the air, making more than one mouth water.

The Tree of Life, Eden thought as the scent tempted her. Forbidden fruit. She kept herself surrounded by girls and tried to remember that the tour was educational.

He explained that the quick-maturing trees were planted in the forty-foot spaces between the slow growers, then cut out when the space was needed. A practical business, she remembered, organized, with a high level of utility and little waste. Still, it had the romance of apple blossoms in spring.

Masses of laborers harvested the summer fruit. While they watched the men and machines at work, Chase answered questions.

"They don't look ripe," Roberta commented.

"They're full-size." Chase rested a hand on her shoulder as he chose an apple. "The changes that take place after the fruit's reached maturity are mainly chemical. It goes on without the tree. The fruit's hard, but the seeds are brown. Look." Using a pocketknife with casual skill, he cut the fruit in half. "The apples we harvest now are superior to the ones that hang longer." Reading Roberta's expression correctly, Chase tossed her half the fruit. The other half Squat took in one yawning bite.

"Maybe you'd like to pick some yourself." The reaction was positive, and Chase reached up to demonstrate. "Twist the fruit off the stem. You don't want to break the twig and lose bearing wood."

Before Eden could react, the girls had scattered to nearby trees. She was facing Chase. Perhaps it was the way his lips curved. Perhaps it was the way his eyes seemed so content to rest on hers, but her mind went instantly and completely blank.

"You have a fascinating business." She could have kicked herself for the inanity of it.

"I like it."

"I, ah…" There must be a question, an intelligent question, she could ask. "I suppose you ship the fruit quickly to avoid spoilage."

He doubted that either of them gave two hoots about apples at the moment, but he was willing to play the game. "It's stored right after picking at thirty-two degrees Fahrenheit. I like your hair pulled back like that. It makes me want to tug on the string and watch it fall all over your shoulders."

Her pulse began to sing, but she pretended she hadn't heard. "I'm sure you have various tests to determine quality."

"We look for richness." Slowly, he turned the fruit over in his hand, but his gaze roamed to her mouth. "Flavor." He watched her lips part as if to taste. "Firmness," he murmured, as he circled her throat with his free hand. "Tenderness."

Her breath seemed to concentrate, to sweeten into the sound of a sigh. It was almost too late when she bit it off. "It would be best if we stuck to the subject at hand."

"Which subject?" His thumb traced along her jawline.

"Apples."

"I'd like to make love with you in the orchards, Eden, with the sun warm on your face and the grass soft at your back."

It terrified her that she could almost taste what it would be like, to be with him, alone. "If you'll excuse me."

"Eden." He took her hand, knowing he was pushing too hard, too fast, but unable to stop himself. "I want you. Maybe too much."

Though his voice was low, hardly more than a whisper, she felt her nerves jangling. "You should know you can't say those things to me here, now. If the children—"

"Have dinner with me."

"No." On this, she told herself she would stand firm. She would not be manipulated. She would not be maneuvered. "I have a job, Chase, one that runs virtually twenty-four hours a day for the next few weeks. Even if I wanted to have dinner with you, which I don't, it would be impossible."

He considered all this reasonable. But then, a great many smoke screens were. "Are you afraid to be alone with me? Really alone."

The truth was plain and simple. She ignored it. "You flatter yourself."

"I doubt a couple hours out of an evening would disrupt the camp's routine, or yours."

"You don't know anything about the camp's routine."

"I know that between your partner and the counselors, the girls are more than adequately supervised. And I know that your last riding lesson is at four o'clock."

"How did you—"

"I asked Roberta," he said easily. "She told me you have supper at six, then a planned activity or free time from seven to nine. Lights-out is at ten. You usually spend your time after supper with the horses. And sometimes you ride out at night when you think everyone's asleep."

She opened her mouth, then shut it again, having no idea what to say. She had thought those rides exclusively hers, exclusively private.

"Why do you ride out alone at night, Eden?"

"Because I enjoy it."

"Then tonight you can enjoy having dinner with me."

She tried to remember there were girls beneath the trees around them. She tried to remember that a display of temper was most embarrassing for the person who lost control. "Perhaps you have some difficulty understanding a polite refusal. Why don't we try this? The last place I want to be tonight, or at any other time, is with you."

He moved his shoulders before he took a step closer. "I guess we can just settle all this now. Here."

"You wouldn't…" She didn't bother to finish the thought. By now she knew very well what he would dare. One quick look around showed her that Roberta and Marcie were leaning against the trunk of a tree, happily munching apples and enjoying the show. "All right, stop it." So much for not being manipulated. "I have no idea why you insist on having dinner with someone who finds you so annoying."

"Me, either. We'll discuss it tonight. Seven-thirty." Tossing Eden the apple, he strolled over toward Roberta.

Eden hefted the fruit. She even went so far as to draw a mental bull's-eye on the back of his head. With a sound of disgust, she took a hefty bite instead.

Chapter 5

Vengefully, Eden dragged a brush through her hair. Despite the harsh treatment, it sprang back softly to wisp around her face and wave to her shoulders. She wouldn't go to any trouble as she had for other dates and dinners, but leave it loose and unstyled. Though he was undoubtedly too hardheaded to notice that sort of female subtlety.

She didn't bother with jewelry, except for the simple pearl studs she often wore around camp. In an effort to look cool, even prim, she wore a high-necked white blouse, regretting only the lace at the cuffs. Matching it with a white skirt, she tried for an icy look. The result was an innocent fragility she couldn't detect in the one small mirror on the wall.

Intending on making it plain that she had gone to no trouble for Chase's benefit, she almost ignored makeup. Grumbling to herself, Eden picked up her blusher. Basic feminine vanity, she admitted; then she added a touch of clear gloss to her lips. There was, after all, a giant step between not fussing and looking like a hag. She was reaching for her bottle of perfume before she stopped herself. No, that was definitely fussing. He would get soap, and soap only. She turned away from the mirror just as Candy swung through the cabin door.

"Wow." Stopping in the doorway, Candy took a long, critical look. "You look terrific."

"I do?" Brow creased, Eden turned back to the mirror. "Terrific wasn't exactly what I was shooting for. I wanted something along the lines of prim."

"You couldn't look prim if you wore sackcloth and ashes, any more than I could look delicate even with lace at my wrists."

With a sound of disgust, Eden tugged at the offending lace. "I knew it. I just knew it was a mistake. Maybe I can rip it off."

"Don't you dare." Laughing, Candy bounded into the room to stop Eden from destroying her blouse. "Besides, it isn't the clothes that are important. It's the attitude, right?"

Eden gave the lace a last tug. "Right. Candy, are you sure everything's going to be under control here? I could still make excuses."

"Everything's already under control." Candy flopped down on her bunk, then began to peel the banana she held. "In fact, things are great. I've just taken a five-minute break to see you off and stuff my face." She took a big bite to prove her point. "Then," she continued over a mouthful of banana, "we're getting together in the mess area to take an inventory of our record collection for the dance. The girls want some practice time before the big night."

"You could probably use extra supervision."

Candy waved her half-eaten banana. "Everyone's going to be in the same four walls for the next couple of hours. You go enjoy your dinner and stop worrying. Where are you going?"

"I don't know." She stuffed some tissue in her bag. "And I really don't care."

"Come on, after nearly six weeks of wholesome but god-awful boring food, aren't you just a little excited about the prospect of oysters Rockefeller or escargots?"

"No." She began to clasp and unclasp her bag. "I'm only going because it was simpler than creating a scene."

Candy broke off a last bite of banana. "Certainly knows how to get his own way, doesn't he?"

"That's about to end." Eden closed her purse with a snap. "Tonight."

At the sound of an approaching car, Candy propped herself up on an elbow. She noticed Eden nervously biting her lower lip, but she only gestured toward the door with her banana peel. "Well, good luck."

Eden caught the grin and paused, her hand on the screen door. "Whose side are you on, anyway?"

"Yours, Eden." Candy stretched, and prepared to go rock and roll. "Always."

"I'll be back early."

Candy grinned, wisely saying nothing as the screen door slammed shut.

However hard Eden might have tried to look remote, icy, disinterested, the breath clogged up in Chase's lungs the moment she stepped outside. They were still an hour from twilight, and the sun's last rays shot through her hair. Her skirt swirled around bare legs honey-toned after long days outdoors. Her chin was lifted, perhaps in anger, perhaps in defiance. He could only see the elegant line of her throat.

The same slowly drumming need rose up inside him the moment she stepped onto the grass.

She'd expected him to look less...dangerous in more formal attire. Eden discovered she had underestimated him again. The muscles in his arms and shoulders weren't so much restricted as enhanced by the sports jacket. The shirt, either by design or good fortune, matched his eyes and was left open at the throat. Slowly and easily he smiled at her, and her lips curved in automatic response.

"I imagined you looking like this." In truth, he hadn't been sure she would come, or what he might have done if she had locked herself away in one of the cabins and refused to see him. "I'm glad you didn't disappoint me."

Feeling her resolve weaken, Eden made an effort to draw back. "I made a bargain," she began, only to fall silent when he handed her a bunch of anemones freshly picked from the side of the road. He wasn't supposed to be sweet, she reminded herself. She wasn't supposed to be vulnerable to sweetness. Still, unable to resist, she buried her face in the flowers.

That was a picture he would carry with him forever, Chase realized. Eden, with wildflowers clutched in both hands; her eyes, touched with both pleasure and confusion, watching him over the petals.

"Thank you."

"You're welcome." Taking one of her hands, he brought it to his lips. She should have pulled away. She knew she should. Yet there was something so simple, so right in the moment— as if she recognized it from some long-ago dream. Bemused, Eden took a step closer, but the sound of giggling brought her out of the spell.

Immediately she tried to pull her hand away. "The girls." She glanced around quickly enough to catch the fielder's cap as it disappeared around the corner of the building.

"Well, then, we wouldn't want to disappoint them?" Turning

her hand over, Chase pressed a kiss to her palm. Eden felt the heat spread.

"You're being deliberately difficult." But she closed her hand as if to capture the sensation and hold it.

"Yes." He smiled, but resisted the impulse to draw her into his arms and enjoy the promise he'd seen so briefly in her eyes.

"If you'd let me go, I'd like to put the flowers in water."

"I'll do it." Candy left her post by the door and came outside. Even Eden's glare didn't wipe the smile from her face. "They're lovely, aren't they? Have a good time."

"We'll do that." Chase linked his fingers with Eden's and drew her toward his car. She told herself the sun had been in her eyes. Why else would she have missed the low-slung white Lamborghini parked beside the cabin. She settled herself in the passenger's seat with a warning to herself not to relax.

The moment the engine sprang to life, there was a chorus of goodbyes. Every girl and counselor had lined up to wave them off. Eden disguised a chuckle with a cough.

"It seems this is one of the camp's highlights this summer."

Chase lifted a hand out of the open window to wave back. "Let's see if we can make it one of ours."

Something in his tone made her glance over just long enough to catch that devil of a smile. Eden made up her mind then and there. No, she wouldn't relax, but she'd be damned if she'd be intimidated either. "All right." She leaned back in her seat, prepared to make the best of a bad deal. "I haven't had a meal that wasn't served on a tray in weeks."

"I'll cancel the trays."

"I'd appreciate it." She laughed, then assured herself that laughing wasn't really relaxing. "Stop me if I start stacking the silverware." The breeze blowing in the open window was warm and as fresh as the flowers Chase had brought her. Eden allowed herself the pleasure of lifting her face to it. "This is nice, especially when I was expecting a pickup truck."

"Even country bumpkins can appreciate a well-made machine."

"That's not what I meant." Ready with an apology, she turned, but saw he was smiling. "I suppose you wouldn't care if it was."

"I know what I am, what I want and what I can do." As he took a curve he slowed. His eyes met hers briefly. "But the opinions of certain people always matter. In any case, I prefer the mountains to traffic jams. What do you prefer, Eden?"

"I haven't decided." That was true, she realized with a jolt. In a matter of weeks her priorities, and her hopes, had changed direction. Musing on that, she almost missed the arching ELLIOT sign when Chase turned between the columns. "Where are we going?"

"To dinner."

"In the orchard?"

"In my house." With that he changed gears and had the car cruising up the gravel drive.

Eden tried to ignore the little twist of apprehension she felt. True, this wasn't the crowded, and safe, restaurant she had imagined. She'd shared private dinners before, hadn't she? She'd been raised from the cradle to know how to handle any social situation. But the apprehension remained. Dinner alone with Chase wouldn't be, couldn't possibly be, like any other experience.

Even as she was working out a polite protest, the car crested the hill. The house rose into view.

It was stone. She couldn't know it was local stone, quarried from the mountains. She saw only that it was old, beautifully weathered. At first glance, it gave the appearance of being gray, but on a closer look colors glimmered through. Amber, russet, tints of green and umber. The sun was still high enough to make the chips of mica and quartz glisten. There were three stories, with the second overhanging the first by a skirting balcony. Eden could see flashes of red and buttercup yellow from the pots of geraniums and marigolds. She caught the scent of lavender even before she saw the rock garden.

A wide, sweeping stone stairway, worn slightly in the center, led to double glass doors of diamond panes. A redwood barrel was filled with pansies that nodded in the early evening breeze.

It was nothing like what she had expected, and yet...the house, and everything about it, was instantly recognizable.

His own nervousness caught Chase off guard. Eden said nothing when he stopped the car, still nothing when he got out to round the hood and open her door. It mattered, more than he had ever imagined it could, what she thought, what she said, what she felt about his home.

She held her hand out for his in a gesture he knew was automatic. Then she stood beside him, looking at what was his, what had been his even before his birth. Tension lodged in the back of his neck.

"Oh, Chase, it's beautiful." She lifted her free hand to shield her eyes from the sun behind the house. "No wonder you love it."

"My great-grandfather built it." The tension had dissolved without his being aware of it. "He even helped quarry the stone. He wanted something that would last and that would carry a piece of him as long as it did."

She thought of the home that had been her family's for generations, feeling the too-familiar burning behind her eyes. She'd lost that. Sold it. The need to tell him was almost stronger than pride, because in that moment she thought he might understand.

He felt her change in mood even before he glanced down and saw the glint of tears in her eyes. "What is it, Eden?"

"Nothing." No, she couldn't tell him. Some wounds were best left hidden. Private. "I was just thinking how important some traditions are."

"You still miss your father."

"Yes." Her eyes were dry now, the moment past. "I'd love to see inside."

He hesitated a moment, knowing there had been more and that she'd been close to sharing it with him. He could wait, Chase told himself, though his patience was beginning to fray. He would have to wait until she took that step toward him rather than away from him.

With her hand still in his, he climbed the steps to the door. On the other side lay a mountain of apricot fur known as Squat. Even after Chase opened the door, the mound continued to snore.

"Are you sure you should have such a vicious watchdog unchained?"

"My theory is most burglars wouldn't have the nerve to step over him." Catching Eden around the waist, Chase lifted her up and over.

The stone insulated well against the heat, so the hall was cool and comfortable. High, beamed ceilings gave the illusion of unlimited space. A Monet landscape caught her eye, but before she could comment on it, Chase was leading her through a set of mahogany doors.

The room was cozily square, with window seats recessed into the east and west walls. Instantly Eden could imagine the charm of watching the sun rise or set. Comfort was the theme of the room, with its range of blues from the palest aqua to the deepest indigo. Hand-hooked rugs set off the American antiques. There were fresh flowers here, too, spilling out of a Revere Ware bowl. It was a touch she hadn't expected from a bachelor, particularly one who worked with his hands.

Thoughtful, she crossed the room to the west window. The slanting sun cast long shadows over the buildings he had taken them through that morning. She remembered the conveyor belts, the busy sorters and packers, the noise. Behind her was a small, elegant room with pewter bowls and wild roses.

Peace and challenge, she realized, and she sighed without knowing why. "I imagine it's lovely when the sun starts to drop."

"It's my favorite view." His voice came from directly behind her, but for once she didn't stiffen when he rested his hands on her shoulders. He tried to tell himself it was just coincidence that she had chosen to look out that window, but he could almost believe that his own need for her to see and understand had guided her there. It wouldn't be wise to forget who she was and how she chose to live. "There's no Symphony Hall or Rodin Museum."

His fingers gently massaged the curve of her shoulders. But his voice wasn't as patient. Curious, she turned. His hands shifted to let her slide through, then settled on her shoulders again. "I don't imagine they're missed. If they were, you could visit, then come back to this." Without thinking, she lifted her hand to brush the hair from his forehead. Even as she caught herself, his hand closed around her wrist. "Chase, I—"

"Too late," he murmured; then he kissed each of her fingers, one by one. "Too late for you. Too late for me."

She couldn't allow herself to believe that. She couldn't accept the softening and opening of her emotions. How badly she wanted to let him in, to trust again, to need again. How terrifying it was to be vulnerable. "Please don't do this. It's a mistake for both of us."

"You're probably right." He was almost sure of it himself. But he brushed his lips over the pulse that hammered in her wrist. He didn't give a damn. "Everyone's entitled to one enormous mistake."

"Don't kiss me now." She lifted a hand but only curled her fingers into his shirt. "I can't think."

"One has nothing to do with the other."

When his mouth touched hers, it was soft, seeking. *Too late.* The words echoed in her head even as she lifted her hands to his face and let herself go. This is what she had wanted, no matter how many arguments she had posed, no matter how many defenses she had built. She wanted to be held against him, to sink into a dream that had no end.

He felt her fingers stream through his hair and had to force himself not to rush her. Desire, tensed and hungry, had to be held back until it was tempered with acceptance and trust. In his heart he had already acknowledged that she was more than the challenge he had first considered her. She was more than the summer fling he might have preferred. But as her slim, soft body pressed against his, as her warm, willing mouth opened for him, he could only think of how he wanted her, now, when the sun was beginning to sink toward the distant peaks to the west.

"Chase." It was the wild, drumming beat of her heart that frightened her most. She was trembling. Eden could feel it start somewhere deep inside and spread out until it became a stunning combination of panic and excitement. How could she fight the first and give in to the second? "Chase, please."

He had to draw himself back, inch by painful inch. He hadn't meant to take either of them so far, so fast. Yet perhaps he had, he thought as he ran a hand down her hair. Perhaps he had wanted to push them both toward an answer that still seemed just out of reach.

"The sun's going down." His hands weren't quite steady when he turned her toward the window again. "Before long, the lights will change."

She could only be grateful that he was giving her time to regain her composure. Later she would realize how much it probably had cost him.

They stood a moment in silence, watching the first tints of rose spread above the mountains. A loud, rasping cough had her already-tense nerves jolting.

"S'cuze me."

The man in the doorway had a grizzled beard that trailed down to the first button of his red checked shirt. Though he was hardly taller than Eden, his bulk gave the impression of power. The folds and lines in his face all but obscured his dark eyes. Then he grinned, and she caught the glint of a gold tooth.

So this was the little lady who had the boss running around in circles. Deciding she was prettier than a barrelful of prime apples, he nodded to her by way of greeting. "Supper's ready. Unless you want to eat it cold, you best be moving along."

"Eden Carlbough, Delaney." Chase only lifted a brow, knowing Delaney had already sized up the situation. "He cooks and I don't, which is why I haven't fired him yet."

This brought on a cackle. "He hasn't fired me because I wiped his nose and tied his shoes."

"We could add that that was close to thirty years ago."

She recognized both affection and exasperation. It pleased her to know someone could exasperate Chase Elliot. "It's nice to meet you, Mr. Delaney."

"Delaney, ma'am. Just Delaney." Still grinning, he pulled

on his beard. "Mighty pretty," he said to Chase. "It's smarter to think of settling down with someone who isn't an eyesore at breakfast. Supper's going to get cold," he added. Then he was gone.

Though Eden had remained politely silent during Delaney's statement, it took only one look at Chase's face to engender a stream of laughter. The sound made Chase think more seriously about gagging Delaney with his own beard.

"I'm glad you're amused."

"Delighted. It's the first time I've ever seen you speechless. And I can't help be pleased not to be considered an eyesore." Then she disarmed him by offering him her hand. "Supper's going to get cold."

Instead of the dining room, Chase led her out to a jalousied porch. Two paddle fans circled overhead, making the most of the breeze that crept in the slanted windows. A wind chime jingled cheerfully between baskets of fuchsia.

"Your home is one surprise after another," Eden commented as she studied the plump love seats and the glass-and-wicker table. "Every room seems fashioned for relaxation and stunning views."

The table was set with colorful stoneware. Though the sun had yet to drop behind the peaks, two tapers were already burning. There was a single wild rose beside her plate.

Romance, she thought. This was the romance she had once dreamed of. This was the romance she must now be very wary of. But, wary or not, she picked up the flower and smiled at him. "Thank you."

"Did you want one, too?" As she laughed, Chase drew back her chair.

"Sit down. Sit down. Eat while it's hot." Despite his bulk, Delaney bustled into the room. In his large hands was an enormous tray. Because she realized how easily she could be mowed down, Eden obeyed. "Hope you got an appetite. You could use a little plumping up, missy. Then, I've always preferred a bit of healthy meat on female bones."

As he spoke, he began to serve an exquisite seafood salad. "Made my special, Chicken Delaney. It'll keep under the covers if you two don't dawdle over the salad. Apple pie's on the hot plate, biscuits in the warmer." He stuck a bottle of wine unceremoniously in an ice bucket. "That's the fancy wine you wanted." Standing back, he took a narrowed-eyed glance around before snorting with satisfaction. "I'm going home. Don't let my chicken get cold." Wiping his hands on his jeans, he marched to the door and let it swing shut behind him.

"Delaney has amazing style, doesn't he?" Chase took the wine from the bucket to pour two glasses.

"Amazing," Eden agreed, finding it amazing enough that those gnarled hands had created anything as lovely as the salad in front of her.

"He makes the best biscuits in Pennsylvania." Chase lifted his glass and toasted her. "And I'd put his Beef Wellington up against anyone's."

"Beef Wellington?" With a shake of her head, Eden sipped her wine. It was cool, just a shade tart. "I hope you'll take it the right way when I say he looks more like the type who could charcoal a steak over a backyard grill." She dipped her fork in the salad and sampled it. "But…"

"Appearances can be deceiving," Chase finished for her, pleased with the way her eyes half shut as she tasted. "Delaney's been cooking here as long as I can remember. He lives in a little cottage my grandfather helped him build about forty years ago. Nose-wiping and shoe-tying aside, he's part of the family."

She only nodded, looking down at her plate for a moment as she remembered how difficult it had been to tell her long-time servants she was selling out. Perhaps they had never been as familiar or as informal as Chase's Delaney, but they, too, had been part of the family.

It was there again, that dim candle glow of grief he'd seen in her eyes before. Wanting only to help, he reached over to touch her hand. "Eden?"

Quickly, almost too quickly, she moved her hand and began to eat again. "This is wonderful. I have an aunt back home who would shanghai your Delaney after the first forkful."

Home, he thought, backing off automatically. Philadelphia was still home.

The Chicken Delaney lived up to its name. As the sun set, the meal passed easily, even though they disagreed on almost every subject.

She read Keats and he read Christie. She preferred Bach and he Haggard, but it didn't seem to matter as the glass walls filtered the rosy light of approaching twilight. The candles burned lower. The wine shimmered in crystal, inviting one more sip. Close and clear and quick came the two-tone call of a quail.

"That's a lovely sound." Her sigh was easy and content. "If things are quiet at camp, we can hear the birds in the evening. There's a whippoorwill who's taken to singing right outside the cabin window. You can almost set your watch by her."

"Most of us are creatures of habit," he murmured. He wondered about her, what habits she had, what habits she had changed. Taking her hand, he turned it up. The ridge of callus had hardened. "You didn't take my advice."

"About what?"

"Wearing gloves."

"It didn't seem worth it. Besides..." Letting the words trail off, she lifted her wine.

"Besides?"

"Having calluses means I did something to earn them." She blurted it out, then sat swearing at herself and waiting for him to laugh.

He didn't. Instead he sat silently, passing his thumb over the toughened skin and watching her. "Will you go back?"

"Go back?"

"To Philadelphia."

It was foolish to tell him how hard she'd tried not to think about that. Instead, she answered as the practical Eden was supposed to. "The camp closes down the last week in August. Where else would I go?"

"Where else?" he agreed, but when he released her hand she felt a sense of loss rather than relief. "Maybe there comes a time in everyone's life when they have to take a hard look at the options." He rose, and her hands balled into fists. He took a step toward her, and her heart rose up to her throat. "I'll be back."

Alone, she let out a long, shaky breath. What had she been expecting? she asked herself. What had she been hoping for? Her legs weren't quite steady when she rose, but it could have been the wine. But wine would have made her warm, and she felt a chill. To ward it off, she rubbed her arms with her hands. The sky was a quiet, deepening blue but for a halo of scarlet along the horizon. She concentrated on that, trying not to imagine how it would look when the stars came out.

Maybe they would look at the stars together again. They could look, picking out the patterns, and she would again feel that click that meant her needs and dreams were meshing. With his.

Pressing a hand to her lips, she struggled to block off that train of thought. It was only that the evening had been lovelier than she had imagined. It was only that they had more in common than she had believed possible. It was only that he had a gentleness inside him that softened parts of her when she least expected it. And when he kissed her, she felt as though she had the world pulsing in the palm of her hand.

No. Uneasy, she wrapped her hands around her forearms and squeezed. She was romanticizing again, spinning daydreams when she had no business dreaming at all. She was just beginning to sort out her life, to make her own place. It wasn't possible that she was looking to him to be any part of it.

She heard the music then, something low and unfamiliar that nonetheless had tiny shivers working their way up her spine. She had to leave, she thought quickly. And right away. She had let the atmosphere get to her. The house, the sunset, the wine. Him. Hearing his footsteps, she turned. She would tell him she had to get back. She would thank him for the evening, and...escape.

When he came back into the room, she was standing beside the table so that the candlelight flickered over her skin. Dusk swirled behind her with its smoky magic. The scent of wild roses from the bush outside the window seemed to sigh into the room. He wondered, if he touched her now, if she would simply dissolve in his hands.

"Chase, I think I'd better—"

"Shh." She wouldn't dissolve, he told himself as he went to her. She was real, and so was he. One hand captured hers, the other slipping around her waist. After one moment of resistance, she began to move with him. "One of the pleasures of country music is dancing to it."

"I, ah, I don't know the song." But it felt so good, so very good, to sway with him while darkness fell.

"It's about a man, a woman and passion. The best songs are."

She shut her eyes. She could feel the brush of his jacket against her cheek, the firm press of his hand at her waist. He smelled of soap, but nothing a woman would use. This had a tang that was essentially masculine. Wanting to taste, she moved her head so that her lips rested against his neck.

His pulse beat there, quick, surprising her. Forgetting caution, she nestled closer and felt its sudden rise in speed. As her own raced to match it, she gave a murmur of pleasure and traced it with the tip of her tongue.

He started to draw her away. He meant to. When he'd left her, he'd promised himself that he would slow the pace to one they could both handle. But now she was cuddled against him, her body swaying, her fingers straying to his neck, and her mouth... With an oath, Chase dragged her closer and gave in to hunger.

The kiss was instantly torrid, instantly urgent. And somehow, though she had never experienced anything like it, instantly familiar. Her head tilted back in surrender. Her lips parted. Here and now, she wanted the fire and passion that had only been hinted at.

Perhaps he lowered her to the love seat, perhaps she drew him to it, but they were wrapped together, pressed against the cushions. An owl hooted once, then twice, then gave them silence.

He'd wanted to believe she could be this generous. He'd wanted to believe his lips would touch hers and find unrestricted sweetness. Now his mind spun with it. Whatever he had wanted, whatever he had dreamed of, was less, so much less than what he now held in his arms.

He stroked a hand down her body and met trembling response. With a moan, she arched against him. Through the sheer fabric of her blouse, he could feel the heat rising to her skin, enticing him to touch again and yet again.

He released the first button of her blouse, then the second, following the course with his lips. She shivered with anticipation. Her lace cuffs brushed against his cheeks as she lifted her hands to his hair. It seemed her body was filling, flooding with sensations she'd once only imagined. Now they were so real and so clear that she could feel each one as it layered over the next.

The pillows at her back were soft. His body was hard and hot. The breeze that jingled the wind chime overhead was freshened with flowers. Behind her closed eyes came the flicker and glow of candlelight. In teams of thousands, the cicadas began to sing. But more thrilling, more intense, was the sound of her name whispering from him as he pressed his lips against her skin.

Suddenly, searing, his mouth took hers again. In the kiss she could taste everything, his need, his desire, the passion that teetered on the edge of sanity. As her own madness hovered, she felt her senses swimming with him. And she moaned with the ecstasy of falling in love.

For one brief moment, she rose on it, thrilled with the knowledge that she had found him. The dream and the reality were both here. She had only to close them both in her arms and watch them become one.

Then the terror of it fell on her. She couldn't let it be real. How could she risk it? Once she had given her trust and her promise, if not her heart. And she had been betrayed. If it happened again, she would never recover. If it happened with Chase, she wouldn't want to.

"Chase, no more." She turned her face away and tried to clear her head. "Please, this has to stop."

Her taste was still exploding in his mouth. Beneath his, her body was trembling with a need he knew matched his own.

"Eden, for God's sake." With an effort that all but drained him, he lifted his head to look down at her. She was afraid. He recognized her fear immediately and struggled to hold back his own needs. "I won't hurt you."

That almost undid her. He meant it, she was sure, but that didn't mean it wouldn't happen. "Chase, this isn't right for me. For either of us."

"Isn't it?" Tension knotted in his stomach as he drew her toward him. "Can you tell me you didn't feel how right it was a minute ago?"

"No." It was both confusion and fear that had her dragging her hands through her hair. "But this isn't what I want. I need you to understand that this can't be what I want. Not now."

"You're asking a hell of a lot."

"Maybe. But there isn't any choice."

That infuriated him. She was the one who had taken his choice away, simply by existing. He hadn't asked her to fall into his life. He hadn't asked her to become the focus of it before he had a chance for a second breath. She'd given in to him to the point where he was half-mad for her. Now she was drawing away. And asking him to understand.

"We'll play it your way." His tone chilled as he drew away from her.

She shuddered, recognizing instantly that his anger could be lethal. "It's not a game."

"No? Well, in any case, you play it well."

She pressed her lips together, understanding that she deserved at least a part of the lash. "Please, don't spoil what happened."

He walked to the table and, lifting his glass, studied the wine. "What did happen?"

I fell in love with you. Rather than answer him, she began to button her blouse with nerveless fingers.

"I'll tell you." He tossed back the remaining wine, but it didn't soothe him. "Not for the first time in our fascinating relationship, you blew hot and cold without any apparent reason. It makes me wonder if Eric backed out of the marriage out of self-defense."

He saw her fingers freeze on the top button of her blouse. Even in the dim light, he could watch the color wash out of her face. Very carefully, he set his glass down again. "I'm sorry, Eden. That was uncalled-for."

The fight for control and composure was a hard war, but she won. She made her fingers move until the button was in place, then, slowly, she rose. "Since you're so interested, I'll tell you that Eric jilted me for more practical reasons. I appreciate the meal, Chase. It was lovely. Please thank Delaney for me."

"Damn it, Eden."

When he started forward, her body tightened like a bow. "If you could do one thing for me, it would be to take me back now and say nothing. Absolutely nothing."

Turning, she walked away from the candlelight.

Chapter 6

During the first weeks of August, the camp was plagued with one calamity after another. The first was an epidemic of poison ivy. Within twenty-four hours, ten of the girls and three of the counselors were coated with calamine lotion. The sticky heat did nothing to make the itching more bearable.

Just as the rashes started to fade came three solid days of rain. As the camp was transformed into a muddy mire, outdoor activities were canceled. Tempers soared. Eden broke up two hair-pulling battles in one day. Then, as luck would have it, lightning hit one of the trees and distracted the girls from their boredom.

By the time the sun came out, they had enough pot holders, key chains, wallets and pillows to open their own craft shop.

Men with Jeeps and chain saws came to clear away the debris from the tree. Eden wrote out a check and prayed the last crisis was over.

It was doubtful the check had even been cashed when the secondhand restaurant stove she and Candy had bought stopped working. In the three days the parts were on order, cooking was done in true camp style—around an open fire.

The gelding, Courage, developed an infection that settled in his lungs. Everyone in camp worried about him and fussed over him and pampered him. The vet dosed him with penicillin. Eden spent three sleepless nights in the stables, nursing him and waiting for the crisis to pass.

Eventually the horse's appetite improved, the mud in the compound dried and the stove was back in working order. Eden told herself that the worst had to be over as the camp's routine picked up again.

Yet oddly, the lull brought out a restlessness she'd been able to ignore while the worst was happening. At dusk, she wandered to the stables with her sackful of apples. It wasn't hard to give a little extra attention to Courage. He'd gotten used to being pampered during his illness. Eden slipped him a carrot to go with the apple.

Still, as she worked her way down the stalls, she found the old routine didn't keep her mind occupied. The emergencies over the past couple of weeks had kept her too busy to take a second breath, much less think. Now, with calm settling again, thinking was unavoidable.

She could remember her evening with Chase as if it had been the night before. Every word spoken, every touch, every gesture, was locked in her mind as it had been when it had been happening. The rushing, tumbling sensation of falling in love was just as vital now, and just as frightening.

She hadn't been prepared for it. Her life had always been a series of preparations and resulting actions. Even her engagement had been a quiet step along a well-paved road.

Since then, she'd learned to handle the detours and the road-blocks. But Chase was a sudden one-way street that hadn't been on any map.

It didn't matter, she told herself as she finished Patience's rubdown. She would navigate this and swing herself back in the proper direction. Having her choices taken away at this point in her life wasn't something she would tolerate. Not even when the lack of choice seemed so alluring and so right.

"I thought I'd find you here." Candy leaned against the stall door to give the mare a pat. "How was Courage tonight?"

"Good." Eden walked to the little sink in the corner to wash liniment from her hands. "I don't think we have to worry about him anymore."

"I'm glad to know that you'll be using your bunk instead of a pile of hay."

Eden pressed both hands to the small of her back and stretched. No demanding set of tennis had ever brought on this kind of ache. Strangely enough, she liked it. "I never thought I'd actually look forward to sleeping in that bunk."

"Well, now that you're not worried about the gelding, I can tell you I'm worried about you."

"Me?" Eden looked for a towel and, not finding one, dried her hands on her jeans. "Why?"

"You're pushing yourself too hard."

"Don't be silly. I'm barely pulling my weight."

"That stopped being even close to the truth the second week of camp." Now that she'd decided to speak up, Candy took a deep breath. "Damn it, Eden, you're exhausted."

"Tired," Eden corrected her. "Which is nothing a few hours on that miserable bunk won't cure."

"Look, it's okay if you want to avoid the issue with every-one else, even with yourself. But don't do it with me."

It wasn't often Candy's voice took on that firm, no-non-sense tone. Eden lifted a brow and nodded. "All right, what is the issue?"

"Chase Elliot," Candy stated, and she saw Eden freeze up. "I didn't hound you with questions the night you came back from dinner."

"And I appreciate that."

"Well, don't, because I'm asking now."

"We had dinner, talked a bit about books and music, then he brought me back."

Candy closed the stall door with a creak. "I thought I was your friend."

"Oh, Candy, you know you are." With a sigh, Eden closed her eyes a moment. "All right, we did exactly what I said we did, but somewhere between the talk and the ride home, things got a little out of hand."

"What sort of things?"

Eden found she didn't even have the energy to laugh. "I've never known you to pry."

"I've never known you to settle comfortably into depression."

"Am I?" Eden blew her bangs out of her eyes. "God, maybe I am."

"Let's just say that you've jumped from one problem to the next in order to avoid fixing one of your own." Taking a step closer, Candy drew Eden down on a small bench. "So let's talk."

"I'm not sure I can." Linking her hands, Eden looked down at them. The opal ring that had once been her mother's winked back at her. "I promised myself after Papa died and everything was in such a mess that I would handle things and find the best way to solve the problems. I've needed to solve them myself."

"That doesn't mean you can't lean on a friend."

"I've leaned on you so much I'm surprised you can walk upright."

"I'll let you know when I start limping. Eden, unless my memory's faulty, we've taken turns leaning on each other since before either of us could walk. Tell me about Chase."

"He scares me." With a long breath, Eden leaned back against the wall. "Everything's happening so fast, and everything I feel seems so intense." Dropping the last of her guard, she turned her face to Candy's. "If things had worked out differently, I'd be married to another man right now. How can I even think I might be in love with someone else so soon?"

"You're not going to tell me you think you're fickle." The last thing Eden had expected was Candy's bright, bubbling laughter, but that was what echoed off the stable walls. "Eden, I'm the fickle one, remember? You've always been loyal to a fault. Wait, I can see you're getting annoyed, so let's take this logically." Candy crossed her ankles and began to count off on her fingers.

"First, you were engaged to Eric—the slime—because of all the reasons we've discussed before. It seemed the proper thing to do. Were you in love with him?"

"No, but I thought—"

"Irrelevant. No is the answer. Second, he showed his true colors, the engagement's been off for months, and you've met a fascinating, attractive man. Now, let's even take it a step further." Warming up to the subject, Candy shifted on the bench. "Suppose—God forbid—that you had actually been madly in love with Eric. After he had shown himself to be a snake, your heart would have been broken. With time and effort, you would have pulled yourself back together. Right?"

"I certainly like to think so."

"So we agree."

"Marginally."

That was enough for Candy. "Then, heart restored, if you'd met a fascinating and attractive man, you would have been equally free to fall for him. Either way, you're in the clear." Satisfied, Candy rose and dusted her palms on her jeans. "So what's the problem?"

Not certain she could explain, or even make sense of it herself, Eden looked down at her hands. "Because I've learned something. Love is a commitment, it's total involvement, promises, compromises. I'm not sure I can give those things to anyone yet. And if I were, I don't know if Chase feels at all the same way."

"Eden, your instincts must tell you he does."

With a shake of her head, she rose. She did feel better having said it all out loud, but that didn't change the bottom line. "I've learned not to trust my instincts, but to be realistic. Which is why I'm going to go hit the account books."

"Oh, Eden, give it a break."

"Unfortunately, I had to give it a break during the poison ivy, the lightning, the stove breakdown and the vet visits." Hooking her arm through Candy's, she started to walk toward the door. "You were right, and talking it out helped, but practicality is still the order of the day."

"Meaning checks and balances."

"Right. I'd really like to get to it. The advantage is I can frazzle my brain until the bunk really does feel like a feather bed."

Candy pushed open the door, then squared her shoulders. "I'll help."

"Thanks, but I'd like to finish them before Christmas."

"Oh, low blow, Eden."

"But true." She latched the door behind them. "Don't worry about me, Candy. Talking about it cleared my head a bit."

"Doing something about it would be better, but it's a start. Don't work too late."

"A couple of hours," Eden promised.

The office, as Eden arrogantly called it, was a small side room off the kitchen. After switching on the gooseneck lamp on the metal army-surplus desk, she adjusted the screen, flap up. As an afterthought, she switched the transistor radio on the corner of the desk to a classical station. The quiet, familiar melodies would go a long way toward calming her.

Still, as always, she drew in a deep breath as she took her seat behind the desk. Here, she knew too well, things were black-and-white. There were no multiple choices, no softening the rules as there could be in other areas of the camp. Figures were figures and facts were facts. It was up to her to tally them.

Opening the drawers, she pulled out invoices, the business checkbook and the ledger. She began systematically sorting and entering as the tape spilled out of the adding machine at her elbow.

Within twenty minutes, she knew the worst. The additional expenses of the past two weeks had stretched their capital to the limit. No matter how many ways Eden worked the numbers, the answer was the same. They weren't dead broke, but painfully close to it. Wearily, she rubbed the bridge of her nose between her thumb and forefinger.

They could still make it, she told herself. She pressed her hand down on the pile of papers, letting her palm cover the checks and balances. By the skin of their teeth, she thought, but they could still make it. If there were no more unexpected expenses. And if, she continued, the pile seeming to grow under her hand, she and Candy lived frugally over the winter. She imagined the pile growing another six inches under her restraining hand. If they got the necessary enrollments for the next season, everything would turn around.

Curling her fingers around the papers, she let out a long breath. If one of those *if*s fell through, she still had some jewelry that could be sold.

The lamplight fell across her opal-and-diamond ring, but she looked away, feeling guilty at even considering selling it. But she would. If her other choices were taken away, she would. What she wouldn't do was give up.

The tears began so unexpectedly that they fell onto the blotter before she knew she had shed them. Even as she wiped them away, new ones formed. There was no one to see, no one to hear. Giving in, Eden laid her head on the piles of bills and let the tears come.

They wouldn't change anything. With tears would come no fresh ideas or brilliant answers, but she let them come anyway. Quite simply, her strength had run out.

He found her like that, weeping almost soundlessly over the neat stacks of paper. At first Chase only stood there, with the door not quite shut at his back. She looked so helpless, so utterly spent. He wanted to go to her, but held himself back. He understood that the tears would be private. She wouldn't want to share them, particularly not with him. And yet, even as he told himself to step back, he moved toward her.

"Eden."

Her head shot up at the sound of her name. Her eyes were drenched, but he saw both shock and humiliation in them before she began to dry her cheeks with the backs of her hands.

"What are you doing here?"

"I wanted to see you." It sounded simple enough, but didn't come close to what was moving inside him. He wanted to go to her, to gather her close and fix whatever was wrong. He stuck his hands in his pockets and remained standing just inside the door. "I just heard about the gelding this morning. Is he worse?"

She shook her head, then struggled to keep her voice calm. "No, he's better. It wasn't as serious as we thought it might be."

"That's good." Frustrated by his inability to think of something less inane, he began to pace. How could he offer comfort when she wouldn't share the problem? Her eyes were dry now, but he knew it was pride, and pride alone, that held her together. The hell with her pride, he thought. He needed to help.

When he turned back, he saw she had risen from the desk. "Why don't you tell me about it?"

The need to confide in him was so painfully strong that she automatically threw up the customary shield. "There's nothing to tell. It's been a rough couple of weeks. I suppose I'm overtired."

It was more than that, he thought, though she did look exhausted. "The girls getting to you?"

"No, really, the girls are fine."

Frustrated, he looked for another answer. The radio was playing something slow and romantic. Glancing toward it, Chase noticed the open ledger. The tail of adding-machine tape was spilling onto the floor. "Is it money? I could help."

Eden closed the book with a snap. Humiliation was a bitter taste at the back of her throat. At least it dried the last of her tears. "We're fine," she told him in a voice that was even and cool. "If you'd excuse me, I still have some work to do."

Rejection was something Chase had never fully understood until he'd met her. He didn't care for it. Nodding slowly, he searched for patience. "It was meant as an offer, not an insult." He would have turned and left her then, but the marks of weeping and sleeplessness gave her a pale, wounded look.

"I'm sorry about the trouble you've been having the past year, Eden. I knew you'd lost your father, but I didn't know about the estate."

She wanted, oh so badly, to reach out, to let him gather her close and give her all the comfort she needed. She wanted to ask him what she should do, and have him give her the answers. But wouldn't that mean that all the months of struggling for self-sufficiency had been for nothing? She straightened her shoulders. "It isn't necessary to be sorry."

"If you had told me yourself, it would have been simpler."

"It didn't concern you."

He didn't so much ignore the stab of hurt as turn it into annoyance. "Didn't it? I felt differently—feel differently. Are you going to stand there and tell me there's nothing between us, Eden?"

She couldn't deny it, but she was far too confused, far too afraid, to try to define the truth. "I don't know how I feel about you, except that I don't want to feel anything. Most of all, I don't want your pity."

The hands in his pockets curled into fists. He didn't know how to handle his own feelings, his own needs. Now she was treating them as though they didn't matter. He could leave, or he could beg. At the moment, Chase saw no choice between the two. "Understanding and pity are different things, Eden. If you don't know that, there's nothing else to say."

Turning, he left her. The screen door swished quietly behind him.

For the next two days, Eden functioned. She gave riding instructions, supervised meals and hiked the hills with groups of girls. She talked and laughed and listened, but the hollowness that had spread inside her when the door had closed at Chase's back remained.

Guilt and regret. Those were the feelings she couldn't shake, no matter how enthusiastically she threw herself into her routine. She'd been wrong. She'd known it even as it was happening, but pride had boxed her in. He had offered to help. He had offered to care, and she'd refused him. If there was a worse kind of selfishness, she couldn't name it.

She'd started to phone him, but hadn't been able to dial the number. It hadn't been pride that had held her back this time. Every apology that formed in her mind was neat and tidy and meaningless. She couldn't bear to give him a stilted apology, nor could she bear the possibility that he wouldn't care.

Whatever had started to grow between them, she had squashed. Whatever might have been, she had cut off before it had begun to flower. How could she explain to Chase that she'd been afraid of being hurt again? How could she tell him that when he'd offered help and understanding she'd been afraid to accept it because it was so easy to be dependent?

She began to ride out alone at night again. Solitude didn't soothe her as it once had; it only reminded her that she had taken steps to insure that she would remain alone. The nights were warm, with the lingering scent of honeysuckle bringing back memories of a night where there had been pictures in the sky. She couldn't look at the stars without thinking of him.

Perhaps that was why she rode to the lake, where the grass was soft and thick. Here she could smell the water and wild blossoms. The horse's hooves were muffled, and she could just hear the rustle of wings in flight—some unseen bird in search of prey or a mate.

Then she saw him.

The moon was on the wane, so he was only a shadow, but

she knew he was watching her. Just as she had known, somehow, that she would find him there tonight. Reining in, she
let the magic take her. For the moment, even if it were only a
moment, she would forget everything but that she loved him.
Tomorrow would take care of itself.

She slid from the horse and went to him.

He said nothing. Until she touched him, he wasn't sure she
wasn't a dream. In silence, she framed his face in her hands
and pressed her lips to his. No dream had ever tasted so warm.
No illusion had ever felt so soft.

"Eden—"

With a shake of her head, she cut off his words. There were
weeks of emptiness to fill, and no questions that needed answering. Rising on her toes, she kissed him again. The only
sound was her sigh as his arms finally came around her. She
discovered a bottomless well of giving inside her. Something
beyond passion, something beyond desire. Here was comfort,
strength and the understanding she had been afraid to accept.

His fingers trailed up to her hair, as if each touch reassured
him she was indeed real. When he opened his eyes again, his
arms wouldn't be empty, but filled with her. Her cheek rubbed
his, smooth skin against a day's growth of beard. With her
head nestled in a curve of his shoulder, she watched the wink
and blink of fireflies and thought of stars.

They stood in silence while an owl hooted and the horse
whinnied in response.

"Why did you come?" He needed an answer, one he could
take back with him when she had left him again.

"To see you." She drew away, wanting to see his face. "To
be with you."

"Why?"

The magic shimmered and began to dim. With a sigh, she

drew back. Dreams were for sleeping, Eden reminded herself. And questions had to be answered. "I wanted to apologize for the way I behaved before. You were being kind." Searching for words, she turned to pluck a leaf from the tree that shadowed them. "I know how I must have seemed, how I sounded, and I am sorry. It's difficult, still difficult for me to…" Restless, she moved her shoulders. "We were able to muffle most of the publicity after my father died, but there was a great deal of gossip, of speculation and not-so-quiet murmurs."

When he said nothing, she shifted again, uncomfortable. "I suppose I resented all of that more than anything else. It became very important to me to prove myself, that I could manage, even succeed. I realize that I've become sensitive about handling things myself and that when you offered to help, I reacted badly. I apologize for that."

Silence hung another moment before he took a step toward her. Eden thought he moved the way the shadows did. Silently. "That's a nice apology, Eden. Before I accept it, I'd like to ask if the kiss was part of it."

So he wasn't going to make it easy for her. Her chin lifted. She didn't need an easy road any longer. "No."

Then he smiled and circled her throat with his hand. "What was it for then?"

The smile disturbed her more than the touch, though it was the touch she backed away from. Strange how you could take one step and find yourself sunk to the hips. "Does there have to be a reason?" When she walked toward the edge of the lake, she saw an owl swoop low over the water. That was the way she felt, she realized. As if she were skimming along the surface of something that could take her in over her head. "I wanted to kiss you, so I did."

The tension he'd lived with for weeks had vanished, leaving him almost light-headed. He had to resist the urge to scoop her up and carry her home, where he'd begun to understand she belonged. "Do you always do what you want?"

She turned back with a toss of her head. She'd apologized, but the pride remained. "Always."

He grinned, nudging a smile from her. "So do I."

"Then we should understand each other."

He trailed a finger down her cheek. "Remember that."

"I will." Steady again, she moved past him to the gelding. "We're having a dance a week from Saturday. Would you like to come?"

His hand closed over hers on the reins. "Are you asking me for a date?"

Amused, she swung her hair back before settling a foot in the stirrup. "Certainly not. We're short of chaperons."

She bent her leg to give herself a boost into the saddle, but found herself caught at the waist. She dangled in midair for a moment before Chase set her on the ground again, turning her to face him. "Will you dance with me?"

She remembered the last time they had danced and saw from the look in his eyes that he did as well. Her heart fluttered in the back of her dry throat, but she lifted a brow and smiled. "Maybe."

His lips curved, then descended slowly to brush against hers. She felt the world tilt, then steady at an angle only lovers understand. "A week from Saturday," he murmured, then lifted her easily into the saddle. His hand remained over hers another moment. "Miss me."

He stayed by the water until she was gone and the night was silent again.

Chapter 7

The last weeks of summer were hot and long. At night, there was invariably heat lightning and rumbling thunder, but little rain. Eden pushed herself through the days, blocking out the uncertainty of life after September.

She wasn't escaping, she told herself. She was coping with one day at a time. If she had learned one important lesson over the summer, it was that she could indeed make changes, in herself and in her life.

The frightened and defeated woman who had come to Camp Liberty almost as if it were a sanctuary would leave a confident, successful woman who could face the world on her own terms.

Standing in the center of the compound, she ran her hands down her narrow hips before dipping them into the pockets of her shorts. Next summer would be even better, now that they'd faced the pitfalls and learned how to maneuver around them. She knew she was skipping over months of her life, but found she didn't want to dwell on the winter. She didn't want to think of Philadelphia and snowy sidewalks, but of the mountains and what she had made of her life there.

If it had been possible, she would have found a way to stay behind during the off-season. Eden had begun to understand that only necessity and the need for employment were taking her back east. It wasn't her home any longer.

With a shake of her head, Eden pushed away thoughts of December. The sun was hot and bright. She could watch it shimmer on the surface of Chase's lake and think of him.

She wondered what would have happened if she had met him two years earlier when her life had been so ordered and set and mapped-out. Would she have fallen in love with him then? Perhaps it was all a matter of timing; perhaps she would have given him a polite how-do-you-do and forgotten him.

No. Closing her eyes, she could recall vividly every sensation, every emotion he'd brought into her life. Timing had nothing to do with something so overwhelming. No matter when, no matter where, she would have fallen in love with him. Hadn't she fought it all along, only to find her feelings deepening?

But she'd thought herself in love with Eric, too.

She shivered in the bright sun and watched a jay race overhead. Was she so shallow, so cold, that her feelings could shift and change in the blink of an eye? That was what held her back and warned her to be cautious. If Eric hadn't turned his back on her, she would have married him. His ring would be on her finger even now. Eden glanced down at her bare left hand.

But that hadn't been love, she reassured herself. Now she knew what love felt like, what it did to heart and mind and body. And yet… How did he feel? He cared, and he wanted, but she knew enough of love now to understand that wasn't enough. She, too, had once cared and wanted. If Chase was in love with her, there wouldn't be any *before*. Time would begin now.

Don't be a fool, she told herself with a flash of annoyance. That kind of thinking would only make her drift back to dependence. There was a before for both of them, and a future. There was no way of being sure that the future would merge with what she felt today.

But she wanted to be a fool, she realized with a quick, delicious shudder. Even if only for a few weeks, she wanted to absorb and concentrate all those mad feelings. She'd be sensible again. Sensible was for January, when the wind was sharp and the rent had to be paid. In a few days she would dance with him, smile up at him. She would have that one night of the summer to be a fool.

Kicking off her shoes, Eden plucked them up in one hand and ran the rest of the way to the dock. Girls, already separated into groups, were waiting for the signal to row out into the lake.

"Miss Carlbough!" In her camp uniform and her familiar cap, Roberta hopped up and down on the grass near the rowboats. "Watch this." With a quick flurry of motion, she bent over, kicked up her feet and stood on her head. "What do you think?" she demanded through teeth clenched with effort. Her triangular face reddened.

"Incredible."

"I've been practicing." With a grunt, Roberta tumbled onto the grass. "Now, when my mom asks what I did at camp, I can stand on my head and show her."

Eden lifted a brow, hoping Mrs. Snow got a few more details. "I'm sure she'll be impressed."

Still sprawled on the grass, arms splayed out to the sides, Roberta stared up at Eden. She was just old enough to wish that her hair was blond and wavy. "You look real pretty today, Miss Carlbough."

Touched, and more than a little surprised, Eden held out a hand to help Roberta up. "Why, thank you, Roberta. So do you."

"Oh, I'm not pretty, but I'm going to be once I can wear makeup and cover my freckles."

Eden rubbed a thumb over Roberta's cheek. "Lots of boys fall for freckles."

"Maybe." Roberta tucked that away to consider later. "I guess you're soft on Mr. Elliot."

Eden dropped her hand back in her pocket. "Soft on?"

"You know." To demonstrate, Roberta sighed and fluttered her eyes. Eden wasn't sure whether to laugh or give the little monster a shove into the lake.

"That's ridiculous."

"Are you getting married?"

"I haven't the vaguest idea where you come up with such nonsense. Now into the boat. Everyone's ready to go."

"My mom told me people sometimes get married when they're soft on each other."

"I'm sure your mother's quite right." Hoping to close the subject, Eden helped Roberta into their assigned rowboat, where Marcie and Linda were already waiting. "However, in this case, Mr. Elliot and I barely know each other. Everyone hook their life jackets, please."

"Mom said she and Daddy fell in love at first sight." Roberta hooked on the preserver, though she thought it was a pain when she swam so well. "They kiss all the time."

"I'm sure that's nice. Now—"

"I used to think it was kind of gross, but I guess it's okay."

Roberta settled into her seat and smiled. "Well, if you decide not to marry Mr. Elliot, maybe I will."

Eden was busy locking in the oars, but she glanced up. "Oh?"

"Yeah. He's got a neat dog and all those apple trees." Roberta adjusted the brim of her cap over her eyes. "And he's kind of pretty." The two girls beside her giggled in agreement.

"That's certainly something to think about." Eden began to row. "Maybe you can discuss the idea with your mother when you get home."

"'Kay. Can I row first?"

Eden could only be grateful that the girl's interest span was as fast-moving as the rest of her. "Fine. You and I will row out. Marcie and Linda can row back."

After a bit of drag and a few grunts, Roberta matched her rhythm to Eden's. As the boat began to glide, it occurred to Eden that she was rowing with the same three girls who had started the adventure in the apple orchard. With a silent chuckle, she settled into sync with Roberta and let her mind drift.

What if she had never gone up in that tree? Absently, she touched her lower lip with her tongue, recalling the taste and feel of Chase. If she had it to do over, would she run in the opposite direction?

Smiling, Eden closed her eyes a moment, so that the sun glowed red under her lids. No, she wouldn't run. Being able to admit it, being able to be sure of it, strengthened her confidence. She wouldn't run from Chase, or from anything else in life.

Perhaps she was soft on him, as Roberta had termed it. Perhaps she could hug that secret to herself for a little while. It would be wonderful if things could be as simple and uncomplicated as Roberta made them. Love equaled marriage, marriage equaled happiness. Sighing, Eden opened her eyes and watched the surface of the lake. For a little while she could believe in poetry and dreams.

Daydreams... They were softer and even more mystical than dreams by night. It had been a long time since Eden had indulged in them. Now the girls were chattering and calling to their friends in the other boats. Someone was singing, deliberately off-key. Eden's arms moved in a steady rhythm as the oars cut smoothly into the water and up into the air again.

So she was floating...dreaming with her eyes open...silk and ivory and lace. The glitter of the sun on water was like candlelight. The call of crows was music to dance by.

She was riding on Pegasus. High in a night sky, his white wings effortlessly cut through the air. She could taste the cool, thin wind that took them through clouds. Her hair was free, flying behind her, twined with flowers. More clouds, castle-like, rose up in the distance, filmy and gray and secret. Their secrets were nothing to her. She had freedom for the first time, full, unlimited freedom.

And he was with her, riding the sky through snatches of light and dark. Higher, still higher they rose, until the earth was only mist beneath them. And the stars were flowers, the white petals of anemones that she could reach out and pick as the whim struck her.

When she turned in his arms, she was his without boundaries. All restrictions, all doubts, had been left behind in the climb.

"Hey, look. It's Squat!"

Eden blinked. The daydream disintegrated. She was in a rowboat, with muscles that were just beginning to ache from exertion. There were no flowers, no stars, only water and sky.

They'd rowed nearly the width of the lake. A portion of Chase's orchard spread back from the shore, and visible was one of the greenhouses he had taken the camp through on the day of the tour. Delighted with the company, Squat dashed back and forth in the shallow water near the lake's edge. His massive paws scattered a flurry of water that coated him until he was a sopping, shaggy mess.

Smiling as the girls called out greetings to the dog, Eden wondered if Chase was home. What did he do with his Sundays? she thought. Did he laze around the house with the paper and cups of coffee? Did he switch on the ball game, or go out for long, solitary drives? Just then, as if to answer her questions, he and Delaney joined the dog on the shore. Across the water, Eden felt the jolt as their eyes met.

Would it always be like that? Always stunning, always fresh? Always immediate? Inhaling slowly, she coaxed her pulse back to a normal rate.

"Hey, Mr. Elliot!" Without a thought for the consequences, Roberta dropped her oar and jumped up. Excitement had her bouncing up and down as the boat teetered.

"Roberta." Acting by instinct, Eden locked her oars. "Sit down, you'll turn us over." Eden started to grab for her hand as the other girls took Roberta's lead and jumped to their feet.

"Hi, Mr. Elliot!"

The greeting rang out in unison, just before the boat tipped over.

Eden hit the water headfirst. After the heat of the sun it seemed shockingly cold, and she surfaced sputtering with fury. With one hand, she dragged the hair out of her eyes and focused on the three bobbing heads. The girls, buoyed by their life jackets, waved unrepentantly at the trio on shore.

Eden grabbed the edge of the upended boat. "Roberta!"

"Look, Miss Carlbough." Apparently the tone, said through gritted teeth, passed over the girl's head. "Squat's coming out."

"Terrific." Treading water, Eden plucked Roberta by the

arm and tried to drag her back to the capsized boat. "Remember the rules of boating safety. Stay here." Eden went for the next girl, but twisted her head to see the dog paddling toward them. Uneasy with his progress, she looked back toward shore.

Her request that Chase call back his dog caught in her throat as she spotted his grin. Though she couldn't hear the words, she saw Delaney turn to him with some remark. It was enough to see Chase throw back his head and laugh. That sound carried.

"Want some help?" he called out.

Eden pulled at the next giggling girl. "Don't put yourself out," she began, then shrieked when Squat laid a wet, friendly nose on her shoulder. Her reaction seemed to amuse everyone, dog included. Squat began to bark enthusiastically in her ear.

Fresh pandemonium broke out as the girls began to splash water at each other and the dog. Eden found herself caught in the crossfire. In the other boats, campers and counselors looked on, grinning or calling out encouraging words. Squat paddled circles around her as she struggled to restore some kind of order.

"All right, ladies. Enough." That earned her a mouthful of lake. "It's time to right the boat."

"Can Squat take a ride with us?" Roberta giggled as he licked water from her face.

"No."

"That hardly seems fair."

Eden nearly submerged before Chase gripped her arm. She'd been too busy trying to restore order and her own dignity to notice that he'd swum the few yards from shore. "He came out to help."

His hair was barely damp, while hers was plastered to her

head. Chase hooked an arm around her waist to ease her effort to tread water.

"You'd better right the boat," he said to the girls, who immediately fell to doing so with a vengeance. "Apparently you do better with horses." His voice was soft and amused in Eden's ear.

She started to draw away, but her legs tangled with his. "If you and that monster hadn't been on shore—"

"Delaney?"

"No, not Delaney." Frustrated, Eden pushed at her hair.

"You're beautiful when you're wet. Makes me wonder why I haven't thought of swimming with you before."

"We're not supposed to be swimming, we're supposed to be boating."

"Either way, you're beautiful."

She wouldn't be moved. Even though the girls had already righted the boat, Eden knew she was in over her head. "It's that dog," she began. Even as she said it, the girls were climbing back into the boat and urging Squat to join them.

"Roberta, I said—" Chase gently dunked her. Surfacing, she heard him striking the bargain.

"We'll swim back. You bring Squat. He likes boats."

"I said—" Again, she found herself under water. This time when she came up for air, she gave Chase her full attention. The swing she took at him was slow and sluggish because of the need to tread water.

He caught her fist and kissed it. "Beat you back."

Narrowing her eyes, Eden gave him a shove before striking out after the boat. The water around her ears muffled the sound of Squat's deep barking and the girls' excited cheering. With strong, even strokes, she kept a foot behind the boat and made certain the girls behaved.

Less than twenty feet from shore, Chase caught her by the ankle. Laughing and kicking, Eden found herself tangled in his arms.

"You cheat." As he rose, he swept her off her feet so that her accusation ended in another laugh. His bare chest was cool and wet under her palms. His hair was dripping so that the sunlight was caught in each separate drop of water. "I won."

"Wrong." She should have seen it coming. Without effort, he pitched her back in the lake. Eden landed bottom first. "I won."

Eden stood to shake herself off. Managing to suppress a smile, she nodded toward the whooping girls. "And that, ladies, is a classic example of poor sportsmanship." She reached up to squeeze the water out of her hair, unaware that her shirt clung to every curve. Chase felt his heart stop. She waded toward shore, with the clear lake water clinging to her tanned legs. "Good afternoon, Delaney."

"Ma'am." He gave her a gold, flashing grin. "Nice day for a swim."

"Apparently."

"I was about to pick me some blackberries for jam." He cast his gaze over the three dripping girls. "If I had some help, could be I'd have a jar or so extra for some neighbors."

Before Eden could consent or refuse, all the girls and Squat were jumping circles around her. She had to admit that a tenor fifteen-minute break would make the row back to camp a little more appealing. "Ten minutes," she told them before turning back to signal to the other boats.

Delaney toddled off, sandwiched between girls who were already barraging him with questions. As they disappeared into a cluster of trees, a startled flock of birds whizzed out. She laughed, turning back to see Chase staring at her.

"You're a strong swimmer."

She had to clear her throat. "I think I've just become more competitive. Maybe I should keep an eye on the girls so—"

"Delaney can handle them." He reached out to brush a bead of water from her jawline. Beneath his gentle touch, she shivered. "Cold?"

More than the sun had taken the lake's chill from her skin. Eden managed to shake her head. "No." But when his hands came to her shoulders, she stepped back.

He wore only cutoffs, faded soft from wear. The shirt he had peeled off before diving into the lake had been tossed carelessly to the ground. "You don't feel cold," he murmured as he stroked his hands down her arms.

"I'm not." She heard the laughter beyond the trees. "I really can't let them stay long. They'll have to change."

Patient, Chase took her hand. "Eden, you're going to end up in the lake again if you keep backing up." He was frightening her. Frustrated, he struggled not to push. It seemed that every time he thought he'd gained her trust, he saw that quick flash of anxiety in her eyes again. He smiled, hoping the need that was roiling inside him didn't show. "Where are your shoes?"

Off-balance, she looked down and stared at her own bare feet. Slowly, her muscles began to relax again. "At the bottom of your lake." Laughing, she shook her wet hair back, nearly destroying him. "Roberta always manages to keep things exciting. Why don't we give them a hand with the berry-picking."

His arm came across her body to take her shoulder before she could move past him. "You're still backing away, Eden." Lifting a hand, he combed his fingers through her sleek, wet hair until they rested at the base of her neck. "It's hard to resist you this way, with your face glowing and your eyes aware and just a bit frightened."

"Chase, don't." She put her hand to his.

"I want to touch you." He shifted so that the full length of her body was against his. "I need to touch you." Through the wet cotton, she could feel the texture of his skin on hers. "Look at me, Eden." The slightest pressure of his fingers brought her face up to his. "How close are you going to let me get?"

She could only shake her head. There weren't any words to describe what she was feeling, what she wanted, what she was still too afraid to need. "Chase, don't do this. Not here, not now." Then she could only moan, as his mouth traveled with a light, lazy touch over her face.

"When?" He had to fight the desire to demand rather than to ask, to take rather than to wait. "Where?" This time the kiss wasn't lazy, but hard, bruising. Eden felt rational thought spiral away even as she groped for an answer. "Don't you think I know what happens to you when we're like this?" His voice thickened as his patience stretched thinner and thinner. "Good God, Eden, I need you. Come with me tonight. Stay with me."

Yes, yes. Oh, yes. How easy it would be to say it, to give in, to give everything without a thought for tomorrow. She clung to him a moment, wanting to believe dreams were possible. He was so solid, so real. But so were her responsibilities.

"Chase, you know I can't." Fighting for rationality, she drew away. "I have to stay at camp."

Before she could move away again, he caught her face in his hands. She thought his eyes had darkened, a stormier green now, with splashes of gold from the sun. "And when summer's over, Eden? What then?"

What then? How could she have the answer, when the answer was so cold, so final? It wasn't what she wanted, but what had to be. If she was to keep her promise to herself, to make her life work, there was only one answer. "Then I'll go back, back to Philadelphia, until next summer."

Only summers? Was that all she was willing to give? It was the panic that surprised him and kept the fury at bay. When she left, his life would be empty. He took her shoulders again, fighting back the panic.

"You'll come to me before you go." It wasn't a question. It wasn't a demand. It was a simple statement. The demand she could have rebelled against; the question she could have refused.

"Chase, what good would it do either of us?"

"You'll come to me before you go," he repeated. Because if she didn't, he'd follow her. There would be no choice.

Chapter 8

Red and white crepe paper streamed from corner to corner, twined together in elongated snakes of color. Balloons, bulging with air from energetic young lungs, were crowded into every available space. Stacked in three uneven towers were all the records deemed fit to play.

Dance night was only a matter of hours away.

Under Candy's eagle eye, tables were carried outside, while others were grouped strategically around the mess area. This simple chore took twice as long as it should have, as girls had to stop every few feet to discuss the most important aspect of the evening: boys.

Although her skills with paint and glue were slim at best, Eden had volunteered for the decorating committee—on the understanding that her duties were limited to hanging and tacking what was already made. In addition to the crepe paper and balloons, there were banners and paper flowers that the more talented members of campers and staff had put together by hand. The best of these was a ten-foot banner dyed Camp Liberty red and splashed with bold letters that spelled out WELCOME TO CAMP LIBERTY'S ANNUAL SUMMER DANCE.

Candy had already taken it for granted that it would be the first of many. In her better moods, Eden hoped she was right. In her crankier ones, she wondered if they could swing a deal with the boys' camp to split the cost of refreshments. For the moment, she pushed both ideas aside, determined to make this dance the best-decorated one in Pennsylvania.

Eden let an argument over which records had priority run its course below her as she climbed a stepladder to secure more streamers. Already, the record player at the far end of the room was blaring music.

It was silly. She told herself that yet again as she realized she was as excited about the evening as any of the girls. She was an adult, here only to plan, supervise and chaperon. Even as she reminded herself of this, her thoughts ran forward to the evening, when the mess area would be filled with people and noise and laughter. Like the girls below her, her thoughts kept circling back to vital matters—like what she should wear.

It was fascinating to realize that this simple end-of-the-summer dance in the mountains was more exciting for her than her own debutante ball. That she had taken lightly, as the next step along the path that had been cleared for her before she was born. This was new, untried and full of possibilities.

It all centered on Chase. Eden was nearly ready to accept that as a new song blared into life. Since it was one she'd heard dozens of times before, she began to hum along with it. Her ponytail swayed with the movement as she attached another streamer.

"We'll ask Miss Carlbough." Eden heard the voices below,

but paid little attention, as she had a tack in her mouth and five feet of crepe paper held together by her thumb. "She always knows, and if she doesn't, she finds out."

She had started to secure the tack, but as the statement drifted up to her, she stopped pushing. Was that really the way the girls saw her? Dependable? With a half laugh, she sent the tack home. To her, the statement was the highest of compliments, a sign of faith.

She'd done what she had set out to do. In three short months, she had accomplished something she had never done in all her years of living. She had made something of herself, by herself. And, perhaps more importantly, for herself.

It wasn't going to stop here. Eden dropped the rest of the tacks into her pocket. The summer might be nearly over, but the challenge wasn't. Whether she was in South Mountain or Philadelphia, she wasn't going to forget what it meant to grow. Twisting on the ladder, she started down to find out what it was the girls had wanted to ask her. On the second rung, she stopped, staring.

The tall, striking woman strode into the mess. The tail of her Hermès scarf crossed the neck of a cerise suit and trailed on behind. Her bone-white hair was perfect, as was the double strand of pearls that lay on her bosom. Tucked in the crook of one arm was a small piece of white fluff known as BooBoo.

"Aunt Dottie!" Delighted, Eden scrambled down from the ladder. In seconds she was enveloped by Dottie's personal scent, an elusive combination of Paris and success. "Oh, it's wonderful to see you." Drawing back from the hug, Eden studied the lovely, strong-boned face. Even now, she could see shadows of her father in the eyes and around the mouth. "You're the last person I expected to see here."

"Darling, have you grown thorns in the country?"

"Thorns? I—oh." Laughing, Eden reached in her pocket. "Thumbtacks. Sorry."

"The hug was worth a few holes." Taking Eden's hand, she stepped back to make her own study. Though her face remained passive, she let out a quiet sigh of relief. No one knew how many restless nights she'd spent worrying over her brother's only child. "You look beautiful. A little thin, but with marvelous color." With Eden's hand still in hers, she glanced around the room. "But darling, what an odd place you've chosen to spend the summer."

"Aunt Dottie." Eden just shook her head. Throughout the weeks and months after her father's death, Dottie had stubbornly refused to accept Eden's decision not to use Dottie's money as a buffer, her home as a refuge. "If I have marvelous color, credit the country air."

"Hmm." Far from convinced, Dottie continued to look around as a new record plopped down to continue the unbroken cycle of music. "I've always considered the south of France country enough."

"Aunt Dottie, tell me what you're doing here. I'm amazed you could even find the place."

"It wasn't difficult. The chauffeur reads a map very well." Dottie gave the fluff in her arms a light pat. "BooBoo and I felt an urge for a drive to the country."

"I see." And she did. Like everyone else she had left behind, Eden knew that her aunt considered her camp venture an impulse. It would take more than one summer to convince Dottie, or anyone else, that she was serious. After all, it had taken her most of the summer to convince herself.

"Yes, and since I was in the neighborhood…" Dottie let that trail off. "What a chic outfit," she commented, taking in

Eden's paint-spattered smock and tattered sneakers. "Then, perhaps bohemian's coming back. What do you have there?"

"Crepe paper. It goes with the thumbtacks." Eden extended her hand. BooBoo regally allowed her head to be patted.

"Well, give them both to one of these charming young ladies and come see what I've brought you."

"Brought me?" Obeying automatically, Eden handed over the streamers. "Start these around the tables, will you, Lisa?"

"Do you know," Dottie began as she linked her arm through Eden's, "the nearest town is at least twenty miles from here? That is if one could stretch credibility and call what we passed through a town. There, there, BooBoo, I won't set you down on the nasty ground." She cuddled the dog as they stepped outside. "BooBoo's a bit skittish out of the city, you understand."

"Perfectly."

"Where was I? Oh yes, the town. It had one traffic light and a place called Earl's Lunch. I was almost curious enough to stop and see what one did at Earl's Lunch."

Eden laughed, and leaned over to kiss Dottie's cheek. "One eats a small variety of sandwiches and stale potato chips and coffee while exchanging town gossip."

"Marvelous. Do you go often?"

"Unfortunately, my social life's been a bit limited."

"Well, your surprise might just change all that." Turning, Dottie gestured toward the canary-yellow Rolls parked in the main compound. Eden felt every muscle, every emotion freeze as the man straightened from his easy slouch against the hood.

"Eric."

He smiled, and in a familiar gesture, ran one hand lightly over his hair. Around him, a group of girls had gathered to admire the classic lines of the Rolls and the classic looks of Eric Keeton.

His smile was perfectly angled as he walked toward her. His walk was confident, just a shade too conservative for a swagger. As she watched him, Eden saw him in the clear light of disinterest. His hair, several shades darker than her own, was perfectly styled for the boardroom or the country club. Casual attire, which included pleated slacks and a polo shirt, fit neatly over his rather narrow frame. Hazel eyes, which had a tendency to look bored easily, smiled and warmed now. Though she hadn't offered them, he took both her hands.

"Eden, how marvelous you look."

His hands were soft. Strange, she had forgotten that. Though she didn't bother to remove hers, her voice was cool. "Hello, Eric."

"Lovelier than ever, isn't she, Dottie?" Her stiff greeting didn't seem to disturb him. He gave her hands an intimate little squeeze. "Your aunt was worried about you. She expected you to be thin and wan."

"Fortunately, I'm neither." Now, carefully, deliberately, Eden removed her hands. She would have been greatly pleased, though she had no way of knowing it, that her eyes were as cold as her voice. It was so easy to turn away from him. "Whatever possessed you to drive all this way, Aunt Dottie? You weren't really worried?"

"A tad." Concerned with the ice in her niece's voice, Dottie touched Eden's cheek. "And I did want to see the—the place where you spent the summer."

"I'll give you a tour."

A thin left brow arched in a manner identical to Eden's. "How charming."

"Aunt Dottie!" Red curls bouncing, Candy raced around the side of the building. "I knew it had to be you." Out of breath and grinning broadly, Candy accepted Dottie's embrace. "The girls were talking about a yellow Rolls in the compound. Who else could it have been?"

"As enthusiastic as ever." Dottie's smile was all affection. She might not have always understood Candice Bartholomew, but she had always been fond of her. "I hope you don't mind a surprise visit."

"I love it." Candy bent down to the puff of fur. "Hi, BooBoo." Straightening, she let her gaze drift over Eric. "Hello, Eric." Her voice dropped an easy twenty-five degrees. "Long way from home."

"Candy." Unlike Dottie, he had no fondness for Eden's closest friend. "You seem to have paint all over your hands."

"It's dry," she said, carelessly, and somewhat regretfully. If the paint had been wet, she would have greeted him more personally.

"Eden's offered to take us on a tour." Dottie was well aware of the hostility. She'd driven hundreds of miles from Philadelphia for one purpose. To help her niece find happiness. If it meant she had to manipulate…so much the better. "I know Eric's dying to look around, but if I could impose on you—" She laid her hand on Candy's. "I'd really love to sit down with a nice cup of tea. BooBoo, too. The drive was a bit tiring."

"Of course." Manners were their own kind of trap. Candy sent Eden a look meant to fortify her. "We'll use the kitchen, if you don't mind the confusion."

"My dear, I thrive on it." With that she turned to smile at Eden and was surprised by the hard, knowing look in Eden's eyes.

"Go right ahead, Aunt Dottie. I'll show Eric what the camp has to offer."

"Eden, I—"

"Go have your tea, darling." She kissed Dottie's cheek.

"We'll talk later." She turned, leaving Eric to follow or not. When he fell into step beside her, she began. "We've six sleeping cabins this season, with plans to add two more for next summer. Each cabin has an Indian name to keep it distinct."

As they passed the cabins, she saw that the anemones were still stubbornly blooming. They gave her strength. "Each week, we have a contest for the neatest cabin. The reward is extra riding time, or swimming time, or whatever the girls prefer. Candy and I have a small shower in our cabin. The girls share facilities at the west end of the compound."

"Eden." Eric cupped her elbow in his palm in the same manner he had used when strolling down Broad Street. She gritted her teeth, but didn't protest.

"Yes?" The cool, impersonal look threw him off. It took him only a moment to decide it meant she was hiding a broken heart.

"What have you been doing with yourself?" He waved his hand in a gesture that took in the compound and the surrounding hills. "Here?"

Holding on to her temper, Eden decided to take the question literally. "We've tried to keep the camp regimented, while still allowing for creativity and fun. Over the past few weeks, we've found that we can adhere fairly tightly to the schedule as long as we make room for fresh ideas and individual needs." Pleased with herself, she dipped her hands into the pockets of her smock. "We're up at six-thirty. Breakfast is at seven sharp. Daily inspection begins at seven-thirty and activities at eight. For the most part, I deal with the horses and stables, but when necessary, I can pitch in and help in other areas."

"Eden." Eric stopped her by gently tightening his fingers on her elbow. Turning to him, she watched the faint breeze ruffle his smooth, fair hair. She thought of the dark confusion of Chase's hair. "It's difficult to believe you've spent your summer camping out in a cabin and overseeing a parade of girls on horseback."

"Is it?" She merely smiled. Of course it was difficult for him. He owned a stable, but he'd never lifted a pitchfork. Rather than resentment, Eden felt a stirring of pity. "Well, there's that, among a few other things such as hiking, smoothing over cases of homesickness and poison ivy, rowing, giving advice on teenage romance and fashion, identifying fifteen different varieties of local wildflowers and seeing that a group of girls has fun. Would you like to see the stables?" She headed off without waiting for his answer.

"Eden." He caught her elbow again. It took all her willpower not to jab it back into his soft stomach. "You're angry. Of course you are, but I—"

"You've always had a fondness for good horseflesh." She swung the stable door open so that he had to back off or get a faceful of wood. "We've two mares and four geldings. One of the mares is past her prime, but I'm thinking of breeding the other. The foals would interest the girls and eventually become part of the riding stock. This is Courage."

"Eden, please. We have to talk."

She stiffened when his hands touched her shoulders. But she was calm, very calm, when she turned and removed them. "I thought we were talking."

He'd heard the ice in her voice before, and he understood it. She was a proud, logical woman. He'd approach her on that level. "We have to talk about us, darling."

"In what context?"

He reached for her hand, giving a small shrug when she drew it away. If she had accepted him without a murmur, he would have been a great deal more surprised. For days now, he'd been planning exactly the proper way to smooth things over. He'd decided on regretful, with a hint of humble thrown in.

"You've every right to be furious with me, every right to want me to suffer."

His tone, soft, quiet, understanding, had her swallowing a ball of heat. Indifference, she reminded herself, disinterest, was the greatest insult she could hand him. "It doesn't really concern me if you suffer or not." That wasn't quite true, she admitted. She wouldn't be averse to seeing him writhe a bit. That was because he had come, she realized. Because he had had the gall to come and assume she'd be waiting.

"Eden, you have to know that I have suffered, suffered a great deal. I would have come before, but I wasn't sure you'd see me."

This was the man she had planned to spend her life with. This was the man she had hoped to have children with. She stared at him now, unsure whether she was in the midst of a comedy or a tragedy. "I'm sorry to hear that, Eric. I don't see any reason why you should have suffered. You were only being practical, after all."

Soothed by her placid attitude, he stepped toward her. "I admit that, rightly or wrongly, I was practical." His hands slid up her arms in an old gesture that made her jaw clench. "These past few months have shown me that there are times when practical matters have to take second place."

"Is that so?" She smiled at him, surprised that he couldn't feel the heat. "What would go first?"

"Personal..." He stroked a finger over her cheek. "Much more personal matters."

"Such as?"

His lips were curved as his mouth lowered. She felt the heat of anger freeze into icy disdain. Did he think her a fool? Could he believe himself so irresistible? Then she nearly did laugh, as she realized the answer to both questions was yes.

She let him kiss her. The touch of his lips left her totally unmoved. It fascinated her that, only a few short months before, his kisses had warmed her. It had been nothing like the volcanic heat she experienced with Chase, but there had been a comfort and an easy pleasure. That was all she had thought there was meant to be.

Now there was nothing. The absence of feeling in itself dulled the edge of her fury. She was in control. Here, as in other areas of her life, she was in control. Though his lips coaxed, she simply stood, waiting for him to finish.

When he lifted his head, Eden put her hands on his arms to draw herself away. It was then she saw Chase just inside the open stable door.

The sun was at his back, silhouetting him, blinding her to the expression on his face. Even so, her mouth was dry as she stared, trying to see through shadow and sun. When he stepped forward, his eyes were on hers.

Explanations sprang to her tongue, but she could only shake her head as his gaze slid over her and onto Eric.

"Keeton." Chase nodded, but didn't extend his hand. He knew if he had the other man's fingers in his he would take pleasure in breaking them, one by one.

"Elliot." Eric returned the nod. "I'd forgotten. You have land around here, don't you?"

"A bit." Chase wanted to murder him, right there in the stables, while Eden watched. Then he would find it just as satisfying to murder her.

"You must know Eden, then." Eric placed a hand on her shoulder in a casually possessive movement. Chase followed the gesture before looking at her again. Her instinctive move to shrug away Eric's hand was stopped by the look. Was it anger she saw there, or was it disgust?

"Yes. Eden and I have run into each other a few times." He dipped his hands into his pockets as they balled into fists.

"Chase was generous enough to allow us to use his lake." Her right hand groped for her left until they were clasped together. "We had a tour of his orchards." Though pride suffered, her eyes pleaded with him.

"Your land must be very near here." Eric hadn't missed the exchange of looks. His hand leaned more heavily on Eden's shoulder.

"Near enough."

Then they were looking at each other, not at her. Somehow that, more than anything, made her feel as though she'd been shifted to the middle. If there was tension and she was the cause of it, she wanted to be able to speak on her own behalf. But the expression in Chase's eyes only brought confusion. The weight of Eric's hand only brought annoyance. Moving away from Eric, she stepped toward Chase.

"Did you want to see me?"

"Yes." But he'd wanted more than that, a great deal more. Seeing her in Eric's arms had left him feeling both murderous and empty. He wasn't ready to deal with either yet. "It wasn't important."

"Chase—"

"Oh, hello." The warmth in Candy's voice came almost as a shock. She stepped through the doorway with Dottie at her side. "Aunt Dottie, I want you to meet our neighbor, Chase Elliot."

Even as Dottie extended her hand, her eyes were narrowed speculatively. "Elliot? I'm sure I know that name. Yes, yes, didn't we meet several years ago? You're Jessie Winthrop's grandson."

Eden watched his lips curve, his eyes warm, but he wasn't looking at her. "Yes, I am, and I remember you very well, Mrs. Norfolk. You haven't changed."

Dottie's laugh was low and quick. "It's been fifteen years if it's been a day. I'd say there's been a change or two. You were about a foot shorter at the time." She sized him up approvingly in a matter of ten seconds. "It's apples, isn't it? Yes, of course, it is. Elliot's."

And, oh my God, she realized almost as quickly, I've brought Eric along and jammed up the works. A person would have to have a three-inch layer of steel coating not to feel the shock waves bouncing around the stables.

What could be done, she told herself, could be undone. Smiling, she looked at her niece. "Candy's been telling me about the social event of the season. Are we all invited?"

"Invited?" Eden struggled to gather her scattered wits. "You mean the dance?" She had to laugh. Her aunt was standing in the stables in Italian shoes and a suit that had cost more than any one of the horses. "Aunt Dottie, you don't intend to stay here?"

"Stay here?" The white brows shot up. "I should say not." She twisted the pearls at her neck as she began to calculate. She didn't intend to bunk down in a cabin, but neither was she about to miss the impending fireworks. "Eric and I are staying at a hotel some miles away, but I'd be heartbroken if you didn't ask us to the party tonight." She put a friendly hand on Chase's arm. "You're coming, aren't you?"

He knew a manipulator when he saw one. "Wouldn't miss it."

"Wonderful." Dottie slid Candy's hand back into the crook of her arm, then patted it. "We're all invited then."

Fumbling, Candy looked from Eric to Eden. "Well, yes, of course, but—"

"Isn't this sweet?" Dottie patted her hand again. "We'll have a delightful time. Don't you think so, Eden?"

"Delightful," Eden agreed, wondering if she could hitch a ride out of town.

Chapter 9

Eden had problems—big problems. But not the least of them were the sixty adolescents in the mess hall. However she handled Eric, however she managed to explain herself to Chase, sixty young bodies couldn't be put on hold.

The boys arrived in vans at eight o'clock. Unless Eden missed her guess, they were every bit as nervous as the girls. Eden remembered her own cotillion days, the uncertainty and the damp palms. The blaring music helped cover some of the awkwardness as the boys' counselors trooped them in.

The refreshment table was loaded. There was enough punch stored in the kitchen to bathe in. Candy gave a brief welcoming speech to set the tone, the banners and the paper flowers waving at her back. A fresh record was set spinning on the turntable. Girls stood on one side of the room, boys on the other.

The biggest problem, naturally, was that no one wanted to

go first. Eden had worked that out by making up two bowls of corresponding numbers. Boys picked from one, girls from another. You matched, you danced. It wasn't imaginative, but it was expedient.

When the first dance was half over, she slipped into the kitchen to check on backup refreshments, leaving Candy to supervise and to mingle with the male counselors.

When she returned, the dance floor wasn't as crowded, but this time the partners had chosen for themselves.

"Miss Carlbough?"

Eden turned her head as she bent to place a bowl of chips in an empty space on the long crowded table. Roberta's face was spotless. Her thatch of wild hair had been tamed into a bushy ponytail and tied with a ribbon. She had little turquoise stars in her ears to match a ruffled and not-too-badly-wrinkled blouse. The dusting of freckles over her face had been partially hidden by a layer of powder. Eden imagined she had conned it out of one of the older girls, but let it pass.

"Hi, Roberta." Plucking two pretzels from a bowl, she handed one over. "Aren't you going to dance?"

"Sure." She glanced over her shoulder, confident and patient. "I wanted to talk to you first."

"Oh?" It didn't appear that she needed a pep talk. Eden had already seen the skinny, dark-haired boy Roberta had set her sights on. If Eden was any judge, he didn't stand a chance. "What about?"

"I saw that guy in the Rolls."

Eden's automatic warning not to speak with her mouth full was postponed. "You mean Mr. Keeton?"

"Some of the girls think he's cute."

"Hmm." Eden nibbled on her own pretzel.

"A couple of them said you were soft on him. They think

you had a lovers' quarrel, you know, like Romeo and Juliet or something. Now he's come to beg you to forgive him, and you're going to realize that you can't live without him and go off and get married."

The pretzel hung between two fingers as Eden listened. After a moment, she managed to clear her throat. "Well, that's quite a scenario."

"I said it was baloney."

Trying not to laugh, she bit into the pretzel. "Did you?"

"You're smart, all the girls say so." Reaching behind Eden, she took a handful of chips. "I said you were too smart to be soft on the guy in the Rolls, because he's not nearly as neat as Mr. Elliot." Roberta glanced over her shoulder as if in confirmation. "He's shorter, too."

"Yes." Eden had to bite her lip. "Yes, he is."

"He doesn't look like he'd jump in the lake to fool around."

The last statement had Eden trying to imagine Eric diving into the cool waters of the lake half-dressed. Or bringing her a clutch of wildflowers. Or finding pictures in the sky. Her lips curved dreamily. "No, Eric would never do that."

"That's why I knew it was all baloney." Roberta devoured the chips. "When Mr. Elliot comes, I'm going to dance with him, but now I'm going to dance with Bobby." Shooting Eden a smile, she walked across the room and grabbed the hand of the lanky, dark-haired boy. As Eden had thought, he didn't have a chance.

She watched the dancing, but thought of Chase. It came to her all at once that he was the only man she knew whom she hadn't measured against her father. Comparisons had never occurred to her. She hadn't measured Chase against anyone but had fallen in love with him for himself. Now all she needed was the courage to tell him.

"So this is how young people entertain themselves these days."

Eden turned to find Dottie beside her. For Camp Liberty's summer dance, she had chosen mauve lace. The pearls had been exchanged for a single, sensational ruby. BooBoo had a clip of rhinestones—Eden sincerely hoped they were only rhinestones—secured on top of her head. Feeling a wave of affection, Eden kissed her aunt. "Are you settled into your hotel?"

"So to speak." Accepting a potato chip, Dottie took her own survey. The powder-blue voile was the essence of simplicity with its cap sleeves and high neck, but Dottie approved the way it depended on the wearer for its style. "Thank God you haven't lost your taste."

Laughing, Eden kissed her again. "I've missed you. I'm so glad you came."

"Are you?" Always discreet, Dottie led her toward the screen door. "I was afraid you weren't exactly thrilled to see me here." She let the screen whoosh shut as they stepped onto the porch. "Particularly with the surprise I brought you."

"I was glad to see you, Aunt Dottie."

"But not Eric."

Eden leaned back on the rail. "Did you think I would be?"

"Yes." She sighed, and brushed at the bodice of her lace. "I suppose I did. It only took five minutes to realize what a mistake I'd made. Darling, I hope you understand I was trying to help."

"Of course I do, and I love you for it."

"I thought that whatever had gone wrong between you would have had time to heal over." Forgetting herself, Dottie offered BooBoo the rest of the chip. "To be honest, the way he's been talking to me, I was sure by bringing him to you I'd be doing the next-best thing to saving your life."

"I can imagine," Eden murmured.

"So much for grand gestures." Dottie moved her shoulders so that the ruby winked. "Eden, you never told me why you two called off the wedding. It was so sudden."

Eden opened her mouth, then closed it again. There was no reason to hurt and infuriate her aunt after all these months. If she told her now, it would be for spite or, worse, for sympathy. Eric was worth neither. "We just realized we weren't suited."

"I always thought differently." There was a loud blast of music and a chorus of laughter. Dottie cast a glance over her shoulder. "Eric seems to think differently, too. He's been to see me several times in recent weeks."

Pushing the heavy fall of hair from her shoulders, Eden walked to the edge of the porch. Perhaps Eric had discovered that the Carlbough name wasn't so badly tarnished after all. It gave her no pleasure to be cynical, but it was the only answer that seemed right. It wouldn't have taken him long to realize that eventually she would come into money again, through inheritances. She swallowed her bitterness as she turned back to her aunt.

"He's mistaken, Aunt Dottie. Believe me when I say he doesn't have any genuine feelings for me. Perhaps he thinks he does," she added, when she saw the frown centered between Dottie's brows. "I'd say it's a matter of habit. I didn't love Eric." Her hands outstretched, she went to take her aunt's. "I never did. It's taken me some time to understand that I was going to marry him for all the wrong reasons—because it was expected, because it was easy. And…" She drew in her breath. "Because I mistakenly thought he was like Papa."

"Oh, darling."

"It was my mistake, so most of it was my fault." Now that

it was said, and said aloud, she could accept it. "I always compared the men I dated with Papa. He was the kindest, most caring man I've ever known, but even though I loved and admired him, it was wrong of me to judge other men by him."

"We all loved him, Eden." Dottie drew Eden into her arms. "He was a good man, a loving man. A gambler, but—"

"I don't mind that he was a gambler." Now, when she drew back, Eden could smile. "I know if he hadn't died so suddenly, he'd have come out on top again. But it doesn't matter, Aunt Dottie, because I'm a gambler, too." She turned so that her gesture took in the camp. "I've learned how to make my own stake."

"How like him you are." Dottie was forced to draw a tissue out of her bag. "When you insisted on doing this, even when I first came here today, I could only think my poor little Eden's gone mad. Then I looked, really looked, at your camp, at the girls, at you, and I could see you'd made it work." After one inelegant sniff, she stuffed the tissue back in her bag. "I'm proud of you, Eden. Your father would have been proud of you."

Now it was Eden's eyes that dampened. "Aunt Dottie, I can't tell you how much that means to me. After he died and I had to sell everything, I felt I'd betrayed him, you, everyone."

"No." Dottie cupped Eden's chin in her hand. "What you did took tremendous courage, more than I had. You know how badly I wanted to spare you all of that."

"I know, and I appreciate it, but it had to be this way."

"I think I understand that now. I want you to know that I hurt for you, Eden, but I was never ashamed. Even now, knowing you don't need it, I'll tell you that my house is yours whenever you like."

"Knowing that is enough."

"And I expect this to be the finest camp in the east within five years."

Eden laughed again, and all the weight she'd carried with her since her father's death slipped off her shoulders. "It will be."

With a nod, Dottie took a step along the rail and looked out at the compound. "I do believe you should have a pool. Girls should have regulated, regimented swimming lessons. Splashing in the lake doesn't meet those standards. I'm going to donate one."

Eden's back went up immediately. "Aunt Dottie—"

"In your father's name." Dottie paused and cocked a brow. "Yes, I can see you won't argue with that. If I can donate a wing to a hospital, I can certainly donate a swimming pool in my brother's name to my favorite niece's camp. In fact, my accountant's going to be thrilled. Now, would you like Eric and me to go?"

Barely recovered from being so neatly maneuvered, Eden only sighed. "Having Eric here means nothing now. I want you to stay as long as you like."

"Good. BooBoo and I are enjoying ourselves." Dottie bent down to nuzzle in the dog's fur. "The delightful thing about BooBoo is that she's so much more tractable than any of my children were. Eden, one more thing before I go inside and absorb culture. I would swear that I felt, well, how to put it? One might almost say earth tremors when I walked into the stables this afternoon. Are you in love with someone else?"

"Aunt Dottie—"

"Answer enough. I'll just add my complete approval, not that it matters. BooBoo was quite charmed."

"Are you trying to be eccentric?"

With a smile, Dottie shifted the bundle in her arms. "When you can't rely on beauty any longer, you have to fall back on something. Ah, look here." She stepped aside as the Lamborghini cruised up. Lips pursed, Dottie watched Chase climb out. "Hello again," she called. "I admire your taste." She gave Eden a quick pat. "Yes, I do. I think I'll just pop inside and try some punch. It isn't too dreadful, is it?"

"I made it myself."

"Oh." Dottie rolled her eyes. "Well, I've some gambler in me as well."

Bracing herself, Eden turned toward Chase. "Hello. I'm glad you could—"

His mouth covered hers so quickly, so completely, that there wasn't even time for surprise. She might think of the hard possessiveness of the kiss later, but for now she just slid her hands up his back so that she could grip his shoulders. Instantly intense, instantly real, instantly right.

She hadn't felt this with Eric. That was what Chase told himself as she melted against him. She'd never felt this with anyone else. And he was going to be damn sure she didn't. Torn between anger and need, he drew her away.

"What—" She had to stop and try again. "What was that for?"

He gathered her hair in his hand to bring her close again. His lips tarried a breath from hers. "As someone once said to me, I wanted to kiss you. Any objections?"

He was daring her. Her chin angled in acceptance. "I can't think of any."

"Mull it over. Get back to me." With that, he propelled her toward the lights and music.

She didn't like to admit that cowardice might be part of the reason she carefully divided her time between the girls and the visiting counselors. Eden told herself it was a matter of courtesy and responsibility. But she knew she needed to have her thoughts well in hand before she spoke privately with Chase again.

She watched him dance with Roberta and wanted to throw herself into his arms and tell him how much she loved him. How big a fool would that make her? He hadn't asked about Eric, so how could she explain? It hummed through her mind that if he hadn't asked, it didn't matter to him. If it didn't matter, he wasn't nearly as involved as she was. Still, she told herself that before the evening was over she would find the time to talk it through with him, whether he wanted to hear it or not. She just wanted to wait until she was sure she could do a good job of it.

There was no such confusion about the evening in general. The summer dance was a hit. Plans between the camp coordinators were already under way to make it an annual event. Already Candy was bubbling with ideas for more joint ventures.

As always, Eden would let Candy plan and organize; then she would tidy up the details.

By keeping constantly on the move, Eden avoided any direct confrontation with Eric or Chase. Of course they spoke, even danced, but all in the sanctuary of the crowded mess hall. Eric's conversation had been as mild as hers, but there had been something dangerous in Chase's eyes. It was that, and the memory of that rocketing kiss, that had her postponing the inevitable.

"I guess you like her a lot," Roberta ventured as she saw Chase's gaze wander toward Eden yet again.

"What?" Distracted, Chase looked back at his dance partner.

"Miss Carlbough. You're soft on her. She's so pretty," Roberta added with only the slightest touch of envy. "We voted her the prettiest counselor, even though Miss Allison has more—" She caught herself, realizing suddenly that you didn't discuss certain parts of a woman's anatomy with a man, even with Mr. Elliot. "More, ah…"

"I get the picture." Charmed, as always, Chase swung her in a quick circle.

"Some of the other girls think Mr. Keeton's a honey."

"Oh?" Chase's smile turned into a sneer as he glanced at the man in question.

"I think his nose is skinny."

"It was almost broken," Chase muttered.

"And his eyes are too close together," Roberta added for good measure. "I like you a lot better."

Touched, and remembering his first crush, Chase tugged on her ponytail to tilt her face to his. "I'm pretty soft on you, too."

From her corner, Eden watched the exchange. She saw Chase bend down and saw Roberta's face explode into smiles. A sigh nearly escaped her before she realized she was allowing herself to be envious of a twelve-year-old. With a shake of her head, she told herself that it was the strain of keeping herself unavailable that was beginning to wear on her. The music never played below loud. Uncountable trips to the kitchen kept the refreshment table full. Boys and girls shouted over the music to make themselves heard.

Five minutes, she told herself. She would steal just five quiet, wonderful minutes by herself.

This time, when she slipped back into the kitchen, she kept going. The moist summer air soothed her the moment she stepped outside. It smelled of grass and honeysuckle. Grateful for the fresh air after the cloying scent of fruit punch, Eden breathed deeply.

Tonight, the moon was only a sliver in the sky. She realized she had seen it change, had watched its waning and waxing more in the past three months than she had in all of her life. This was true of more than the moon. She would never look at anything else exactly the same way again.

She stood for a moment, finding the pictures in the sky that Chase had shown her. With the air warm on her face, she wondered if there would ever be a time when he would show her more.

As she crossed the grass, the light was silvery. From behind her came the steady murmur of music and voices. She found an old hickory tree and leaned against it, enjoying the solitude and the distance.

This was what warm summer nights were for, she thought. For dreams and wishes. No matter how cold it got during the winter, no matter how far away summer seemed, she would be able to take this night out of her memory and live it again.

The creak and swish of the back door cut through her concentration.

"Eric." She straightened, not bothering to disguise the irritation in her voice.

He came to her until he, too, stood under the hickory. Starlight filtered through the leaves to mix with the shadows. "I've never known you to leave a party."

"I've changed."

"Yes." Her eyes were calm and direct. He shifted uncomfortably. "I've noticed." When he reached out to touch her, she didn't step back. She didn't even feel his touch. "We never finished talking."

"Yes, we did. A long time ago."

"Eden." Moving cautiously, he lifted a finger to trace her jawline. "I've come a long way to see you, to make things right between us."

Eden merely tilted her head to the side. "I'm sorry you

were inconvenienced, but there's nothing to make right."
Oddly, the anger, even the bitterness, had become diluted. It
had started weakening, she knew, when he had kissed her that
afternoon. Looking at him now, she felt detached, as if he were
someone she'd known only vaguely. "Eric, it's foolish for either of us to drag this out. Let's just leave things alone."

"I admit I was a fool." He blocked her exit, as if by simply continuing in the same vein he could put things back in
the order he wanted. "Eden, I hurt you, and I'm sorry, but I
was thinking of you as well as myself."

She wanted to laugh, but found she didn't even have the
energy to give him that much. "Of me, Eric? All right, have
it your way. Thank you and goodbye."

"Don't be difficult," he said, displaying a first trace of impatience. "You know how difficult it would have been for you
to go through with the wedding while the scandal was still
fresh in everyone's mind."

That stopped her, more than his hand had. She leaned back
against the tree and waited. Yes, there was still a trace of
anger, she discovered. It was mild, and buried quite deep, but
it was still there. Perhaps it would be best to purge everything
from her system. "Scandal. By that I assume you mean my
father's poor investments."

"Eden." He moved closer again to put a comforting hand
on her arm. "Your position changed so dramatically, so
abruptly, when your father died and left you..."

"To earn my own way," she finished for him. "Yes, we can
agree on that. My position changed. Over the past few months
I've become grateful for that." There was annoyance now, but
only as if he were a pesky fly she had to swat away. "I've
learned to expect things from myself and to realize money had
very little to do with the way I was living."

She saw by his frown that he didn't understand, would never understand the person who had grown up from the ashes of that old life. "You might find this amazing, Eric, but I don't care what anyone thinks about my altered circumstances. For the first time in my life, I have what I want, and I earned it myself."

"You can't expect me to believe that this little camp is what you want. I know you, Eden." He twined a lock of hair around his finger. "The woman I know would never choose something like this over the life we could have together in Philadelphia."

"You might be right again." Slowly, she reached up to untangle his hand from her hair. "But I'm no longer the woman you knew."

"Don't be ridiculous." For the first time he felt a twinge of panic. The one thing he had never considered was driving hundreds of miles to be humiliated. "Come back to the hotel with me tonight. Tomorrow we can go back to Philadelphia and be married, just as we always planned."

She studied him for a moment, trying to see if there was some lingering affection for her there, some true emotion. No, she decided almost at once. She wished it had been true, for then she could have had some kind of respect for him.

"Why are you doing this? You don't love me. You never did, or you couldn't have turned your back on me when I needed you."

"Eden—"

"No, let me finish. Let's finish this once and for all." She pushed him back a foot with an impatient movement of her hands. "I'm not interested in your apologies or your excuses, Eric. The simple truth is you don't matter to me."

It was said so calmly, so bluntly, that he very nearly believed it. "You know you don't mean that, Eden. We were going to be married."

"Because it was convenient for both of us. For that much, Eric, I'll share the blame with you."

"Let's forget blame, Eden. Let me show you what we can have."

She held him off with a look. "I'm not angry anymore, and I'm not hurt. The simple fact is, Eric, I don't love you, and I don't want you."

For a moment, he was completely silent. When he did speak, Eden was surprised to hear genuine emotion in his voice. "Find someone to replace me so soon, Eden?"

She could almost laugh. He had jilted her almost two steps from the altar, but now he could act out the role of betrayed lover. "This grows more and more absurd, but no, Eric, it wasn't a matter of replacing you, it was a matter of seeing you for what you are. Don't make me explain to you what that is."

"Just how much does Chase Elliot have to do with all of this?"

"How dare you question me?" She started past him, but this time he grabbed her arm, and his grip wasn't gentle. Surprised by his refusal to release her, she stepped back and looked at him again. He was a child, she thought, who had thrown away a toy and was ready to stamp his feet now that he wanted it back and couldn't have it. Because her temper was rising, she fell back on her attitude of icy detachment. "Whatever is or isn't between Chase and me is none of your concern."

This cool, haughty woman was one he recognized. His tone softened. "Everything about you concerns me."

Weary, she could only sigh. "Eric, you're embarrassing yourself."

Before she could rid herself of him again, the screen door opened for a second time.

"Apparently I'm interrupting again." Hands in pockets, Chase stepped down from the porch.

"You seem to be making a habit of it." Eric released Eden, only to step between her and Chase. "You should be able to see that Eden and I are having a private conversation. They do teach manners, even here in the hills, don't they?"

Chase wondered if Eric would appreciate his style of manners. No, he doubted the tidy Philadelphian would appreciate a bloody nose. But then, he didn't give a damn what Eric appreciated. He'd taken two steps forward before Eden realized his intent.

"The conversation's over," she said quickly, stepping between them. She might as well have been invisible. As she had felt herself being shifted to the middle that afternoon, now she felt herself being nudged aside.

"Seems you've had considerable time to say what's on your mind." Chase rocked back on his heels, keeping his eyes on Eric.

"I don't see what business it is of yours how long I speak with my fiancée."

"Fiancée!" Eden's outraged exclamation was also ignored.

"You've let some months slip past you, Keeton." Chase's voice remained mild. His hands remained in his pockets. "Some changes have been made."

"Changes?" This time Eden turned to Chase, with no better results. "What are you talking about?"

Calmly, without giving her a glance, he took her hand. "You promised me a dance."

Instantly, Eric had her other arm. "We haven't finished."

Chase turned back, and for the first time the danger in his eyes was as clear as glass. "Yes, you have. The lady's with me."

Infuriated, Eden yanked herself free of both of them. "Stop

it!" She'd had enough of being pulled in two directions without being asked if she wanted to move in either. For the first time in her life, she forgot manners, courtesy and control and did what Chase had once advised. When you're mad, he'd said, yell.

"You are both so *stupid*!" A toss of her head had the hair flying into her eyes to be dragged back impatiently. "How dare you stand here like two half-witted dogs snarling over the same bone? Don't either of you think I'm capable of speaking my own mind, making my own decisions? Well, I've got news for both of you. I can speak my own mind just fine. You." She turned to face Eric. "I meant every word I said to you. Understand? *Every single word.* I tried to phrase things as politely as possible, but if you push, let me warn you, you won't receive the same courtesy again."

"Eden, darling—"

"No, no, no!" She slapped away the hand he held out to her. "You dumped me the moment things got rough. If you think I'll take you back now, after you've shown yourself to be a weak, callous, insensitive—" oh, what was Candy's word? "—weasel," she remembered with relish, "you're crazy. And if you dare, if you *dare* touch me again, I'll knock your caps loose."

God, what a woman, Chase thought. He wondered how soon he could take her into his arms and show her how much he loved her. He'd always thought her beautiful, almost ethereal; now she was a Viking. More than he'd wanted anything in his life, he wanted to hold that passion in his arms and devour it. He was smiling at her when she whirled on him.

"And you." Taking a step closer to Chase, she began to stab him in the chest with her finger. "You go find someone else to start a common brawl over. I'm not flattered by your Neanderthal attempts at playing at the white knight."

It wasn't quite what he'd had in mind. "For God's sake, Eden, I was—"

"Shut up." She gave him another quick jab. "I can take care of myself, Mr. Macho. And if you think I appreciate your interference in my affairs, you're mistaken. If I wanted some—some muscle-flexing he-man to clean up after me, I'd rent one."

Sucking in a deep breath, she turned to face both of them. "The two of you have behaved with less common sense than those children in there. Just for future reference, I don't find it amusing that two grown men should feel it necessary for their egos to use me as a Ping-Pong ball. I make my own choices, and I've got one for you, so listen carefully. I don't want either one of you."

Turning on her heel, she left them standing under the hickory, staring after her.

Chapter 10

The last day of the session was pandemonium. There was packing and tears and missing shoes. Each cabin gave birth to its own personal crisis. Gear had to be stored until the following summer, and an inventory had to be made of kitchen supplies.

Beds were stripped. Linen was laundered and folded. Eden caught herself sniffling over a pillowcase. Somehow, during the first inventory, they came up short by two blankets and counted five towels more than they'd started with.

Eden decided to leave her personal packing until after the confusion had died down. It even crossed her mind to spend one last night in camp and leave fresh the following morning. She told herself it was more practical, even more responsible, for one of them to stay behind so that a last check could be made of the empty cabins. In truth, she just couldn't let go.

She wasn't ready to admit that. Leaving the laundry area

for the stables, she began counting bridles. The only reason she was considering staying behind, she lectured herself, was to make certain all the loose ends were tied up. As she marked numbers on her clipboard, she struggled to block out thoughts of Chase. He certainly had nothing to do with her decision to remain behind. She counted snaffle bits twice, got two different totals, then counted again.

Impossible man. She slashed the pencil over the paper, marking and totaling until she was satisfied. Without pausing, she started a critical study of reins, checking for wear. A good rubbing with saddle soap was in order, she decided. That was one more reason to stay over one more night. But, as it often had during the past week, her confrontation with Chase and Eric ran through her mind.

She had meant everything she'd said. Just reaffirming that satisfied her. Every single word, even though she had shouted it, had come straight from the heart. Even after seven days her indignation, and her resolve, were as fresh as ever.

She had simply been a prize to be fought over, she remembered as indignation began to simmer toward rage. Is that all a woman was to a man, something to yank against his side and stretch his ego on? Well, that wasn't something she would accept. She had only truly forged her own identity in recent months. That wasn't something she was going to give up, or even dilute, for anyone, for any man.

Fury bubbling, Eden crossed over to inspect the saddles. Eric had never loved her. Now, more than ever, that was crystal clear. Even without love, without caring, he'd wanted to lay some sort of claim. My woman. My property. My *fiancée*! She made a sound, somewhere between disgust and derision, that had one of the horses blowing in response.

If her aunt hadn't taken him away, Eden wasn't sure what she might have done. And, at this point, she was equally unsure she wouldn't have enjoyed it immensely.

But worse, a hundred times worse, was Chase. As she stared into space, her pencil drummed a rapid rat-a-tat-tat on the clipboard. He'd never once spoken of love or affection. There had been no promises asked or given, and yet he'd behaved just as abominably as Eric.

That was where the comparison ended, she admitted, as she pressed the heel of her hand to her brows. She was in love with Chase. Desperately in love. If he'd said a word, if he'd given her a chance to speak, how different things might have been. But now she was discovering that leaving him was infinitely more difficult than it had been to leave Philadelphia.

He hadn't spoken; he hadn't asked. The compromises she might have made for him, and only him, would never be needed now. Whatever might have been was over, she told herself, straightening her shoulders. It was time for new adjustments, new plans and, again, a new life. She had done it once, and she could do it again.

"Plans," she muttered to herself as she studied the clipboard again. There were so many plans to make for the following season. It would be summer again before she knew it.

Her fingers clutched the pencil convulsively. Was that how she would live her life, from summer to summer? Would there only be emptiness in between, emptiness and waiting? How many times would she come back and walk along the lake hoping to see him?

No. This was the mourning period. Eden closed her eyes for a moment and waited for the strength to return. You couldn't adjust and go on unless you'd grieved first. That was something else she had learned. So she would grieve for Chase. Then she would build her life.

"Eden. Eden, are you in there?"

"Right here." Eden turned as Candy rushed into the tack room.

"Oh, thank God."

"What now?"

Candy pressed a hand to her heart as if to push her breath back. "Roberta."

"Roberta?" Her stomach muscles balled like a fist. "Is she hurt?"

"She's gone."

"What do you mean, gone? Did her parents come early?"

"I mean gone." Pacing, Candy began to tug on her hair. "Her bags are all packed and stacked in her cabin. She's nowhere in camp."

"Not again." More annoyed than worried now, Eden tossed the clipboard aside. "Hasn't that child learned anything this summer? Every time I turn around she's off on a little field trip of her own."

"Marcie and Linda claim that she said she had something important to take care of before she left." Candy lifted her hands, then let them fall. "She didn't tell them what she was up to, that I'm sure of. You and I both know that she might only have gone to pick some flowers for her mother, but—"

"We can't take any chances," Eden finished.

"I've got three of the counselors out looking, but I thought you might have some idea where she could have gone before we call out the marines." She paused to catch her breath. "What a way to round out the summer."

Eden closed her eyes a minute to concentrate. Conversations with Roberta scattered through her memory until she focused on one in particular. "Oh, no." Her eyes shot open. "I think I know where she's gone." She was already rushing out of the tack room as Candy loped to keep up.

"Where?"

"I'll need to take the car. It'll be quicker." Thinking fast, Eden dashed to the rear of their cabin, where the secondhand compact was parked under a gnarled pear tree. "I'd swear she's gone to say goodbye to Chase, but make sure the orchard gets checked."

"Already done, but—"

"I'll be back in twenty minutes."

"Eden—"

The gunning of the motor drowned out Candy's words. "Don't worry, I'll bring the little darling back." She set her teeth. "If I have to drag her by her hair."

"Okay, but—" Candy stepped back as the compact shot forward. "Gas," she said with a sigh as Eden drove away. "I don't think there's much gas in the tank."

Eden noticed that the sky was darkening and decided to blame Roberta for that as well. She would have sworn an oath that Roberta had gone to see Chase one last time. A three-mile hike would never have deterred a girl of Roberta's determination.

Eden drove under the arching sign, thinking grimly of what she would say to Roberta once she had her. The pleasure she got from that slid away as the car bucked and sputtered. Eden looked down helplessly as it jolted again, then stopped dead. The needle of the gas gauge registered a flat *E*.

"Damn!" She slapped a hand on the steering wheel, then let out a yelp. Padded steering wheels weren't part of the amenities on cars as old as this one. Nursing her aching wrist, she stepped out of the car just as the first blast of thunder shook the air. As if on cue, a torrent of rain poured down.

For a moment, Eden merely stood beside the stalled car, her throbbing hand at her mouth, while water streamed over her. Her clothes were soaked through in seconds. "Perfect," she mumbled; then, on the heels of that: "Roberta." Casting one furious look skyward, she set off at a jogging run.

Lightning cracked across the sky like a whip. Thunder bellowed in response. Each time, Eden's heart leaped toward her throat. As each step brought her closer to Chase's home, her fear mounted.

What if she'd been wrong? What if Roberta wasn't there, but was caught somewhere in the storm, wet and frightened? What if she was lost or hurt? Her breath began to hitch as anxiety ballooned inside her.

She reached Chase's door, soaked to the skin and terrified.

Her pounding at the door sounded weak against the cannoning thunder. Looking back over her shoulder, Eden could see nothing but a solid wall of rain. If Roberta was out there, somewhere… Whirling back, she pounded with both fists, shouting for good measure.

When Chase opened the door, she nearly tumbled over his feet. He took one look at her soaked, bedraggled figure and knew he'd never seen anything more beautiful in his life. "Well, this is a surprise. Get you a towel?"

Eden grabbed his shirt with both hands. "Roberta," she managed, trying to convey everything with one word.

"She's in the front room." Gently, he pushed the hair out of her eyes. "Relax, Eden, she's fine."

"Oh, thank God." Near tears, Eden pressed her fingers to her eyes. But when she lowered them, her eyes were dry and furious. "I'll murder her. Right here, right now. Quickly."

Before she could carry through with her threat, Chase stepped in front of her. Now that he'd had a good taste of her temper, he no longer underestimated it. "I think I have an idea how you feel, but don't be too rough on her. She came by to propose."

"Just move aside, or I'll take you down with her." She shoved him aside and strode past him. The moment she stood in the doorway, Eden drew a breath. "Roberta." Each syllable was bitten off. The girl on the floor stopped playing with the dog and looked up.

"Oh, hi, Miss Carlbough." She grinned, apparently pleased with the company. After a moment her teeth dropped down to her lower lip. Though perhaps an optimist, Roberta was no fool. "You're all wet, Miss Carlbough."

The low sound deep in Eden's throat had Squat's ears pricking. "Roberta," she said again as she started forward. Squat moved simultaneously. Drawing up short, Eden gave the dog a wary glance. He sat now, his tail thumping, directly between Eden and Roberta. "Call off your dog," she ordered without bothering to look at Chase.

"Oh, Squat wouldn't hurt you." Roberta scurried across the floor to leap lovingly on his neck. Squat's tail thumped even harder. Eden thought for a moment that he was smiling. She was certain she'd gotten a good view of his large white teeth. "He's real friendly," Roberta assured her. "Just hold your hand out and he'll sniff it."

And take it off at the wrist—which was giving her enough trouble as it was. "Roberta," Eden began again, staying where she was. "After all these weeks, aren't you aware of the rules about leaving camp?"

"Yes, ma'am." Roberta hooked an arm around Squat's neck. "But it was important."

"That isn't the point." Eden folded her hands. She was aware of how she looked, how she sounded, and she knew that if she turned her head she would see Chase grinning at her. "Rules have a purpose, Roberta. They aren't made up just to spoil your fun, but to see to order and safety. You've broken one of the most important ones today, and not for the first time. Miss Bartholomew and I are responsible for you. Your parents expect, and rightfully so, that we'll…"

Eden trailed off as Roberta listened, solemn-eyed. She opened her mouth again, prepared to complete the lecture, but only a shuddering breath came out. "Roberta, you scared me to death."

"Gee, I'm sorry, Miss Carlbough." To Eden's surprise, Roberta jumped up and dashed across the room to throw her arms around Eden's waist. "I didn't mean to, really. I guess I didn't think anyone would miss me before I got back."

"Not miss you?" A laugh, a little shaky, whispered out as Eden pressed a kiss to the top of Roberta's head. "You monster, don't you know I've developed radar where you're concerned?"

"Yeah?" Roberta squeezed hard.

"Yeah."

"I am sorry, Miss Carlbough, really I am." She drew back so that her freckled, triangular face was tilted to Eden's. "I just had to see Chase for a minute." She sent Eden an intimate, feminine glance that had Eden looking quickly over at Chase.

"Chase?" Eden repeated, knowing her emphasis on Roberta's use of the first name would get her nowhere.

"We had a personal matter to discuss." Chase dropped down onto the arm of a chair. He wondered if Eden had any idea how protectively she was holding Roberta.

Though it was difficult, Eden managed to display some dignity in her dripping clothes. "I realize it's too much to expect a twelve-year-old to show a consistent sense of responsibility, but I would have expected more from you."

"I called the camp," he said, taking the wind out of her sails. "Apparently I just missed catching you. They know Roberta's safe." Rising, he walked over and grabbed the tail of her T-shirt. A flick of the wrist had water dripping out. "Did you walk over?"

"No." Annoyed that he had done exactly what he should have done, Eden smacked his hand away. "The car..." She hesitated, then decided to lie. "Broke down." She turned to frown at Roberta again. "Right before the storm."

"I'm sorry you got wet," Roberta said again.

"And so you should be."

"Didn't you put gas in the car? It was out, you know."

Before Eden could decide to murder her after all, they were interrupted by the blast of a horn.

"That'll be Delaney." Chase walked to the window to confirm it. "He's going to run Roberta back to camp."

"That's very kind of him." Eden held her hand out for Roberta's. "I appreciate all the trouble."

"Just Roberta." Chase caught Eden's hand before she could get away from him again. Ready and willing, or kicking and screaming, he was holding on to what he needed. "You'd better get out of those wet clothes before you come down with something."

"As soon as I get back to camp."

"My mother says you catch a chill if your feet stay wet." Roberta gave Squat a parting hug. "See you next year," she said to Chase, and for the first time Eden saw a hint of shyness. "You really will write?"

"Yeah." Chase bent down, tilted her head and kissed both cheeks. "I really will write."

Her freckles all but vanished under her blush. Turning, she threw herself into Eden's arms again. "I'll miss you, Miss Carlbough."

"Oh, Roberta, I'll miss you, too."

"I'm coming back next year and bringing my cousin. Everyone says we're so much alike we should be sisters."

"Oh," Eden managed weakly. "Wonderful." She hoped one winter was enough time to recharge.

"This was the best summer ever." Roberta gave one last squeeze as tears began to cloud Eden's eyes. "Bye!"

The front door was slamming behind her before Eden had taken the first step. "Roberta—"

"It was my best summer ever, too." Chase took her free hand before she could try for the door.

"Chase, let me go. I have to get back."

"Dry clothes. Though, as I may have mentioned before, you look wonderful wet and dripping."

"I'm not staying," she said, even as he tugged her toward the stairs.

"Since I just heard Delaney pull off, and your car's out of gas, I'd say you are." Because she was shivering now, he hurried her up. "And you're leaving puddles on the floor."

"Sorry." He propelled her through his bedroom. Eden had a fleeting impression of quiet colors and a brass bed before she was nudged into the adjoining bath. "Chase, this is very nice of you, but if you could just drive me back—"

"After you've had a hot shower and changed."

A hot shower. He could have offered her sable and emeralds and not tempted her half so much. Eden hadn't had a hot shower since the first week of June. "No, I really think I should get back."

But the door was already closing behind him.

Eden stared at it; then, her lower lip caught between her teeth, she looked back at the tub. Nothing she'd ever seen in her life had seemed so beautiful, so desirable. It took her less than ten seconds to give in.

"Since I'm here anyway..." she mumbled, and began to peel out of her clothes.

The first sizzle of hot spray stole her breath. Then, with a sigh of pure greed, she luxuriated in it. It was sinful, she thought as the water sluiced over her head. It was heaven.

Fifteen minutes later, she turned the taps off, but not without regret. On the rack beside the tub was a thick, thirsty bath towel. She wrapped herself in it and decided it was nearly as good as the shower. Then she noticed her clothes were gone.

For a moment, she only frowned at the empty rail where she'd hung them. Then she gripped the towel tighter. He must have come in and taken them while she was in the shower. Lips pursed, Eden studied the frosted glass doors and wondered how opaque they really were.

Be practical, she told herself. Chase had come in and taken her clothes because they needed to be dried. He was simply being a considerate host. Still, her nerves drummed a bit as she lifted the navy-blue robe from the hook on the back of the door.

It was his, of course. His scent clung to the material so that she felt he was all but in the room with her as she drew it on. It was warm and thick, but she shivered once as she secured the belt.

It was practical, she reminded herself. The robe was nothing more than an adequate covering until her clothes were dry again. But she tilted her head so that her chin rubbed along the collar.

Fighting off the mood, she took the towel and rubbed the mist away from the mirror. What she saw was enough to erase any romantic fantasies from her mind. True, the hot water from the shower had brought some color to her cheeks, but she hadn't even a trace of mascara left to darken her lashes. With the color of the robe to enhance them, her eyes dominated her face. She looked as though she'd been saved just before going under for the third time. Her hair was wet, curling in little tendrils around her face. Eden dragged a hand through it a few times, but couldn't bring it to order without a brush.

Charming, she thought before she pulled the door open. In Chase's bedroom she paused, wanting to look, wanting even more to touch something that belonged to him. With a shake of her head, she hurried through the bedroom and down the stairs. It was only when she stopped in the doorway of the front room and saw him that her nerves returned in full force.

He looked so right, so at ease in his workshirt and jeans as he stood in front of a nineteenth-century cabinet pouring brandy from a crystal decanter. She'd come to realize that it was his contradictions, as much as anything else, that appealed to her. At the moment, reasons didn't matter. She loved him. Now she had to get through this last encounter before burying herself in the winter months.

He turned and saw her. He'd known she was there, had felt her there, but had needed a moment. When he'd come into the bath to take her wet clothes, she'd been humming. He'd only seen a shadow of her behind the glass but had wanted, more than he could remember wanting anything, to push the barrier aside and take her. To hold her with her skin wet and warm, her eyes huge and aware.

He wanted her as much, as sharply, now as she stood in the doorway dwarfed by his robe.

So he'd taken a moment, for the simple reason that he had to be sure he could speak.

"Better?"

"Yes, thanks." Her hand reached automatically for the lapels of the robe and fidgeted there. He crossed the room to offer her a snifter.

"Drink. This should ward off the danger of wet feet."

As she took the glass, Chase closed the doors at her back. Eden found herself gripping the snifter with both hands. She lifted it slowly, hoping the brandy would clear her head.

"I'm sorry about all this." She made certain her tone was as polite and as distant as she could manage. She kept her back to the doors.

"No trouble." He wanted to shake her. "Why don't you sit down?"

"No, I'm fine." But when he continued to stand in front of her, she felt it necessary to move. She walked to the window, where the rain was still pouring from the sky. "I don't suppose this can keep up for long."

"No, it can't." The amusement he was beginning to feel came out in his voice. Wary, Eden turned back to him. "In fact, I'm amazed it's gone on this long." Setting his brandy aside, he went to her. "It's time we stopped it, Eden. Time you stopped backing away."

She gave a quick shake of her head and skirted around him. "I don't know what you mean."

"The hell you don't." He was behind her quickly, and there was nowhere to run. He took the snifter from her nerveless fingers before turning her to face him again. Slowly, deliberately, he gathered her hair in his hands, drawing it back until her face was unframed. There was a flash of fear in her eyes, but beneath it, waiting, was the need he'd wanted to see.

"We stood here once before, and I told you then it was too late."

The sun had been streaming through the glass then. Now the rain was lashing against it. As she stood there, Eden felt past and present overlap. "We stood here once before, and you kissed me."

His mouth found hers. Like the storm, the kiss was fierce and urgent. He'd expected hesitation and found demand. He'd expected fear and found passion. Drawing her closer, he found hunger and need and shimmering desire. What he had yet to find, what he discovered he needed most, was acceptance.

Trust me. He wanted to shout it at her, but her hands were in his hair, entangling him and pulling him to her.

The rain beat against the windowpanes. Thunder walked across the sky. Eden was whirling in her own private storm. She wanted him, wanted to feel him peeling the robe from her shoulders and touching her. She wanted that first delirious sensation of skin meeting skin. She wanted to give her love to him where it could be alive and free, but knew she had to keep it locked inside, secret, lonely.

"Chase. We can't go on like this." She turned her head away. "I can't go on like this. I have to leave. People are waiting for me."

"You're not going anywhere. Not this time." He slid a hand up her throat. His patience was at an end.

She sensed it and backed away. "Candy will be wondering where I am. I'd like to have my clothes now."

"No."

"No?"

"No," he said again as he lifted his brandy. "Candy won't be wondering where you are, because I phoned her and told her you weren't coming back. She said you weren't to worry, that things were under control. And no—" he sipped his brandy "—you can't have your clothes. Can I get you something else?"

"You phoned her?" All the fear, all the anxiety, drained away to make room for temper. Her eyes darkened, losing their fragility. Chase almost smiled. He loved the cool woman, the nervous one, the determined one, but he adored the Viking.

"Yeah. Got a problem with that?"

"Where did you possibly get the idea that you had a right to make my decisions for me?" She pushed a hand, covered by the cuff of his robe, against his chest. "You had no business calling Candy, or anyone else. More, you had no business assuming that I'd stay here with you."

"I'm not assuming anything. You are staying here. With me."

"Guess again." This time, when she shoved, there was enough power behind it to take him back a step. He knew that if he hadn't already been mad about her, he would have fallen in love at that moment. "God, but I'm sick to death of dealing with overbearing, dictatorial men who think all they have to do is want something to have it."

"You're not dealing with Eric now, Eden." His voice was soft, perhaps a shade too soft. "You're not dealing with other men, but with me. Only me."

"Wrong again, because I'm through dealing with you. Give me my clothes."

He set the shifter down very carefully. "No."

Her mouth would have fallen open if her jaw hadn't been clenched so tightly. "All right, I'll walk back in this." Ready to carry out her threat, she marched to the door and yanked it open. Squat lay across the threshold. As they spotted each other, he rose on his haunches with what Eden was certain was a leer. She took one more step, then, cursing herself for a coward, turned back.

"Are you going to call off that beast?"

Chase looked down at Squat, knowing the dog would do nothing more dangerous than slobber on her bare feet. Hooking his thumb in his pocket, he smiled. "He's had his shots."

"Terrific." With her mind set on one purpose, she strode to

the window. "I'll go out this way then." Kneeling on the window seat, she began to struggle with the sash. When Chase caught her around the waist, she turned on him.

"Take your hands off me. I said I was leaving, and I meant it." She took a swing, surprising them both when it landed hard in his gut. "Here, you want your robe back. I don't need it. I'll walk the three miles naked." To prove her point, she began fighting the knot at the belt.

"I wouldn't do that." As much for his sake as hers, he caught her hands. "If you do, we won't spend much time talking this through."

"I'm not spending any time at all." She squirmed until they both went down on the cushions of the window seat. "I don't have anything else to say to you." She managed to kick until the robe was hitched up to her thighs. "Except that you have the manners of a pig, and I can't wait until I'm hundreds of miles away from you. I decided the other night, when I was given the choice between a boring fool and a hardheaded clod, that I'd rather join a convent. Now take your hands off me, or I swear, I'll hurt you. No one, but no one, pushes me around."

With that, she put all her energy into one last shove. It sent them both tumbling off the cushions and onto the floor. As he had done once before, Chase rolled with her until he had her pinned beneath him. He stared at her now as he had then, while she fought to get her breath back.

"Oh God, Eden, I love you." Laughing at them both, he crushed his lips to hers.

She didn't fight the kiss. She didn't even move, though her fingers stiffened under his. Each breath took such an effort that she thought her heart had slowed down to nothing. When she could speak again, she did so carefully.

"I'd appreciate it if you'd say that again."

"I love you." He watched her eyes close and felt that quick twinge of panic. "Listen to me, Eden. I know you've been hurt, but you have to trust me. I've watched you take charge of your life this summer. It hasn't been the easiest thing I've ever done to stand back and give you the space you needed to do that."

She opened her eyes again. Her heart wasn't beating at a slow rhythm now, but seemed capable of bursting out of her chest. "Was that what you were doing?"

"I understood that you needed to prove something to yourself. And I think I knew that until you had, you wouldn't be ready to share whatever that was with me."

"Chase—"

"Don't say anything yet." He brought her hand to his lips. "Eden, I know you're used to certain things, a certain way of life. If that's what you need, I'll find a way to give it to you. But if you give me a chance, I can make you happy here."

She swallowed, afraid of misunderstanding. "Chase, are you saying you'd move back to Philadelphia if I asked you to?"

"I'm saying I'd move anywhere if it was important to you, but I'm not letting you go back alone, Eden. Summers aren't enough."

Her breath came out quietly. "What do you want from me?"

"Everything." He pressed his lips to her hand again, but his eyes were no longer calm. "A lifetime, starting now. Love, arguments, children. Marry me, Eden. Give me six months to make you happy here. If I can't, we'll go anywhere you like. Just don't back away."

"I'm not backing away." Her fingers entwined with his. "And I don't want to be anyplace but here."

She saw the change in his eyes even as his fingers tightened on hers. "If I touch you now, there's no going back."

"You've already told me it was too late." She drew him down to her. Passion and promises merged as they strained closer. She felt again that she had the world in the palm of her hand and held it tightly. "Don't ever let me go. Oh, Chase, I could feel my heart breaking when I thought of leaving here today, leaving you when I loved you so much."

"You wouldn't have gotten far."

Her lips curved at that. Perhaps, in some areas, she could accept a trace of arrogance. "You'd have come after me?"

"I'd have come after you so fast I'd have been there before you."

She felt pleasure grow, and glow. "And begged?"

His brow lifted at the glint in her eyes. "Let's just say I'd have left little doubt as to how much I wanted you."

"And crawled," she said, twining her arms around his neck. "I'm almost sorry I missed that. Maybe you could do it now."

He took a quick nip at her ear. "Don't press your luck."

Laughing, she held on. "One day this will be gray," she murmured as she trailed her fingers through his hair. "And I still won't be able to keep my hands out of it." She drew his head back to look at him, and this time there was no laughter, only love. "I've waited for you all my life."

He buried his face in her throat, fighting back the need to make her his, then and there. With Eden it would be perfect, it would be everything dreams were made of. He drew away to trace the line of her cheekbone. "You know, I wanted to murder Eric when I saw him with his hands on you."

"I didn't know how to explain when I saw you there. Then, later…" Her brow arched. "Well, you behaved very badly."

"You were magnificent. You scared Eric to death."

"And you?"

"You only made me want you more." He tasted her again,

feeling the wild, sweet thrill only she had ever brought to him. "I had plans to kidnap you from camp. Bless Roberta for making it easy."

"I hope she's not upset you're going to marry me instead. You have a neat dog, and you're kind of cute." She pressed her lips to the sensitive area just below his ear.

"She understood perfectly. In fact, she approves."

Eden stopped her lazy exploration of his throat. "Approves? You mean you told her you were going to marry me?"

"Sure I did."

"Before you asked me?"

Grinning, Chase leaned down to nip at her bottom lip. "I figured Squat and I could convince you."

"And if I'd said no?"

"You didn't."

"There's still time to change my mind." He touched his lips to hers again, letting them linger and warm. "Well," she said with a sigh, "maybe just this once I'll let you get away with it."

* * * * *

MILLS & BOON®

Pure reading pleasure

Visit millsandboon.co.uk and discover your one-stop shop for romance!

★ Choose and buy books from an extensive selection of Mills & Boon®, M&B™ and MIRA® titles.

★ Receive 25% off the cover price of all special releases and MIRA® books.

★ Sign up to our monthly newsletter to keep you up-to-date with all news and offers.

★ Take advantage of our amazing FREE book offers.

★ In our Authors area find titles currently available from all your favourite authors.

★ Get hooked on one of our fabulous online reads, with new chapters updated regularly.

Visit us online at www.millsandboon.co.uk

...you'll want to come back again and again!!

WEB/RS2

Romantic reads to
Need, Want

...International affairs, seduction and passion guaranteed
10 brand-new books available every month

Pure romance, pure emotion
6 brand-new books available every month

Pulse-raising romance – heart-racing medical drama
6 brand-new books available every month

From Regency England to Ancient Rome, rich, vivid and passionate romance...
6 brand-new books available every month

Scorching hot sexy reads...
4 brand-new books available every month